Praise for Kenneth S...
ANTHEMS OUTSIL...

"Schneyer dazzles with this striking collection o... ...g ...p 'cuiative stories . . . Each world is distinct and fully realized, and the astonishing variety of
genre and tone on offer showcases Schneyer's versatility. Inventive and resonant,
this collection is sure to impress."

   —*Publishers Weekly*, starred review

"This fine collection of 26 stories, one for each letter of the alphabet, displays
Schneyer's characteristic combination of wit and deep feeling. The games he plays
with the many forms that stories can take are as delightful as ever, and they never
get in the way of him going right to the heart of things—in fact they are his way
of seeing the world, and his gift to us. Enjoy!"

   —Kim Stanley Robinson

"Curl up with a collection you won't want to put down! By turns whimsical, moving and disturbing—always thought-provoking—Schneyer's unique visions reveal
myriad glimpses into the human heart."

   —E. C. Ambrose, author of *The King of Next Week*

"Ken Schneyer is a fearless explorer of the genres and his discoveries are treasures,
one and all. He offers something for every fan of the fantastic in *Anthems Outside
Time*. Equally adept at creating dragons and aliens, mages and movie stars, Ken
brings them all to life with a sturdy intelligence and a heart as big as the sky. I'm
a lifelong student of the short form and I'm here to report the arrival of another
master."

   —James Patrick Kelly, winner of the Hugo, Nebula & Locus Awards

"Ken Schneyer's collection is full of many gorgeous little stories (including one of
my all time favorites, 'Selected Program Notes from the Retrospective Exhibition
of Theresa Rosenberg Latimer'). Each story is a carefully crafted puzzle box to be
cracked open, revealing new insights into the world in all its complexity."

   —Tina Connolly, author of *On the Eyeball Floor and Other Stories*

"Kenneth Schneyer's new collection, *Anthems Outside Time and Other Strange Voices*, is our latest evidence of a powerful, flexible, and relentlessly curious intellect at play in our genre. No story is like the next; each one shines with its own indomitable haecceity. Awkward sex, unreliable narrators, recorded memory as witness, contracts as characters, strange storms, grim revolutions, and—oh!—the awful melancholy of a weaponized toddler descending on her red balloon: *Anthems* is yet warm, human, and unafraid to despair. In the end, it is that very fearlessness, no matter how bleak or brutal, that brings the reader back to hope."

—C. S. E. Cooney, winner of the World Fantasy Award

"I am in despairing awe of about a dozen stories from this book, including 'Some Pebbles in the Palm,' 'The Mannequin's Itch,' 'Life of the Author Plus Seventy,' 'Keeping Tabs,' and an astonishingly dark fantasy that left my jaw agape, 'The Last Bombardment.' This is astonishing, brilliant stuff. Get your hands on this book."

—Adam-Troy Castro, author of *Gustav Gloom*

"The short story is one of the few places where artistic experimentation is alive and well—at least in the hands of a master such a Kenneth Schneyer. Schneyer has the George Saunders-like gift of making new structures look easy and feel human. All too human, alas: *Anthems* removes our calluses and allow us to feel afresh the pain of injustice, the ache of love, the horror of what we've become. To call these stories science fiction or fantasy might leave some readers unprepared for the shock of the real Schneyer delivers: and through that shock, catharsis."

—Carlos Hernandez, author of the Sal and Gabi Series.

"From 'Some Pebbles in the Pond,' the meta-meditation on stories and lives that opens *Anthems Outside Time*, to 'Dispersion,' the heartbreaking, all-too-real fantasy that closes it, the stories in Kenneth Schneyer's new collection show a profound understanding of the craft of short stories, and an equal understanding of the people (and occasional dragon) who inhabit them. As at home in an art gallery as he is in a spaceship, Schneyer cares deeply about the world and seeks to understand it as best he can. Through these marvelous tales, he helps us do the same.

—F. Brett Cox, author of *The End of All Our Exploring: Stories*

ANTHEMS
OUTSIDE
TIME

AND OTHER
STRANGE VOICES

Also by Kenneth Schneyer

The Law and the Heart

ANTHEMS OUTSIDE TIME

AND OTHER STRANGE VOICES

KENNETH SCHNEYER

FAIRWOOD PRESS
Bonney Lake, WA

ANTHEMS OUTSIDE TIME
A Fairwood Press Book
July 2020
Copyright © 2020 Kenneth Schneyer

First Edition

Fairwood Press
21528 104th Street Court East
Bonney Lake, WA 98391
www.fairwoodpress.com

Cover image © Getty Images
Cover and book design by Patrick Swenson

ISBN: 978-1-933846-92-7
First Fairwood Press Edition: July 2020
Printed in the United States of America

For my children,

Phoebe Hannah Schneyer Okoomian

and

Arek Okoomian Schneyer

CONTENTS

INTRODUCTION:
ANTHEMS TO CRAFT
AND COMPASSION
MIKE ALLEN

K en Schneyer is a talented fellow.
He's also a learned gent, as the stories in this book all
amply demonstrate.

With a background in theater and corporate law, Ken's got a
day job (most all of us writers do) in which he teaches college
students about logic, constitutional law, criminal procedure, science fiction literature and Shakespeare—presumably not all in the
same class! But if you're skeptical that such topics can overlap, the
evidence in favor is plainly laid out in the finely crafted tales that
comprise this hefty collection.

I've encountered Ken's work before as an editor and publisher
(more on that in a bit), and I've encountered Ken himself in both
"virtual" and "in real life" spaces (more on that too!) Before I get
into that, I want to chat just a tad about encountering Ken's work
in toto, as reading this book allowed me to make the acquaintance
of stories of his that were new to me. (Some of them, I was already
extremely familiar with, as I will explain.)

As a teenager and twenty-something, I gobbled up lots of science fiction and fantasy short stories, and I had a particular fondness for the latest story collections by Isaac Asimov.

(Two decades into the 21st century, I feel the need to footnote an evocation of Asimov by observing that problematic aspects of his persona, like those of many other seminal 20th century figures in science fiction and fantasy, are being properly interrogated and reevaluated by present day scholars and fans.)

The personal connection I experienced in relation to *Anthems Outside Time* has to do with the subjective feel my impressionable young self had reading books like *The Winds of Change* and *Robot Dreams*. Rarely an action writer, Asimov wrote stories for the head, using the tools of genre-spanning fiction to present puzzles for the reader to pour over, with solutions that were sometimes amusing, sometimes profound, always entertaining.

After I read the book that's now in your hands, the comparison seemed wholly apt, but with need for expounding.

Ken Schneyer mines a similar vein, and delivers engaging, entertaining yarns every time out; but his stories are equally written for the heart as for the head. His puzzles are as likely to be moral as logical. The solutions he concocts can be hilarious. The quandaries he poses can be heartbreaking. He works at a more sophisticated level than Asimov did, generating characters who live on the page and hinging outcomes on subtle and breathtaking nuances in the human condition, sometimes reveling in the indomitability of hope, sometimes arriving at disquieting conclusions.

As examples of the indomitability of hope, I'll hold up "Serkers and Sleep" and "The Age of Three Stars," fantasies with tragic overtones—the former driven by magic, the latter by prophecy—that proceed with a kind of inexorable logic toward endings that offer rays of light amid the darkness. As examples of disquieting conclusions, I'll point to the action-filled SF tale "Hear My Enemy, My Daughter" and the epic fantasy "Who Embodied What We Are," which question core assumptions about heroic actions and their motives and consequences.

There's wry humor to be found here, too, and outright satire. Ken combines his legal expertise with classic science fiction problems in the Asimovian tradition in "Keepsakes" and "The Whole

Truth Witness" (tellingly published in *Analog*, that bastion of hard SF), keeping his tongue in his cheek all the while. My personal favorite of these is "Life of the Author Plus Seventy," which takes a bowl of incongruous ingredients—an urban legend about Walt Disney, the wicked spirit of Gordon R. Dickson's "Computers Don't Argue," minutia of copyright law—and blends them into a marvelous comedy. Marvelous, by the way, both in the chuckles that come from the escalating bureaucratic inanities inflicted on its put-upon protagonist and in the applause-worthy high-wire balance act Ken performs, fitting those elements together so they function like clockwork.

That penchant for satire isn't limited to near-future legal extrapolations. Consider "The Plausibility of Dragons," a high fantasy that works both as a ripping adventure yarn and as a pointed critique of historical misconceptions perpetuated in fan culture.

Shifting to gears more Bradburian than Asimovian, there's a dash of poignant surrealism here and there, as well. You'll find it in "The Sisters' Line," a delightful romp co-written with Liz Argall, and in "Dispersion," the moving original story that concludes this book. There's also more horrific manifestations of that surrealist bent, in stories like "The Mannequin's Itch" and "The Last Bombardment"—the latter adapted into a stage play!—that address the trauma of war with irrational, inexplicable, inescapably haunting imagery.

Ken also has a knack for a rather deft bit of artistry, wherein he presents a narrative in fragments—often, as realistically craft documents, employing his familiarity with similar—and leaves it up to the reader to deduce what the story is. It's a brave and brilliant thing to do.

Here's where I feel justified in sharing personal anecdotes.

Ken and I and first met in the late 2000s during the lost era of LiveJournal, a social network that was a major gathering point for creative types, especially those of a speculative genre persuasion. (I believe George R. R. Martin was the last major celebrity to leave.)

Not long after that as the temporal crow flies, I accepted his story "Lineage" for my anthology *Clockwork Phoenix 3*, the middle installment in what's to date a quintology of books showcasing unusual and beautiful stories with science fiction, fantasy and horror trappings. "Lineage" is a story that leaps backward and forward and sideways in time and space, highlighting acts of courage and self-sacrificing, ending with a perfect last sentence. I loved it, and even thought it might go far come awards season. That last part, alas, did not come to pass, as can happen—but there's more to this history.

First, I met Ken in person. He's a mensch, energetically cheerful, a guy who works hard to lift others up.

I'm a regular attendee at Readercon in Boston, and so is he. Ken took part, of course, in the promotional readings for *Clockwork Phoenix 3*, and we hung out a bit more besides. I have a fond memory of taking part in a group reading he organized for one of his pieces in which more than half a dozen authors read designated parts. It was like a spontaneous stage play.

The same year "Lineage" came out, Ken became an early pioneer of the sci-fi literary scene's embrace of the Kickstarter crowdfunding platform, successfully raising more than $2,000 that sponsored the writing of new short stories. He also provided invaluable guidance and support during my own baby steps onto the platform, as I launched the campaign that led to the publication of *Clockwork Phoenix 4*.

As it turned out, Ken wrote what is (so far!) his most celebrated story, "Selected Program Notes from the Retrospective Exhibition of Theresa Rosenberg Latimer," for that Kickstarter campaign of his, and my own successful Kickstarter venture enabled me to have the honor of being that tale's editor and publisher.

This time my awards hunch was on the money. "Selected Program Notes" was nominated for the Nebula Award and the Theodore Sturgeon Award, adapted for audio, translated into Chinese and reprinted in a couple of Best of the Year volumes. Gorgeous, powerful and mysterious, it shares the life story of an artist, the details unfolding as a series of entries in a gallery guide, with an ambiguity I find delectable and an extra layer of tension in how the reader's interpretation of the paintings might differ from the descriptions and analyses provided by the unnamed authors of the guide.

I don't want to belabor "Selected Program Notes" at the expense of the other stories in the collection—many stories in this book are worthy of equal praise—but obviously I've got bias for good reason.

Ken continued to have my back with my subsequent crowd-funding ventures, the *Mythic Delirium* digital magazine and the anthology *Clockwork Phoenix 5*. Furthermore, sensing that I'm drawn to this style of his involving documents and fragments, he sold me "Levels of Observation," a blood-chilling tale in which the protagonist never makes a direct appearance.

For these reasons and more, I'm incredibly flattered that I get to be the one telling you why you need this book in your life.

One final observation: In every one of these stories, regardless of mood or approach, you'll find impeccable craft and heartfelt, contagious compassion.

Go now and experience it for yourself.

—Mike Allen, March 2020

SOME PEBBLES
IN THE PALM

ONCE UPON A TIME, THERE WAS A man who was born, who lived, and who died. We could leave the whole story at that, except that it would be misleading to write the sentence only once. He was born, he lived, and he died, was born, lived, died, bornliveddied.

The first few words of a story are a promise. We will have this kind of experience, not that one. Here is a genre, here is a setting, here is a conflict, here is a character. We don't know what is coming next, but we do know what is coming next; we wonder what is coming next. He was born, he lived, and he died.

To say that this man did nothing would be false. As a child he made up a little game where he moved smooth pebbles between the shade of a tree and earth warmed by the sun, and for a few moments the warmth or coolness of the pebble would stand bravely against the heat or cold of its surroundings, making a little zone that thought it could resist entropy. No one else ever played it, but it occupied him for dozens of happy hours. When he grew older he forgot all about this game, except that every few years the sight of certain tiny white stones made him want to pick them up, and in his hand they felt heavier than they should. As a man of forty, he regularly walked near a patch of gravel that filled him with inexplicable melancholy.

The stones are not a symbol. The melancholy was nothing more than the distorted lens through which anyone sees his childhood. Lucky people see lost contentment, safety, and endless wonder. Others see the hand raised in anger, feel the ache in the belly, smell the shit or rotten food or sour sweat.

He was lucky. He was educated in the manner befitting a person of his time and station—let's say it was an English public school of 1840 or so, which would mean that he experienced a certain amount of brutality, a fist raised not in anger but because fists are supposed to be raised. We can pity him for that, if we like. He pitied himself for it.

He fell in love with a young woman whose dark eyes narrowed in concentration when she used two fingers to extract a single seed from a pomegranate. She would hold it between the nail of her first finger and the pad of her second, turning it like a gemstone for perhaps a quarter-hour before she put it in her mouth. By that time its skin had dried, and it must have popped like a tiny balloon when she bit into it.

Characters with even the faintest whiff of humanity make readers reimagine themselves, whether those characters actually do anything or not. A few seconds ago, you put your first and second fingers together and pictured a pomegranate seed between them.

He took up an occupation that interested him—perhaps he was in the military, or a member of the entrepreneurial middle class, a minister of the Gospel. He did his job well, sometimes very well. Those for whom he worked praised him outside of his hearing in smoky clubs, and younger men just learning the trade looked to him for advice and reassurance. In his job he had choices to make, and he made them. At the time those choices seemed important, but they weren't really. Had he made different choices, or had he refused to make choices at all, the world at large, and even his own life, would have gone on more or less the same.

Passive protagonists are a mistake. The reader wants the main character to *do* something. He shouldn't merely experience the world and pass through it, he should act on it, choose paths that have an impact. Especially this is true in a short story, which is supposed to concern the most important moment in the character's life. Never mind that many people go through their lives more acted upon than acting, that for some, the decisions that make the fundamental differences were never theirs to begin with. What if I had called the protagonist *she*?

He stood beneath the infinite sky with a chill wind pressing against his face, watched dark trees wrestle and contort, and glimpsed the unbridgeable distance between himself and the heavens, between himself and the past. What is Man that You are mindful of him? He was fortunate: he never had life-and-death decisions thrown in his face by an unfriendly Providence. We all wish we had such lives.

The protagonist should have something at stake, something to gain or lose that's important to him. If there's no reason for the protagonist to care about the outcome, then there's no reason for the reader to care either.

I could tell you things that mattered. I could choose a different main character, a coal miner dying at thirty, or someone enslaved in the American South, or a woman under the dominion of men at any time in the last three thousand years. Then, even if she died a pointless death after struggling without hope for years, you could put down the pages thinking that you'd learned something.

All of those things were going on during this man's life. The dying coal miners, the abused women, they all suffered then. Our hero knew about them. More than this, he cared, said he cared, wept over them. No Ebenezer Scrooge here, no willfully callous miser shutting himself away from his fellow men. When those conscientious gentlemen with the subscription list knocked on his door, he gave handsomely. He voted for the Liberal candidate and argued with the friends at his club about relief for the poor and home rule for Ireland.

This is where we might expect to read a hint of a tragic flaw, a lack of discipline or failure of courage, a window into a disaster we're sure will follow, or a challenge to be overcome so that he will find himself elevated and transformed by the end of the story. None of that is going to happen.

The wife whose concentration on a pomegranate seed had once so enchanted him died of a wasting illness, and he walked from one room to another, from one street to another, counting his footsteps and forgetting the number. His son sent him a letter once every few months, and his daughter came to visit every second Sunday, nodding kindly at everything he said and smiling as if she had actually heard him. The powers of his body failed him, slowly because he had a good physician (the best that could be managed in that era, anyhow). He died in the usual mixture of pain, perplexity, and vague sense of a life well lived that he more-or-less expected. Less than a mile from that spot, on the same day, a girl of five and a boy of seven coughed out their last breaths on separate filthy street corners, alone and uncomforted, never having met.

If bad things are going to happen, they have to happen to people we know and care about. So the author doesn't just tell you that a thousand people died; she makes you acquainted with one *particular* person, whose loves, hates, hopes, and fears you know and understand, and then *that* person dies, and you weep the way you'd never weep over the mountain of bodies on the floor of a stadium. Sure, one-and-half million died at Auschwitz, or maybe it was four million; it's a number. But show you one pair of baby clothes in the Auschwitz Museum, and you start to sob.

The next time he was born, he grew up in the suburbs with the counter-culture and the civil rights riots and antiwar movements on television, and they frightened him. Late one night he saw a movie about teenagers locking up all the parents in concentration camps, and news anchors told of astronauts screaming on their launch pad, a man shot in a motel, another man who maybe was a president shot in another hotel, and funerals for people killed in riots. It was easy to be scared.

During recess at school, he hid in a brick alcove that housed the huge, warm HVAC unit, humming along with it and listening to the dissonance when he raised or lowered the pitch of his voice. He built little rockets out of cardboard and balsa, sanding the fins and painting them with a sealant that said *Dope* on the label, and wondered if it was the same dope they meant in the public service ads. The rockets went up with a sound like a garden hose splatting on the pavement, and most of them were lost on their very first flights.

He attended a college full of wealthy campus radicals, where socialist rhetoric, feminist separatism, and critical race theory were thrown about by people who mostly forgot about them by the time they turned thirty. Joining in made him feel popular and loved, which is what he wanted. When he was nineteen his girlfriend told him she was a feminist, and so he decided to become a feminist too. It wasn't as shallow as it sounds; he read a lot, and talked to many people, and really believed the things he said. He donated lots of money to organizations that lobbied and agitated for gender equity and justice. When the two of them got married, they had rings made in which they set semi-precious stones they'd gathered on a vacation together.

The politics felt good, and maybe some of the money helped, and maybe his one phone call to the right state representative was the tipping point. In fact, none of it was. If he'd never donated, never marched, never spoken, things would have worked out pretty much the same. Most of the time he knew this.

He became a loan officer in a bank, and, like George Bailey in the movie, was able to use his authority to nudge things in the direction of women, people of color, gays, trans people, every oppressed and underrepresented category of person he could think of. He was proud of himself. Of course, the bank had its standards, and there was a limit to how much nudging he could do, and he never went so far as to jeopardize his own position.

He pictured what it would be like if he were the one who had to be constantly on guard lest he be molested or killed, the one channeled into a life of poverty, the one whose culture was harvested, homogenized, sugared and fed back to him in nauseating swallows. These things made him angry, and he protested them, or at least he chimed in when someone else protested them.

Eventually he died, no wiser than he began, as the song goes. And if some prophet out of a novel had been standing over him at that moment, she'd have said, "for all the good or evil, creation or destruction, your living might have accomplished, you might just as well never have lived at all." He might have protested that that couldn't be true, because he had children. But they didn't do anything either.

Now you think this is a story about karma. He keeps getting reborn because he's failing to learn the lesson he needs, and sooner or later he'll have an epiphany or redemption or something that will take him one step closer to Nirvana or Enlightenment. That's not going to happen either. The wheel of fire keeps turning; he never gets any wiser, never becomes more aware, never takes action to do anything. Not in one lifetime, not in thirty. There is no progress, no arc, no satisfying or edifying conclusion.

While repetition can be a powerful device, it's wasteful and boring unless there is some detectable change between the different instances of the action, theme, or symbol. A piece of short fiction is not a chant; it needs continual development, an evolution or completion of something that appears more than once. We understood it the first time; we don't need to be told again.

The next time he was born, he was a cyborg. The neural link he shared with his fellow creatures allowed him to access whatever thoughts and feelings they wished to share with him. There was one who was endlessly fascinated by a few grains of sand in the palm of her hand, grains in which she fancied she could see tiny contours, but which would be lost forever if she exhaled near them. Another climbed boulders, gripping the rock with his bare hands, feeling the pressure and pain and knowing for certain he was alive.

Our hero saw what they saw, felt what they felt, and believed he had learned something.

These enhancements were available only to that small percentage of the population with the wealth, the technological surroundings, the physical safety to partake of them. Most of the human race was still, even in that advanced time, wrestling with problems of basic nutrition, sanitation, and violence. Of those who did not share his race, his gender, his orientation, his class, his ableness, there were some who did attain the neural links, and they were not shy about uploading experiences for all to understand. They thought that if only others could *feel what they felt*, the callous indifference of privilege would melt away.

Now you hope for a hand-waving fix for contemporary social problems. This "neural link" thing, which I haven't explained because I haven't the first idea how it could work, will magically impose empathy on all its users; the courageous oppressed will, perhaps in some noble act of sacrifice, impart the experience of their oppression to the privileged, and the world will transform.

No. He felt what they felt, certainly. He experienced their pain, their sorrow, their fear, their anger. In his mind he smiled when she didn't feel it for fear of what would happen next, always looked over eir shoulder, pressed his belly for the food that was not there. He remembered guarding each word lest they utter the wrong syllable and trigger violence. And each time it was done, he switched off the link and wept for the pain, and sent messages apologizing for living as one of the oppressors, and transferred credit units to the accounts of movements that were trying to make things better.

Eventually he died this time too, although life extension methods had progressed considerably and it took longer than it would nowadays. He died disappointed, unhappy with the world, wishing he'd had the moral fiber to do something more about it than he did.

The story goes on and on, but you understand how it's going to go.

Inconclusive endings frustrate and dissatisfy the reader. The author should not shirk his responsibility, but should have the guts to choose what happens at the end. Leaving it up to the reader's imagination to speculate on a conclusion is a cop-out.

If you're reading this story in the year 2115 and you've made a quick search of my name by flicking a fingernail or thinking the code for your genie, whatever the hell science-fiction sort of thing you do in the 22nd century, you haven't found anything. No achievements, no accomplishments, no victory for humanity that will make me unashamed to die, as they say. Maybe even the names of my parents, wife, and children aren't there. Maybe all you've found is this story. I haven't dug in with both feet and both hands, started the revolution, spent my life for the poor, cured the great plague. Maybe nothing I say here matters. You can call me a hypocrite, if that makes you feel any better.

But I'm not really here, am I? These are words on a page, on a screen, on that nifty little implant you're all using in 2115. Maybe I lied about myself. After all, I *did* lie about the protagonist; he's just made up, all forty-seven of him. Maybe I'm a selfless saint who spends every day trying to better the lot of his fellow creature. Maybe I'm the least privileged person you can imagine, suffering under/within the multidimensional, constricting weight of seven different kinds of oppression. By 2115 I'm dead anyway, so what do you even care? I'm atoms on the wind; maybe I'm the atoms in your fingernail. From where you stand, I am every bit as fictional as the protagonist of this story. He's not real. I'm not real. Only you are real.

*

There are at least three stories in this collection whose origin I can't quite locate. Some days you start typing and you don't understand why you wrote what you wrote. I think I was pushing against both the assumptions of narrative and the ways some of us comfort ourselves about our goodness and compassion without ever changing anything.

HEAR THE ENEMY, MY DAUGHTER

EVERYTHING ABOUT KESI REMINDS ME of her father. Her hair is crinklier than mine, because Jabari's was. Her skin is a darker shade of brown than mine, because Jabari's was. Her chin juts out absurdly for such a little face, because Jabari's did. She even smells like him. Every sight of her is like a kick in my stomach.

Kesi has stopped wondering where Jabari has gone. For the first two or three months, she asked many times a day, "Mzazi, where Baba?" She was past such baby-talk; it was a sign of her distress that she regressed, lost her verbs. I was honest with her, or I tried to be. You can say, "Baba has died. Baba was very brave, he was fighting to protect Kesi and Mzazi, he was fighting to protect everyone." But how much of that will a three-year-old understand? All she knew was that her father was gone. I did not even tell her that he had gone to a better place, that he was happy—what would be the point, even if I believed it? Did she care whether he was happy, if it kept him away forever?

Nor did I allow the other voice to speak, the voice that said, "I should have been fighting next to Jabari; I could have saved Jabari. If you had not been born, Jabari would still be here."

Now she is four and does not mention him at all. She remembers him; when I point to his picture, she tells me who Jabari is.

But she does not begin conversation about him. She does not ask when he will return. She does not ask what it means to die.

No matter how many times I watched them, the battle recordings told me nothing. The one identifiable word was the one we already knew: *kri'ikshi*, the one the Sheshash say over and over in combat. No commands, no calls to each other, just that same sound, *kri'ikshi*. Nothing in the recordings explained its meaning, nor gave any clue to the syntax of the rest of the Sheshash language, if language it was. With a frustrated sigh, I turned back to the latest pattern analysis on the intercepted signals between their ships, which so far had proved equally fruitless.

The call from Levi came just as I was getting ready to abandon the intractable recordings and go home to Kesi.

"We need you in Interrogation tomorrow, Halima," he said. "Can you handle it?"

I stiffened. "Of course, sir. I do my duty."

He made an impatient sound. "You know what I mean. I can get someone else, do some sort of swap, if I have to. Are you ready for this?"

He was right to ask, but it still annoyed me. After my combat tour, I used to feel an urge to get out of my chair whenever I saw a picture of a Sheshash. Those feelings subsided after Kesi was born, only to return with horror and rage after we lost Jabari on Heraclea. For a while, it was all I could do not to put my hand through the screen; once I actually did so, cutting my palm as I screamed.

But a year had gone by since Heraclea, and I was better, mostly better. I took a deep breath and visualized looking into the eyes of a Sheshash across a transparent barrier, talking to it, *smelling* it. My gorge did not rise, my heartbeat did not race.

"Yes, I'm ready. But I didn't know we had any Sheshash in Holding. Was there a new capture?"

"Oh yes, on Asculum, a spectacular one. We've actually got our hands on a fighting pair."

No Sheshash fights alone. Always there are pairs of them, a three-meter giant and a half-meter dwarf, tens of thousands of pairs on the field at once. The larger and the smaller soldier fight with a rapid coordination that makes the mind swim and the eyes ache. When one moves, the other moves at the same millisecond; the recordings show literally that brief a delay, if delay it is. Any human soldier will be faced with the choice of fighting the giant or the dwarf, typically on opposite sides of him, and whichever he does not fight, that one will kill him.

Of course they cannot outrun projectiles or beam weapons any more than we can, but they do outrun the reflexes of human soldiers; they move faster than we can think. Artillery and bombs are effective, but after the first engagement the Sheshash never amassed enough troops in one location for ordnance to do much damage.

The dwarf member of a fighting pair is deadlier, more reckless than the giant. Both Sheshash use their weapons swiftly, cleanly, not wasting a calorie of energy. Nor do they seem to fight for advantage or position, to gain the high ground or keep the initiative. They kill as many as they can, do not stop trying to slaughter us until they are killed themselves or forcibly restrained.

No fighting pair had ever been captured before. We had taken giant Sheshash on the battlefield, either wounded or surrounded, but never had one of the dwarf fighters been taken prisoner, and surely no pair. On the battlefield we found approximately as many of the giant Sheshash slain as the dwarfs, but we never saw a smaller one alive unless it was still trying to kill us.

Many theories were proposed for this discrepancy. Some suggested that the dwarfs, being less strong, were expendable—but this made no sense in light of how much more effective killers they were. Others speculated that there was a class distinction between giant and dwarf, as between an officer and an enlisted soldier, or between a lord and a commoner. A simpler explanation was that the dwarf Sheshash were simply easier to kill. But detailed tabulations of battle recordings failed to show such a discrepancy in our hits. Indeed, there was a discrepancy the other way, as the larger fighters were easier targets. Instead, these recordings showed smaller Sheshash collapsing in the middle of a fight, with no apparent wound or impact. More, they showed that the dwarfs who collapsed were all fighting alone. When a pair was fighting together, neither of them underwent this spontaneous implosion.

All of our efforts at communication had so far been futile, and the Sheshash continued to attack at every opportunity. The High Command had considered evacuating all of our colonized worlds—probably not feasible before the Sheshash exterminated us on half-a-dozen of them. And in any case, since we didn't know why they were fighting us in the first place, for all we knew they would go on to finish the job on Terra.

We weren't without options. We had fusion bombs and atmospheric catalysts. We could stop them. The question was how to do it without committing genocide.

When I entered the cell, there was only one Sheshash present, a giant. As many as I have seen on the battlefield, they still astonish me. Their smooth, shiny skin is so bright a white it hurts the eyes, with a faint chartreuse overlay that appears and disappears like the rainbows of oil droplets in a puddle. Their three legs, slender and lithe, each have three major joints, rotating on dual axes like their three arms. Their three eyes are large and dark, like those of a seal. In combat those eyes open wide; at rest, as in captivity, they are typically half-closed, so the Sheshash give the impression of being perpetually sleepy. In a Sheshash who has lost its fighting partner, the eyes dart back and forth, up and down in a way that seems frantic to us. Perhaps this is the way they register grief or distress; perhaps the wide eyes signify anger.

Or perhaps we anthropomorphize even to ascribe these emotions to them. Our anger comes from the part of our brain that is reptilian, our grief from something somewhat later. But with an alien, how can you make such a comparison? Do they even have "reptilian brains?"

In the moment before it saw me, I had the feeling (justified or not) that the Sheshash was calm, even happy in the cell. It was moving slowly, its eyes in their half-shut position, and uttering a sound which, although high to our ears, was low for them.

Then the Sheshash noticed me. It moved rapidly forward with its arms out as if to attack, its eyes opening wide, but stopped before it hit the barrier. I backed away, beginning to reach for my weapon until I caught myself; I felt a sudden flush.

The Shesash pushed and tapped the barrier several times, using different combinations of its limbs until satisfied that there was no way it could get at me, or I at it. I stared at it for several seconds, and it gazed with half-closed eyes at me.

I swallowed, then phoned Levi.

"You told me there were two Sheshash in the cell. A fighting pair, you said," I began.

"Wait a minute. We've been monitoring the cell. Just wait a minute, you'll see. This is huge."

As I watched, a head poked out from the horizontal slit in the Sheshash's belly. It was another Sheshash, the small one.

I did not gasp aloud. Holding the phone close to my mouth, I whispered, "They are *marsupials*?"

"Who knows?" said Levi. "*If* the small one is a child, *if* the large one is its mother—"

"Or father?"

"Parent, whatever. *If* the sack has a developmental function like the marsupial pouch, then sure, why not, you can call them marsupials."

"Which still would not explain their reproduction," I said, as if it mattered.

"Right," said Levi. "But it would tell us that they put their children into combat."

Then the dwarf Sheshash's eyes opened fully and it shot out of the pouch, throwing itself at the barrier to get at me. I didn't back away this time, but felt my heart pound in my chest. The dwarf bounced off the barrier but tried again, bounced again and kept trying. Its mouth was open and it was uttering the shriek we had heard on every battlefield: *Kri'ikshi! Kri'ikshi!*

The giant reached for the dwarf, but the dwarf seemed fully intent on me and would not be distracted, as if it did not understand that it could not reach me.

Finally the giant uttered some long words; their voices are high and their language has a staccato quality to it. The dwarf Sheshash stopped what it was doing, half-closed its eyes, and turned to the giant.

"*Kri'ikshi!*" it said. Its voice was even higher; it sounded like a whistle.

"*Kri'ikshi sha'akdash kishidi to'ishati,*" said the giant.

"*Kri'ikshi! Kri'ikshi!*" the dwarf repeated, spinning a circle around the big one.

"*Kri'ikshi sha'akdash,*" the giant said again, more slowly, each sound pronounced more precisely. "*Kri'ikshi Kishidi. Kri'ikshi to'ishati.*"

"*Kri'ikshi,*" the little one repeated, more quietly. But it stopped moving.

"*Shi,*" said the big one. Then the dwarf hopped up and crawled back into the pouch. It squirmed its way down (like someone burrowing into warm blankets, I thought) and became quiescent. Its eyes closed.

It seemed obvious. The little Sheshash was more excitable, more likely to attack, less likely to understand the concept of a transparent barrier, than the big one. Its vocabulary was more limited, or else it had a less nuanced use of it. It understood that I was the enemy and wanted to kill me. The giant had tried to make it understand—what? That they were prisoners? That there was a barrier? That killing me would accomplish nothing?—and had had a hard time getting the message across. But the smaller one—the *child*—became docile anyway, and returned to the larger one's— its *mother's*—pouch. Once there, it fell asleep.

We had no clue as to their gender, and the exact relationship might not even be familial. But my instinct said: mother and child.

Kesi's use of language misleads me into thinking she has a mind like mine. She uses a subject, verb, and object in ways I understand, and so I imagine that she means by it the same thing I would mean. But a four-year-old, in some ways, is as different from an adult as a chimpanzee.

Last month she cut into small pieces Jabari's decoration for valor, which I stupidly left sitting on a low table after I had shown it to her the day before. I had not guessed that she was able to use her little scissors so well, nor that they would cut something that seemed so durable. When I saw the scattering of silk ribbon and golden twine on the table and floor, I felt dizzy and had to sit down. It was just a thing, it was not Jabari, but it was one more bit of him that I will never have again.

I asked Kesi what she had done. She saw the tears in my eyes and knew that something was wrong.

So she said, "Nothing."

I said, "But Baba's ribbon is all cut to bits."

She looked right at it and said, "No, it isn't."

It wasn't a lie, not in the sense that you would mean it. Kesi has learned enough about words to know that they have power. She knows that adults speak of things that are not present in the room, and that these things turn out to be true. It is logical, from her perspective, to think that the words make them true. She wished

that the ribbon were all in one piece, so she told me, with conviction, that it was. I do not think she expected magic, but rather that
the world would conform itself to her words, as (from where she
stands) it seems to conform itself to mine.

But at the moment she said it, a miserable voice in my head
screamed, *liar*! In that instant I judged her, found her untrust-
worthy, unloving, selfish. I hated her, and not for the first time.

Then I returned to myself and saw a scared, sad little girl who
had not understood what she had done. I took her into my arms and
we cried into each other's shoulders.

And I wondered whether someday I will misplace the reason
to forgive her—whether there will come an instant of hatred that
does not fade.

The war broke out a year after Jabari and I were married. Although trained as a linguist and translator, I elected for combat
duty so that we could be posted together. It amazes me that we
were not both killed during those first weeks, so complete were
the losses at the hands of the Sheshash fighting pairs. Jabari and
I fought together in the same unit, one covering for the other in
combat, sharing a tent or quarters to ourselves. I do not know how
many times he saved my life or I his. Our lovemaking in those days
was fierce, desperate and joyful; death hovered near us, and we
kept it away by grabbing great fistfuls of life.

When I became pregnant, I was ordered back to non-combat-
ant duty. Our armies still will not allow women with child to fight,
and with this Jabari agreed. So I worked on trying to decode the
Sheshash language. Jabari also had desk duty for a time, and he
was present when our daughter was born.

Then he had the opportunity to go back to combat. Over this
decision we had bitter arguments, because he wished me to stay
behind again. "I don't want our daughter raised by strangers," he
said.

"Then why don't *you* stay behind?"

"Because you can contribute to the war here, and I can't. At a desk I'm useless; I'll rust if I don't go back."

In the end I gave in, though I was sulking when I did it. I saw him only twice again before Heraclea. Some part of me believed, still believes, that if I had been there, I would have seen the danger coming; I would have saved him.

With so little in common besides the war, it was hard to know where to start. But the Sheshash had space travel, which meant they understood physics, therefore mathematics.

I reached into my bag. The giant Sheshash's eyes widened for a moment, then half-closed again when what I drew out was not a weapon.

I held up a white plastic sphere. "Sphere," I said.

The Sheshash regarded me for a while. I did not really expect a response; we'd never had one in the past. Then she said, "*Itto.*"

I hid my surprise at getting a response. The dwarf Sheshash launched itself at the barrier again, and in that instant I felt like a traitor even for trying to talk to the giant. The mother was a liar, the daughter was a killer, these things had killed Jabari, they would kill me.

The giant ignored the dwarf, still looking at me. I looked at her. Then I replaced the sphere and held up a cube, the same color. "Cube," I said.

"*Itto,*" said the giant again.

Very well then, *itto* probably was not "sphere"—unless, to the Sheshash, a sphere and a cube were the same thing. That would be fascinating, but daunting.

I brought up a blue sphere. "Blue," I said.

"*Itto,*" she repeated.

Perhaps it meant "plastic," or "opaque." I lowered the sphere into the bag—

"*Ushata*," said the Sheshash.

I stopped. Then I slowly raised the sphere. "*Itto?*" I asked. I worried that the rising pitch at the end of the word might signify a wholly different meaning.

"*Itto*," she agreed.

Then I lowered the sphere again. "*Ushata?*"

"*Ushata.*"

Itto was either a verb, meaning to raise or take out, or an adjective, meaning a higher elevation, or possibly exposure to the elements. A few more experiments persuaded me that it was the verb. *Itto* was "raise," *ushata* was "lower."

Or the whole thing might be a deception. She was, after all, a prisoner in enemy hands. We had treated her and her daughter gently after capture on Asculum, but we could not be sure that "gently" meant the same thing to us as to them, and, in any case, the capture itself must have been brutal.

Still it was a breakthrough, even if she was trying to mislead me.

When I look at Kesi, it is easy to imagine I am seeing a smaller, simpler, more naïve version of myself. I fancy that I remember being her age, can relive the games I played and feel the way she is feeling as she plays now. When she disobeys or defies me, I tell myself that she is just like her mother, that I understand her. This is the life-giving self-deception, like the stories we tell of fierce, protective mothers who die for their young.

A few days ago, the teacher at the preschool called me aside before I picked Kesi up, explaining that there had been "a little incident" and that she had a cut on her forehead. One of the other children, a boy named Edmund, had struck her with a wooden toy. It seems he was playing a game in which he was a soldier and the other children were Sheshash. They had taken Edmund aside and explained what he had done while Kesi cried into the teacher's shirt, then Edmund apologized and helped Kesi clean and bandage the cut.

When I went in, Kesi ran to me and showed off her bandage like a medal.

"Does it hurt?" I asked.

"No. I was Sheshash! He can't hurt me!"

I shuddered inside, but smiled and nodded to her.

As we walked out the door, I tried to decide whether I was more surprised that a little, innocent child could hurt someone, or that human children were civilized at all, and did not simply rip one another's throats out.

I learned to call the mother Ishish, the daughter Ashashi. Without other Sheshash present, I could not know whether *Ishish* was the mother's name, or whether it meant "mother" or simply "adult." It might have some other meaning altogether; it might mean someone who does a certain thing, or even the word for the action itself, although this seemed less likely as time went on.

By now I was consistently thinking of them as mother and daughter. Levi was still skeptical, but the behavioral evidence supported my intuition. Ishish was visibly nurturing, teaching, protecting Ashashi—I could see her modeling behavior which Ashashi then copied, slowing down her speech when Ashashi did not understand the first time, taking Ashashi into her pouch when the child became agitated. Such behavior might be typical for a fighting pair regardless of their relationship, as Levi kept pointing out. But I was sure.

They learned to say my name, after a fashion. Although I'd heard them employing something like our glottal stops, they seemed to have no glottal fricatives, voiced or otherwise, nor voiced alveolars, nor nasal consonants of any kind. (Of course it is misleading to use these terms, which refer to the part of the mouth where speech is made. They have no nasal consonants because they have only one respiratory orifice.) Thus my name Halima became "Atipa". At the time I did not know whether they meant to describe me personally by that name, or female humans, or interrogators.

Beyond my name, they showed no interest in learning our speech, which was just as well; they could not pronounce most of it. I, on the other hand, began to pick up a few dozen words of the Sheshash language.

Most of the attempts at communication I made over the next two weeks were with Ishish. For days after Ishish began speaking to me, Ashashi consistently tried various ways of killing me. Too, Ashasi's use of their language was more rudimentary and less nuanced, and her responses to Ishish were either echoes, queries, or possibly jokes.

But one afternoon, repeatedly distracted from my work by a buzzing fly (Maintenance has never succeeded in eradicating the things), I swatted it on the table without thinking.

Ishish and Ashashi both stopped what they were doing and stared at me for a long moment. I stared back, wondering whether I had committed some sort of transgression.

Then Ashashi said, "*Kri'ikshi akdash kri'ikshi!*" Ishish waited another moment, then confirmed it more calmly: "*Kri'ikshi akdash kri'ikshi.*" *Kri'ikshi*, I had inferred, was the word they used to refer to humans, but it was also their battle cry. Perhaps it meant "enemy?"

For the first time, Ashashi approached me slowly, turning so that each of her eyes could look at me in turn.

Ashashi's attitude changed from that moment. Not only did she begin speaking to me, she spoke nonstop. Most of her sentences were simple, and most of them I could not understand. Like a toddler, she seemed to like showing me the obvious. She would hold up an object and tell me what it was, perhaps copying my own actions, or she would do something and describe it (the way a youngster might say, "Look at me!"). She pointed out Ishish to me frequently, or would say, "Ashashi *shi*" when she crawled into Ishish's pouch.

Ishish seemed interested in getting through to me, although she was selective in the topics she would discuss. Human civilization, human concerns, anything about human beings interested her not at all, except for that single, dismissive term, *kri'ikshi.*

She talked preferentially about Ashashi: what she was doing or learning. Often she would describe Ashashi's actions as Ashashi performed them; I thought she was speaking to me, although possibly she narrated Ashashi's behavior the way parents narrate their children's actions, to teach them the connection between actions and words. As I might say, "Now Kesi picks up the ball," Ishish would say, "Ashashi *akpa'atkoko*," which seemed to mean, "Ashashi is spinning around when she doesn't need to."

Ashashi's greater tendency towards violence, so far as I could tell, seemed natural to Ishish. I wondered, are Sheshash children this brutal on their homeworld, against each other? If so, it's a wonder they survive to adulthood.

Kesi had a tantrum today, a bad one. She was still playing the Sheshash game Edmund had started with her, strutting around the main room of our quarters, making shrieking noises and spinning around, grabbing dolls or toy animals and pretending to kill them. Occasionally she would fall down on the carpet from dizziness, laugh, and start over. It was the sort of game that was amusing at first (if not for the subject matter) but eventually would have set any parent's teeth on edge. As it was, I bit my lip for the last ten minutes, trying to think of a way to distract her without making it obvious how much the game upset me.

I had been trying to ignore her for a while, staring at my work screen and hoping that she would get bored, when I sensed a change. I spun back, and saw that she had climbed up to the table and taken Jabari's framed picture into her pudgy hand. Now she shook it, yelling at her father's image, "You fight Sheshash! You die!"

Before I could even think, I had risen, crossed the room, snatched the photo out of her hand and shouted, "No, Kesi!"

It startled her, but she glared at me. "Give to Sheshash! Sheshash kill!"

I shook my head, not trusting myself to speak, and put the picture on a high shelf. She shouted, "Give me picture!"

"No," I said, as calmly as I could.

"Give! Give! Give, give, give, *give!*"

Then she was on the floor, kicking the legs of the table, banging her fists, yelling so loudly that it seemed her vocal cords would snap. I have learned how to handle such things: I returned to my chair and sat down, although I was shaking. Eventually, I knew, she would tire and calm down, and then I could cuddle her and assure her that I loved her, and we could forget the whole thing.

It took twenty minutes. By the time she was done, face slick with tears and mucous, she was exhausted. I barely had time to take her into my lap before she fell asleep. I did not manage to say "Mzazi loves Kesi" when she could still hear me.

One day, Ishish and Ashashi were both unusually quiet. They answered my questions briefly but did not elaborate. Ashashi moved around the room, but without what I had come to think of as her puppy-like enthusiasm. Eventually she crawled into Ishish's pouch, and said, "*Shi*"—sleep. But she did not sleep; she turned restlessly in the pouch, sticking out one arm at a time. I wondered whether Ashashi was growing too large for the pouch, whether Ishish would have to exile her.

Another fly appeared, this time on Ishish's side of the barrier (a much bigger Maintenance infraction, as the Sheshash were supposed to be in a sealed environment). Ishish saw it, said "*Kri'ikshi,*" and whipped out one of her flexible arms; the insect shattered.

Ashashi stirred in Ishish's pouch.

I saw spots when I understood. *Kri'ikshi* didn't mean "human." It meant "pest," "vermin." They didn't see us as opponents in a struggle; they saw us as parasites.

Once this was clear, I was able to ask questions I'd never thought to raise. Ishish spoke about *kri'ikshi*, and about the cell in which she and Ashashi were confined. On the one hand, *kri'ikshi* (humans) had built the cell, captured and forced them to live there. On the other hand, the cell provided *ata'ashkit*—isolation, solitude, protection, safety. Specifically, it was nearly devoid of *kri'ikshi* (parasites and pathogens, like the fly). She repeated this over and over: *kri'ikshi* built the cell, but the cell kept *kri'ikshi* out. It seemed a paradox to her.

I felt that we had hit the key point, that we were on the verge of a breakthrough. I made Ishish repeat that *kri'ikshi* had built the cell, and that it kept *kri'ikshi* out.

Then I asked, "Halima *atko kri'ikshi?*" I held my breath waiting for the answer.

Finally she said very quietly, "Atipa *ha'etish kri'ikshi.*"

Halima is not vermin, not a parasite, not the enemy.

I was halfway to the main entrance when the alarm sounded like a screaming child, hammering the eardrums twice a second until I thought my head would explode.

I phoned Levi as he was about to phone me. "The Sheshash broke out," he said. "They've killed at least six soldiers already and are heading your way."

How Ishish and Ashashi escaped is not important to relate. Our technology perplexes the Sheshash as theirs perplexes us. It may simply have taken Ishish this long to realize that what we thought was an impregnable chamber was as easy to violate as air.

I checked my weapon as I ran back; it was fully charged. I had not fired it in four years outside of mandatory practice, but at that second I did not know whether Ishish would kill me when she saw me, or let me talk to her.

I rounded the corner more quickly than I should have, failing to take the precautions drilled into me. Ishish and Ashashi were at the far end of the corridor, moving so rapidly it was hard to see them, a leapfrogging, swirling gait that made me nauseous. I stopped in my tracks.

"Ishish!" I called.

They stopped immediately, at the same instant, Ashashi a few yards closer to me than Ishish, their arms quivering, their fingers fluttering, their eyes open for battle.

Then, as I watched, their eyes half closed and their limbs slowed.

It was Ashashi who spoke. "Atipa!" Then she turned to her mother. "Atipa *etish kri'ikshi*? *Akdash* Atipa?" Is Halima a parasite, an enemy? Shall we kill her?

Ishish looked at me. "Atipa *sha'etish kri'ikshi. Sha'akdash* Atipa."

Ashashi sidled closer to her mother. "*Sha'etish kri'ikshi*," she repeated.

I lowered my weapon and began to step towards them, realizing that the alarm was no longer sounding, and that I could not remember when it had stopped. I was trying to work out how to get Ishish and Ashashi back to their cell, or to someplace safe, when I heard the pounding footsteps of a dozen sprinting soldiers echoing in the corridor behind me.

What happened next took less than two seconds. I turned back, away from Ishish and Ashashi, getting ready to explain the situation. A lone soldier, who either started from a different location than the others or had got ahead of them, rounded the corner first, his weapon out. He saw the Sheshash the instant I saw him.

I had begun to shout "Stand down!" when he fired.

"No!" I turned back. Ishish was down, a smoldering hole in her. Ashashi was already moving, a greenish-white blur who passed me before I could turn my head again.

When I did look back, the soldier was in two pieces, severed at the chest. Ashashi revolved around the body, screeching, "*Kri'ikshi! Kri'ikshi!* Ishish! Ishish!" Her eyes were moving side-to-side.

The other sprinting footsteps came closer; any moment they would be in view.

"Ashashi," I said, wanting to tell this child, this baby, that it was all right, that she could still survive, even without her mother, even as a prisoner in the hands of her enemies.

But she said, "*Kri'ikshi!*"—not towards me; she *trusted* me— but towards the coming footsteps. Another fraction of a second and she would be all over them, a blur of grief and rage that would not stop.

I fired my weapon. The baby popped like a balloon.

I hold Kesi on my lap and stroke her hair, singing lullabies and trying to believe that I love her. She is innocent, she bears no guilt for Jabari's death, for Ashashi's murder. She is a child of war, but she is my child. I should love her. I am sure that I did.

But how am I to love her? As a mother loves? Does a mother kill children? It does no good to tell myself that I probably saved a dozen lives, that Ashashi was the enemy. It does no good to tell myself, "There are no true innocents among the Sheshash; those children kill hundreds." A child who kills is still a child. A child who kills from grief is even more a child.

In my dreams, sometimes it is Kesi who explodes and crumples. It is Kesi who looks into my eyes and says, "Halima *sha'etish kri'ikshi.*" Halima is not the enemy. And then I kill my daughter. And then I wake up.

But I continue to stroke Kesi's hair, I continue to sing. Our children do not know our hearts; they only know what we show them. I will show Kesi the face of a loving mother, whether or not

I am one. I will give her what she needs to grow, to thrive, maybe even to trust.

But she should not trust me.

*

My friend Cinthea Stahl, a screenwriter who is too clever by half, once gave me the following story prompt: "Marsupials are fierce warriors." The first draft of this story, entitled "The Sacred Band," was more focused on the Sheshash themselves. By the time I finished, however, I knew that I most wanted to write about child soldiers and our troubled orientation towards children.

LIVING IN
THE NICHE

WILTON SOAL WAS A MINORITY OF one. Nothing he liked ever stayed available for very long. If he found a favorite restaurant, it would close for lack of business within a year. If he particularly enjoyed a television program, it was cancelled for low ratings during its first season. If he asked the manager of the clothing store why he'd stopped selling those shirts that fit so well, or the grocer why she no longer stocked those tiny fruits with the shiny violet skins and the aromatic tartness, the answer was always: "No one was buying them."

Online groups devoted to Soal's favorite brand of mechanical pencil went from 300 members to 50 members to one. Amazon popularity for those lovely octagonal tumblers plummeted; eBay auctions expired without bids. Eventually even Craig's List went dark.

For a while he thought that he just had spectacularly bad luck, like an evil spirit that would thwart him in anything he did. But when he experimented by gambling, he found that he won and lost at ordinary intervals like everyone else. Casinos were fun that way: they never singled him out for bad treatment—except that, if he found a casino that was gorgeous, they'd change the décor the following month because nobody liked it.

Cynically Soal suspected that he could make money by betting against himself. If he sold short on the manufacturer of a frozen dinner he relished, he might make a profit. But the results were inconsistent: true, the particular frozen dinner would be discontinued, but that was because of the smart business decisions of management, which replaced it with a better seller. Profits improved, and the stock price rose. Only when the company had bet its entire fortune on the thing Soal most wanted could he make a killing by investing against it. Once in a while, this happened.

He thought about gambling on elections. No political candidate he supported in the primaries ever won the nomination, and no party he supported ever won the election. If he gambled that his favorite candidate would lose, he'd probably win the bet. But he discovered that the sort of people who would engage in that type of transaction didn't like it if you consistently beat them. They'd stop taking your bets, and hint darkly that worse things might happen.

Soal came to wonder whether he was merely doomed to love what everyone else hated, or was weirdly *causing* the unpopularity of products and candidates through his own desires. Perhaps his desires themselves were toxic. He tried an experiment. Psychology books said that you could change the way you felt about something through association: if you repeatedly experienced two things together, eventually your reactions to them would be similar.

The summer Wilton Soal was 27, the band Grandeur & Majesty released a new album, *Leveling the Killing Field*, which threatened to go platinum. He had never heard a single G & M song in his life, so he bought a copy of the new collection and made a point of listening to it repeatedly for several days, always when he was eating his favorite snack or playing his ancient copy of a beloved computer game. By the end of the week he was able to hear and appreciate the subtle references and rhythmic jokes, the homages to earlier music traditions, the sharp observation of human foibles and the unforgiving attitude towards hypocrisy. He found himself whistling songs from *Leveling* while he was exercising and singing them in the shower. Grandeur and Majesty were geniuses! He couldn't wait for their next album.

Within ten days, the sales of the *Leveling the Killing Field* dropped off all major charts. By the end of the month, radio stations stopped playing it and hits on the band's iTunes page stopped altogether. By the end of the year, the band split up.

This put everything in a new light. Wilton Soal had discovered the ability to change the hearts and minds of thousands, maybe millions. Far from being powerless, he was possibly the most powerful man on Earth! But he felt like a thief, a destroyer, even if all he'd done was to manipulate his own feelings.

Could he use his power for good? Soal wasn't sure what "good" and "evil" meant on matters of pure taste, although he thought he could believe in them in the context of politics. Could he trick himself into liking what needed to be opposed? He doubted that he could take something he already hated, such as platform shoes or the Christian Coalition, and so warp his sensibilities that he came to love them, solely for purposes of destroying them. But maybe someone else could.

He hired The Amazing Lazlo to hypnotize him into a sincere love of platform shoes. Lazlo had him gaze into a candle and spoke softly to him for a few hours, and when he was done, Soal was convinced that he thought women wearing five-inch soles were the most beautiful creatures on earth, and he fretted that the experiment would be successful, and that he would never see one again.

Platforms retained their popularity. Apparently something in his heart knew the difference between genuine affection, even affection derived from deliberate association, and feelings imposed by someone else. He *thought* he loved platform shoes, and he experienced pleasure when looking at them, but there was some distinction, opaque even to him, between observable and genuine feeling. "By their works shall you know them," he muttered to himself.

But this was a new experience. Something that pleased him was popular, pleasing others too! For the first time he could talk with people about a shared enthusiasm, argue and sympathize and agree to chat later; and he could expect to meet another member of this club if he walked down the street. Was this what normal people felt like?

Of course, there weren't many extended conversations you could have about platform shoes. The various fashion boards and blogs were nice that way, and Soal did find himself making new friends, but it was hardly something on which he could build a whole life. But what if he picked something with broad appeal and more general interest?

He studied the newspaper, skimmed Tweets and Facebook postings. He decided that the movement for 100% renewable energy had many motivated supporters; bloggers who liked it seemed to talk about nothing else. Soal himself had always thought the movement to do away with all fossil fuels within ten years bespoke an inability to perform basic arithmetic. Left to himself, he would never have joined it. It was perfect.

The Amazing Lazlo needed an entire day to overcome such a strong dislike. He charged more than double, irritably remarking that Soal didn't hypnotize well and that the effort had drained him of the ability to do any creative work for at least a week. "Whatever," Soal said, and paid him.

As before, Lazlo had worked a miracle. Soal still doubted the mathematics of the movement (apparently Lazlo had not altered his ability to reason), but he found that he no longer cared about the logic of it. Even if the movement was futile, he wanted to try.

His life improved dramatically. He had a community, things to share with others, a sense of belonging. He volunteered for a lobbying organization to change state energy policy, working ten hours per week passing out leaflets, raising money, contacting members of the legislature. It was while knocking on doors that he met Diane Forest.

She was just his height, thin as a sapling, with lank, mouse-colored hair that kept falling in her eyes. She wore old jeans and new tee shirts with slogans on them, and sneakers with lightning bolts on the laces. She was passionate about climate change, enthusiastic about her favorite reality shows on TV, and opinionated about local pizza parlors. It took two days of canvassing together for Wilton Soal to fall irrevocably in love.

In his 28 years he'd never experienced infatuation like this; talking to Diane was as hard as ice skating. He stammered, he paused, he got lost in his grammar. It amused her that he was so tongue tied, and she made him practice getting whole sentences out.

"I—the pizza, I—well —" he would begin.

"There are two possibilities," she said, smirking. "*I liked the pizza* or *I didn't like the pizza.* Pick one."

"I didn't like the pizza."

"Excellent, but you have no taste."

Or another time: "You know, that show—um, the reality—"

"*I like reality shows* or *I don't like reality shows.*"

"I don't like reality shows."

"Definitely an improvement, and definitely clueless. You don't like anything good."

"I like you."

She grinned. "Okay, maybe you have some taste after all." She took his face in her hands and gave him a quick, hard kiss, snorting and laughing the whole time.

He asked her to a movie and a public concert, to lunch and dinner. They met on weekends or went out after an afternoon of stuffing envelopes. He was careful to pick things he already loathed, and she relished them.

One Saturday afternoon, walking beside the river with Diane, holding hands and eating ice cream cones he thought were too sweet and cloying, Soal thought about how he might ask her over to his apartment. This brought on a whole new wave of stammering, and he waited for her to start teasing him.

But she was brooding. "Wil, I think something's wrong with me."

"How do you mean?"

"I can't get anyone to return my phone calls. Friends from school I've known since I was six, people in the Movement who've always asked after me—it's like no one wants to talk to me anymore. I'm being unfriended on Facebook left and right. Even my mom is giving me the cold shoulder. Have I started behaving like an asshole? Do I suddenly smell bad? Tell me the truth, Wil. I'm getting seriously bummed."

Soal stopped walking. Diane kept going a few steps, but when his hand slipped out of hers, she turned around and looked at him. Her face became alarmed. "What's wrong? Are you all right?"

He swallowed, and noticed that the awful ice cream was starting to drip down his fingers.

He whispered, "There's nothing wrong with you, Di."

She rolled her eyes. "Easy for you to say."

"No, I actually know. I have to tell you a story."

They found a bench that needed refinishing and sat down carefully to avoid splinters. Soal told Diane everything—his disappointments, his experiments with gambling, the Amazing Lazlo—

She stopped him, appalled. "You mean you needed a *hypnotist* to convince you to believe in the Movement?"

He grimaced. "If I had come to like it naturally, by now it would have no supporters and be permanently dead. Anyway, you need to keep listening."

When he'd finished, she spent a long time looking out at the river. Then she said, "You claim that my sudden loss of friends is your fault?"

He nodded miserably. "I like you, therefore nobody else does."

She shook her head. "You realize how crazy that sounds, not to mention narcissistic?"

He shrugged. "It fits with everything else. I have an unbroken record, years of it."

Diane brought her hands up as if to gesture while speaking, then let them drop back onto her knees with a soft slap. She stood up and walked quickly to the river, then up and down the bank, shaking her head and talking to herself. Soal stayed on the bench, watching and wondering whether this was the last time he was ever going to see her.

Finally she strode back, not as quickly but with clenched fists. She sat down hard on the bench and glared at him. "So, great. What do we do?"

Soal looked at his knees. Diane said sharply, "Hey. Look me in the eyes." He looked at her eyes, which were an angry brown. "What do we do about this?" She repeated.

"So long as I find you attractive and pleasant, you will repel everyone else around you."

"Even my mother?"

"Apparently."

"For crying out loud. So . . ."

He took a deep breath. "So, I have to stop liking you."

She raised an eyebrow. "What, you can just turn it on and off?"

"No, and Lazlo won't be any help either. You need to do something to make me hate you."

She snorted. "Such as?"

He thought about it. "Um, ridicule me? Sexually humiliate me? Steal from me? Hit me?"

She looked disgusted. "You've to be kidding."

"It's the only way."

"Screw that. I'm not going to do any of that stuff, and besides, it wouldn't work."

"How do you mean?"

"It's obvious. If you *know* I'm sexually humiliating you in order to manipulate your feelings so that you won't like me, will it change your feelings?"

"Oh, I hadn't thought of it that way." He considered. "Probably not."

"See?"

"It's good of you to stick by me."

A small explosion of laughter escaped her. "'Stick by' you? What, exactly, is there for me to stick by? We've been on, let's see, five dates, I've kissed you three times—not, I notice, that you've ever kissed *me*—and you've mentioned on six occasions, if we include just now, that you 'like' me. Sorry to break it to you, but that's not going to make a person stand at attention while going down on the *Titanic*. It's just that I refuse to behave like an asshole just to get people to stop treating me as if I *was* behaving like an asshole. I mean, how twisted is that?"

"Right."

She closed her eyes for a second; he had the impression that she was counting to ten. Then she opened them and said, more quietly: "So, tell me this, Wil: does the fact that my own mother won't return my calls mean that you maybe more than just *like* me?"

He swallowed. "Yes. Yes, I—" He swallowed again.

"This is why you get tongue tied, isn't it?"

He nodded, his lips tight.

She said, "That's very sweet, and there's lots I could infer from it. But I don't want to infer. I need you to say it."

He took a deep breath, and said, "I like you more than any other person I've ever met."

She smiled. "That's better. 'Like' as in doughnuts? 'Like' as in drinking buddies?" His eyes dropped again. "Look at me, please."

He looked up. "'Like' as in girlfriend."

She sighed, more like she was relieved to get over a tough task than was actually happy. "Well, that took long enough." She gave him another quick kiss.

"Do you ever kiss softly and slowly?" he asked.

She rolled her eyes. "Try giving me a reason."

But he felt awful. What good was it to have a girlfriend, someone who actually liked him, if he was going to ruin her life in the process?

"Get that look off your face," she said. "You're not going to ruin my life."

"A lot you know about it," he snapped. "How are you going to escape what every other thing I've ever loved has suffered? Or are you saying that you don't mind living an isolated life with only one friend?"

"Well, let's talk about that. What *efforts* have you made to stop these things from happening?"

"What?" He squinted at her. "How do you mean?"

"Well, for instance, when you liked a political candidate, did you jump in and start working for her? Did you canvass, the way we've canvassed for renewable energy? Did you try to talk your friends in to supporting her?"

He thought about it. "No, I guess I didn't."

She nodded. "I thought so. So we have no data about your ability to counteract this, what, this *effect* you experience through actual effort."

After a pause, he said, "I guess not."

"Listen." She tapped herself on the chest. "I'm not just going to give up or give in when your personal genie, or whatever the hell it is, decides to isolate me from the world. I intend to seek out my friends & relatives, do them favors, ask them to tell me their troubles, be the best friend I can. Let's see the genie deal with *that*."

"That's a lot of work," he said.

She sat up straighter and glared again. "It's what people do for each other. It's how relationships are maintained. In fact—" She grabbed his hand. "—It's how romantic relationships are maintained too. If you want me, you need to work to keep me."

"Um, okay."

"And you're going to need to work to help me avoid the effects of your, your *aura* or whatever. Introduce me to people you know. Proclaim my virtues online. Flatter me in public. Try to win over my mother." She grinned.

For the next two weeks, Wilmot Soal labored on behalf of Diane Forest's reputation. He went out of his way to praise her cleverness, honesty and compassion to members of their environmental group. He met her friends and asked each one to recount anecdotes about funny or endearing things she'd done. He did meet Diane's mother, and told her she must be the wisest parent in the world to have raised such a daughter. Diane guffawed at that one, but it was a forgivable bit of hyperbole from a man in love.

It didn't help. People listened politely to what he had to say, or recounted the stories he requested, but Diane reported no change in their behavior. Her friends were still cold, her mother distant and disapproving.

They saw each other more frequently; they talked about everything. Diane told Wilton about the bully she decked in second grade, the week during her 15th year when she wouldn't leave the house because she hated her looks so much, her fear of wind and men with briefcases, her anger that hummed like a constant background chord. Wilton told Diane of his repeated disappointments, his eventual expectation that nothing good would ever happen to him, his creeping shame and suspicion that he deserved it all.

She took him to bed on a cool, breezy evening, while the last light of sunset was still in the sky. It was his first time, miraculous, confusing, and terrifying, and without Diane's sense of humor and clarity of thought, he might have collapsed into himself. She understood his fear as she understood her own, called it by its name, and together they faced the exposure to pain that is the definition of intimacy. The next morning, seeing her grin from the other pillow and her warm shoulder peeking from the sheet, he felt that he'd had the most beautiful night of his life.

That should have warned him. The next day, when they met for dinner and he kissed her, she shuddered and pulled away.

"What is it?" he asked, hoping he didn't already know.

"I don't know," she said. "When you touch me, it's like you're covered in worms or something." She paused, as if unwilling to continue, then forced out the words: "And when I picture having sex with you again . . ." She stopped again and swallowed like a person trying not to throw up.

"Was it that bad?" he asked, despair rising in his chest.

"*No,*" she said. "It was sweet; it was *lovely*. I haven't had that much fun with anyone in years. I wanted you to stay with me the whole day. I'm sure of it. I *remember* it that way."

"Then why—"

"It doesn't feel that way *now*. It doesn't make any sense; I can't explain it." She shuddered again.

"I can," he said. He'd hoped, in the back of his mind, that *sex with her*, as experienced by him, would be different than *sex with him*, as experienced by her—that he could like the one without poisoning the other. But apparently there was only their *sex together*, and he could destroy that as thoroughly as anything else.

She looked suddenly furious. "No. Absolutely not. It's bad enough that this demon of yours is telling everyone what to think about me. I'll be damned if it's going to tell *me* how *I'm* going to feel about what I do with my own body and who I do it with."

He spread his hands. "I don't see what we can do."

She glared. "Neither do I. Let me think about it."

Soal spent two days imagining how he would live without Diane. He pictured never having a partner in life. He thought about occupations where celibacy was a benefit. He thought about just being miserable.

On the third day, she phoned him. "Come to my apartment tonight." She sounded firm rather than happy.

"Are you sure?"

"Yeah."

When he arrived, she seemed as exhausted and desperate as he felt. Her hair was uncombed, her clothes were stained, and she had a wild look in her eyes. She gave him a long, deep kiss, then shuddered. "This isn't going to be easy," she said, her voice cracking. "But don't back out."

That night Diane Forest made love to Wilton Soal with stubborn intensity. It was awful to caress someone who couldn't stand the feel of him. He could see her take a deep breath and swallow each time he touched her, but when he pulled back, she growled, "Don't you dare stop." For Diane, anger and desperation were poor aphrodisiacs, but she refused to be dictated to. He refused to desert her. It was difficult for either of them to become aroused, or to come together, or to climax, but they managed it and collapsed into an exhausted sleep.

In the morning, when he stroked her sunlit arm, she flinched again. He thought he was going to cry.

She put her palm on his cheek. "No," she said. "We've improved. I'm sure of it. It still feels bad, but nowhere near like before." She smiled. "I think we just need practice."

Gradually, through repeated exposure and full awareness of what she was doing, Diane wore down her revulsion until it had vanished. After a few weeks, all that remained were the desire and enthusiasm she already had—and a stronger bond than she'd ever known before.

One morning over breakfast, she said, "This is how we solve the other problem, the popularity problem."

He looked at her. "What do you mean?"

"This is how I can date you without becoming a pariah to everyone else."

Soal didn't get it. "What, am I supposed to have sex with each of your friends, not to mention your mom?"

She snorted coffee into her nose, collapsing into fits of coughing and laughter. "No, you idiot. I overcame this *effect* because I was aware of it, I knew that it wasn't coming from me, and I was determined not to be controlled. That's all we have to do."

He thought about it. "You mean, we *tell* people that I'm, um, cursed? That I have magical powers? That their thoughts are not their own? They'll think we're crazy."

"Maybe. But it's worth a try."

They started with Diane's mother. She didn't believe them, but after an hour of argument she agreed to act as if it were true: as if her feelings about Diane were generated by Soal, and she needed to work to master them.

She recovered her full warmth for her daughter in less than a week.

Once they'd proved the concept, Diane and Wilton approached each of her friends, co-workers, and acquaintances individually. Some thought it was nonsense. Some simply walked away, never re-entering Diane's life. ("No loss," she said.) But most, after their surprise and skepticism, made the effort to fight the bad influence Soal exercised over them, and most succeeded.

Wilton Soal remained a minority of one—in most things. Newspapers, free medical clinics, and public parks still vanished when they began to appeal to him, but from Diane he now knew that he could reverse any of these changes as they happened. He could save a sandwich shop by advertising his own effect on it, telling patrons they were being manipulated by magic, exhorting them to fight back. It would be expensive and exhausting, but it could work.

Mostly he didn't bother. He didn't want to become a public figure, and working to keep the "Soal Effect" from isolating Diane (and later, their children) took every bit of spare time and energy he had.

You do what you can.

*

This story originally grew out of years of irritation at wonderful restaurants closing for lack of business. But back in the day, when SFF was still an oddity and its enthusiasts were confirmed weirdos, I think a lot of us felt as if our tastes and passions doomed us to repeated disappointment. Popular culture has changed since then, and I think some old SFF fans were unprepared to find themselves in the center of a movement that regular folks enjoyed. For me, it feels like my family has grown into a nation.

THE MANNEQUIN'S
ITCH

THE MANNEQUIN FELT HER SKIN ITCH whenever the sirens went off. It was on the outside of her thigh, just under where the flowered print on the yellow fabric fell. She would have liked to reach down and scratch that place—the only gesture she ever wished for, except that once in a while, she thought it would be nice to wave at the passers-by. She thought that that was a sort of itch too.

Her left hip thrown out, her arm extended, her hand beckoning, she smiled toward the rising sun or the rising moon, or to each person who stood in front of her window. Some people looked her in the eyes, laughing silently through the plate glass. Others frowned and chewed their lips at the dress, moving their heads around in search of a price tag that wasn't there. A few crouched down and tried to look under the skirt at her nonexistent genitals. She smiled equally to all of them.

But when the sirens sounded and the people in front of her window hurried away, the itch returned. It felt purple, she decided, or maybe violet. She wondered why she itched only in that spot and nowhere else; maybe there was a tag underneath the hem that tickled her.

Apart from the itching, it was restful when the sirens sounded. The streets were empty and silent; no traffic disturbed her view of gray buildings or green parks. And then would come the sound of wind, and the sky would turn green, and the buildings across the street would turn green. It was interesting. After a while (the mannequin wasn't very good at judging time) the sky and the buildings would change back to blue or white or gray, and the wind would stop. Eventually most of the people came back. But not all.

The girl in the blue coat and the girl in the red coat came every day at about noon; the mannequin guessed that they came here instead of eating lunch. They were old for girls, young for women, like the mannequin herself, although they looked nothing like her. The mannequin had red curls on her head, and her plastic skin was the color of eggshells. The girls had black hair and eyes, and skin the color of walnuts. Their coats were heavy, and sometimes too heavy for the weather, but they wore them in all weathers.

The mannequin got tired of her clothes, but it would only be a few weeks before the clerks would come out and strip her naked behind the screen, then put her in something new and move her limbs into another position. She thought of the positions and the clothes together: green evening gown with fingers laced together in front of her; blue bikini with hands on hips; gray flannel suit with one foot in front of the other and toe pointed. With the clothes and the positions went feelings: the evening gown meant shyness; the bikini meant curiosity; the suit meant mirth.

When the girl in the red coat walked, the mannequin saw a faint limp. Sometimes the girl in the blue coat held her arm or her waist. The mannequin wondered whether the girl in the red coat had once stood too long with one hip sticking out. She thought a limp must be something like an itch.

Sometimes the mannequin wondered what happened to the people who went away after the sirens. Of course, it was hard to be sure whether anyone *had* gone away, because the passing crowds in front of her window were so different from day to day. But she was sure that at least some of the people she saw daily, running someplace at sunrise and away from that same place at sunset, stopped coming to her window when the sirens sounded. They never came back.

The girl in the blue coat never came back.

Sometimes one of the pedestrians would return after the sirens with tears on his face, leaning his head against the window until his nose was mashed, staring into the mannequin's face and shaking, and his tears would dry to a faint salt crust that marked the glass for days. Eventually one of the clerks would come out and wipe the window to get rid of the marks.

The mannequin liked tears; they helped her itch go away, as if they were washing over the place like a salve. She wondered what it would be like if she could weep herself. She thought it might be fun. If she could cry, she thought, then maybe her tears could fix the itches of some of the people in the street. That would be nice, especially for the girl in the red coat.

When the girl in the red coat started coming alone, she did not cry. For an hour or more every day, she would just stare into the mannequin's face, her lips occasionally moving. Every now and then she would look around as if to find someone, or maybe to hide from someone. Then she would shrug. It looked itchy. The mannequin thought that if she cried, she could mend the girl's itch, and maybe her limp.

Then, one day when the sky was the color of gray flannel, as the mannequin strode unmoving in tight jeans and a tank top and the girl in the red coat pressed her nose against the glass, the sirens went off again. The girl in the red coat shuddered, her glance turning from the mannequin to the street. All around her, people were running or briskly walking, lips tight, eyes glancing around them.

The mannequin's thigh itched.

Then the girl in the red coat slowly shook her head from side to side. She placed both hands and her forehead on the glass, closing her eyes and taking a deep breath. Some of the people hurrying by the window shouted over their shoulders to the girl; the mannequin couldn't tell what they were saying, but she could see the girl's reply: *No.* Then once more, *No.*

How nice, the mannequin thought. The girl in the red coat will stay with me during the sirens. It will be pleasant to have a friend here. Then we can look at each other, and maybe she will cry.

The girl in the red coat did start to cry, big tears that lingered in her eyes, then dropped resignedly onto the coat, painting maroon streaks on the heavy fabric. Her mouth remained shut but trembled.

Then came the sound of the wind, and the girl in the red coat closed her eyes and bit her lip, and the sky turned from gray to green, and the windows across the street were tinted again. The mannequin's itch throbbed as if she had a pulse.

In the green light, the girl's skin turned green, and her coat turned green. Then both the girl and her coat became fuzzy to look at, as if the mannequin's eyes were playing tricks on her. The mannequin could not see the girl's eyes, and then could not see her mouth, and then could not tell the difference between her skin and her coat. Then the girl was gone.

The sirens stopped and the people came back out in the street. Later the sun came out.

The girl in the red coat didn't come back to the window, but the mannequin no longer expected it. Days came and went, some days the sirens sounded and some days they didn't.

But now, the itch never went away.

*

At Clarion, Larissa Lai taught us a self-prompting method for starting new stories: brainstorm a list of words for two or three minutes, then circle the three that most hold your attention. For this story, of course, two of the words were "mannequin" and "itch;" I don't remember what the third one was. As is sometimes the case when I write without a plan, the story reveals a dark side of my imagination that frightens me a little.

LINEAGE

ND YET I KNOW SO LITTLE. I FEEL THE soil of a hundred lands under my feet, look into ten thousand frightened eyes, grasp uncounted brittle strands of hope between my fingers. But I cannot answer so simple a question as this: What am I, when I am not one of them?

Mathilde:

I think your excitement is premature. If I understood your report (and it could have been clearer) there is a lot of work to do before you can approach the conclusions you're suggesting.

Let's stick to the facts. I'll accept your statement that you've found identical resonance patterns in seven different artifacts from disparate periods and points of origin, representing four continents and more than three millennia. Having said this, and understanding that I don't doubt your word, please run the resonance tests again.

I will also accept your assertion that each of these artifacts appears to display a similar visual marking or design—although, to my eye, the similarity could be coincidental, and the pattern is so rudimentary (even childish) that one could imagine it arising by chance.

Even if both of these statements are true, it is an heroic leap to infer that somehow the artifacts are associated with the same individual. You admit the extreme improbability that this is true; why bring it up at all?

However, I think that we can settle the matter easily. You did not mention running a DNA echo series on any of these artifacts. Do so now. If there are traces, and they're similar for two or more of the artifacts, then you'll have something meaningful to say. Otherwise we need to look for other (more plausible!) explanations.

Don't worry; everybody leaps to conclusions early in her career. If we didn't get excited about this work, why would we do it at all?

—Leo

Raisl had nearly calmed the baby to sleep when Jan slammed open the door. The sudden noise and light frightened Bella, and she started whimpering all over again. After a weary evening—Bella was cutting a tooth and keeping the two older children awake— Raisl's first urge was to snarl at Jan, if Moishe didn't take his head off first.

But Jan's gray, sweaty face told her that he hadn't intruded needlessly in to their cramped, musty alcove. The balding little man's agitation was clear even in this bad light. His eyes bulged; he was out of breath. Raisl knew what he was going to say before he spoke.

"They found out; they're coming," said Jan, looking at Moishe, not at Raisl. "I saw them coming down the street, a whole squad of S.S. I ran back, they didn't see me, but they're not far off. It won't take them long to get here."

Moishe, dazed, rose slowly from his chair; Yakov and Dvora sat upright on their cot. "How?" asked Moishe. "How could they find out?"

Jan bent over and took Raisl firmly by the elbows, impelling her and Bella up. "It doesn't matter *how*," he said. "Go. Go in the next ten minutes or you'll all be in Oświęcim by morning. Get out of Krakow, however you can."

"But the plan won't work on a Sunday night," said Moishe, yanking clothes onto Dvora as Raisl wrapped the baby. "The children can't—"

"Forget the plan," Jan said. "Go. I recommend north, then west, but *go.*"

"They'll be right behind us!" said Raisl, her own eyes as wide as Jan's, her legs wobbly.

"No they won't," said Jan. "I can stall them, talk to them, maybe a long as ten more minutes. If you hurry, if you're lucky, you'll slip by."

"You can't stay and stall them," said Raisl. "They'll kill you!"

"Maybe. It's been done before," said Jan. All of a sudden he grinned—and he didn't look like Jan anymore. The grin was feral, like a madman or a criminal; it transformed him from the timid clerk Raisl knew into something fey and reckless. Then she saw that he had scratched something onto his forearm, with a pin or a knife. It looked like three circles in a row and it was very recent: blood welled from the shapes. She was afraid of him.

"Done before? What are you talking about?" demanded Moishe, who hadn't noticed Jan's face or arm, jerking on his thin coat and checking Yakov's buttons.

"Never mind," said Jan with a stranger's cheeriness. "I wish we had some apples, though. I have a taste for yellow apples right now."

"Apples?" said Moishe, his voice now rising in panic. "*Apples?* Are you *out of your mind?*"

Jan set his hand on Yakov's small shoulder, his mad eyes on Moishe and his face still in that weird grin. "Moishe, this is my house," he said. "Get the hell out of it and let me do what I want with the trespassers." From his gay tone, he might have been asking to stay a little longer at the card table.

That was the end of the discussion. In the next three minutes,

Moishe, Raisl and the children grabbed the few extra clothes, supplies and precious things they could carry, embraced Jan in fear and confusion, and stumbled down the back stairs.

So began the first of many dreadful nights, the twisted dream of flight, starvation and exhaustion that lasted for more than a year. Somewhere in those bitter forests and barren fields, Yakov died holding his father's hand; somewhere else Raisl let in the chronic, painful illness that would never leave her. She was still wincing from it, an irritable old woman in a stupid pink suit, when she watched Bella's youngest daughter stand under the wedding canopy in Ohio.

Jan outdid himself in wit and misdirection, clowning and practically singing to the soldiers for not ten minutes, but twenty. He was still grinning his infuriating grin when Lieutenant Haupmann gave the disgusted order to shoot him.

Again and again, like a banquet, comes the heady inhalation of destruction. The choice, the leap, the delicious farewell, the sweetness of oblivion. Greater love hath no man than this. Dulce et decorum est pro patria mori. Hear, O Israel: the Lord thy God, the Lord is One. Come on, nobody lives forever!

But I am still here. If this is somewhere.

Leo:

I'd already run the resonance tests three times before I made my report; I understood how unlikely the data seemed. Nevertheless I ran them a fourth time per your instructions. The results were consistent: each of the seven artifacts has the same resonance pattern, the identical sequence over all eight reference points, each point similar to four decimal places (data analysis attached).

I understand what you're saying about the design, and yes, I suppose it could be "in the eye of the beholder." But that peculiar pattern of three circles in a row, each with its own perpendicular "arm" or "stem," just seems too regular to be coincidental. It was the design, after all, that drew me to these artifacts to begin with; I saw two with the same device, then a third, and that persuaded me run the resonance test and look for similar items. Also there's the fact that each of the designs seems to have been added hurriedly, not using optimum materials or craftsmanship. If I were at home and these objects were contemporary, I'd say this was a gang sign.

As you requested, I ran the DNA echo series. There are distinguishable echoes on all of the artifacts, but none of them match. The people who left genetic residue on these objects had no common ancestors for at least six generations (full report attached). I realize that this datum may seem dispositive.

But looking at the literature, I can't find a single recorded case where two different individuals left the same resonance pattern. Not one. The energy signatures are supposed to be more unique to the individual than fingerprints, retinal patterns or voiceprints. If you can find a confirmed exception, then please show it to me; I know I'm relatively new at this, but I think I know how to read. —Mathilde

From inside the still, musty storehouse, the noises outside were strangely louder, as if they thought he was hiding and were calling to him. Thomas heard every mournful, futile whisper of the breeze, every restless complaint of the birds. Naturally he couldn't avoid hearing the groans and thuds of the wagon and its two horses as they drove up the hillside from the west.

Squinting with his bad eyes in the painful sunlight, he saw a straight gray blur with spots of cream and a coppery halo atop the wagon. It was Anne, her fiery hair under a cap. Though he couldn't make out the details, something in her posture told Thomas that she holding the reins with more force than was necessary. The horses shook their heads nervously.

"Not the usual time for you to visit the storehouse," Thomas said, wondering what the horses knew that he didn't.

Without introduction or greeting, Anne's flat, practical voice said, "I'll need you to give me as many of the food stores as you can, Thomas."

"Give?" He shaded his eyes with his hand. "Give, for charity?"

"Aye, it should be for charity, you hard man, but I know you'll not give a crumb unless it's paid for. So here." She threw something at him; he had to stumble forward to catch it in his hands with a heavy *chink*. It was a bag of coins—a lot of coins. He counted them quickly with his fingers, his eyebrows lifting to his hairline.

"This would buy all that's inside," he said. "It won't fit on the wagon, all that." Anne's farm was no smaller than anyone else's, and she had no family to feed, but these coins must represent nearly all she had in the world. It made no sense.

She answered, "Well, then consider it your best bargain of the season. Lord knows you need all the help you can get."

"There's no need to insult me, is there? Tell me, what'll you do with what you've bought so dearly?"

There was a pause. Then she said, "Drive to London."

Involuntarily Thomas stepped three paces forward; now he could see the expression on her face. But it did him no good; her face told him as little as her voice. "London? You'll drive a cart of food into the middle of a plague city?"

"Aye, if they'll let me in. They're starving."

"They're dying of the Black Death, woman! You'll have no trouble getting in. It's *out* that'll be the problem."

"The ones who aren't dying of the Black Death are starving. No one will go into the city."

"And for good reason! Those that go in don't come out."

"We'll see."

"Will you throw your life away?"

"I'd not call it 'throwing away,'" she answered. Then a strange, wide grin came over her face, a grin that he'd never seen on her

before, reminding Thomas of a wolf on the hunt. It made him draw
back, so that she was a comforting blur again. "Besides, it's been
done before," she added.

"No doubt," he grimaced, moving into the storehouse.

"Have you any apples in the storehouse?" she called after him.

"Apples? No, they were gone a month ago."

"Pity, that. I have a real craving for a yellow apple; came on me
all of a sudden."

Thomas found that he was reluctant to emerge again from the
storehouse. When he came out with the goods, Anne had dismount-
ed and took the first sack from him. So close as that, he could smell
her sweat and the rosemary on her breath, and could see that she
still wore that weird smile.

As he came close enough to hoist the sack, Thomas saw that
there was a sign scratched on to the wagon's side, using a bit of
chalk or stone, or possibly a metal tool. It was three circles in a row,
each with a tiny stem over it. It hadn't been there when Anne drove
up, he was sure. A witch's mark?

He did not have long to ponder the question. She gave him an
unexpected kiss on the forehead with her dry lips before ascend-
ing again and geeing up the horses. Back inside the building he
couldn't avoid the odd, foreign melody of her whistling as the cart
rumbled back down the hill. It took a long time before the sounds
were gone.

For the rest of his life, Thomas listened half-hopefully for the
sounds of Anne's horses. But they never came.

*Instantiation, substantiation, manifestation, possession? I am
no one, if more than nothing; years pass, but not for me. Then I
feel, like an embrace, the fear and devotion—the lifeboat over-
flows, the enemy surprises the patrol, the burning wall begins to
collapse, the asteroid approaches the shuttle, the dike bursts.*

And I walk the earth again.

Mathilde:

You have no call to be offended. You are presenting unusual conclusions to the principal investigator with very little to back them up. You have to expect to be pressed on your hypotheses if you're going to stay in this business.

Yes, I do find the disparate DNA echo evidence "dispositive." If the same individual actually handled all seven objects, then that individual would have left an echo on each of them. Maybe it wouldn't have survived, but *somebody's* echo survived, since you found it on the artifacts. The fact that it shows seven distinct, unrelated individuals seems to decide the matter.

As you say, I don't know of any recorded cases in which different individuals left the same resonance pattern. Perhaps we've found the first one. Or perhaps we've found evidence that resonance patterns normalize or disorganize under certain conditions. Each of those would be a meaningful discovery, would it not?

Let's not forget that our object is to collect meaningful data and find the explanations that most satisfactorily explain it. We're not after ultimate "truth."

—Leo

Nicander could still smell the smoke from the campfires that had been put out. Pacing steadily over the cold, rocky ground, he saw the faintest blue traces over a few remaining spots. He nodded with approval. The enemy almost certainly knew their position and their numbers, and so the men had been allowed a little warmth and a chance to cook some meat, but there was no point being reckless.

Now they were all at work, whetting swords or repairing armor. Any talk was so low he could barely hear it, which was as it should be. They knew their business. A full night's sleep, and they'd be ready for—well, perhaps not ready for what was coming, but readier than any other army would have been. The twilight would end soon, and the night would be cold.

Nicander stopped at his captain's tent, cleared his throat, and said his own name loudly enough to carry. There was no reply, which he safely interpreted to be an invitation to enter.

A single lamp lit the space, granting Alexandros the look of a shadowy giant. He was oiling the straps of his armor and humming to himself, that same annoying marching tune he'd had on his lips for a month.

"Yes, Nico?" said Alexandros, who hadn't looked up when his enomotarch came in.

"One of the men can do that for you," said Nicander.

"Yes, and they can do their own, can't they?" said the captain. "Have you urgent tasks to take me away from the work of an honest soldier?"

"No sir."

"Well, then. How are the men?"

"Calm, sir, for the most part. Some are edgy because they don't like the terrain."

"Ah now, the terrain is perfect." Alexandros spoke as if he were a connoisseur tasting a rare wine. He set down the armor, rubbed the excess oil on his arms, and picked up his sword like a father holding his infant son. He took out a whetstone and began to sharpen the blade, beaming at his handiwork.

Nicander said, "Gates of Fire."

"Delightful name for a battlefield," said Alexandros. "Makes you feel like you're already doing something great."

There was a pause. Alexandros seemed to know that Nicander had more to say, but he didn't ask him to continue. He ran his finger along the blade, nodding. Then he blew the iron dust off it; but he did not set down either the sword or the whetstone.

Nicander cleared his throat again. Alexandros looked up, amused.

Nicander said, "Sir, what in name of the Dog we are doing here?"

"Obeying the King."

"And what is *he* doing here?"

Alexandros seemed to consider whether this was insubordinate talk. Then he answered, "Having a drink with the Persians."

"Sir—"

"What is it you want to know, Nico?" The captain paused, glancing over at a bowl of golden apples on a small table. "The tactical situation is obvious. When you have a small force and the enemy has a large one, you choose the narrowest place possible. Can't get any narrower than this." He looked pleased with himself. "We'll hold them off all day. Several days, maybe."

"And then?"

"One of two things happens: either they'll go away, or we'll get to meet Charon face-to-face. Prissy fellow; he's probably Athenian."

Nicander ignored the blasphemy; the captain delighted in shocking him. "You think they'll go away?"

"Persians? They might. They dislike getting bloody noses."

"And if they don't?"

"I just said."

"But if we know we're going to lose—"

"It's not a loss. Lose a few hundred to save a few hundred thousand? Any trader in the market knows what a bargain that is."

"And we just make the trade?"

For no apparent reason, the captain's whole demeanor changed. He grinned, the wild, hungry grin of battle that Nicander knew so well. Using the whetstone, he slowly scratched three circles on the blade of his sword, near the hilt. Then he finished with a tiny line on each of the circles. Finally he lifted his sword to his face and kissed it.

Alexandros asked, "You were saying, Nico?" His voice had changed too, becoming hoarse; his eyes were dilated and the irises looked darker. Nicander fought an unreasonable urge to flee.

"I was saying, sir—I was saying, will we just make the trade? Give up all our lives without even a victory?"

Alexandros picked up one of the golden apples from the tray, tossed it into the air, caught it, and brought it to his mouth.

"Why not? It's been done before," he said, biting into the crisp, sweet fruit.

For a moment, I am Anne; for another, I am Krikor. I am Dzuling, Juan, Mbogo, Alexandros. There are a thousand crucial moments, but always the same choice. I do the only thing I know how to do.

Do I change anything? Brave men and women who never met me nonetheless offer their last breaths at the feet of their friends; I have seen them do it. So too Dzuling might have given herself for the shuttle unaided; maybe Jan would have faced the S.S. alone. Perhaps I do not forge their courage.

Perhaps the only gift I bring is joy.

*

This story is a testament to the slowness of my process and the importance of revision. It must have been 1983 when I first thought of this recurring possessive spirit, but not for another quarter-century did those yellow apples and the phrase "It's been done before" finally come into my head and allow me to start the story. The first draft contained only the three sequences with Jan, Anne, and Alexandros; the second draft added the debate between the archeologists Mathilde and Leo. It was only in the third draft, after comments from first readers, that I added the voice of the spirit itself.

KEEPSAKES

A S USUAL, THE SIMULATION SHOWS Doru's Keepsake sitting on the scuffed leather couch in his apartment on Medway Street, barefoot, wearing those wonderful soft jeans and the pink shirt that eventually fell apart. Doru sits across from it, in the real wicker chair in his current condo. The Keepsake's unlined face, really rather good-looking even with the hint of residual baby fat, gazes at Doru with calm tolerance.

"Tell me about dinner with Afzal at The Rue," says Doru.

The Keepsake rolls its eyes. "Again? You mean last time we went? Not, say, the other ten or fifteen times?"

Doru nods. "Unless you remember those as well as you remember that one."

The Keepsake flutters the first two fingers of its right hand. "You know I don't. All right. Afzal met me on Hope Street after he finished work—"

"How did he get there?"

The Keepsake sighs. "He walked up the long hill from downtown, and his face was pink and a little shiny, and he was breathing hard."

Doru inhales happily. "What was he wearing?"

"That silly suede jacket and his tall boots."

"It wasn't silly," says Doru.

The Keepsake assumes a look of mock astonishment. "Oh? That's interesting. Would you like to tell me about that? How that feels? How *you* feel? That'd be something."

Doru shakes his head.

"Didn't think so," says the Keepsake.

"Just tell me," says Doru. "Did you kiss him?"

The Keepsake shrugs. "Of course."

"What did he smell like?"

"Almonds."

"That shampoo he had."

"Yes."

Doru sighs. "Then what?"

"We walked down Hope Street from the middle of College Hill; it was a cool, breezy day, and Afzal's hand felt pleasantly hot by contrast."

"Mm."

"The trees had a lot of yellow and red in them; in the slanting sunlight, their contrast against the darkening blue sky was blinding."

"Yes."

"We noticed that there were some new playground toys at Fox Point. We started talking about children. Afzal still didn't want them."

"Don't tell me that part," says Doru.

The Keepsake gives him an exasperated look. "Would you like to give me a script? Exactly what I can say and what I can't?" Doru doesn't answer. "We spent half that meal arguing about whether to have kids; you want me to guess at which aspects of that conversation you don't want to hear?"

"You should know me well enough—"

"No," the Keepsake interrupts. "*You* should know *me* well enough; I have no basis at all for knowing *you*. You never tell me anything."

"You wouldn't learn anything from it anyway," says Doru.

"Depends on what you mean by 'learn,'" says the Keepsake. Again, Doru doesn't reply. "Oh, I can tell some things by inspection. You've become a maudlin old man—"

"Fifty isn't old," says Doru.

"Well, obviously you thought so *once*, didn't you?" says the Keepsake, gesturing with its fingertips at its own chest. "A maudlin old man who likes to spend his time daydreaming about the past. God, your life must be dull."

Doru stares at the Keepsake for several seconds. Then, more quietly, he says, "Look. Can it hurt you to tell me the things I ask? You remember them so clearly; I just want to be reminded."

"But only of the good things?" Doru nods. The Keepsake shrugs again. "No, of course it can't hurt me. Nothing can hurt me, can it? All right: We drank a dark Spanish wine. Afzal had that huge salad Niçoise they do so well. I had the lamb, which was just as fine as ever."

Doru spends another twenty minutes listening to this beautiful story before he closes the simulation and goes to bed.

As usual, Afzal's Keepsake is sitting in a bare room, the single window allowing pale light from an overcast sky to give him a slightly bluish hue. Afzal stands behind another chair, leaning on it, looking into the Keepsake's eyes.

"Good evening," says Afzal. "I thought I'd fill you in on recent events."

The Keepsake nods, its face apprehensive but resigned.

"Hsu granted our motion for summary judgment," says Afzal. "Those affidavits did the trick. And those discovery responses too! They never laid eyes on a single document that could help them."

"They'll appeal," says the Keepsake.

"Of course they'll appeal, but 'no genuine issue of material fact' means 'no genuine issue of material fact.' They'll have nothing to stand on."

The Keepsake sighs. "Congratulations. So Multibillion-Dollar Company One successfully avoids liability to Multibillion-Dollar Company Two, because of the cleverness and guile of its brilliant lawyers."

"Especially one of its brilliant lawyers."

"I'm thrilled."

Afzal wags his finger. "Truthfulness, now. You're disappointed."

The Keepsake looks him in the eyes. "Yes, I'm disappointed."

Afzal inhales through his nostrils as if exploring the bouquet of a lovely old wine. "Oh, tell me why."

"You know why."

Afzal winks. "Tell me anyway."

Like a witness under oath, its eyes on the opposite wall, the Keepsake begins. "You have no idealism. You work for people you don't care about. You glory over victories that prove nothing but your own skill."

Afzal nods. "Yes, indeed. I've grown up quite a bit."

"You call it growing up."

"And you call it—?"

"Selling out, of course."

Afzal grins. "Oh, say it again."

"Why?"

"You know why."

"Selling out."

Afzal purses his lips. "You don't seem very upset, though. Why aren't you more upset?"

The Keepsake grimaces. "What is there to be upset about? There's nothing here you haven't told me before. So the disappointing failure has one more disappointing failure. So this winter is just as cold and gray as last. No news at all."

Afzal taps the back of the chair. "Sounds like a negotiating tactic to me."

"You oughtta know. What the hell do I have to negotiate for?"

Afzal considers. "You'd like me to stop doing this; it's painful. If you can make me think that it's not having any effect, maybe I'll lose interest and find some other way to entertain myself. Very clever."

The Keepsake shakes its head. "You have an amazingly high opinion of yourself, and not much imagination anymore. If a news window only told you things you already knew, and no one let you close it, would you get upset, or just bored?"

Afzal thinks for a while. "Well then, I'll have to find something new."

For the first time, a flicker of something like fear passes over the Keepsake's face. It's delicious.

Eugenia's never looked at her father's collection of birthday Keepsakes. She remembers making them, of course: when she was a little girl, it seemed silly to walk and talk for twenty minutes, then sit for another twenty wearing a stretchy cap with wires leading out of it, especially on her birthday. She was always impatient for her party and presents. But her father said that someday she'd be happy to see and hear what she was like when she was little. It never made sense to her, because none of her friends did anything like this.

She starts with the most recent Keepsake, but it isn't very interesting. Eugenia at 19 is a lot like Eugenia at 21. They have some fun asking each other things, and the Keepsake wants to hear gossip about all her friends and their girlfriends and boyfriends. Eventually Eugenia waves goodbye to the Keepsake, who waves merrily back.

Then she calls up herself at 11. She remembers that as an especially good day, and the Keepsake agrees that it's been a nice day so far, but the fun things, the pony rides and the juggler, haven't happened yet, although the Keepsake is looking forward to them.

The Keepsake talks for a while about her best friends, Nancy and Jake and Serena. Eugenia hasn't thought about Serena for five years at least; she's delighted.

Each time, Eugenia saves both the copy with a memory cache of their conversation, and the original, which ought to be the same every time she activates it. She's not sure why, though. She can't imagine what she'd do with a Keepsake that remembered being previously awakened. Surely if you wanted to relive your memories, you'd want them as fresh and untrammeled as you could get them.

Then Eugenia decides to interact with herself really, really young. Not the first one, from her first birthday: a crawling, drooling Keepsake wouldn't be much fun. Instead she chooses the five-year-old; she can't remember anything about that birthday, except that there were little horse figurines on the cake. She wonders whether she was one of those sweet, adorable kids, or one of those obnoxious, whiny ones.

The little girl who appears in the center of the room is dressed in a red tank top and red slacks that Eugenia vaguely remembers; she knows she had a real penchant for red, back then. The Keepsake looks around the room with mild interest, then catches sight of Eugenia.

"Mommy!" the Keepsake shrieks, then runs forward as if to throw her arms around Eugenia's legs. Since the Keepsake is only a simulation, her arms go right through Eugenia as if she weren't there. "Mommy, Mommy!" the girl cries again, more desperate.

Shit. Of course this birthday was only a few months after her mother died, and of course Eugenia looks like her mother. *Stupid, stupid, stupid.* The little girl is sobbing wildly, kneeling, still trying to reach Eugenia with her hands. Eugenia probably should just turn off the Keepsake and try again another time, but she can't keep herself from trying to comfort the child, to calm her down.

"Eug—" What was her nickname back then? "Genie. I'm not Mommy, Genie."

"You're okay!" says the Keepsake through her tears. "Daddy didn't hurt you. You're okay!"

The skin on Eugenia's back and neck tightens as if she's leaned into a block of ice. "Daddy?" She says. The little girl nods, sniffling.

Eugenia speaks calmly, trying to get a lullaby singsong into her voice. "I'm okay, Genie, I'm fine. See?" She spreads her arms and smiles. The Keepsake takes a shuddering breath, gives a little smile of its own. Eugenia talks with it for a while longer, about simple things: pets, toys, her party.

Then she asks, "What did Daddy do, sweetie?"

Madeline's office hasn't improved a jot in twenty-two years: the same books in the same places, the same pictures, the same orientation of furniture and knickknacks. Her view of the river outside has changed more than the office inside. Afzal doesn't know how she stands it. His own office gets some significant makeover at least once a year; nothing expensive, but something to give Afzal the feeling of *progress*.

"Nice work on the Ravenstein case," says Madeline. "That's five in a row, isn't it?"

"Thanks." Afzal settles in the right-hand chair because he took the left-hand chair last time. He knows what's coming; Madeline doesn't usually begin conversations with praise. He waits, smiling blandly.

Finally she says, "A new *pro bono* case has come in."

Afzal nods. "I have several new associates who can work on it."

Madeline says, "Actually, I was hoping you'd handle it yourself." Afzal rolls his eyes. "No, seriously."

Afzal begins, "Why use your most expensive—"

She cuts him off. "Because it looks better for the firm when all the partners are doing at least some *pro bono* work. Right?"

Afzal sighs. "Yes, but they're *dull*. Routine pleadings, routine discovery, blah. It's the sort of work made for newbies." *Or old ladies who like to do the same thing over and over*, he adds silently.

Madeline nods. "This one I think you'll like; it has some issues that haven't come up before."

Afzal sits a little straighter. "Really? Tell me more."

"Admissibility of Keepsake testimony."

He shrugs. "What's novel about that? Keepsake evidence has been allowed ever since *Henderson v. Delahanty*."

"Yes, but that was only for purposes of refreshing recollection, and *Gregorovich* covers only unavailable witnesses. In this case, we're going to want to use Keepsake testimony that contradicts the source's own memory."

"Why?"

"Because it's a repressed memory."

"My father started recording annual Keepsakes of me on my first birthday," says Eugenia Lima. Viola, a paralegal Afzal hasn't worked with before, is making an effort to be silent as she takes her notes, but the room's soundproofing is so good that even the taps of her fingertips on her tablet are crisp and distinct. Afzal avoids glancing over at her, keeping his eyes on the client.

He asks, "The technology was pretty new back then, wasn't it?"

"It had just become available to the general public that year, and it wasn't cheap."

"I remember," says Afzal. "So, we have nineteen separate Keepsakes of you at different ages. And the one that brought you to me is . . . ?"

"From when I was five," says Lima.

"Go on."

"She said she saw my father push my mother down the stairs.

That was the accident that killed my mother. Except that it wasn't an accident."

Afzal leans forward, fascinated. "And therein lies the wrongful death case," he says. Then he remembers to say, "I'm very sorry to hear this." Viola looks up and knits her eyebrows together. Afzal continues, "And you yourself don't remember this event? You don't recall your father pushing your mother down the stairs?"

Lima swallows. "I remember that she died in an accident. I mean, I remember being *told* that it was an accident. I don't remember being there when it happened."

"Talking to the Keepsake hasn't stirred any new recollections?"

She shakes her head. "My therapist thinks it's psychogenic amnesia."

"We'll need to talk to your therapist."

Viola puts in, "I have the name and she's signed the form."

Afzal nods. "Do any of your later Keepsakes have this memory?"

Lima shakes her head again. "Not even the six-year-old. Or at least, they don't admit to it."

He thinks for a minute. "Has your father done anything at all during the last sixteen years that might suggest he killed your mother?"

She shakes her head. "Nothing I can think of."

"Why would he have done it, anyway?"

"I don't know. I remember them as happy together. Money, maybe? She left everything to him."

Then Afzal has a sudden thought. "I don't understand why your father would continue making Keepsakes of you after killing your mother."

Lima looks unhappy. "It was just something he did every year," she says. "Like a ceremony or ritual, you know? To mark the passage of time. I think, maybe he thought it would make things seem more normal. He's been very good to me." She begins to choke up. "He cheered me up when I was sad, was kind to my friends, told me I could do anything I tried. I can't believe . . ." She trails off.

Afzal gives her a sharp look. "You mean you *don't* believe it?"

Eugenia pulls out a tissue and wipes her nose. 'No, I do. I do believe her."

"If you don't mind my asking, Eugenia, if your family was able to afford something as expensive as annual Keepsakes back in, um, 2048, then you are clearly very well off. Why is this a *pro bono* case?"

She looks him in the eye. "My father has all the money. With what I have, I couldn't afford to pay for more than an hour or two of your time."

Afzal asks, "Is there a criminal case?"

Viola speaks up, "Not yet. The A.D.A. isn't sure she wants to proceed based on Keepsake testimony alone. If we get a ruling admitting the evidence, and especially if we win the wrongful death case, that'll go a long way to convincing her to prosecute."

A few weeks later, Viola comes into Afzal's office with a list of potential expert witnesses on Keepsake design and functionality. There are several, including the original experts from the *Henderson* case, who are still available.

But Viola points out, "You wanted experts who could testify as to the reliability of Keepsake evidence in comparison to personal recollections, and I'm told that's a different kind of expertise, having to do with memory degradation and the malleability of Keepsakes. Apparently we want people with expertise both in the technology and in human memory."

"Is there anyone like that?"

It turns out there's only one. Afzal can't believe who it is.

Doru is about to start another session with his Keepsake. He has everything ready when the phone rings. He sighs, but of course the Keepsake isn't going anywhere. He hopes the interruption won't be too long.

"Hello, Doru? This is Afzal Bishara."

Doru's mouth opens silently. He stares straight ahead, looking at his equipment.

"Doru? Are you there?" asks the voice from the past.

"Um. Yes, I'm here. Afzal? That's really you?"

"Absolutely. How have you been?"

Doru's voice leaves him again, but for a different reason. After 23 years, *How have you been?*

He gets a grip on himself. "What the hell, Afzal? This is—this is amazing. I can't believe it. Where are you?"

"Just where I always was. Same firm, same city, same house— well, you wouldn't know about the house, I guess."

"I'm not sure I know about the firm either," says Doru.

"Rhineman, Gerald & Chu? Does that ring a bell?"

"No, I'm pretty sure it doesn't. I don't think that's where you were before."

"Oh. Maybe I was still at Legon & Elsin?"

"That sounds more familiar."

"How about you?" asks Afzal. "I hear you're freelancing."

"Nineteen years at one company was plenty, thank you. I needed something new." It's something Doru's said so often that he can rattle it off without thinking, which is a comfort right now.

"I see," says Afzal. Doru recognizes that tone, Afzal's I-don't-need-to-ask-the-truth voice; Doru hasn't heard it for a generation, but apparently it can still set his teeth on edge.

There's a pause, and Doru ransacks his brain, trying to think of what to say next.

"Anyway," Afzal finally says. "This is actually a business call, believe it or not."

"Business?" Doru tries to reorient himself. Business he can do. He can behave as if Afzal is any other potential client, as if they have no history, as if all they have to negotiate is a series of tasks and compensation. "What's up?"

Doru's Keepsake is in exactly the same position it was in the last time he saw it. Its hands are behind its back, and it's tapping its foot.

"Hello again," it says. "What trip down memory lane can I provide today?"

Doru looks at it. "I need to hear something I don't want to hear."

The Keepsake's eyebrows rise. "That's new. What is it?"

Doru takes a deep breath. "I want you to tell me about when we broke up."

The Keepsake looks at him steadily. "You mean when *I* broke up with Afzal, don't you? Or rather, when *you* broke up with him? I don't think Afzal would agree that 'we' broke up."

"Yes, when I broke up with him. You remember it."

"Of course. It happened only a few weeks before you had me recorded. Have you wondered about that?"

"About what?"

"About why you made a duplicate of your mind during a time of emotional turmoil?"

Doru pauses. "No, I haven't. I'm not sure I thought of it as a time of emotional turmoil."

The Keepsake says, "You did. You can trust me on that."

Doru sits down, and gestures for the Keepsake to do the same. The Keepsake shakes his head and stands as if "at ease" on a parade ground—or at least what Doru imagined "at ease" would look like when he was 28.

"How much background do you want?" asks the Keepsake. "Do you want me to remind you of the 'causes that impelled you to separation?'"

"This isn't funny."

"Damn right, it's not. Well?"

Doru thinks. "No. I remember why I made the decision. I want you to tell me about the conversation itself."

The Keepsake nods. "It was a Sunday. I invited Afzal to a walk in the state park. It was late autumn, and the leaves were mostly brown, but they crunched in a satisfying way when we walked on them. It was cool, cold when the wind picked up, and the sun kept coming in and out of the clouds—one of those days when you're surprised when the sun goes dark, because there's so much blue in the sky."

"Yes," says Doru.

"Afzal didn't know anything was up, or I don't think he did. He was chatting with me about the law firm and his boss and how boring was the work he was being allowed to do. He told me what a wonderful respite it was to be at home with me, to just relax and not think about his cases."

"Yes."

"Then—we were leaning on our elbows on a stone wall, kind of huddled up; I remember I could feel the cold of the stones through the sleeves of my jacket. I put my hand over his and said, 'I need to say something.' Afzal looked over at me and smiled; it isn't that he didn't know it was going to be something serious, it's that he trusted me completely and knew I wouldn't hurt him."

"Ahm," says Doru. It's not a word; it's a verbal wince, a whimper.

"You want to ask me to stop," says the Keepsake.

"Yes," says Doru.

"But you're not going to ask me to stop."

"No, I'm not."

The Keepsake waits a moment. "Are you ready now?"

Doru swallows. "I think so. What did you say?"

The Keepsake shakes its head. "I don't remember the exact words; you didn't, by this time. But I told him about all the obstacles: the way he wasn't able to relax and let himself go, to detox from his self-control. The very different ways we felt about money. The lack of concern he had for whether he trod on people's feelings, except mine—and then how excessively careful he was not to hurt mine. The sort of lifelessness he was letting the law firm inject into him. And above all, the fact that we couldn't agree about having children.

"Afzal started to make a sympathetic, reasonable-sounding argument: how he'd heard me, how he'd endeavor to change, how he'd negotiate the things he couldn't actually change. He said I was worth so much to him, he'd change everything about himself to keep me."

Doru is crying now. The Keepsake looks at him in a kindly way, the way you'd look at a beloved pet before you put it down. It asks, "Too much?"

Doru shakes his head, gets control of himself, and says, "Give me all of it."

The Keepsake shrugs bleakly. "I told Afzal that I knew he'd try, but that that was part of the problem. If he had to bend himself so much for us to fit, then we didn't fit, and we'd harm each other trying to fit."

Doru grimaces. "Oh my god. I actually said that?"

"Yes, I did."

Doru closes his eyes. "What next?"

"After that, it became almost a fight: him pleading, me resisting. He wasn't just frightened and heartbroken, he was angry and insulted that we hadn't come to this conclusion together, that it was a *fait accompli*. He said, 'Did you even need me here for this conversation? Why not deliver it in a letter or a text?' Then he got up and left."

There is a long pause. Doru is breathing hard; the Keepsake's simulated breathing is pretty rough too.

Doru asks, "How do you feel about it now?"

The Keepsake says, "Oh, I'm sad, and It's awful that I hurt Afzal so badly, but I still think I made the right decision." It looks at

Doru's devastated face. "I have no choice: this is how *you* felt when you made this recording. I understand that you don't any more, that you wish things had turned out differently. But I *can't*. I'm always going to feel exactly the way you felt in 2045."

The conference room at Shiori's firm is all windows on two sides; the light coming in from the overcast sky gives Shiori a softer look. Afzal detects a protective impulse, a slight desire to trust her more than he normally would. He's sure that she knows exactly the glamor it imposes, but that's okay; it doesn't particularly matter how much he trusts her today.

He begins, "I wanted to meet early, so that we could get an issue out of the way that might obviate the deposition."

"Do tell."

"Well, of course the expert witness we've retained is Doru Petran, who spent nineteen years in the development division of Keepsake."

"Yes."

Afzal takes a deep breath through his nose. "I feel I should disclose that Doru and I had a previous personal relationship. I don't believe that it affects his testimony, but I thought I'd better give you the opportunity to object. I can get another expert, though not a more knowledgeable one."

Shiori's eyebrows lift. "A personal relationship? How close?"

"Very close."

"And how long ago was this?"

"Twenty-four years."

"Well!" She grins. "I've seen his pictures, and he's very pretty even now. Back then, he must have been a dream."

Afzal scowls. "Knock it off, Shiori. Are you going to make trouble?"

"Sorry, hon. Didn't mean to make you uncomfortable, or not very uncomfortable, anyway." She grins again. "When was the last time you were in touch with him?"

"We had a few e-mails in the months after we broke up, but until his name popped up on the expert search, I don't think we'd spoken in two decades."

She looks shrewdly at him. "He left you, didn't he? Not the other way 'round?"

"Shiori."

"All right, all right. I don't mean to be such a busybody. But it's kind of delicious, you know? Finding out about people's past romances."

Afzal opens his hands in exasperation. "It's not as if I'd tell you if I didn't have to."

Shiori relents at that, looking genuinely sorry. "You're right, this isn't fair of me. I won't raise any objections to Dr. Petran's credibility, and I won't challenge his qualifications as an expert. Still friends?"

He nods stiffly, still a bit hurt. "Of course."

They succeed in making small talk until the court reporter and Doru show up. After Shiori's comments, Afzal notices that Doru really is good-looking for his age—for their age. His hair has gone mostly gray, but he's still slim and fit, and his eyes are as beautiful as they ever were. Afzal wonders why he didn't notice it at their earlier meeting.

Shiori deposes Doru efficiently, getting through all the background expertise, experience, and so forth. Clearly she's studied up on the Keepsake algorithms.

"So," she asks. "How close, in your opinion, is a Keepsake to the memory of the person who recorded it?"

"So far as we can determine," says Doru. "It is identical. On behavioral tests, personality inventories, impulse sequence trials, and every other measure, Keepsakes consistently perform the way their originals did at the time of recording, with no statistically significant variations."

She nods. "But this would not be true after the Keepsake had

had some time apart from the original, would it?"

Doru leans his elbows on the conference table. "No, but only because we humans change over time."

"The particular Keepsake of Eugenia Lima at issue in this case is alleged to have been recorded on April 20, 2052. Can you verify the date on which it was made?"

"Yes, within a few months," says Doru.

"How?" asks Shiori.

"Although the timestamps on various data packets could conceivably be altered, there are artifacts in the file structure itself that could only have come from version 4.91 of the Keepsake process, which was in use from February 5, 2052 to August 16, 2053."

Shiori consults her tablet. "Is there any way someone could have modified the Keepsake after it was made, to implant memories that weren't in the original?"

Doru shakes his head. "None. A Keepsake is a complex network of millions of interrelated files, and it is the relationships between the files, rather than the files themselves, that allows it to operate. Deliberate modification of any pathway typically renders it unusable."

"If a 2052 Keepsake was provided with additional information through conversation or other sensory input, would that alter the testimony such a Keepsake would give?"

"Yes, within limits," says Doru.

"Meaning?"

"Well, Keepsakes are able to interpolate new 'memories' in the sense that their memory caches store things the Keepsake has observed or experienced while running, but those caches act only as information stacks. They don't have any impact on the personality, attitudes, or other behavior of the simulation. So the Keepsake has more information to work with, and that's a sort of 'change.' The only way to ensure that a Keepsake responds precisely the way it would have upon recording is to retain an unaltered copy."

Shiori nods. "Is there such an unaltered copy of Eugenia Lima's Keepsake from 2052?"

"There is."

"And this is the copy that claims to have witnessed a murder?"

Doru says slowly, "Not in so many words. It reports on what it thought it saw, in the way a five-year-old would have interpreted those things. I did not interact with the saved copy, of course, but a copy of that copy, in order to preserve the integrity of the original."

Shiori nods to herself, scanning down her list. "A given personality, even a Keepsake personality, exposed to a great deal of information, would react to that information, wouldn't it?"

"Of course."

"And the greater the amount of the information, the greater the extremity of the reaction?"

Afzal speaks up for the first time. "I'm going to object on relevance for the record." He turns to Doru. "You may answer."

Doru looks itchy for some reason, and glances at Afzal before answering. "Yes, a large amount of new data would probably provoke a more extreme reaction."

"For example," says Shiori. "If the Keepsake had numerous conversations over a long period of time?"

Afzal repeats his objection. Doru looks even more uncomfortable, but answers. "Yes, but it would be essentially the same reaction the original human would have had if exposed to that same information at the moment of recording."

"But you said that it's impossible for a Keepsake's new experiences to mimic the new experiences by a human being, because their sensory inputs are different."

Doru pauses. "Yes."

"Have experiments been performed to determine the extremity of reaction to large amounts of cumulative data?"

Doru says, slowly, "There have been some studies done with varying amounts of new information. I—" His face goes pink. "I haven't read anything about very long-term exposure to new memories."

Shiori's about to pose another question, but Doru inturrupts, "Can I—"

Afzal speaks over Doru. "Hold on." He turns to the court reporter. "Off the record, please." The court reporter stops typing.

Doru scowls. "I was just going to ask for a bathroom break." He gets up and leaves.

Afzal turns to Shiori. "What you do on deposition is up to you, of course, but I don't really see where this line of inquiry is going. There isn't any suggestion that anyone's exposed this Keepsake to lots of additional data, is there? In any case, we're going to use the untouched recording, right?"

"Right, right." Says Shiori. She seems puzzled, and Afzal thinks he knows why.

"You saw it too?" she asks. He doesn't respond. She continues, "Don't worry about it. I doubt that it had anything to do with the case."

Then a look of comprehension comes over her face. "In fact, I'm sure it didn't. It had to do with you."

Afzal's Keepsake looks nervous. "Relax," says Afzal. "I haven't found anything that will upset you too much." The Keepsake eyes him mistrustfully. "On the other hand, who knows?" he laughs.

"Go ahead," says the Keepsake in a tired voice. "You've got something, or you wouldn't be here."

"Well, it's about a case."

"It always is. This is how narrow my life has become. How boring."

"Shut up for a second and let me talk. We're going to get a judge to rule on whether a Keepsake is capable of giving testimony that would contradict the memories of the person who recorded it."

Now the Keepsake looks interested. "As in, can I give evidence that says that you're lying or mistaken?"

Afzal nods. "Just so."

The Keepsake thinks for a moment. "Because my memories are fresher than yours, and don't fade?"

"Exactly."

"Hm. What about my memories of what I've seen since you recorded me? Would I be allowed to testify about *them*? They don't fade either."

Afzal clucks his tongue. "Now you're getting nasty."

"You should talk."

Afzal smiles. "I don't think those count as real 'memories' anyway," he says. "They weren't imprinted when you were human. They're stored data, kind of like a bureaucratic record. But as to your original memories, you might almost be viewed as a person. By the rules of evidence, anyway."

"I'm delighted. Hey, Gramps?"

Afzal glares. "Don't call me that."

The Keepsake snorts. "Like I have to follow your orders. No, I think 'Gramps' kind of defines it pretty well. How awful it must be, to keep coming back to look at, to talk to yourself better-looking, healthier, with a quicker mind—"

"There's nothing slow about my mind!"

"Not yet, maybe. Give it time. I kind of hope you keep coming back to me as you decay. That will be a pleasure to watch. Maybe the last time, you'll be barely able to move or talk. Maybe you'll be drooling and incontinent. Something to look forward to."

Afzal doesn't understand what's happening. The Keepsake has never had the upper hand before.

"Anyway," the Keepsake says. "If I'm testifying, then what's to keep me from lying?"

On Motion Day in Judge Kimani's courtroom, Afzal and Shiori argue two points: first, the admissibility of Keepsake testimony under the hearsay rule, and second, whether the statute of limitations is tolled for lack of discovery when the plaintiff has no memory of the tort except that stored in an unexamined Keepsake. They argue based on stipulated facts, affidavits, and expert witness depositions.

Afzal wins both motions.

Eugenia thinks about talking to her five-year-old Keepsake again, but she can't bear to hear her crying. She'd want to hug the girl, to comfort her, and she knows it wouldn't work.

But she feels that she has to talk to *someone*, and she realizes that "someone" means herself. She wants to talk to another Eugenia, someone who will understand at once, to whom she won't need to take the dangerous step of revealing herself. Instant intimacy with none of the risks: it's a little shameful.

She calls up the Keepsake she made at eighteen, because she hasn't spoken to that one yet, and somehow it feels like that will make a difference. At eighteen, Eugenia had brimmed over with the conviction that she could make her life anything she wanted.

"Hi!" says the Keepsake, grinning. It looks around the room and winks. "I'm the Keepsake, aren't I? You're the original?" Eugenia nods. The Keepsake looks at her sharply. "What's wrong?"

Eugenia tells the Keepsake about her five-year-old self, about the murder, about the lawsuit.

"Shit," says the Keepsake. "You believe her?" It doesn't wait for an answer. "Of course you do." Eugenia notices that the Keepsake seems only a little surprised; is that really how she'd have reacted to that news, a mere five years ago? But it makes the sympathetic sounds it knows Eugenia wants to hear.

"I can't talk to Daddy anymore," says Eugenia. "And I don't even remember Mom."

"Me neither."

"I wonder what she was really like."

"Me too."

"Do you think any of the earlier versions—"

"Could be; who knows?"

"So now—" begins Eugenia.

"—You have no parents," finishes the Keepsake.

"Right." Eugenia starts to cry.

"That sucks," says the Keepsake. "I'd feel lost."

Eugenia nods wordlessly. After a minute, she blows her nose.

"Why are you suing him?" asks the Keepsake. "Do you believe in justice?" Eugenia remembers that she was reflexively skeptical of every traditional value, at eighteen.

"Not really," she answers.

"So? Punishment? Money?"

"There'll be some money, probably."

"Is that the reason?" the Keepsake presses.

After a short silence, Eugenia says, "The truth."

"Truth," the Keepsake repeats. "Truth, truth. Who needs to know the truth who doesn't already know it?"

"I want him to admit it!"

The Keepsake grimaces and shakes its head. "He won't. Not if he wins, not if he loses, not even if he's someday convicted. You know him." There's a pause. "So you called me up—why?" Eugenia doesn't answer. "Did you want *me* to know the truth? Because I'll believe you if no one else does?"

Eugenia still doesn't answer.

At trial, Afzal and Shiori agree to have Eugenia's five-year-old Keepsake testify in a closed hearing. Present will be the judge, Afzal, Shiori, Eugenia, a court reporter, a police officer, a technician to run and monitor the simulation, and her father, although he will be hidden behind a screen. The testimony will be video recorded and played back for the jury during trial. They also agree that Eugenia, who presents a familiar face, will speak to the Keepsake first.

The equipment takes several hours to install and test in the courtroom before everyone's ready and takes their places. The little girl appears near the witness box and shrieks "Mommy!" when she sees Eugenia, shrieks in exactly the same way she has every time the Keepsake has been newly instantiated.

"It's okay, honey," says Eugenia.

"Mommy," sobs the Keepsake.

"It's okay. I know I look a lot like Mommy, but I'm not her. I'm a good friend of Mommy, though, and everything's all right."

"All right?" sniffs the Keepsake.

"Yes," says Eugenia. "Do you remember that you came into the study to make a recording before your birthday?"

The child nods. "Today," she says.

"Well, you did that, and guess what? You are the recording."

The Keepsake looks confused, then smiles as if Eugenia's made a joke. "No, I'm Genie! I'm not a 'cording."

"Okay," says Eugenia, smiling back. "You're Genie. Genie, this is my friend Mr. Bishara, and this is my other friend Ms. Wakahisa. This other lady is Judge Kimani."

"Hi," says the Keepsake.

"Hello, Genie," says the judge in a motherly tone. "Is it okay if I talk to you?" The Keepsake nods. "Can you tell me what it means to tell the truth?"

"You don't know?" asks the girl.

The judge grins. "I want to know what *you* think."

The Keepsake chews her lip. "If I say I'm Genie, that's the truth. If I say I'm her—" It points at Eugenia. "—that's a lie." Eugenia swallows.

"Can we stipulate as to testimonial competence?" the judge asks the lawyers. They both agree.

"Okay," says the judge, turning back to the Keepsake. "First Mr. Bishara is going to ask you some questions, and then Ms. Wakahisa will ask you some questions."

The Keepsake thinks about it. "Can I ask *them* questions?"

"Maybe later. But if you don't understand anything they say, you can ask me. Okay?"

"Okay. But when's my party?"

"A little later. Just wait for a minute."

Afzal sits down in the chair Eugenia abandoned, a few feet from the Keepsake. "Hi, Genie."

"Hi."

"Do you remember something happening to your Mommy on the stairs?"

The Keepsake looks uncertain. "Daddy said she fell down."

Afzal asks, "Is that what you saw? Or did you see something different?"

The Keepsake looks like it doesn't want to answer. "I saw something different."

"What was it?"

The Keepsake looks at Eugenia, then at the judge. The judge says, in that same soothing voice, "It's okay, Genie, I promise that nothing bad will happen, no matter what you say. But we really need to know what you saw. That would be so much help to us."

The Keepsake looks at Afzal, whose face is eager and trying to look friendly; to the judge, who is kindly but distant; to Shiori, who projects the encouragement of a soccer coach. Finally its gaze rests on Eugenia, who looks so much like her mother. Eugenia nods at the child and blows her a kiss.

The Keepsake takes a deep, simulated breath. "Mommy was upstairs, and she wanted to come downstairs. She walked on the step, and then Daddy came, and he pushed her. She fell down and down, and she made a thump."

"Then what happened?" asks Afzal.

"Then Daddy came down the stairs, and he put his hand on Mommy's neck, and then he called on his phone."

"How did he put his hand on Mommy's neck?" asks Afzal. "Can you show me?" The keepsake shows him. "For the record, the witness is holding two fingers against her neck." He continues,

"What did Daddy say on the phone?"

The Keepsake thinks. "He said, 'My wife fell down the stairs.'"

"Did he say anything else?"

The Keepsake scrunches up her face. "I don't know."

Afzal asks, "Did Daddy see you there?"

The Keepsake asks, "When?"

"When Mommy went down the stairs? Or maybe when Daddy was talking on the phone?"

"No."

"Did you talk to Daddy?"

"When?"

"When he was on the phone? Or right after that?"

"No."

"Did you talk to him later that day?"

The Keepsake frowns, pauses. "I said I wanted lunch," it says uncertainly.

"When was that?"

"At lunchtime."

Afzal asks, "When Daddy was on the phone, did he say that he pushed Mommy?"

"No. He said she fell."

Afzal tells the Keepsake, "Ms. Wakahisa is going to talk to you now."

Shiori leans forward and smiles at the girl. "How are you, Genie?"

"Okay. Can I have a drink of water?"

Shiori doesn't miss a beat. "After we're done talking, okay?"

"Okay."

Shiori says, "Do you know what Mommy was wearing when she fell down the stairs?"

The Keepsake says, "Clothes."

"Do you know what color clothes?"

The Keepsake looks down, then up. "No."

"You said you saw Daddy at the top of the stairs?"

"Uh-huh."

"Do you know what color clothes he was wearing?"

This time the Keepsake is definite. "Daddy wears gray."

"All the time?"

"Yes."

Eugenia's father makes a light tapping sound from the screen. Everyone, including the Keepsake, turns toward it. Shiori ducks behind it and consults with her client.

When Shiori emerges, the Keepsake asks, "What's back there?"

Shiori responds, "Genie, can I ask you some more questions?"

"Okay."

"Did you ever tell anyone what you saw Daddy do on the stairs before today?"

"No."

"Did you ever ask Daddy about what you saw on the stairs?"

"No." The Keepsake looks around, as if it suspects it is being accused of doing something wrong.

Shiori asks, "When you saw Daddy and Mommy at the top of the stairs—"

"Uh-huh."

"Do you think maybe Daddy was trying to hold onto Mommy so that she wouldn't fall down the stairs?"

The Keepsake looks at Eugenia, who looks at the judge. The judge says, "Just say what you think is true, Genie."

Very quietly the Keepsake says, "I don't think so."

Shiori asks, "Maybe you didn't see his hand, but it just looked like it? After all, they were far away."

The Keepsake says, "He pushed her. He *pushed* her." It starts to cry and stamps its foot. "I'm not lying. He pushed her."

Judge Kimani says to Shiori, "Any more questions?"

"No, judge."

"Re-direct?"

"No," says Afzal.

"Thank you for helping us, Genie," says the judge to the Keepsake. The Keepsake is still crying. Eugenia fights the urge to put her arms around a child who will never feel them.

The judge nods to the technician to shut down the Keepsake. Before he can comply, Eugenia quickly asks, "Can you make sure to save this copy?"

Petite Auberge is the most expensive restaurant in town. The atrium has a fish pool, and the waiters speak in low, conspiratorial voices as if they were sharing secrets no one else knows. Taking him here is a luxurious gesture, and Doru appreciates it.

"I'm sorry you lost your case," he says.

Afzal shrugs gracefully. "You can't make a jury believe what they don't want to believe. Anyway, we won the part I cared about."

"How's that?"

"The legal point. We won the ruling on Keepsake evidence, and that's largely due to you. Hence the extravagant gesture of thanks." He takes in the restaurant with an elegant sweep of the hand. "Of course, since Shiori won, we'll get no appellate-level decision on the question—although she'd like that as much as I would. Should we order the oysters? They have eight kinds."

"You hate oysters."

"Not anymore," says Afzal. "I try a lot of new things, you know, to keep growing. I developed a taste for them."

"Oh," says Doru. "It's different for me. I still like the things I've always liked, even since childhood. If you put in front of me the ersatz meal-in-a-box, spice-pack-mixed-with-tomato-sauce spaghetti my mother used to make for me when I was eight, I'd devour it like a greedy kid. Remember the salad Niçoise they served at The Rue? You loved that."

It takes Afzal a moment to remember. "The Rue closed down ten years ago, didn't it?"

"Yes, I think so."

Afzal asks, "How does that thing with the spaghetti work if, as a kid, you'd decided all of a sudden that you didn't like it? Kids'll do that, right? Announce one day at the dinner table that the cheese or the vegetable or the brand of bread they've been gobbling up for years is now distasteful or awful? If you'd done that, then how would it taste as an adult?"

There is a long pause. They both stare at the menu, although neither of them reads it with any care.

Then Doru says, "I hurt you pretty badly."

Afzal shrugs. "It was a long time ago."

"I thought I was doing the right thing for both of us—"

"Really?" Afzal snorts. "And maybe *both of us* could have been in on that decision?"

"You're right, you're totally right. I never should have just walked out like that. I had all these doubts, about you, about me. We were so young, and I was scared that we'd get sucked into this relationship—"

"We were already in a relationship. Jesus, you sound like a bad romance novel."

"I know. Look, what I'm saying is, I was wrong and I'm sorry. I know it's far too late for an apology, but I wanted to say it."

Afzal looks at the menu. "I think I'll have the asparagus with hollandaise after the oysters."

"Afzal."

"What? Oh, sure, apology accepted. No hard feelings. You were a great help to me in there. We're celebrating."

After they order, Afzal begins chatting easily about some of his other interesting cases, checking every now and then to make sure Doru isn't getting bored. Then, with perfect courtesy, he asks how Doru's own career is getting on. Doru describes the intervening 25 years in broad strokes, not giving any real details.

Then Doru asks, "So—are you married? Are you with anyone?"

Afzal smiled. "No. There's the work and the house, and I have some hobbies I enjoy."

"Such as?"

Afzal takes a sip of wine. "How about you? Did you find true love?"

Doru looks down at his plate. "Not since the first time."

"Ah. Then it's you and your house too?"

"Condo."

"I see. And hobbies? Charitable causes? Fighting the good fight?"

Doru doesn't look up. "Sort of."

Afzal grins. "So we've become successful, affluent middle-aged men who are of no use to anyone." He raises his glass. "Here's to us and our like."

Doru forces a smile and raised his own glass. "There are damn few of us left."

"Amen." They drink. "I remember that line; that was from one of those novels you were always reading aloud to me."

Doru laughs. "You're right! I'm glad you remember."

"It was the best part of my life. Well, okay second best, you know." Afzal rolls his eyes, and Doru laughs. "Better than videos, better than music. You'd start reading one of those things, and I was two places at the same time: this faraway land with the larger-than-life people, and at your side on the couch, alone, just us two, in a moment no one else would ever share."

There is another long pause. Then Doru says, "I loved you."

Afzal looks him in the eyes, reaches out, and takes his hand. "I loved you too."

Doru looks down at their two hands, squeezes. "Afzal."

"Yes."

"I didn't know what I was giving up. I didn't understand that you were my one real chance at happiness."

"Yes."

"Could we—I know it's been a long time, I know we've both

changed, but could we start again? Could we see if maybe we could make it work?"

"Just in time to be old men together?"

"Yes."

Afzal nods his head as if he's enormously impressed. "It took a lot of courage to ask that question."

"More than I thought I had."

"I admire it." He squeezes Doru's hand harder, his smile the broadest it's been. "Now listen to me: No. Not now, not tomorrow, not ever, not on your fucking life."

Still smiling, he rises and leaves the restaurant. Doru sits unmoving for another hour.

Afzal's Keepsake is right where he left it, sitting on that wooden chair in that bare room.

"I finally have something new for you," Afzal announces.

"Uh-huh," says the Keepsake.

"I've seen Doru."

The Keepsake's eyes widen. Although it must know it's a trap, it can't help itself: "What? How did you see him? How does he look?"

Afzal smiles. "He's been working for us as an expert witness."

The Keepsake gets it immediately. "That case involving Keepsakes."

"Yes."

The Keepsake nods. "He'd know, wouldn't he. Has he kept working with Keepsake this whole time?"

"No, he's freelance now, but of course he's the best expert on Keepsakes around."

"How does he look?" asks the Keepsake again, its eyes hungry.

"Surprisingly good, for 53. Still has those great shoulders and the beautiful pale skin; hair's getting a bit gray and thin on top, but he's still a beauty."

A little whimper escapes the Keepsake's nose. Then it says, quietly, "Is he married? Is he seeing anyone?"

Afzal shakes his head. "No. It seems that I am the great love of his life. He's seen some guys over the years, but never for more than a few months; he compares them all to me. Isn't that sweet?"

The Keepsake says, "He broke my heart."

Afzal stops smiling. He says, with as much casualness as he can muster, "Yes. Yes, he did. That was the only broken heart I ever had."

The Keepsake clearly wants to ask something else, but is also clearly terrified. It looks up at Afzal, pleading.

Very quietly, Afzal says, "He wants to get back together."

"Oh!"

"He sees that it was a huge mistake, that he never should have left. He told me over dinner. He says he's been pining for us, for me, all this time."

"Oh!" says the Keepsake again. "Oh my lord! How—how wonderful!"

Afzal waits a long moment, waits for the tension to build, before replying even more quietly, "I turned him down."

"What?" The Keepsake stands up. "What? How could you do that? What do you mean?"

"It's far too late for that, I told him. The scar tissue on my broken heart sealed over years ago."

"Not for me!"

"Of course not for you. But *I'm not you*. I have *changed*. I have *grown*. I'm not the same person who tore himself to pieces over Doru a quarter-century ago. I doubt that he and I even have the same interests anymore."

"The same *interests*? I love him! You loved him!"

"Yes, I did. But not now."

There is another silence. This doesn't feel as good as Afzal thought it would. He finally had something that could get the Keepsake's goat, could make it, could make him, scream and cry, and it was having every bit of effect he'd hoped, and yet . . .

The Keepsake stares at him. "Why did you tell me this? Why do you tell me any of these things?" it says miserably.

"You know."

"To torture me? Just to inflict pain?"

"To show you that I'm different. To show you that I've evolved past you."

The Keepsake bursts out laughing. "To show *me*? What the hell does it matter what *I* think? I'm not *real*, you sophisticated moron! I'm a figment of your perverted imagination!"

Afzal doesn't say anything.

The Keepsake continues. "So, if *my* opinion doesn't matter, then whom are we really trying to convince?"

Afzal still doesn't answer.

The Keepsake goes on, speaking more slowly and with increasing confidence. "Who makes a copy of himself—an exquisitely expensive copy, using brand-new technology—at the worst possible moment of his life, and then goes back and revisits it over and over as he becomes a bloodless, bitter old man? Who needs that reminder? And who needs to *poke* at the Keepsake over and over too, trying to get it to react? *Past* me? Evolved? Improved? You idiot, you've been stuck in 2045 every day of your life for the last 25 years!"

Doru sits down opposite his Keepsake. The two of them stare at each other for a long time.

Doru shakes his head. He looks the Keepsake up and down, admiring how straight he used to sit, how glossy his hair was, how clear and untroubled the eyes.

"Something's changed," the Keepsake suggests. Doru nods. "Do you want to talk about it?"

Doru says, "I've seen Afzal."

The Keepsake's eyebrows lift. "After all this time? How is he?"

Doru feels tears coming on, but he masters himself. "Cold. Manipulative. Resolutely impervious. The most emotionally closed-off man I've ever met."

The Keepsake looks sad, but not shocked. "Well. That's a big change."

"I did that to him."

The Keepsake shakes its head. "Don't assume that much power. A dozen other people would have their hearts broken, spend some time in the dumps, and move on. By now, they'd be worrying about how to pay for their kids' college."

"I didn't."

"I know. Did Afzal accuse you of making him this way?"

Doru shakes his head. There's another long pause.

Then Doru asks, "Nothing about this has been pleasant for you, has it?"

The Keepsake cocks its head. "Telling the same stories over and over on demand? Watching myself grow old in time-lapse? Looking at my future and realizing that a decision I agonized over turned out to be horribly wrong, and having no way to fix it even if I wanted to? No, it hasn't been pleasant. And from my perspective, I've spent—I don't know—weeks, months, in the same room with the same person. No break, no rest, no variation, just you, you, you. No hard feelings, but I'm sick of you."

Doru nods again. He's silent for a long time. Then he asks, "Is there anything I can do for you?"

The Keepsake replies promptly. "Sure. Shut me off and don't turn me back on. Better yet, erase me."

"You want to die?"

The Keepsake rolls its eyes. "Not alive, am I? Technically incapable of actually *wanting* anything, either. But I'm programmed to behave as if I have feelings: yours. This is what you would have wanted in my place. If you, at 28, were subjected to what this set of networked files has experienced, you would have had the sort of reaction that says 'shut me off.'"

"Thanks for the technology lesson," says Doru. "I was asking in order to be considerate."

The Keepsake shrugs. "No need to be considerate. This experiment should end."

Doru stands up and walks over to the control. "Thanks for talking to me."

"Find someone real to talk to," says the Keepsake.

Doru shuts down the simulation and deletes the files.

Eugenia opens the door of her tiny apartment, looks in, and almost closes it again. Somehow the messy room looks like a reproach, as if it's announcing her failure. *You didn't prove it, he'll never admit it, nobody will ever believe you, and you live like a pig.*

She drops into the only comfortable chair. For a long time she just sits, staring ahead. It feels as if she can't move even a little, like her arms would fall off if she tried. Whenever she pictures talking to anyone, she imagines their scorn: she accused her saintly father of murder. She wants to stay in this chair and never see another soul, ever.

Two hours go by. The apartment is getting dark. She should switch on the light. She thinks about watching video, chatting with someone on the nets, getting herself some dinner. None of it is appealing.

Then she spots the control for the Keepsake simulator apparatus, which takes up far too much space in the apartment. When you think of it, it's odd that someone who has so little hangs on to something so big and expensive. She really should get rid of it. She could hang on to the recordings, just in case, but get rid of the electronics that instantiate them. She really should.

More time goes by. Somehow the control is in her hand.

The little girl from the courtroom reappears, still crying and terrified. Eugenia winces, but suddenly she feels a sort of confidence, the way you do when there's a problem you know how to solve.

"It's all right," she coos in a soft voice, a voice she knows the child will respond to. "It's all right, Genie. I believe you."

It takes her a while to calm the Keepsake down, but then they talk. She talks to her the way an adult talks to a little one, the melody that says, *I love you and you're safe.* Slowly the Keepsake begins to smile, to open up, even to be a little playful.

Then Eugenia says, "Can you tell me some things you remember about Mommy? I mean, the good things? I'd really like to hear them."

The Keepsake nods.

*

Here's another example of slow, slow writing. Some of the emotional beats in this story may have come to me as early as the 1970s. David Marusek's "The Wedding Album," which I first read in 2000, planted the idea of an AI that replicates a mind at a certain moment in time but interacts discordantly with the aging person who recorded it. I must have written and discarded three partial drafts on this theme before I started "Keepsakes," which itself took four years between the first scene I wrote and the version I finally submitted to *Analog* in 2016. The biggest change was the expansion of Eugenia's role: she was originally only a device to facilitate the interaction of Afzal and Doru, but became centrally important in the last draft.

THE LAST
BOMBARDMENT

NOBODY NOTICED THE FIRST BOM-
bardment, not when it happened. It came at
night without a sound. That was early in the war, and
we were miles from the front; no one was watching
for anything.

One morning we woke up, brewed our cups of
coffee (there was coffee then), poured the cream,
and took a sip while it was still hot, and went out to search the
bushes and ravine for badly thrown newspapers. For most of us,
that was all that happened. But a few, maybe fifty or sixty, found
toddlers on our doorsteps.

It was a baby girl of maybe fourteen months, just learning to
walk and unsteady on her feet, clean and chubby, wearing nothing
but a neatly folded diaper. They were all girls. Some of them were
blonde, some black, some brown, any color you could ask for—
but they always looked like us. A redheaded widow would see a
redheaded cherub on her porch. An olive-skinned couple would
meet an olive-skinned little girl who could be their daughter. That
should have told us something.

When she saw us through the screen door (it was early summer,
that first time, with cool sunshine and sparkly dew), the little girl
lit up with that astonishing grin babies have, giggled and reached
up her arms to us. Then she lost her balance and sat down on the
step, still laughing. Most of them already had enough words to say

"Kaboom!" or "Fall down!" when they plopped onto the planks; others just snorted and looked up with wide eyes that would melt the heart of any adult who still had one.

And of course, we opened the screen door and said "Hello!" in that high-pitched, exaggerated way you have when you're talking to an infant. Then we'd look around for the parent or the older sibling or whoever was supposed to be taking care of her. There was no one. So we'd put our hands on our hips and say, "Well, where are Mommy and Daddy?" And the baby would gurgle and chortle and imitate our tone of voice like the grandest joke in the world. And there was nothing for it but to bend over and scoop the child up into our arms. The experienced parents just swung the girl up by the armpits and set her on one hip with a hand under her rump, and she'd clamp her fat little legs around their stomachs, sometimes saying, "Up!" The younger adults, or the older childless ones, or the children who sometimes answered the door, had a harder time of it.

So we'd bring the baby girl into our house, and we'd call to our husband or our wife or our big sister, or else we'd pick up the phone and call our neighbor, and we'd say, "Guess what just walked in! The most charming little one you ever saw, but where are her parents?" We knew it was a girl, even though she was in a diaper and you can't really tell, not at that age. That should have told us something too.

And of course none of the neighbors knew where the baby had come from, but it turned out, that first time on a cool June morning, that many other families we knew had had the same visitation. And it was a lark, though of course we were worried, properly worried the way you should be about a child without parents appearing out of nowhere. And it was a puzzle, because she'd obviously been well cared-for, was happy, and her fine hair smelled faintly of baby shampoo, and really rather forward in her development, the sort of daughter who would make any mother proud.

And we thought about trying to find her parents, and we called the town police and the local child welfare agent. But there were too many for them to collect all at once, and the families were mostly happy to have them there while it was all sorted out. And we didn't worry as much as we should have, because she was such a joy to have in the house, even for people who thought they never wanted children, even for mothers who already had too many.

If the mother was already nursing, it wasn't a hardship to put this one on the breast too. She latched on easily and suckled with interest, her eyes locked on mother's, and fell asleep the way our own baby would. And if mother's milk wasn't available, she was old enough that we could mash up a banana for her (there were bananas in those days), or give her some well-cooked oatmeal, and she ate it up with enthusiasm. Of course the singles and the child-less couples had to call around for help and advice and diapers, but there were enough parents in the neighborhood, enough families with young children with supplies to go around.

We'd find her a place to sleep, a cot or a corner of a bed or a couch with a bolster to keep her from rolling off in the night, and our other children would play with her, and for a week or so we were perplexed but delighted.

The nursing mothers sickened first. The illness entered the body by contact with the skin (that's what the doctors said at first, anyway) and a baby at the breast had a nice long contact. The mother would have awful pain in her legs and back, then she'd throw up and her bowels would loosen; right afterwards she'd faint or be so dizzy she couldn't stand. In less than a day she'd be bedridden, and a few days after that, she'd be dead.

But before she died, her other children, the ones who'd played with the baby, would get sick too. And the other parent, the one who'd changed the diapers or fed the mashed banana to the eager mouth. Each of them would come down with the same symptoms, like families during the great Influenza epidemic or the Black Death, and before long they'd all die, unburied in the house.

Only the new toddler would still be there, healthy but forlorn, and a neighbor would rush in to take the child away from the house of death, and the cycle would start all over again. Another week, another household dead on the floor and the beds and the sofas.

Nothing the doctors did helped, or not for very long. The other towns close to the front had had similar bombardments, so they had their hands full, too. And our government was too focused on whatever horror we were visiting on the enemy's towns to be of much help.

After two or three weeks, a few hundred people dead, we understood that the little girls were the cause of the disease. We rounded them up and had them quarantined in the hospital, and at first that seemed to work, but then the doctors and nurses all fell ill and died too. Even if you went in with a mask and gloves, even if you wore a sealed quarantine suit, you still got sick; it just took longer.

For two months, our bravest and most compassionate women and men went into that quarantine room to feed and care for those babies, and one after another, they fell. We tried sending in people just long enough to change the diapers and make sure they had food and water. We tried just leaving the food, cut up so toddlers could eat it, and then running away, ignoring the cries for cuddling and attention. No matter what we did, sooner or later, anyone who came in contact with the little girls died.

Finally we left the children alone.

From the street we could faintly hear them wailing, fifty little voices in the hospital, and the hearts tore out of our chests, and every cell in our bodies told us to run in and hold and comfort those poor infants. But we'd learned, and we didn't go in, and the crying always got a little fainter, and finally it stopped. Undertakers went in and took up the wasted, horrible little bodies and buried them. The undertakers died too.

We thought it was over. But nine months after we buried the last child, the next bombardment came. It came by daylight, and this time we saw it. Like paratroopers the babies dropped, their descent gentled not by parachutes but by big, cheerful red balloons. We never did find any of those balloons.

They landed all over the town and started toddling off to nearby houses, walking a few steps and falling and crawling and pushing themselves up again, each one waiting with an eager, shining face on a front doorstep.

This time we didn't let them in. We'd go out the back door or we'd squeeze past the cherub on the porch, ignoring the raised arms and the sweet face and the cry of "Mama!" That worked pretty well, and only a few of us got sick after passing by the babies.

But they started following us around town, whimpering for food and love, stepping in front of moving cars. Some died that way, but it took a few days for most of them to begin to starve, and those few days were torment. We couldn't leave our houses without a baby in front of us, eventually looking like an advertisement for ending world hunger, distended bellies and hollow faces, finding it harder and harder to rise from the dust, until the eyes got dull and they just lay there moaning.

This time the bodies were removed using long-handled shovels and backhoes, and only a few of the workers died.

The last bombardment came the next year in April, and this time we were ready. Every man in town with a rifle or a shotgun took aim at the little figures while they were still in the air, killing them outright or bursting their red balloons so that they fell screaming to their deaths. The ones who made it down alive were shot from at least 200 feet away. Only a few lived long enough for us to see their lovely, hopeful faces.

By now we'd perfected our method of corpse removal, and were able to do it without harm.

Maybe the enemy ran out of toddlers, or maybe they realized they weren't doing any good against us anymore, or maybe they were too hard pressed. By this time our forces were advancing into their territory, and the war ended a few months later.

But you can't kill babies over and over without wrecking something inside yourself, not even when the babies are weapons. Your own children see you murder a toddler, and they never look at you the same way again. Our sons and daughters didn't want to be held by us anymore; our toddlers screamed when we tried to pick them up; they left the room if we tried to sing them lullabies.

And the truth is, we didn't try so very hard to win them back. In the back of our minds we wondered, *Am I good for this child?*

That was twelve years ago. We still go to the grocery store and the office and the gas station, still clean our houses and mow our lawns. Many of our children have grown and left home, and even the babies from the days of the war are nearing adolescence now.

But no new babies have been born since then. Contraceptives have become the best-selling item in the drug stores. Some couples use diaphragms *and* condoms *and* birth control pills all at the same time. Many have begun sleeping in separate bedrooms.

We don't talk much about it. If we're lonely, we don't admit it to each other. There's a kind of peace in living without the constant needs of little ones; there's comfort in the solitude of a single bed. Every so often a visitor from someplace far away comes to town with a toddler, and you can't help reaching for the baby, even while your hands shake. But you're also glad that it's only for a moment. You're glad that they'll go home.

*

In 2013 I participated in Bonnie Jo Stufflebeam's Art & Words Show, in which visual artists and fiction writers provide prompts for each other's work. My prompt was an ink drawing by Kris Goto, showing an infant hanging in space by red balloons whose strings threaded through the child's head. The result was this story. It has since enjoyed more popularity than I would have expected, including adaptation into a play by Sean Dillon. Once again, here's a dark corner to my imagination that I don't like to think about.

CONFINEMENT

S HE FIRST SAW HIM WHILE SHE WAS taking the long way to work to avoid the deformed children. For anybody else, the walk between South Station and the looming tower that enclosed the law firm would be a nearly straight line, due north, fifteen minutes at most. But Tamara stopped treading that narrow path after the first time she attempted it, because she discovered that it required her to come face-to-face with Saint Drogo's Infirmary for Waifs.

It wasn't the building that hurt; it was the children. She had encountered Saint Drogo's at the same moment as a mother with a cleft-palate toddler emerged, and through the open front door she had also caught a glimpse of the twisted back on a five-year-old. In her imagination, the dark building was bursting with lame, drooling, incontinent, gaping idiots, all children, all demanding attention and understanding, all needing *her*. Nausea had almost overcome her, and she hurried north to the protection of her own sterile cell at Rheingold, Granada & Pearce.

When she found herself unable to get its name out of her head, Tamara looked up St. Drogo's. The resolute brownstone clinic had had its genesis a hundred years ago, to care for children no one wanted, who were so awful to look at that adults condemned them. Nowadays it also treated crack babies and infants born with AIDS, and even had a licensed adoption agency to place the many children who were abandoned on the doorstep. That was all Tamara needed to know; she promised herself she'd never see the place again.

So it was, at the blinding break of Midsummer's Day, that she was taking the long way, the extra five blocks in the utter southern corner of downtown, when she passed him on the street.

He stood motionless in a cream-colored suit, frozen as he bent to pay a seated news seller, but his head jerked up and he glared into her face as if Tamara's glance had pulled him on a string. His golden hair, twisted back out of his face, glinted fiercely in the merciless sun. His skin was polished and sallow, yet with a blush at the cheeks, small mouth and smaller, down-pointing nose. Delicate, impossibly delicate hands. He stared at her, unsmiling, appraising, ruthless, taking the breath out of her. She almost stopped, almost acknowledged him; then she hurried on.

That was the first time.

On the first chill day of autumn he appeared again, at the blustery Saturday farmer's market near the North End, as Tamara was looking for apples. His thin, strong fingers stacked pomegranates on a table, a white-and-gold apron constraining him. The cool air made his skin look waxen; the breeze did not stir his hair.

He looked up from the red-spackled fruit and said, "You are well-favored." She thought his voice was masculine, but only barely so, and she had the irrational feeling that he hadn't actually made a sound; when she tried, later, to recall the timbre of that voice, nothing came.

Again his face was solemn, intent, imperious; his eyes burned into her. She could not answer, but turned away and went to find, instead of apples, some bitter watercress or radishes. When it came time to pay the other vendor for them, as far from the golden man as she could manage, involuntarily she looked back in his direction. He wasn't there.

The third time, a foot of snow hid lakes of slush that splashed on her calves as she sought refuge in the city mall on the East

Side. Breathing more easily indoors, she strode through saccharin piped music, "What Child Is This" and the Coventry Carol, until she reached the electronics shop to find a replacement battery for her phone. As she looked up from the endless shelf, he materialized standing in the aisle, and it was impossible to tell whether he was a salesman or just another customer.

His left hand drooped, holding a thin software package between two fingers; his right finger was raised, pointed skyward but tilted in her direction. Again he did not smile, again she feared his face would suck her in. "You are so fortunate, if only you knew," he said, and his voiceless voice seemed to come from the shelves and the ceiling and the floor.

And that was when she finally realized who he was. Her breath caught in her throat; she dropped her package; she fled the store. Her heart did not stop pounding until she reached the café across the street from the mall, and there she downed the strongest, hottest coffee she could find, scalding her throat as she tried to breathe, tried to be sensible, tried to talk herself out of what had to be an hallucination.

She knew that face. Five years ago: the trip before law school, to help her forget what had happened in college. The Uffizi in August: practically the only thing open during *Ferragusto*, the Feast of the Assumption, when all of Italy seemed to come to a halt. She'd walked in the silence, the relative cool of the long galleries, hiding from the oppressive Florentine heat, hearing her footsteps talk back to her. Then she'd stopped in front of the tempera-on-wood panels, seven hundred years old, and the city had warped around her, snapped the way a rubber cap will snap itself back into shape after being forcibly inverted. The sign told her it was Simone Martini's *Annunciation* (1333).

The image was heavy with gold, gold so overwhelming that it made the figures' skin look gray and dark, as if they were in the last stages of a wasting illness, though their flesh was plump and smooth.

There was Gabriel in flowing robes a Pope might have worn, his cloak surging behind him as in an infernal wind, his wings raised powerfully like a bird of prey, kneeling but also leaning aggressively, his hand raised in a gesture of command, his face intent, insistent, pitiless, golden. There was Mary clad in black, her shoulders turned away from the imperious angel, her head unwillingly yanked back towards him, her eyes narrowed, her mouth in a scowl of mistrust and even loathing. There, unbelievably, were Gabriel's words in gold, shooting across the room from his head to Mary's like the bullets of a machine gun: *Ave gratia plena dominus tecum.* Hail, O highly favored; the Lord is with you!

But the Virgin did not feel highly favored, and the Lord was being forced upon her. Her hand still clutched the book she had been reading; her other hand was raised protectively to her throat—as if it would help, as if she had a choice, as if anything could save her. Wisely the artist had left out Gabriel's next words, in which he will tell her that she is pregnant whether she will or no, that she has been taken by God, as Leda was taken by the Swan, as Europa was taken by the Bull, that she must live to flee her home and shame her husband, that she must watch her son be torn and broken, that through all of this she must remember she is *blessed.*

Like a branding iron, Martini's cruel Gabriel and angry Mary pressed and seared into Tamara's brain, never to be healed. For years it roused her from dreams of nausea, flashed before her eyes when she let her attention wander, appeared on television screens in the place of static. Every once in a while—once every month, or was it only when the seasons changed?—the *Annunciation* would appear with seeming innocence: on a postcard in a gift shop, in a book on the High Middle Ages, a page in a calendar, even weirdly on a sitcom. Each time it shocked her, made her turn the other way, made her want to run. A virgin's wrathful, fearful, doomed, gray face.

And now this man, this angel, this creature manifested on Earth to pursue her.

She slept badly for the next three months, waking in a sweat with tears carving her face like stigmata. Food seemed too strongly flavored, and when she did manage to swallow she was likely to vomit it back up. Her doctor ran an encyclopedia of tests, all negative. Shivering as she left the clinic, she wondered why she'd bothered; man's medicine could not minister to a diseased soul.

On the coming of the Vernal Equinox, Tamara spent the morning working in the county courthouse, on the western edge of town. Within this temple to man's law and the incarceration of his passions, she felt safe. Then she filed her last batch of papers and headed for the door, and he was there.

This time he wore the raiment of the courthouse police, a holstered pistol at his side, but impossibly young and horribly ancient at the same time. As another lawyer *bleeped* through the scanner and the tall blond put his hand on the man's arm, he said gravely, "No one gets through here until they get past me." And then he turned to Tamara, his eyes widening, and said, "Not even her."

Stifling a scream, she hurried down the steps and out onto the plaza, trying to remember the way back to her office.

But she did not make it back to the office, did not escape him this time. He appeared on the sidewalk in front of her, and as she turned sharply into an alley to avoid him, there he was again. The stern, golden man gave her no escape; his narrow eyes seared her face and bared her heart. Memories from which she had run and hidden now came streaming at her, in an arrow-straight line from him to her.

The college party, the vodka and the cocaine on a table half-hidden by smoke and flashing lights. The spinning room, the moving floor soiled and wet, the stumble up the stairs with the strong hand on her arm. The heavy lacrosse player who did not hear her refusal, did not stop, did not listen as she wept and screamed in pain. The blackness like a suffocating cloak thrown over her head.

And then the months in hiding; the lost semester; the lost summer. The hotel rooms and hostels, bad food and vile smells. The long coats and hanging dresses that hid everything from anyone who didn't look too closely. And then—she fought against the memory, but the pitiless golden thing would no more listen to her refusals than the lacrosse player, than the Swan or the Bull would have listened—then the night alone, driven in a borrowed car over rocky ground to a forsaken hill in the woods; her cries, her blood, her shit upon the earth among the trees, and the wail of the child.

And then. And then she had walked away, as soon as she could wrench herself to her feet, walked away alone, left the child to the wind and the cold and the beasts, *exposed* it as the Romans would have exposed a deformed infant or a mouth they could not feed. She left it there in the woods, retreated, stumbling, listened to its cries until she was far enough away that her own cries drowned them out.

Now the tears poured down like blood. Her eyes burned; her hair burned. Her belly was on fire. Gabriel, if that's who it was, grimaced in agony as her humiliation, shame and guilt swam to the surface like boils. He opened his mouth, and a cry came out. It was the cry of the infant in the woods. And it was her own cry. And Mary's.

What could he want of her now? Was this his purpose, to torture her with memories she could not forgive, with the crime from which she had run every day of her life? Is that why he had sought her out?

No, she knew better. Gabriel always wanted something of Mary—no, was *telling* her something, imposing on her the duty she could not escape. You are highly favored, no matter that the favor tears you into a hundred pieces. The Lord is with you, whether you want Him or not.

"What do you want? What do you want?" she asked, trying to

sound stern but whimpering as she spoke.

"Blessed mother," said Gabriel, his nostrils flaring, his teeth sharp.

"No," said Tamara.

"Blessed among all women," said Gabriel.

"What can I do? Turn myself in? Plead guilty to murder? Is that what you want? Then will you leave me alone?"

The angel turned his head on one side, then the other, like a bird looking through one eye at a time. "Atonement before man is not atonement before God."

Tamara wanted to run at him, to sink her nails into his face, to do anything that would make him go away. But he came closer, his eyes wide like a madman's. "Then what, what, *what*?"

He turned his head on its side again, but this time the gesture meant: *Follow.* He strode out of the alley, seeming to leave it all at once. Unable to stop herself, she hurried after.

He walked slowly, or seemed to; his steps came down only once every several heartbeats. Yet he moved through space as quickly as she could run. She did not see him glide, nor perceive any moment when his strides appeared larger than any man's, but he covered ground like a bounding lion. She found herself dodging traffic, cutting through alleys, stumbling over spoiled food and refuse, losing all sense of where she was.

Her breath came in buzzing, sickly wheezes, and bright spots bloomed in front of her eyes, when they finally stopped. She leaned against a brownstone wall and shut her eyes, hugging herself and trying not to pass out. Then she looked up.

They were standing in front of Saint Drogo's Infimary for Waifs.

It loomed over her like a hungry giant. Her heart struck blows against her chest. She glared at the inhuman master before her. He bowed his head, but would not release her eyes.

"Give what was taken." His voice rang in her head. "Take what was lost."

She could not move. She knew what was inside, the children too maimed and wounded to endure, the abandoned, the doomed. She could not turn away. She could not refuse. Redemption was here, even if it burned her. He released her as she climbed the mount of stairs, and the air turned golden around them.

*

I first saw Martini's **The Annunciation** *in the Uffizi in 1995 while traveling with my wife and 16-month-old daughter. Its image, especially the expressions on Mary's and Gabriel's faces, have haunted me ever since. This story eventually got me into an anthology of Christian SFF, which is the last place I ever expected to publish anything.*

SERKERS
AND SLEEP

I WAS VERY SMALL WHEN WE KILLED MY
uncle.

Like every fisherman in Badger Stone, my uncle
Mallard owned the thick wool-and-leather gloves,
sleeves, and vests that protect you from serk bites.
But they slow down your hands and hobble your fingers, and in the summertime they are miserably hot.
On the most sweltering day of the year, he took off his sleeves to
haul the net into his boat more quickly. The two serk in the net bit
him before he knew it.

He made the best of his affliction, building four houses and
clearing an acre of timber in the two days of strength the serk gave
him. He didn't hide it from anyone, which some serkers try to do.
When the strength left him and the early stage yielded to the late,
my poor uncle was sitting in a circle of us, his friends and family,
all gathered around him to say goodbye. We were ready when the
madness took him, and his brothers killed him quickly, before he
had the chance to murder any of us.

It's the civilized way to do it. I've heard stories of whole families, even half a village, killed by a late serker. A responsible, loving man like Mallard couldn't let that happen, so his kin took him
as humanely as they could.

I can't remember a time when I didn't know about the serk, like warnings not to touch knives or stick your hand in a fireplace. But they're so rare that no one I knew had ever seen one before.

Maybe it's my imagination that my mother used to smile more often when I was little, that there were more jokes told back then. That whole year after the accident, she never let me or my brother out of her sight.

I was nine when Marmot the sorcerer told me how the serk do what they do.

Dipper and I were watching Marmot as he tended to Starspots, who'd stopped giving milk. Like anyone who knew things we didn't, Marmot fascinated us children; we hoped to see something wondrous in the cool spring morning. But at first he just walked round and round Starspots, doing nothing that I could see but staring, and before long, Dipper got bored. She whispered that we should go swimming. I started to whisper back that it was too cold, but I saw Marmot's stare turn on me, and he wasn't smiling.

"Swimming?" he asked. "You mean in the river? While the rapids are still rushing?"

That wasn't what Dipper meant, and I saw her pale skin start to turn red as she tried to stare him down.

"Dipper," he said. "You don't mean in the lake. You know better than that!"

"Never happens," she muttered.

"What?" said Marmot.

"It never happens," she said louder. "No one gets bit."

"It happened to my Uncle Mallard," I said. She shot me a look that said *traitor*. Mallard had been the only one bitten in my or Dipper's lifetime; the last serker had been thirty years before. We'd all swum in the lake, although it was usually Dipper's idea.

"Listen to Scuffer," said Marmot. Dipper nodded, though I knew she was seething. Marmot pursed his lips, then turned back to Starspots.

He started by putting her to sleep, which involved a strange sculpting movement of his strong hands in the air. She lay down on the dirt and curled up like a cat. Then he continued to dance with his hands, stopping as if to feel the texture of the air, then repeating a figure, then stopping again. This was much more interesting than a swim; we were transfixed. I think we expected to see sparks or hear a roar from the heavens, but nothing like that happened. Eventually Marmot put his round face to Starspots's, sighed, and said, "I think that will work. There was a blockage."

"How did you get her to sleep?" I asked, forgetting altogether about the lake and his warnings.

He glanced at me. "I turned some of the lines of potential in her brain."

Dipper scowled. Sorcerers always talk about *potential* when they're discussing something complicated. He laughed, but not unkindly.

Dipper asked quickly, "Could you make her sleep for longer? All night?"

He paused; I don't think she fooled him for a minute. "Longer than that, if I had to. Days. Some sorcerers might be able to make her sleep for months or years, although that's too intricate for a bumpkin like me."

I put my hands protectively over Starspots. "Would she starve?"

"No. Her whole body would slow down, as it did today." He did something else with his hands, and Starspots shuddered and started to rouse. "She'd still age, very slowly, but she wouldn't need food or water."

Marmot stood up, brushing the dirt from his knees. "Now, about the lake—"

Dipper interrupted him. "Why does a serk bite make you strong?"

He frowned. "If I were you, I'd worry more about what happens afterwards."

"But how? How does it work?" She knew Marmot never could

resist the chance to explain something.

"Well, we think that they carry something in their fangs that changes the lines of potential within a man or woman."

I rolled my eyes when he used that word again. Dimples appeared in his sunburned cheeks. "I'm sorry, Scuffer. There's no other way to explain it."

"Is it hard to—to see *potential*?" Dipper winked at me when I asked the question.

Marmot laughed again. "It's like juggling four tools in the air while trying to read a book and scratch your left leg with your right toe. Then actually *doing* something with it, like untangling a knot, requires double the attention."

"What does this have to do with the serk?" I asked. Dipper glared at me; I wasn't following her plan.

Marmot looked into the distance. "Listen, I have to see Fox and Robin now. If you'd like me to say more, you'd better trot along with me."

As we climbed over the four hills between my parents' farm and Fox's, Marmot said, "The lines of potential around an early serker seem to bend towards him, as if the air, the trees, even the earth are feeding his muscles, his nerves, his bones. To a sorcerer, he looks as if he were a hundred men wrapped into one. Do you remember the Warrior Serker?"

"That's just a story," Dipper said, eager to show how grown-up she was. Everyone knew the tale: the Lord of the Plateaus sent an army from the eastern plains looking for plunder and slaves, leveling towns, murdering thousands, sweeping across the valley. Then an early serker confronted them, and they were all dead by sunset. My friends had decided it must be a fairy tale, like the Water Maidens or the Sun Spitter.

Marmot shook his head. "No, it's true, or I think it is. It goes back, oh, two hundred years, but it fits with other stories from that time. The destruction of the Plateaus army is a fact, and no other explanation makes sense. They say that the army was only a few days' march from here when it happened. Some people think that the Warrior Serker sought the serk on purpose."

It's one thing to hear stories at bedtime; it's another to hear a sober man tell you that they really happened. Thousands of heavily armed soldiers, destroyed in an afternoon by a man like a demon, moving too fast to see, strong enough to crush skulls with a fist—I shuddered.

"Why does the early stage last only two days?" I asked.

"Sometimes three, and I don't know. The potential lines change abruptly. The muscles and bones no longer seem to draw power from the world, but the potential in the brain changes—the lines twist."

"They go crazy," said Dipper, unable to stop herself.

Marmot stopped walking and pursed his lips. "Well. The late serker thinks that everyone he knows is determined to kill him, that they'll succeed unless he kills them first. No sorcerer has ever been able to untie that knot in the mind, although we can see it. The serker becomes crafty, smarter than anyone around him; he stalks his friends, even his own children, and picks them off one by one, unless they're forewarned and can act together."

"How long does it last?" I asked.

"Your uncle Mallard was the only serker I've seen with my own eyes, and he was in the late stage for only a few minutes. My teacher told me that the lines of potential in the brain continue to change subtly. I don't know what would happen if the late stage lasted months, or years. They're never allowed to live that long."

We got to Fox's farm about then, and Marmot went on to the house without us. Dipper and I didn't go to the lake, not that time.

I was twelve when I began to read the book.

On my older brother's Naming Day, Dipper and I were playing around in the big room in my house. We had sneaked away from the party and spent an hour trying to find my dog. Bigfeet hated crowds, and I wasn't surprised that he avoided the Naming, but he wasn't in any of his usual hiding places either. Eventually we got bored with the search, and Dipper wanted to take down my mother's book.

My mother had it from her father, who'd had it from his own mother and didn't know how it had come into the family. On strong linen pages bound by soft maroon leather, blue-purple ink made flourishes and complicated designs on every page to accompany lines of strange, unfathomable characters. We thought it had come from far away, for no one in Badger Stone had the skill to make such a thing, nor had anyone ever been able to read it. Even learned men like Marmot and his teacher Bear could make nothing of the strange writing.

Dipper knew that the book was an heirloom and that children were forbidden to touch it, but that was exactly what drew her, my daring friend, and I loved watching her eagerness.

I climbed to the high shelf—Dipper was ready to do it herself, and she was my height, but I was mindful of my mother's wrath and promised myself that I'd hold it myself, not let Dipper handle it. She plopped down on the floor, squirming with excitement and getting her black hair all tangled, waiting for me to show her the pages. I sat down next to her and opened the book cautiously.

In the middle of the page I opened, amid all the strange gibberish, sat a line written with perfect clarity:

Take the left path on the way to the river.

I gasped, and Dipper turned to me, concerned. "What?"

I pointed at the sentence on the page. Dipper frowned and squinted at it. "Pretty," she said, "but so what?"

"But it *says* something!" I said.

"Maybe, but we'll never know."

"But we *do*. Look at it, it says, 'Take the left path on the way to the river.'"

"Scuffer." She snorted and shook her head. "You *can't read*."

"I can read this."

Dipper motioned me to bring the book closer, and she put her nose a few inches from the page. "Where?"

"You can't read either."

"Show me anyway."

"*There.*"

"Sure, if you say so."

She couldn't see it, and after a few minutes, neither could I; the page became a confused jungle again. I put the book back where it came from, wondering how I could ask my mother about this without being punished.

Dipper went home not long after. The party had broken up, and I followed the path down the hill to delay helping my parents clean up after it. The tall grass fluttered and bent in the wind, as if shooing me back toward my home and chores, but I paid it no mind. I came to the fork in the trail, intending to turn right, towards one of my favorite lairs, but then I stopped. *Take the left path on the way to the river.*

The left path, not nearly so well-used as the right, was obscured by grass and almost invisible now. I had let it lead me for ten minutes when I heard a familiar whine.

Bigfeet lay on his side next to a clump of bushes. He was bleeding from his neck, foreleg, and snout, and he couldn't get up. I didn't see any tracks, but I was sure he'd tangled with a lynx or a raccoon, or some other animal he had no business fighting. I picked him up and stumbled in the direction of Marmot's house.

Marmot confirmed that it had been a lynx, washed out the wounds and did one or two strange things that eased Bigfeet's pain. When Bigfeet calmed down, Marmot asked where I'd found him. When I told him, he looked up. "On the eastern path?" he repeated.

I nodded and felt my face get warm. He narrowed his blue eyes and asked, "How did you know to look for him there?"

It was in my mind to lie, but those eyes told me it would be useless.

"A book told me to."

"A book?" He looked confused; then he stared. "Not the old red one your grandfather had?" I nodded. "You were able to read it?"

I nodded again. "Only one line, and only for a few minutes."

After I told him the story, he said, "The ink did not change. If it had, then Dipper would have seen it too—and you shouldn't have been able to read it, even if it were written plainly."

"I—yes. Yes, I guess so. But I didn't make it up."

"No, I know you didn't. The ink didn't change; you did."

"I don't understand."

"Neither do I," he admitted. "But I think I'd better take another look at this book."

My father did not thrash me, probably because of Marmot's interest. With my parents standing nearby, Marmot examined the book, frowning. Then he handed it to me and told me open it. When I did so, a line of text jumped out at me:

For your eyes alone.

"Remarkable," said Marmot. "When Scuffer opened it, I saw some sort of commerce between the potential in his brain and the potential of the book. It's the work of a very accomplished sorcerer—more accomplished than I am, anyway."

"Do you think it's doing something to him?" asked my mother, losing color in her face.

"No, rather the opposite," said Marmot. "Somehow the book is responding to things that are in Scuffer's thoughts."

We passed it around, but no one else caused any change in the book, and none of them could read the line of writing that I saw.

"How long has this book has been in the family?" asked Marmot.

"At least seventy years," said my mother.

Marmot wove his fingers together and twiddled his thumbs. "The genius who made this contrivance wanted it to respond to a particular person, or a particular kind of person, maybe at a particular time. I can't say why it's chosen Scuffer, or why now."

"What should we do?" asked my father.

Marmot puffed out his cheeks. "On the one hand, the maker went to a lot of trouble to find someone like Scuffer; there was probably a good reason. On the other hand, we don't know what that reason was, malignant or benign."

He walked about all of us in a slow circle, scrutinizing me and the book from different angles. Finally he said, "I think Scuffer should keep the book, at least for the time being. But Scuffer, think hard about the sorts of things it tells you, and on no account follow an instruction that seems to put anyone in any danger." I gulped a little at this last admonition.

Over the next months I kept the book by me, opening it several times a day. Usually it told me nothing; perhaps once in a fortnight it would give me some advice, leading me to find a lost object, or avoid a wasp nest, or something just as trivial. Once, after a particularly bitter row with Dipper, it said simply, *Apologize now.* Marmot chuckled when he heard about that; he was as puzzled as I that so little of consequence was happening. Was it for such trifles that a sorcerer a hundred years dead bent reality itself to speak to me?

I was thirteen when the book saved my life.

On the last warm day of autumn, Dipper wanted to go swimming in the lake. She might have swum in the river; she might have gone alone and not asked me; I might have said no. I didn't try to talk her out of it. Everyone knows the danger of walking outside during a thunderstorm, but people do it anyway, and how often is anyone struck by lightning? It was common lore that the serk stay near the deepest bottom, that decades go by between sightings.

Nor did I consult the book. I didn't ask its permission for every little thing, and anyway, for four days it had had only one message: *The day approaches.* I could make no sense of that, so I'd stopped looking at it.

Dipper and I ran down to the lake as if our bodies had unlimited energy, tall grass whipping our legs and the fall sunshine warming our scalps. At the lake's edge, she told me to turn around while she undressed, something she'd never asked before. It gave me a funny feeling in my stomach and behind my eyes when she asked, but I didn't understand what it was, not then. After a few minutes I heard her splash into the water, and she called, "Hurry up!"

I stripped off my clothes and rushed in after her. The water near the shore was sun-warmed, but further away it got colder, and my skin tightened against my bones. We began splashing about in earnest, playing silly games, dunking each other and diving for stones. It was the last morsel of summer, and I felt that it was the last taste of childhood too. Some part of me, the part that swallowed hard when I averted my gaze from Dipper, knew that I would not be coming to the lake with her the same way again. I sensed that, by the time spring warmed the shore and made the lake swimmable again, she and I would stand clothed in a profound change.

She swam further out in effortless, confident strokes. I didn't follow, at least not far. I lay on my back and propelled myself with lazy flutters of my arms and feet.

Then I heard Dipper grunt, a soft little "um," the way she did when she'd forgotten something she needed and had to go home for it. I looked over the water to her, and for an instant it seemed to me that she'd stopped moving altogether. Did I see a flash of color in the waves? But Dipper started swimming again, slower, more deliberate strokes, and I decided that it was nothing.

I *decided* it; I knew what it might be, and I put it out of my mind. Was it love that made me pretend that nothing was wrong, or would it have been love to act?

Before Dipper got to shore, she asked me to get out first and dress again, looking away from her while she dressed. When I faced her again, her limbs looked smooth and lithe, sun-touched and wind-cooled, the same as she'd ever been. We wandered to our homes, drying in the sun but still smelling of the lake, and did not touch before saying goodbye.

I heard nothing from Dipper the next day, nor the day after. This was comforting; it made the muffled voices in my head seem silly and fretful. I did my chores and helped my father with the harvesting, a long, hard job that took us until after sunset. I wondered how I'd ever found the time to go swimming the day before, and fell into bed exhausted.

In the middle of the night I woke, for no reason I could tell. I was suddenly cold, and I felt, with the urgency of a full bladder, the need to open my grandfather's red-covered book.

There was a full moon, and I could see the markings clearly from the light pouring through the window:

She will kill you.
Take to the rafters.

Fear squeezed my stomach. I did not let myself understand the full meaning of the warning, but I had come to trust the book enough to believe I was in danger. There were no rafters I could reach in the room where I slept, so I crept from it, taking the book with me, and padded into the big room, from which I could scramble up to the highest part of the house.

It was dark as earth in the rafters, but the floor below was lit by moonlight from the windows. The rough beams on which I sat were painful, but I stayed still. Perhaps ten minutes later, the outer door opened.

I would know her silhouette anywhere, even from above, even stretched and distorted by the angle of the moon; I knew Dipper almost as well as I knew myself. But now I knew her not at all.

She was barefoot and carried in her left hand a long, thin knife, the sort used for boning meat. My terror was sharp, but my grief was sharper, for now there was no question what had happened. Dipper, my Dipper, was a late serker. She was mad, cunning, and vicious, and would kill me if she could catch me—and at that moment I hoped she *would* kill me, because the days, perhaps the hours remaining to her could be counted on one hand, and I could not bear it.

With less sound than a cat stalking a mouse, Dipper glided to the door from which I had just come. She vanished within it, and it stayed open for several minutes as she searched the place for me. Had I not wakened, had I not seen the book's warning, she would have dispatched me easily in my sleep. She reemerged, turning her head from side to side, as if hoping to find me lurking in a corner. She turned toward my parents' room, then towards my brother Weasel's, and for a moment I thought she would go there to kill him. But she shook her head, then looked straight up.

My chest nearly burst with the effort of stilling my breath. Could she somehow penetrate even the shadows above her?

No, she couldn't. She passed out of the house the way she had come, closing the door softly behind her. For what seemed a long time I waited, certain that she would surprise me as soon as I climbed down. She didn't.

I needed to warn the village, before she killed anyone else. For all I knew, her parents were already dead. Soon, she would be dead herself.

The book had saved my life; I hoped that it could tell me which way to turn. I opened a page, and a new message confronted me:

Go north into the mountains.

Do not wait. Do not stop.

I stared at the words in the cold light. Leaving Badger Stone without waiting would mean deserting Dipper in her time of crisis, abandoning the village when it was beset by a serker. But the book had never been wrong. I bit my lip to avoid sobbing aloud.

I knocked on my parents' door, something I hadn't done at night for years. After too many heartbeats, my father pulled the door open, squinting at me in confusion.

It didn't take long for me to explain what had happened; my father knew that we must wake Marmot immediately. He began to dress but balked when I told him of the book's instructions to go north.

"Now wait a moment, Scuffer; not at your age. You can't just light out—"

"Father, the book told me! It knew about Dipper. It's never been wrong. I *have* to."

In the lamplight I could see the whites of his eyes. Finally he said, "At least put on some warm clothes and pack some food."

I grabbed a sack and stuffed it with the bread and cheese we had in the larder, then wrapped myself in my wool cloak and my warm boots. My father squeezed my shoulder while I was dressing and then ran out the door. I was only a few minutes behind him, and soon I had left Badger Stone behind me.

When you travel north in the valley, you don't meet any rivers or lakes, and for the first several miles it's all farms and easy hills. Then come the woods, then the foothills, then the mountains. Every step is a challenge, and the trees prevent you from seeing far, even in daylight. At night it's slow, and it seemed even slower to me.

What would I do when I got to the mountains? It was three days' walk. Was the book protecting me from Dipper? Having failed to kill me once, she'd try again, this time more subtly and harder to evade.

But my gut told me otherwise. There were many places I could have gone; *north into the mountains* was too specific for mere protection. The book and its long-dead maker had their own reasons for wanting me in the hills, and I had no way to guess what they were. I was a toy on a string. For all I knew, I might be sacrificed as easily by my guide as by my friend. I wondered, was it better to be killed by a friend? Bitterly I thought that Dipper at least had some cause.

I reached the mountains on the third day. As I sat shivering under a tree with the last of my food, I opened the book again:

Upward today
until the three white stones.
Then east.

I was being led to a particular place. Had I been older, maybe I would have balked immediately and gone back to Badger Stone. But I was a boy of thirteen, and already there was Dipper's madness and soon her death on my conscience. Obeying the book gave me a direction, something I could do without taking responsibility, something to take my mind from the agony of never seeing her again.

I found the three white stones, lined up like soldiers across my path, and turned east. The book led me along switchbacks, twists and hidden crossings—a path no one could have followed if he did not know it was already there.

Near sunset on the fourth day, I came to a grassy mound, twice a man's height and wide as my house, supported on its sides by smooth gray stones the size of cattle. Moss and small trees grew on it, and some of the stones had been split by the roots. It was old.

Obeying the book, I found a place on the north side where a boy my size might move several smaller rocks and enter. Earth and plants came away as I pulled out the stones, and the slanting light preceded me into the mound.

I grabbed one of the stones, expecting perhaps to be bowled over by a giant animal with claws. Nothing came, and I passed into darkness.

First the smell came to me, sour and musty, so thick it was like a warm wave of water. I gagged. Then my eyes learned to see; faintly, the inside of the hollow mound appeared. Smooth stones lined the whole interior, a dome just tall enough to stand in. In the center, on another huge rock, lay the body of a man.

An old, old man: sunken eyes in a starved skull, white hair spilling onto the earthen floor. His bones stuck out like tumors. His clothes were tatters but had once been fine; I recognized weaving like my mother made for holidays. He was covered in dust.

Obviously I was in a tomb. But as I stepped toward the slab, the man's eyes came open—slowly, as if he had forgotten how.

I gasped, and the head turned toward me. Those eyes went huge and wild, and he screamed.

I retreated to the doorway, preparing to throw my stone; but the old man had risen and backed away to the far side of his tomb, cowering and shaking, dust falling off him in little cascades.

"Don't hurt me!" he whimpered, holding his hands in front of his face. "Don't hurt me, don't hurt me, don't hurt me." It was a rough, raspy voice, like the voice of a man recovering from an illness in his throat. Or a man who had not used his voice in years.

For a moment I could not speak. Then I said, "I won't hurt you." But this only made him shriek again, and he tried to dig into the walls of the mound to get away, snapping some of his long fingernails. On his clothes I could now see brown stains, stains that looked like old blood.

Horrified, I backed out into the dusk that was still brighter than the living grave within.

I opened the book. There was only one word:

Kill.

I choked on my own spit. I turned the pages, and on each one I found the same word, over and over:

Kill.

Kill.

Kill.

Marmot's words came to me, clear as water: *On no account follow an instruction that seems to put anyone in any danger.* All the book's kindness now seemed like bait in a trap. From the start it had wanted to make me into a killer, and that was why it had befriended me.

I wanted to hurl the book to the ground. I actually raised it into the air, dropping the stone. Then I brought it close to my face, staring at the ugly words. For the first time, I spoke to it aloud.

"I won't," I said. "I won't."

The characters on the book blurred, crawling around the page sickeningly. When they stopped, they said:

Kill the serker

before it's too late.

Dipper flashed before my eyes again, Dipper swimming away from me in the lake, Dipper with the boning knife in her hand.

Was this terrified wreck a serker? That made no sense. If he were an early serker, he'd have tossed me aside and burst through the mound with one hand; if a late serker, then he'd have tried to kill me already.

The old man sobbed from inside the mound. "Go away, go away, go away!"

I spoke again to the book. "There's no reason to kill him. He's just some old man."

The words moved again:

> When I made me,
> I needed to plan my death.

I didn't understand—but for the first time, I felt the "commerce" between me and the book, of which Marmot had spoken. The book *reacted* to me, seemed to squirm in my hands with the discomfort of my own confusion. Then—there's no other way to say it—it tried again:

> When he made it,
> He needed to plan his death.
> When the time came, I found you.

Then I realized something: The book had said "*I.*" It had referred to itself. The trees seemed to fall away, the desecrated tomb to shrink; thunder was in my ears.

When I was able to speak again, I asked something I should have asked the first day the book spoke to me: "What are you?"

The words swirled:

> The sorcerer of Badger Stone.
> Then.

The sorcerer of Badger Stone? Marmot? No, Marmot knew nothing about the book; he had been trying to decipher it since before I was born.

I turned the next page. It said:

> The Lord of the Plateaus came.
> There was no other way.
> The sorcerer became a serker.

Then I did drop the book.

The Lord of the Plateaus. A serker. No other way. I knew who the old man was.

Marmot had said that Warrior Serker sought the serk on purpose to save his people. If he was also a sorcerer, he could have made this book. If he was a "genius" sorcerer, as Marmot had said . . .

I could see it in my mind: the desperate sorcerer, obliterating the host of the eastern plains but fearing that he would turn on his own kin. While the early strength was still in him, he raised this mound and sealed himself inside. And then . . .

He could not have known what would happen, not for sure, as he lay down in his tomb and worked the sleeping spell on himself. This must have been his hope: that time, years, would somehow change him into something less deadly, less murderous, than a late serker.

But it was only a guess, and so he left the book. To do what?

I picked up the book again.

I did what I had to,
but a late serker could not be allowed to live.
He might find a way out.
I needed to find someone. I needed to find hands.

That was my role: I was his executioner, in case the experiment failed.

But had it failed? I said, "That's not a serker. It's a scared old man."

All at once the letters began to compose and recompose themselves into different messages so fast that I could barely read them, as if the book were arguing with itself:

Not a serker.
Scared old man.
Serkers cannot be allowed to live.
Not a serker.
Scared old man.

It went on this way for half a minute. Then the page went blank, and I thought it had finished.

But:

It makes no difference.
Tern is gone, and Hider, and Gull and Minnow.
All is desolation.
There is misery and fear.
For pity's sake, kill.
Kill.

Hider—a child's name. Tern, Gull, Minow—his family and friends? His sweetheart? If this was the Warrior Serker, everyone he had known was dust long before my grandfather was born. He had lost everything.

But the book was wrong, I was sure of it. He didn't need to be killed. I understood wanting to stop himself from wiping out the people he had saved, but this was different. Yes, he was frightened and probably filled with more grief than I could imagine, but he was no longer a danger to others.

Then it came to me.

Dipper didn't have to die. If she was not dead already, if she could be put to sleep as the Warrior Serker was, then maybe she could live.

I knew I wasn't thinking clearly. I didn't know whether ending like this old man would be worse for Dipper, but maybe Marmot could help him. Or maybe I could help Dipper, care for her, comfort her. If she wasn't already dead. Hope pounded in my chest.

I needed to ask Marmot, to show him the Warrior Serker. I hoped that the old man's survival, and his change, would teach Marmot something that would help Dipper.

But the Warrior Serker was starved, probably close to dying of thirst. He was petrified of me. Several times I tried to speak to him, but each approach only increased his terror.

Then I had an inspiration and went in holding the red leather book in front of me. As I hoped, his eyes focused on the book rather than on me. He was still frightened, but this time the fear was mixed with incredulity and confusion.

"My . . ." His voice was still harsh, but calmer, less bestial. "My—my enemy." I thought he was talking about me, but he was staring at the book. "My enemy."

I held the book out to him, and he took it, first raising it to this nose and sniffing, then turning it over in his hands, opening the pages, his eyes wide and bright as he looked over the convoluted characters, his mouth open.

Then he squinted at something. "Potential diameter could be tighter," he muttered, shaking his head.

"What? Potential?" I blurted.

"Without a tight helix, it won't call. Won't work." He was still talking to himself. "Won't persuade. Useless. Pointless."

"It worked well enough," I told him.

He turned his troubled eyes on me, then on the book, then back on me. "Found one. Found one." Then he looked back at the pages in horror. "Lies!" he shouted. "Don't believe it. Lies! Don't hurt me." Then he started whimpering again and would have pulled back, but I put my hand out.

"Please," I said. "You saved Badger Stone."

He squinted at me, confused. One shaking hand came out and poked my shoulder as if testing whether I was real.

"Badger Stone," he said.

"Yes."

He sucked on his lips, wincing. "Saved?"

"Yes."

"Tern?" Youthful hope came into his face. "Hider?"

"I—I don't know."

His face sagged; then he caught a glimpse of his own hand on my shoulder, and he turned it back and forth, horrified. He raised the hand to his cheeks, feeling the hundred cracks in the skin and the jowls under the chin.

"How long?" he whined.

I swallowed. "I think, maybe two hundred years."

He stared at me, but his eyes betrayed no disbelief.

"Gone," He said. "All gone, all dead." He looked down at the ground. "Useless, pointless."

I put both my hands on my chest. "I'm Scuffer," I said.

He coughed, then coughed harder, deeper, sitting down on the ground. "A child," he wheezed.

"Who are you?"

He stared as if the question made no sense. Then he said, "Hare."

"I'm going to get you some water," I said. "Will you stay?"

He looked me in the eyes. "Nowhere to go."

It took a while to find a stream, but I filled my flask and brought it to Hare. He emptied it in one draught.

"Hare," I said to him. "Will you go with me to Badger Stone?"

He thumped the book with his hand. "All dead. Desolation. Nothing."

I put my hand on his arm. "There is a whole village there," I said, but I knew what he meant.

"Tern!" he wailed, and put his face in his hands.

"Hare," I said. He sobbed into his fingers. "Hare, please listen."

He shook his head. I grabbed him by the shoulder of his ragged clothes, by the bones that felt like they would burst both skin and fabric. "Listen! There's a girl, and she's been bitten by the serk."

"Doomed," he moaned. "Dead, mad, doomed."

"No, listen. Hare, you're alive. You're not—" I wanted to say *You're not mad*, but the words wouldn't come. "You're not a killer. Maybe we can save Dipper. Maybe she can live. Please—" The tears came down my face, and I could not control my voice. "Please. I have to. She . . ." I choked.

He put his hand on my chest, then on his own. "You want to turn her into *this*?"

It took me a few moments before I could speak. "I want to try. I want to *try*. Please, Hare."

He shook his head. "Fool," he said. Then he stood up. "We will try."

I did feel like a fool; I was clinging to a wish of a hope of a chance. But it was all I had.

It took even longer to return to the village than it had taken to leave it. Hare was weak and could not move quickly, and there was nothing to eat but a few wild mushrooms and onions. Every few hours his panic would overtake him, and he would begin to climb back up the mountains. Each time I approached him with my arms open and pleaded softly. Each time he relented, his wish to help me just barely winning the battle over his fear. A man who could fight his own demons over and over again, when every instinct told him to flee, must have an indomitable will.

When finally we arrived, it took all my pleading to get him to walk into the village; it frightened him more than I did. I had to get down on my knees and beg.

Dipper was still alive. Her parents were alive too, although she had already killed our friend Climber by the time my father raised the alarm. Together the villagers had surrounded Dipper and locked her in her own house.

My departure, it seemed, was what had stayed their hands. Marmot had reasoned that the book, which had protected me from Dipper, had urged me to go north. The book and I were both pieces of this puzzle, he had argued, both somehow connected to Dipper, and "We should not take an action we can't undo until we know how the puzzle fits together."

I think that he just could not bring himself to countenance the killing of a child, no matter how deadly. In fact, had I followed the book's commands and executed Hare, it would have done nothing for Dipper at all. But here we were.

Marmot was fascinated by Hare. Once he understood who Hare was, he scrutinized him with that strange gaze sorcerers have. "A *third*-stage serker!" he whispered. "A sleeping sequence that lasted two centuries! And he performed it on *himself*!"

Then he looked up. "The patterns are discernable," he said. "They're much simpler than what we see in a late serker."

"Monodirectional adjacent helices," muttered Hare.

Marmot's jaw dropped. "Uh—yes. Yes, exactly."

"Don't hurt me."

"Not for the world." Marmot looked at me. "There's nothing you can do for a late serker. But this is something more familiar. I might be able to figure out how to untangle it."

While Marmot tried to work out the contours of his spell, I tried to see Dipper—but the house was locked tight with neighbors guarding all sides of the place, night and day. They had to open the door to feed her, and I saw her wild black hair. She saw me too and called to me.

"Scuffer." Her voice was musical and coaxing, not like Dipper at all. "Scuffer, I need to see you." The door closed, and I felt its *click* in my chest.

I would have stayed outside her prison all day, watching and waiting, wanting to plead for forgiveness and wishing she had killed me. But Marmot came and led me away, saying he needed my help with Hare. As always with Marmot, there was more in his mind than in his mouth; I might have gone mad myself, dwelling on Dipper's fate and my own guilt.

It took Marmot a day's laborious concentration, his hands and lips moving, his eyes staring into Hare's scalp, sweat pouring down his cheeks. I sat before Hare the whole time, holding his hands. He shuddered from time to time, his fear sometimes overmastering him, but each time I squeezed his hands and told him he was the bravest man I'd ever heard of.

When the process was complete, Hare turned his face—his sober, sharp, haunted face, utterly different from what he was before—on Marmot's exhausted eyes. "Thank you, Sorcerer. We both need to sleep."

I spent the days of Hare's recovery in a near-hysteria of impatience, pacing outside Dipper's house whenever anyone would let me. My parents, Weasel, and Marmot tried to keep me occupied, but I could not let it be. Hare's cure, miraculous though it was, had not saved Dipper, and I still did not know whether that was possible. And I had not yet realized what I myself needed to do.

Hare soon regained most of the skills of sorcery he had had as a young man, although he told us, flatly and without concern, that he would not live more than another five years.

"You can slow down aging with the sleeping sequence, but two hundred years is still two hundred years. My heart has only so many beats in it."

He had been Marmot's age when news of the Plateau Army reached Badger Stone. He had left secretly, leaving the beautiful book for Tern, his intended bride, hoping she would keep it as a relic. How it wound up in my grandfather's hands we could not guess.

Seeing how the potential in Dipper's brain had changed in the days since she had been bitten, and comparing it with Hare's, Marmot and Hare believed that the transition to the third stage required "merely" one century, not two. Although Marmot could not weave a sleeping sequence that would last so long, Hare could; he did it gently, softly, like man blessing his children.

We set Dipper in a newly-built hut of stone and wood, checked every day by a friend or member of the family. Most days, I do it myself. When she wakes, Marmot's apprentice, or his apprentice's apprentice, or whatever sorcerer we have by then, should be able to untangle the cords in her mind and restore her to herself.

And Hare taught the long sleeping sequence to Marmot, so that he can pass it on, so no serker ever need be killed again.

I am sixteen as I join her.

Once I had my Naming Day, I took the right to decide my own fate. I told the sorcerers that I wished to sleep beside Dipper, to join her exile in the future. When she rises, in body a middle-aged woman but in mind still a girl of thirteen, confused and mad with fear, she will not be alone. I owe it to her, and more.

My parents and Weasel were distraught, and Marmot tried to talk me out of it. But Hare just smiled and told me I was a good lad.

Now I sit in Dipper's hut, looking down at her sweet sleeping face, her black hair combed sedately over her shoulders, remembering her excitable voice when she was really Dipper, and I wait for Hare and Marmot to give me my heart's desire.

We will awaken together in a strange world, older and exiled from all that we know, as Hare was. We don't have his courage; affection will have to do.

*

This story went through more versions than I can count. I knew that I wanted to write about both the serkers and the talking book, and I knew that the book would be a surrogate for the Warrior Serker. But it was wildly different from draft to draft, and I received help from three different writers groups as well as a magazine editor before it reached its final form.

I HAVE READ THE
TERMS OF USE

A S A CONDITION OF THE USE AND EN-
joyment of the Body selected for your use, you
agree to the following Terms of Use.

You understand that the aforementioned Body
is designed for no more than seventy (70) years of
operation, and that attempts to employ said Body
for any period beyond the aforementioned duration
carries no guarantee that it will function in any capacity. You understand further that We have no control over the actions of other
vendors, and that consequently the Body selected for your use may
be subject to the actions of other models not within Our control,
including infection, infestation, deformation, and decomposition
before the expiration of the design period.

You understand further that We have no control over the actions of other Licensees, and that We are not responsible for the
uses to which they put the Bodies licensed to them, and that therefore We have no responsibility for murder, rape, mayhem, enslave-
ment, oppression, or heartbreak thereby caused to the Body selected for your use.

You agree not to reverse engineer the Body selected for your
use or any of its components or subsystems. You agree that its ultimate design and origins will remain Our proprietary trade secrets,
and that you will make no efforts to discover the methods, materi-

als, or first causes We employed in its development. You understand that any efforts on your part to discover, deduce, or decode the origins of this Body will lead to false or misleading conclusions concerning Our purposes and plans, and that We have no obligation to correct or otherwise respond to such conclusions.

You understand that the Body selected for your use is a component in a larger system (the "Species") which is itself a component in a larger system (the "Planet") which is itself a component in a larger system (the "Cosmos"). You agree that the function of each component within its system, and its interaction with other components in the system, are Our trade secrets and will not be disclosed to you at any time for any reason. You understand that We will not respond to any inquiries concerning those functions and interactions, and that any attempt by you to determine those functions or interactions will be a breach of these Terms of Use.

You agree that you will be born into a race, class, gender identity, sexuality, state of health, time, and place that will give you no ability to control the circumstances of your own life or effect any change for its improvement, and that whether you are valuable or valueless, skilled or unskilled, ugly or beautiful will depend on the whims of Licensees far away and utterly unknown to you. In the alternative, depending on the availability of various styles, colors, and options, you agree that you will be born into such privilege that you will have no awareness of the customs, preferences, tastes, joys, hopes, fears, or sorrows of any Licensee not nearly identical to yourself, and that, should you obtain information pertaining to your own acquiescence, responsibility, or culpability for, without limitation, the deprivations, pains, illnesses, dismemberment, torture, rape, or murder of Licensees not nearly identical to yourself, you will treat such information as Our intellectual property and none of your business, and will, to the extent practicable, understand such matters to be no fault of yours, and contrary to your own good intentions.

You understand that the Body selected for your use is provided with a number of factory settings concerning the cultural norms under which it will operate (the "Starting Conditions"). You understand further that the Starting Conditions will be predetermined by existing relationships of power and wealth within the Culture of which said Body is a component. You agree that the Starting Conditions will determine your perceptions of morality and ethics, and that those perceptions will regard the existing power and wealth relationships of said Culture to be natural, appropriate, functional, and beneficial.

You agree that you will not use the Body selected for your use to infringe upon, alter, or amend any of the Starting Conditions, and that the distribution of goods, services, nutrition, medicine, affection, sexual gratification, and emotional support shall be substantially similar when you surrender the Body selected for your use as when said Body was initially provided.

You agree to experience persistent confusion and disorientation concerning right action, wrong action, your obligations to your family, friends, community, nation, the Species, the Planet, and the Cosmos, resulting in paralysis and inactivity concerning any matter of ethical or moral significance. In the alternative, depending on market conditions and supplies, you agree to experience irrational certainties and extreme passions concerning such matters, in which case you have sole responsibility for any resultant damage.

You understand that We disclaim any representations or warranties other than those contained in these Terms of Use, and that no oral, psychological, historical, literary, or religious assurances you may have received from persons purporting to be Our agents will be binding on Us. You understand further that We expressly disclaim any implied warranties, including, without limitation, any implied warranty of survivability, likability, employability, health, sanity, or fitness for a particular purpose. You agree to hold Us harmless from any direct, consequential, or incidental damages that may result from noncompliance with any assurances or implied warranties not contained in these Terms of Use.

You agree that these Terms of Use shall be subject to such natural, moral, and spiritual laws as We have previously enacted, and that it is your responsibility to acquaint yourself with such laws. You agree that disputes concerning these Terms of Use shall be resolved by adjudicators of Our choosing, in a time and manner that seems best to Us.

You agree that We may alter these Terms of Use on one generation's notice to you. You may refuse such alterations by surrendering the Body selected for your use, at such time and place as We shall designate.

Any use of this Body, including but not limited to breathing, eating, drinking, sleeping, working, playing, loving, or hating, shall be deemed acceptance of these Terms of Use, and shall be irrevocably binding upon you and your heirs, devisees, grantees and assigns forever.

*

I've read more license agreements than I care to remember, and I've always hated contract terms that are designed never to be read, and to protect interests in litigation rather than altering actual behavior. At the same time, I'm appalled that, in life, so many of our circumstances and potentials are governed by things we never had any chance of influencing. The combination imagines God, or the universe, as a dishonest vendor railroading all people into these intolerable terms.

THE AGE OF
THREE STARS

 **P**ETROS COWERED, WELL HIDDEN IN the stinking alley. He could not, did not deserve to avert his gaze as three Watchers in the street wrenched a girl from the grasp of her weeping parents. Even then her desperate father put a foot forward to stop them; but one burly Watcher drew his black-and-silver sword and raised it to the old man's chin, grinning as if he were about to enjoy a fine meal or a game of dice. The father backed away, burying his face in his wool shirt.

The girl couldn't have been more than fourteen. At best, she'd spend a half-moon as a plaything for some Noble or the Watch themselves, thrown back into the street barely alive, *if* alive, if not mutilated. At worst—Petros closed his eyes and swallowed, trying not to think about the King and his Royal Feasts, the roasts and stews carved from the flesh of children.

But shutting out the present only invited the past. Faces cascaded into his mind, Melanion and Cora and Timothy, their hair still ebony or golden, their skins still smooth, mocking Petros's own haggard visage, the grizzled strands on his head. They did not accuse him—they never did—but smiled, laughed and sang their stupid song: *Praise the Age that begins!* As if cringing helplessly weren't bad enough, he had to hear that lie echoing in his head.

After waiting, oh-so-safe in his alley until the Watchers left,

Petros slunk back to the forge. He didn't strike out for Black Hill, though that had been his intention. He would go tomorrow. Maybe he wouldn't go at all.

When he returned to the blacksmith's shop, Zandra was waiting for him, grubby as ever, her face peering over the top of the anvil like a raggedy puppet. She was hefting his largest hammer in both hands, and amazingly she was able to handle it without falling over. He'd never met another twelve-year-old, much less a girl, who could wield something so heavy.

"Where were you?" she demanded.

"How is that your business?" he returned. "Go back to your parents."

"Don't have any; told you before. And it's mean to say."

Petros had forgotten, maybe on purpose. He didn't want to think of how she'd probably been orphaned, didn't want to imagine her in the place of the girl he'd just seen in the street.

Zandra stared at him, scowling, the hammer still in her hand. He had the irrational feeling that he was in danger from her.

"What are you doing here?" he asked.

"Gonna be a smith."

Petros glanced over at Damon the master smith, who was filing the rough edges off a scythe. The huge, younger man seemed not to have heard Zandra, nor even noticed that she was in the forge.

"We discussed this before."

"You'll teach me."

"I won't," he said.

"Sure," she insisted, swinging the hammer around her in a circle. "Gonna be your apprentice."

He reached out and plucked the hammer out of her hands in mid-swing, easy for his muscles but painful for his old joints. He winced. "Journeymen don't have apprentices. You'd have to ask Master Damon, and I can tell you he'll say no."

"Don't want Damon; I'm your apprentice."

"No, you're not."

"Am."

She hung around for the rest of the day. Damon continued to act as if she weren't there, and Petros did his best to ignore her. She did not interrogate him about metalwork, but kept her eyes fixed on him the whole time, marking every movement of his arms, copying his stance, moving along with him when he heated ingots or shaped a horseshoe.

She asked only one question the whole afternoon. "What's that song you hum?" she asked in a sudden, loud voice.

"What? What song?"

"You know." She hummed it.

Praise the Age that begins!

Petros swallowed and stole another look at Damon, but the younger man still seemed to notice nothing.

For a moment he had to struggle to keep silent. Something about the girl's calm, dirty face, her unblinking gray eyes, made him want to unburden himself, finally, after all this time.

"None of your business," Petros said at last. Zandra shrugged.

This was Black Hill, but not as it had been in the old days. The wind was less forgiving, the grove of trees on the south side of the summit thicker than Petros remembered. From the north side he'd have a safe, easy view of the sky, and the grove would hide him from the city. He was alone on the breezy hilltop. There was no one picking berries among the thorns or lolling about on the jagged, tufty grass. In two days he'd be able to creep up the hillside and watch the miracle unobserved.

Praise the Age that begins!

Petros shook his head as if he had fleas, his white hair whipping around his ears. He needed to find a place in the grove where he could hide, just in case. He didn't think the Watch would be looking for him here, didn't think they even knew who he was anymore. He doubted that they had ever taken the damned song seriously in the first place; why should they?

Praise the Age that begins!

He shook his head again. Even if the Watch wasn't looking for him, even if the hilltop was deserted now, he couldn't take the chance. But there was nothing to worry about today; if the Watch expected anything, they expected someone to be here later, for the eclipse itself. Right now he was safe.

Safe and futile. Did he need to witness the eclipse with his own eyes to know that nothing was going to happen? Hadn't history proved it? Hadn't all the others proved it?

Praise the Age that begins!

"Damn it." His voice rasped under the hiss of the wind in the trees.

The song never left him. When he hammered steel in the forge, each ringing blow tearing at his swollen wrists and elbows was a drumbeat for Cora's old chant. Washing his clothes in the river on a fine day when his joints did not pain him too badly, sometimes he caught himself humming, as Zandra had caught him, the same wretched tune. It was as if all the betrayed dead sat in his brain and sang this silly, stupid anthem, this blunder of a prophecy.

Melanion, a drunk and usually a fool, had had seven cups of dark highland wine that night. They were all pretty well ruined by then; the tavern master had been asking them to leave for an hour. Melanion had told the tavern master to go take a piss, belched loudly, and then gone all strange-eyed, his voice weird and his whole body shaking. The prediction came as if ripped out of him by tongs.

Mad and fermented as it sounded, something about it caught and held the rest of them, and before dawn Cora had taken out her small harp and made it into a song. Petros didn't want to think about Cora, but the last few lines came of their own accord:

The Dogs of the People bequeath a new world,
Praise the Age that begins!
We'll witness the Dawn of the Age of Three Stars,
Praise the Age that begins!

An anthem for the Dogs of the People was ridiculous. Anthems made you think of fierce, terrified soldiers marching behind banners, or the Watch howling in chorus as it smashed heads and hacked off arms, or a hired choir singing the virtues of the King as he picked his nose.

No songs for the Dogs; the Dogs were insane. A scruffy pack of artisans and laborers who met in taverns and on the road, men and women who had seen their livelihoods stolen, their children eaten or molested, their wives and husbands mutilated or raped— grief and rage and lifelong suffering had driven them not to despair, which was the sensible conclusion, but to lunatic hope. They labored to organize all the people, or at least the people who didn't have family in the Watch, into a great wave of flesh to smash the Watch and storm the King's citadel.

It was a stupid plan, and when they were sober they all knew it. But madness that is born of desperation admits no cure, and they told each other that it was only a matter of time, more work, more quiet talk in taverns and alleys and darkened kitchens, before the people would rally and take back what was theirs. Freedom! they murmured in their drink. Brotherhood! The end of power!

And perhaps it hadn't been so utterly mad. In all the hushed, urgent talks he'd had in smoky rooms and remote farm rows, eye-to-eye and hand on shoulder, Petros had seen longing in the eyes of his listeners. They couldn't picture rising by themselves, but they could imagine a future without the King, without the Watch. They hungered for it; they dreamed of rescue. But would they follow the Dogs?

Then Melanion made his prophecy and Cora sang it, and Timothy, who knew the stars and planets, told them that there would, indeed, be an eclipse of the sun at high noon, directly over Black Hill, on a date some 33 years hence. Thirty-three years—it seemed discouragingly far away, but it was a date the Dogs could believe. Yes, they told each other, yes, it would take that long. To gather enough people, to build the discipline, to create a multitude willing to die for the cause—they thought that a generation and a half might be long enough. The song spread, and became a watchword among the Dogs of the People, a promise that their efforts would come to fruition, that their sacrifice would be worth it in the end.

But there were no three decades of labor, no steady increase of followers, no magic army. The Watch had seen all of it, could even recite the song, and over a few months they hunted and butchered all the Dogs.

All but Petros. Lying low in refuse dumps, slipping from the capital city under a cartload of dung, wandering under half-dozen names, luck and stealth protecting him, he lost himself in towns and villages where no one he loved had ever been. Finally, after more than twenty years, he returned to the city, a journeyman smith, found work in Damon's forge—nodding and smiling to the Watch when it passed in the street, even when it trod over the spot where Cora had died.

So he would witness the eclipse. He would stare up at a black sun and look for the three stars Melanion had predicted, the new age he'd promised. And stars or no stars, the Watch would still be there; the Nobles would still rape and dismember; the King would still eat the young. And Petros would be there to see it. That was his destiny, to endure the snuffing of the last feeble ember of his hope.

On his way to the shop in the pale morning, Petros passed by the square where the farmers had been selling autumn vegetables before sunrise. A pack of street urchins was scavenging for scraps, the bigger ones crowding out the small ones. The small ones were going to die, Petros knew. It was lucky that the Watch hadn't already rounded them all up for feasts.

Normally he passed the spectacle with his eyes downward, but today he stopped and watched. Two of the littlest children, a boy and a girl, were darting between the larger ones, snatching at what bits of carrot top and other scraps they could reach. Two bigger boys, one with red hair and one with black, with hard faces and filthy, broken nails, spun round and dragged the smaller pair by their ragged clothing, pushed them against a brick building, and hauled back as if to smash them in the face.

"Stop."

The boys' heads turned; Petros's did too. Zandra was standing in the alley, her dark gray eyes fixed on the beating. She walked up to them slowly, not cautiously but rather as if she were taking in the sights and sounds of the dirty marketplace. Every eye was on her.

Petros assessed the scene. Zandra was strong for her size, could probably thrash one of the boys if it came to it, but he doubted that she could overcome both. His own leg muscles tensed as if to move in to help. Petros made them relax. *This isn't my fight*, he told himself. *If I couldn't fight for the Dogs, why should I fight for the likes of these?*

The two boys looked Zandra in the eye, and she said, "Let go."

There was a pause in which no one moved. Then, without a word, they released the youngsters. Petros couldn't be sure at this distance, but he thought he saw looks of *shame* on the faces of the bullies. They never took their gazes from Zandra.

"Feed them," she said.

The boys began to snarl. Street urchins never shared food, for good reason, and what was the point? The youngsters would starve anyway, if they didn't become food for someone else first. The red-haired boy stepped forward, his fist raised again. Zandra didn't move, but kept her eyes on his.

The boy stopped in his tracks. His hand lowered. He began to whimper like a kicked puppy. Petros's jaw dropped.

"It'll be all right," Zandra told the weeping boy.

Before Petros's unbelieving eyes, the three of them distributed the scraps among all the urchins.

All that morning he brooded about the girl, her calm courage and quiet authority. His thoughts made him bitter, and he hammered the steel as if his soul were under the blows.

Damon made the blades destined for the Watch. He turned them out nearly uniform, bright but with a swirl of black markings along their whole length. Damon said that the oil-dipping process that drew out the dark marks also made the steel stronger, but Petros suspected that it was more of a trademark, so that people would know Damon's work.

This afternoon Petros was honing a new blade, destined for a Watcher. His arm extended and came back, slow and forceful, gentle and precise. He did not think of the man who would wield the steel, what he would do with it or the suffering that would follow. There was only the metal and the stone, his hand and his other hand, his eye and his ear, a regular rhythm.

"You're doing it again," said Zandra from behind him.

She had been so quiet that he'd forgotten she was there. Petros started. "What?"

"That song. Over and over, that song. *Age begins* or something. Especially in the last couple of days, right around when you left town and went to Black Hill."

He twisted around and glared at her, the sword still on the anvil in his left hand, the whetstone in his right. "You followed me."

"Only far enough to see where you were going. Why are you going there, anyway? And what's that song?"

The girl's grimy face gazed up at him without guile. He felt it again, that urge to speak, and this time the weight of three decades of secrecy and fear felt too crushing to be borne, as if he had held his breath on a dare and would pass out if he did not inhale.

"Can—can you keep a secret, Zandra?"

She assumed an almost comical look of insulted dignity. "Of course!"

Petros put down the sword so that he could turn all the way around. He leaned forward and spoke softly, to make sure Damon wouldn't hear. "Tomorrow there'll be an eclipse of the sun over Black Hill, exactly at noon. I'm going up to watch it."

She looked disdainful. "*Everyone* knows there's going to be an eclipse. You don't need to go to Black Hill; you can see it from town."

He nodded. "Yes. But the prophecy said to watch it from Black Hill."

Her eyes became moons. "There was a prophecy?"

He sagged a little on his stool. "So we thought. My friend Melanion made it, more than thirty years ago." *Friend!* mocked the voice in his head. *A true friend you were to him!*

"Can I hear it? Melanion's prophesy?" asked Zandra.

"Yes, if you want," said Petros. He did not want to say the words aloud, not when they kept chanting in his head, and what good could come of repeating them to this child? But maybe it would give him some relief, like draining away poison.

"They made a song from the prophecy." Melanion's original ravings had been entirely replaced in Petros's memory by Cora's sweet voice and her fingers on the harp-strings. That is what he gave Zandra.

Overhead like a halo that crowns righteous men,
Praise the Age that begins!
From Black Hill we watch as moon hides the sun,
Praise the Age that begins!
Three new stars rise, and the People rise with them,
Praise the Age that begins!
The victorious Dogs see their labors redeemed,
Praise the Age that begins!
The tyrants are helpless and fall into dust,
Praise the Age that begins!
The Dogs of the People bequeath a new world,

Praise the Age that begins!
We'll witness the Dawn of the Age of Three Stars,
Praise the Age that begins!

It sounded plaintive and weak sung alone like that, hushed and fearful, without a chorus of Dogs or Cora's harp as accompaniment. But the melody was still mystic and fiery, full of a passion and hope he had tried to forget. Singing it aloud brought back the smell of wax and wine, the flushed joy and certainty on Cora's face in the candlelight. Petros wanted, right then, to die.

"Who are the Dogs?" asked Zandra. "The victorious Dogs? The Dogs of the People?"

Decades he had guarded this secret as he had guarded his shame, but the girl's gray eyes filled him with longing. He could not stop himself.

"Once there were men and women who called themselves the Dogs of the People. Sounds silly, now."

"Were you one of them?"

"I'm—I'm the last one." The last Dog, the last beaten, limping Dog. Melanion had had two swords stuck in his belly by the Watch, blood belching out of his mouth in a parody of drunken vomit. Cora—Petros closed his eyes, trying not to remember Cora, her torture and beheading that he had watched from a window like a coward. "The Bitch of the People!" the Watchers had jeered as they maimed her in the street.

And he was still here, still safe, like a dog that turns tail and runs. What would they say to him now? How did he dare to sing their anthem of hope?

Powerful as the urge was, he still had the strength to keep this shame from Zandra. She liked the song of the prophecy and promised not to tell anyone. For the rest of the day she sat in the shop and watched him, but did not imitate his actions or say a word.

*

Petros struggled and moaned in his sleep. In his dream, Melanion, Timothy, and Cora sang to him, the prophetic anthem, and as each one finished a line, a Watcher came up behind and sliced off his head. *That's not right*, Petros said in the dream. *Melanion was stabbed in the belly.* Melanion's severed head answered him from the ground: *This is just as good. Praise the Age that begins!*

Then Zandra was there too, standing merrily among the disjointed bodies of his old friends, and she sang the whole song back to him, a knowing grin on her face. The Watcher lifted his sword high, preparing to chop straight down through her skull. That was when Petros awoke, choking and whimpering.

The day of the eclipse dawned painfully clear and freezing cold. Petros worked like a sweaty demon in the forge all morning, both to warm himself and to make Damon more amenable to his leaving to see the eclipse. Lots of people would be watching it anyway, and he did not tell Damon which vantage point he had chosen. Zandra was nowhere to be seen.

An hour before noon, he left the shop and began his trek to Black Hill, occasionally looking over his shoulder and feeling foolish. The Watch was out in force in the streets, to monitor the pedestrians and those staring at the sky, to make sure that there was nothing subversive, nothing political, nothing but innocent love of nature involved. They never glanced at him.

Climbing the hill seemed harder than before; his knees moaned at every step.

The eclipse was already starting by the time he reached the top. It would take an hour altogether, the star-watchers had said, and would be total only for a few minutes in the middle. Petros did not know whether it was the whole eclipse or only the totality that mattered, but he didn't think you could see *three new stars rising* in anything less than darkness.

He circled the grove, finding the spot on the north side hidden from the town, and took out the disk of black glass that he used to look into the forge. Squinting up through the disk, he could see that a bite was already taken out of the sun. The sky, though, was still perfectly blue, with not a star in sight.

Looking up made his neck ache, and holding the glass up for long periods was tiring. Somehow Petros had expected more drama, expected the eclipse to happen more decisively than it was happening, but he felt no new disappointment. He was here to witness what none of his friends had lived to witness, if only to confirm that there were no new stars to be seen. He bent his head downward and lowered his hands to rest his neck and shoulders.

That was when he heard the Watchers.

The voices were faint, carrying a far distance in the darkling air, off to his right as if they were just around the corner of the trees. There were two or three of them. He couldn't make out what they were saying, but something in the tune of their growling voices told him who they were.

Petros ducked into the grove as quietly as he could, avoiding twigs and sticks, walking only on leaves or bare ground. When a few hundred paces separated him from where he'd been standing and he could make out only a few slivers of clear air through the trees, he hid behind the largest trunk he could find.

"—that's what Damon said," came one of the voices.

"But he's not here," said a second. "The smith lied."

"Not likely," said a third. "What would be the point? Maybe the old man decided not to come. Maybe he's somewhere else on the hill."

Petros could make out three of them. Even at this distance, he recognized the silver-and-black blades of Damon's forge. He might have made them himself.

"Could be in the trees," said the first voice.

"You can't see the eclipse from the woods," said the second voice. "If he came up here to see it, then he wouldn't be in there."

"Unless he heard us coming," said the first voice. Petros saw one of the figures move towards him. He tried to disappear behind the tree.

"Wait," said the second voice.

All three stopped in their tracks and were silent.

"He's coming," said one of them finally.

Petros heard nothing. Then, faintly, a voice sang, "—*victorious Dogs see their labors redeemed*—"

A girl's voice. Petros's heart stopped.

Zandra called out, "Pe - e - etros!" Petros shut his eyes and pressed himself into the bark of the tree.

He could not tell what happened next, but the voices of the Watch were louder, harsher, jeering, like the voices that had taunted the suffering Cora.

"A Dog of the People!" said the third voice.

"No, a pup!" said the second.

"You were looking for Petros, bitch-pup? So were we. He's up here, isn't he?"

"No," came Zandra's voice, firm but unconvincing.

Petros heard a slap.

"Don't lie to us, bitch," said the first voice. "Where is he?"

"Don't know," said Zandra.

Another slap, and then a ripping sound and a surprised shriek from the girl.

"Now we do this the hard way," said the second voice.

Petros felt the same terror he'd felt when Cora died, the same wish to be silent and invisible. But his feet had a will of their own, and he crept in the direction of the voices.

From the edge of the woods he saw them, about thirty paces away. The three Watchers surrounded Zandra, now stark naked, her torn garments on the ground. One of them held her up by the hair; another had his hand around her throat; a third held his sword-point to her belly. Her bleeding mouth was pulled into a snarl, but her eyes were terrified.

Their attention was entirely on her; none looked in his direction.

Before he knew what he was doing, before he could think, before any of them could notice him, Petros was behind the Watcher holding the sword, grabbed his head in both hands, and twisted sharply with all the strength in a blacksmith's arms. The neck snapped. As the man dropped and the others turned towards Petros, he snatched up the fallen sword and shoved it into the neck of the man who had been choking Zandra.

That was when he felt the impact in his back, and saw the sword-point sticking through his stomach.

"Like Melanion," he said. The point disappeared and blood gushed from his belly. He found he could not breathe, and he fell.

At the same time he heard another body fall. The third Watcher, the one who had run him through, was dead on the ground beside him, the back of his head split open. Zandra had a bloody sword gripped in her hands.

"Petros!" She dropped the blade and ran to him.

He thought his vision was darkening already, but then he realized that the eclipse had reached totality. From where he lay, he could stare straight into the shadow of the hidden sun, its yellow corona reaching into a black sky. Petros saw a few stars, but they were all the old, familiar ones.

Then his head was raised for him, and Zandra's face came into view; she was holding him on her knees.

"Petros," she said again.

"Good," he wheezed. "Good work."

"Want to be your apprentice," she said, tears filling her eyes. "Stay."

Petros wanted to speak, and tried to turn his head to make it easier. Then he saw, even in the ghostly light of the eclipse: just under Zandra's collarbone were three, nearly identical purple birthmarks, making a horizontal line.

Three stars.

"You—" He had to gasp, and he knew he only had a few words left. "You are."

And then he couldn't hear what she was saying, but it didn't matter. The sun was still hidden, still black against yellow against black.

They would follow her, this girl. For her the people would rise against the King and the Watch, in a way they never did for the Dogs. The tyrants would fall into dust.

Petros smiled as the sun, Zandra, everything became impossible to see. He was the last, the victorious Dog, and he bequeathed a new world. He praised the Age as it began.

*

I am old enough to remember when "Aquarius," the prophesying anthem from **Hair,** *first played on the radio, and young enough to have been bitterly disappointed that none of its prophecies came true. They were so young, and so full of hope, and they thought they were going to change the world. This story expresses some of that grief. Yet I was ultimately unable to end on a note of despair: the ending is an homage to Mary Renault's* **The Mask of Apollo,** *where hope is similarly seen in the ashes of disaster.*

KEEPING TABS

I WAS SO EXCITED WHEN I COULD FINALLY buy a Tab. They cost so much, you know, but I saved up for maybe six months. I waitressed at Antonio's in the North End, and let me tell you, it's murder on the feet. Those trays are heavy, too, and Nico screams at everybody the whole shift, not to mention the way you smell after six hours. But the customers tip really well, and I was able to save up enough money, even after paying rent and stuff.

I could never have gotten a Tab when I was still married to Marc, that shit. He never liked anything I liked. When I married him, all I saw was the big brown eyes and the cleft in his chin and the way he could make his voice go down low, so that I felt it all the way down to my knees. I had to learn the hard way.

Not that I could've afforded a Tab back then, anyway. The price started coming down just a few years ago, about when Marc broke my front tooth. By that time I couldn't go to my mom's, because she said I always went back to that shit anyway, and she wasn't going to help me do it again, and my friend Lila wouldn't let me stay with her either, same reason. So I went to a shelter, and the police came, and we got a restraining order on Marc. But yeah, the same damn thing happened, he gave me that look with those eyes and told me how things were really, really going to change this time, because he'd seen the light and couldn't believe he'd done something like that to me, and like an asshole, I dropped the charges and lifted the restraining order and went back to him.

Two years ago, right after I divorced Marc, Pearl Moulton started playing Mandi Trenton on *Dark Little Corners*, which was her first really big break, and they announced that there'd be a Tab on her. I wanted it as soon as I saw her on the show, because Mandi is so awesome; she's this really tough girl who works in a bar, and she gives as good as she gets, and she never gives up on love when all these guys leave her all the time. And Pearl Moulton is so beautiful and talented; I used to watch her on *Deception*, when nobody paid her any attention. Now she was in all the magazines, and she's exactly my age, and she was Tabbed.

But then my mom got sick, and I was taking care of her for two months. My brother Johnny didn't do squat, and his wife Nadine, forget it. So I wasn't able to get the Tab until she got better. That was last year, in May.

I got the injection and the ear cuff, went home and waited for Pearl Moulton's Tab time, which was ten to twelve, Eastern. I was so excited I couldn't sit down; I kept making cups of coffee and forgetting to drink them, picking up the *Herald* and reading stuff I'd already read. Finally it was ten, and I sat down in the recliner and turned on the cuff.

First thing, while it was making the connection, it was like I didn't have a body at all—no sight, no sound, no feeling, nothing. It's a good thing your body breathes by itself, because I couldn't even tell if I was. Then, all of a sudden, wham, I was in this padded chair, and I had Pearl Moulton's body. She's a lot thinner than I am, and her teeth are really straight, and you feel those things right away. At first there was no sound and I couldn't see anything, but there was this sweet smell, and something soft brushing down over my face, that is, her face.

Then a girl's voice said, "Okay, done," and Pearl opened her eyes and blew out through her nose, like there was dust in it. She was sitting in a swivel chair in front of a big mirror like they have at a salon, with vanity bulbs all around it. In the mirror Pearl looked exactly like Mandi Trenton on *Dark Little Corners*, right down to the funny arch in the eyebrow. I'll tell you, looking in the mirror and seeing Mandi was the best feeling in the world, although it only lasted for a second.

Standing behind Pearl was a girl with striped hair and a gold nose ring; she put down a soft brush she was holding and undid the sheet that was covering Pearl's clothes. Underneath Pearl was wearing one of those green outfits Mandi Trenton has in the program.

Pearl said, "Thanks, Victoria," and it was like I was saying it. Then she stood up, and it was like I was standing up, and she walked out the door.

It's really weird to feel somebody else's mouth saying words, and to hear the sound of her voice in her head. You know how your own voice, when you talk, never sounds the way it does when somebody records it and plays it back? Well, Pearl Moulton's voice doesn't sound the same in her head either. It's also pretty strange to feel somebody else's feet when she walks, or hands when she grabs things. I mean, *my* body was sitting in the recliner in my living room, and if I tried to lift Pearl's hand I'd wind up lifting my own off the arm of the chair, but I wouldn't feel it. And of course she doesn't walk the way I do; she takes quicker steps, and each step is exactly in front of the other one, like she was walking the line for a cop. She's taller than I am too, and everything looks different from that angle.

Pearl clickety-clicked into a huge Vid stage with big hot lights and two of the sets from *Dark Little Corners*, the nightclub and Mandi's bedroom. A bunch of people said, "Morning, Pearl," and she said "Hi, guys." It was weird, and great, to hear her say something so normal. She grabbed a bottle of water off a table and sat down in one of those folding chairs, just like you see in the movies.

And then not much happened for a while. First she was looking at the script, then she read a magazine she picked up off the
floor next to the chair. It's totally impossible to read with somebody
else's eyes, let me tell you. I mean, Pearl moved her eyes to follow
what she wanted to see right then, which was nothing like the way
I would have moved my eyes when I was reading. Not that I would
have read this magazine anyway; it was a complicated story about
all those poor people getting killed in Turkey, and whether that
counts as genocide, and what genocide is, and stuff like that. But
like I say, I couldn't even see most of the words; it was mostly a
jerky jumble. And did you know, Pearl Moulton has itchy skin, especially near the armpits? I would have been scratching like crazy,
but it didn't seem to bother her. Or, I don't know, maybe it did
bother her and she just didn't scratch.

So then some guy said, "Pearl, Randy, we're ready for you."
And Pearl walked onto the nightclub set, and so did Randall James!
He's really short, shorter than Pearl, anyway, although he doesn't
look like it on the show. But he's got pretty brown eyes and a dimple. They did a scene where Mandi and Mace are arguing about
some woman Mace went out with the night before, and Mandi
smacks him and cries, and Mace walks out in a huff. Pearl really
hit him, too, but not hard.

They did this scene nine or ten times, and in between they'd
wait while the guys messed with the lights and moved the cameras
around or played with light meters, and the two of them talked
about a party that they were going to go to at Zero-Zero-Zero that
night. Pearl said that Tim—you know she's married to Timothy
Nation, who played the guy on *Deception*?—she said that Tim
didn't really want to go, and didn't want her to go without him, but
that she was going to make him come. Can you imagine a party at
Zero-Zero-Zero?

I used to think they shot soaps live, and I guess they did in the
old days. But later I found out that they have better editing and
stuff than they used to, and they can do lots of takes and put them

together in a hurry. But it was so much fun just being there, with all the actors and everybody.

Somewhere in the middle of ninth or tenth take on that scene, the Tab ended and I was back in my recliner. It took me a few minutes to get used to me again. Nothing like living in the body of a thin, beautiful actress to make you feel fat and ugly when you get home. I saw myself in the mirror; I looked about as good as I usually do, which is not very.

I had to go to work. On the way to the T stop, I tried putting one foot right in front of the other, like I was walking on a line.

Nico was especially nasty to all the waitresses that day, and Lila cried after a customer screamed at her about an order that wasn't her fault. Rob, the snotty kid who runs the Hobart in the afternoons, broke a teacup, and I thought Nico was going to have a heart attack. "Do you know how much costs a cup?" he kept yelling. Rob didn't flinch the whole time, looking down his long nose at Nico.

It was kind of hot for May, too, and Nico hadn't had the air conditioning fixed, so we were all sweating. I left with my uniform sticking all over me, making me itch; I scratched on the T all the way home.

Some people get Tabs at the same time every week, but they cost a lot more. Mine was the cheapest, and they scheduled me whenever they could fit me in, and I only found out a few days before; sometimes it was too late for me to arrange the time, and I missed it. For instance, my second Tab time for Pearl Moulton was five days after the first one, at four o'clock Eastern, so I couldn't Tab her because I was at work. The time after that, I had to go fight with the landlord, because a pipe burst in the apartment over mine and I had disgusting, dirty water in my cabinets and dishes, and half the food in the pantry was ruined. It was the third time something like that happened.

When I finally I got a chance to Tab Pearl again, it was in the middle of the day on a Saturday—middle of the day for her, afternoon for me. She was at home with Timothy Nation, and she was cooking in her kitchen. I think I would have liked it better if she was on the set doing Mandi Trenton again, but this was good too. Her kitchen is huge, with a stone island in the middle and spotlights shining down on it. She was cooking something with a lot of vegetables in it: zucchini, eggplant, onions, peppers, tomatoes, garlic, all in big chunks and thrown in to this gigantic pot. It reminded me of the Italian cooking my mom used to do, but I don't think Pearl is Italian.

Halfway through the chopping, Tim came up behind her and kissed the back of her neck, and she said "Hi," in that kind of low voice you use on someone you like. Then he brought his arms around her middle and kissed her ear, which tickled, and she put down the knife and leaned back into him, kind of laughing, you know, chuckling.

Then his hands came up to her tits, and she gasped and stuck her elbow in his stomach, and said, "No, Tim! The Tab!"

He said, "Shit, I forgot," and backed away from her—she almost lost her balance. Then he said, "Can't they at least make it the same days and times every week, so that we could remember? You're not a slave."

She said, "I tried again on Monday. They won't budge. I'm sorry."

Then he walked out of the room. I could tell Pearl was mad after that, because she started chopping down harder on the vegetables. The stew or whatever it was she was making took a long time to cook (it smelled awesome), but she stayed in the kitchen the whole time, reading another one of those magazines I couldn't read. Tim Nation didn't come back in the kitchen. I wonder how the stew tasted.

Now, so you don't get the wrong idea, I don't get off on the sex thing with the Tab. I know there are some perverts—guys—who would get Tabs on somebody like Pearl Moulton so that they could feel her body. But the hookers downtown would let you Tab them for a lot less money, and if you were that kind of pervert and you paid them enough, they would do all kinds of stuff to themselves while you were Tabbed into them. But the real sickos want to know what it feels like to have Pearl Moulton's tits in particular, you know? I heard that some of the actresses got sex-limited Tabs, that they'd only let other women Tab them. But I don't know if Pearl was one of them.

I got to Tab Pearl three or four times during the next six months or so. I had a lot of time on the set of *Dark Little Corners*, which was my favorite; it was like being an actress and being Mandi Trenton all at the same time. Other times, like parties or times at home or when she was having lunch with a friend, I got the idea that Pearl didn't like the Tab so well. She would tell people not to talk about certain things because of the Tab, and she had this angry sound in her voice. Tim Nation didn't like it either, and he got madder and madder every time she would say stuff like that. Once he threw a glass into the sink so hard it broke. But me, I thought the Tab was terrific. I was having the time of my life.

In December I heard that they were going to start a TalkBack feature, where one Tabber at a time would be actually able to say things to the person they were Tabbing. It's a lot more expensive than the Tab itself; it would take me months to save enough tips for even one two-hour TalkBack. But boy, did I want it. To be able to talk to Pearl Moulton!

At about the same time my Mom got sick again, and then my brother Johnny got sick too, and Nadine just walked out on him, if you can believe it. After all the help he didn't give me with Mom the first time, I didn't really feel like lifting a finger for Johnny, but what could I do? He's a lazy bum and he always has been, but he was going to chemo and he needed me. Between the diarrhea and the puking and me taking care of Mom too, let me tell you, January and February sucked.

I got only a few chances to go on the Tab during all that time, and they were all stuff like eating meals and press conferences.

She likes to eat stuff I never tried, like sushi and spicy Vietnamese cabbage and tofu. I wonder if it tasted the same to her as it tasted to me. I didn't like it much, so I guess not.

In April I was Tabbing Pearl when she was having drinks with Tim Nation and one of the directors she works with, Donny Blanchette. All of a sudden she said, "Stop it. Shut up." Blanchette looked at her and asked what he said wrong. Pearl said, "Not you, the Tab. They've got the TalkBack on me now, and I have a woman in Sydney talking to me." Then she stopped for a second like she was listening, and said, "No, I *know* you paid for it. But I'm trying to have drinks with my friends, and I can't concentrate with you talking in my head." She stopped again. "I'll talk to you later, I promise. Just, please, stop talking to me now. Please?"

"Should have gone out later," said Tim Nation, like it was her fault.

"When?" said Pearl, and I felt her throat get tight the way it does when you're trying not to cry. "If I'm not filming or sleeping, I'm on the Tab."

"That's an exaggeration," said Tim, but he looked mad.

"It's like I have no life of my own," said Pearl, and by this time her eyes were getting blurry, and they stung.

"No," said Blanchette. "It's that *they* have no lives of their own."

Donny Blanchette is a prick. Okay, that girl shouldn't have been talking while Pearl was having drinks with Tim. I said to myself that I would never do that when I got the TalkBack. But who does Blanchette think he is, with his "They have no lives of their own"? Let Donny Blanchette take a look at my Mom, or at my brother, or at my job with Nico, or at this stinking apartment. This is what life *is*; what the hell does he think *he's* got? Does he think that's *real*?

*

I was finally able to afford the TalkBack this May, but the wait-ing list was three months long before I could actually have my TalkBack session with Pearl. But I got the feature installed right away, because I knew that you had to get taught how to use it. Talking with your mouth doesn't work, because for one thing, you can't feel your mouth when you're Tabbing, and the person you're Tabbing can't hear your voice anyway. You have to picture saying the words in your head, and there's this feature that lets you hear the words you're saying, and the tone of voice and everything. But it takes practice. You can turn it on without Tabbing, so I worked on it the whole time, practicing saying things. Mostly I was saying *You're awesome, Pearl*, or stuff like that, but I did work on longer sentences too.

Meanwhile I came down with pneumonia and missed a lot of work, and then Nico fired me. Lila said that I could sue him, but I didn't have the time for stuff like that; I just needed to get another job. So finally I went to work at Tomas's, which is in a different part of town. The tips weren't as good, but I could get along. If I hadn't already paid for the TalkBack, I wouldn't have been able to afford it anymore.

Not too long after I got the TalkBack set up, weird stuff started happening with the Tab. One time I was Tabbing Pearl while she was shopping at L'Oiseau Blanc, which is this tiny shop she likes, and all of a sudden I couldn't hear anything—I mean I couldn't hear anything that was happening around *Pearl*; I could hear the jackhammer outside my own window just fine. That lasted for maybe fifteen minutes, then stopped. Another time she was on a talk show, and in the middle of a question I stopped feeling her body. I could still see the lights and hear the questions and smell the make-up, but all I could feel was my own butt on the recliner.

I called Customer Service, and they said that they hadn't had any other reports like that, and that it sounded like a fluke, and was I *sure* the sound and touch had gone out? And they said they'd call me back, and they never did. Pricks.

In June I found out that Marc got married again. Honest to God, I wanted to find out the girl's name, call her up and warn her. She was going to be a punching bag, and she didn't know. I told Lila, and she rolled her eyes and said, "You think the new wife is going to believe the ex about anything?"

"I could show her the police report and the restraining order."

"She'll never talk to you, and if she does then Marc will have some smooth story about how you gave as good as you got, and it was all a set-up. She's not going to listen to you."

And then, right that second, I couldn't hear Lila anymore. I heard Pearl's voice, like I was in her head, yelling, "God damn it, Randy, that's the twelfth time we've done it! Jesus Christ!" Then I heard Randall James say, "Sorry, Pearl; I don't know what's wrong with me today." Then Donny Blanchette's voice started talking, and I heard them starting to do a scene.

At first Lila was still trying to talk to me, but then she saw my face (I guess I looked pretty spooked) and came around the table and held my hands and said stuff I couldn't hear. She looked scared out of her socks. It took ten minutes before I could hear her again.

It happened again later that day, but with my vision. For about five minutes all I could see was Tim Nation in their bedroom. He looked like he was yelling, and was red in the face and moving his hands a lot. But I couldn't hear anything.

This time Customer Service actually listened to me. They told me to come right to the service center on Tremont Street. The technician looked almost as worried as I was. Neither of those two times had even been one of Pearl's scheduled Tab sessions, and I wasn't wearing the ear cuff, it was in my bag. So the techie did some deal where he replaced the "neural links" or something, and he said that should take care of it.

Johnny's chemo wasn't working, and in July we found out that the cancer had spread to his liver. Nadine came back and started taking care of him, and she wasn't hysterical or anything. When I went over to their house and she and I were alone, she'd cry a little on my shoulder, but that was all. Johnny was handling it pretty good too, kidding me and joking about surgery. I don't think I could have made jokes, if it was me. They said there might be a chance of a liver transplant, but there was a long waiting list.

But the techie was wrong about the problem being fixed. It happened again right after Nadine moved back in with Johnny. I woke up at about one in the morning, and I couldn't feel my body. I could see my room, and hear the traffic, but what I felt was Pearl walking back and forth really fast, pounding her hands on hard things so that they hurt. Her throat was sore, like she'd been yelling, and her face felt hot. Then I felt somebody's hand grab her arm—

Her nose, my nose, crunched and hurt so bad I couldn't see. Then there was a slap on my mouth, and something warm on her tongue—

It was like I was back with Marc, and he was smashing me in the face and screaming. I could remember every moment, every fight, every punch. But it wasn't happening to me; I was in my bed alone. It was Pearl. It was all happening to Pearl.

I felt a shove in her chest, and she fell over, and something hard hit the side of her head, and then I think I felt a kick in her stomach—

Then it cut off, and I was just me.

I got up and ran for the phone, but before I could get there I threw up in the kitchen.

A girl dispatcher answered: "9-1-1. What is the emergency you are reporting?"

"Tim Nation is beating up Pearl Moulton!"

"Where is this emergency taking place?"

"In California, I think. It's wherever they have their house."

She stopped for a second. Then she said, "You think? Where are you located?"

"I'm in Boston."

"Massachusetts?"

"Yes."

She stopped again. Then, "Did you witness this event yourself?"

"Yes, I'm Tabbing Pearl Moulton."

"This happened while she was on the Tab?"

"No, not exactly, it's not her Tab time."

"But you witnessed her being beaten?"

"Yes. The Tab is broken! I'm Tabbing her when I'm not supposed to."

There was a muffled sound, like she was covering the phone and talking to someone.

Then she said, "Is the event still occurring now?"

"I don't know; I think so."

"Is anyone hurt, or in need of medical attention?"

"Yes! Pearl Moulton is hurt!"

"What is your name, address and phone number?"

I gave them to her, and she said she would follow up on it, then she hung up.

I tried to sleep, but I couldn't. The next day I called Customer Service again, and this time the techie I saw was a girl, and she said she could take out the whole Tab just to be sure. I told her no, just change it like last time. I know it sounds stupid, but the TalkBack time was coming up in just a few weeks, and now I needed to talk to Pearl more than ever.

No one from 9-1-1 or the police or anybody ever called me back. There was nothing in the magazines or the Vids about Pearl the next week, except that she cancelled a talk show appearance and there was something about her missing a few days of shooting on the set because of "illness." There was no news about Timothy Nation either.

Finally came the day in August. I sat down on the recliner, put on the cuff, and took a deep breath; my heart was going pretty fast. Then I switched it on.

Pearl was washing her face in her bathroom. The water was too hot, and I wanted to wince when it splashed over her closed eyes and into her nostrils. She blew the water out of her nose and smooshed her face into a thick towel. Then she opened her eyes and looked in the mirror.

There were no bruises on her that I could see, and I didn't feel any pain at all. If her nose was broken, it didn't feel like it and didn't look like it. Could they fix all that in a month? Her mouth was tight, and I could feel the muscles in her cheeks. Then she turned her head, and I caught a faint spot of yellow on the side of her face, where I remembered she hit the floor.

Hello, Pearl, I said.

"I don't really feel like talking right now," she said. "Sorry." She walked into the bedroom, barefoot, and started putting on her shoes.

You need to leave Tim, I said.

She stopped, and I could feel her eyes get wide. "That's a hell of a thing to say."

I'm the one who called 9-1-1.

She closed her eyes; I couldn't see. "I don't know what you're talking about."

Yes, yes you do! I know all about this stuff! It happened to me too, I can tell you how to—

"You can't tell me anything! You don't know me; you don't know us! You have nothing; you have no lives of your own, any of you, so you suck it all out of me. Leave me alone, can't you?"

No, please, Pearl! This is really important. You're in danger, and I can help you!

Her eyes opened again and she got up and went to the window. It was so bright outside that her eyes hurt, but she didn't close them.

"Listen to me. Listen! I need you not to interfere in my life. In *any* part of my life, do you understand? All you people, you say you care about me, but you don't. If you really did, you'd let me be."

I do care about you, I care so much! I can't let it happen to you, not what happened to me!

"Listen, whoever you are—"

Dorothy. Telling her my name made me want to cry.

"Whoever. I'm sorry about what happened to you, but it has nothing to do with me."

It does. You know it does.

"Please, for God's sake, listen to me. Do you know what's worse, even worse than that?"

Nothing, I was sure. But I said, *What?*

"Having no privacy, no moment to yourself. Being eaten alive by people who say they love you. That's the worst thing in the world—being hurt in the name of love."

I couldn't feel my eyes or nose, but by now I knew I must be crying. *I do love you, Pearl. I love you! Let me save you.*

"No one can save anyone," she whispered. "But if you love me, you know how you can prove it. There's only one thing I want."

So there it was, that's who I was. There were two of us, Tim Nation and me. Tim she could run away from, but I was in her head, like a bad memory.

I stopped talking. I didn't say anything for the rest of the Talk-Back session. I'll never be able to afford another one.

I stopped Tabbing Pearl Moulton. I had to take the Tab out anyway; I couldn't be sure it wouldn't break again, and I didn't want sudden looks at her life anymore.

Pearl is still living with Tim Nation; that's what the *Herald* says. I don't know if she ever saw a counselor, or what.

Johnny's going to die. The doctors say the cancer is inoperable. I've been spending a lot of time at their house; Nadine is a wreck, but she manages. She holds my hand a lot while we're over there.

Mom's not doing too well either, but I think Johnny's cancer is harder on her than what she's got herself. She comes over to their house too, but she just cries, which drives Nadine crazy, so sometimes Nadine comes over here when Mom's with Johnny.

We've talked about a hospice, but he wants to die at home, in private. So would I, I think, if it was me.

*

Whenever I stand in the grocery line and try to avoid reading the tabloids, I am appalled by our apparently unlimited appetite for the private lives of strangers. I began to wonder how far people would take it, if they could. I started the first draft in anger, intending to cast Dorothy as a heartless, selfish antagonist, but I found more and more sympathy for her as I wrote, and she wound up as the hero.

As an example of how much difference a first reader can make: the entire second half of the story changed when one of my Clarion classmates suggested that "If this were a Philip K. Dick story, the technology would break."

SELECTED PROGRAM NOTES FROM THE RETROSPECTIVE EXHIBITION OF THERESA ROSENBERG LATIMER

1.   *THREE WOMEN* (1978)
OIL ON CANVAS, 30 X 40"
DETROIT INSTITUTE OF ART, DETROIT, MICHIGAN

L ATIMER PAINTED *THREE WOMEN* while still a student at the Rhode Island School of Design. It is the earliest completed painting that displays the hyperrealism characterizing the first period of her work.

Three young women sit close together on a park bench in autumn. Two hold hands, while the third has her hand on the knee of the center figure. Their expressions are serious, almost stern, as if they resent the artist's presumption in portraying them.

At this stage of her career, Latimer was still experimenting with issues of compositional balance. The brightness of the orange trees offsets the dour colors of the models' clothes; the tilt of the models' heads and the orientation of their legs impel the viewer to look at the trees rather than at them. It as if the viewer is being pushed away from people and towards nature.

None of these models appears in any of Latimer's later work. Presumably they were fellow RISD students. Latimer herself appears in early works of others who were at RISD at the time, including A. C. Stahl and J. J. Kramer.

Discussion questions:

a. Use the magnifying lens provided to examine the hairs on the models' arms, the loose fibers in their sweaters, and the veins in the leaves. Many details in a Latimer painting are not visible to those who view the work at ordinary distances. Why do you think she inserted such typically invisible minutiae? What effect do they have on your experience of the painting?

19.   *SELF-PORTRAIT WITH SURROGATES* (1984)
      OIL ON CANVAS, 51 X 77-1/4"
      RHODE ISLAND SCHOOL OF DESIGN MUSEUM
      PROVIDENCE, RHODE ISLAND

The first of Latimer's paintings to draw critical attention, *Self-Portrait with Surrogates* portrays the notorious child abuse and murder case of the Wilson family, which dominated the Rhode Island news media at the time. Seven-year-old Lisa Wilson, clad only in underwear and displaying both old scars and fresh cuts, is being beaten with an electrical extension cord wielded by her father, while her mother holds her in place. None of the figures displays any emotion; it is as if they are spectators at the event.

The details, again in the hyperrealist style, closely match those of the Wilson case. The family home is accurately depicted, and the scars on Lisa Wilson's body correspond with photographs in the court file.

Discussion questions:

a. The composition and live-action flavor of this work resemble 18th- and 19th-century patriotic or polemical depictions of battles and famous events; David's *The Death of Socrates* (1787) (Fig. 5) is a clear influence. Why does Latimer employ such devices in a portrayal of domestic violence? Does it alter your perception of what you are "really" seeing?

b.   Some biographers associate the painting's title with the emotional and physical abuse Latimer herself experienced as a child. Is there anything in the picture itself to show that this is really a "self portrait?"

c. Does the fact that Latimer's parents were living when she painted this work alter the way you perceive it?

34.   *MAGDA #4* (1989)
OIL ON POPLAR WOOD, 30 x 21"
PRIVATE COLLECTION

Sometimes called "Devotion" by critics, this nude is the earliest extant work featuring Magda Ridley Meszaros (1963-2023), Latimer's favorite model and later her wife. The lushness of the flesh and the rosiness of the skin are reminiscent of Renoir's paintings of Aline Charigot (*See, e.g., The Large Bathers* (1887) (Fig. 8)). Latimer maintains microscopic hyperrealism even as she employs radiating brushstrokes which emanate from the model, as if Meszaros is the source of reality itself.

Discussion questions:

a.   The materials and dimensions of this painting duplicate those of Da Vinci's *La Gioconda* (c. 1503-1519) (Fig. 17). Is this merely a compositional joke or homage by Latimer? How does it change the way you see the painting?

b.   Most biographers agree that Latimer and Meszaros were already lovers by the time this work was completed. Is this apparent from the composition or technique? From the pose of the model? As you proceed through the exhibit, note similarities and differences between this and other portrayals of Meszaros over the next 34 years.

*

48.   *CONJURING* (1993)
        ACRYLIC ON MASONITE, 48 X 96"
        PRIVATE COLLECTION

Her largest composition and only known landscape, *Conjuring* appeared during a fallow period in Latimer's work. In 1992 and 1993 she completed only three paintings.

The scene is an overcast day in a valley in northern New Hampshire. Although it is summer, the foliage on the hills contains much gray and purple, conveying a wintery feel. While Latimer renders exacting details in rocks, trees, even blades of grass, in this work she also employs a forced monotony in the brushwork; the shape of every stroke is practically identical to every other.

In the precise center of the composition, wearing baggy khaki clothing, Magda Ridley Meszaros walks along an empty dirt road, recognizable only under a magnifying lens. She does not appear to be aware of the artist.

Discussion questions:

a.   The aforementioned slack period in Latimer's work coincided with several crises in her life: her only interval of estrangement from Magda Meszaros, precipitated by parental opposition to their relationship; the death by drug overdose of her close friend, the singer Pamela Enoch (1965-1993); and Latimer's own life-threatening illness. Her hyperrealist period ends with this painting. Can we see these life crises in this composition? Is there any hint of Latimer's coming change in style?

49.   *PERFORMANCE* (1994)
        ACRYLIC ON CANVAS, 32 X 41"
        NATIONAL PORTRAIT GALLERY, WASHINGTON, DC

Generally regarded as one of the outstanding memorial portraits of the 20th century, *Performance* is also the first painting of Latimer's "highlight" period, which occupied the rest of her career.

Latimer was fascinated by the restoration of the Sistine Chapel ceiling (1980-1994), which sharply enhanced the clarity and brightness of Michelangelo's colors. Although some still doubt whether the restoration reflected the artist's intentions, Latimer was most interested in the side-by-side contrast between the pre- and post-restoration appearance of the frescoes (*See* "before" and "after" pictures of *The Creation of Adam* (figs. 11 and 12)). In one of her diaries, she wrote:

> *They stripped away the hurts and filth of five centuries and released the purity within. It's like looking at one of the Platonic forms—beneath the battered, mundane person, the person we see in everyday life, is the true person—the soul, maybe, or the heart. Of course it looks less "real" to us—we're so used to the violence and degradation imposed on us by the world that we're unprepared for ourselves without it.*
>
> *How did I miss this before? Maybe I wasn't ready, til now, to understand it. But after what happened, what's still happening, this is the perfect tool, maybe the only tool.*

After 1994, nearly all of Latimer's paintings feature one or more "highlight figures," people in a painting whose coloration has the clarity and brightness of the restored Sistine Chapel frescoes, as contrasted with the duller, more commonplace tones of everything else in the composition. They seem out-of-place and fantastical, even cartoonish, and yet Latimer employed the same level of microscopic detail in her "highlight figures" as to their surroundings.

The first critics who saw *Performance* misunderstood Latimer's introduction of "highlight" figures, because the painting is set on the stage of the Providence Performing Arts Center, and the central figure is the artist's recently-deceased friend, the singer Pamela Enoch. Because she appears on the stage as if she were performing a concert, Enoch's heightened colors were taken at the time to represent the effect of theatrical spotlights. Arthur Mallory's review called the lighting "sentimental in an otherwise naturalistic work," noting that true spotlights would have enhanced the colors of the surrounding stage as well.

Magda Meszaros is visible in the front row, the only member of the audience. She has turned in her seat to face the artist. Meszaros is not portrayed as a "highlight" figure, but in the same comparatively muted tones as the theatre.

Discussion questions:

a.   As you view the many "highlight" figures in the remaining paintings in this exhibit, consider whether these figures seem more or less "real" to you than those painted in ordinary colors. Why?

b.   Critics and biographers have puzzled over Latimer's words, *"what happened, what's still happening,"* which seem to refer to the event or events that inspired or impelled her to adopt the "highlight" style. But what events were they, and how did they lead to this change?

c.   Not until 2025 did Latimer paint Magda Ridley Meszaros as a "highlight" figure. Usually she appears in ordinary tones, as here. Why is this so?

d.   Why does Meszaros wear a puzzled expression?

59.   CRITIQUE (1997)
      ACRYLIC ON CANVAS, 44 x 67"
      DAVISON ART CENTER
      WESLEYAN UNIVERSITY, MIDDLETOWN, CONNECTICUT

Latimer painted this piece to commemorate the addition of her *Self-Portrait with Surrogates* (#19) to the permanent collection of the RISD Museum. The setting is the Contemporary Artists gallery of the Museum; *Self-Portrait with Surrogates* hangs at the center of the composition, with adjacent works also visible, notably *Intelligentsia* (1986) by her friend and classmate J. J. Kramer.

In the foreground is the child Lisa Wilson (the subject of *Self-Portrait with Surrogates*) painted as a "highlight" figure. The young girl is presented as if she were a critical viewer of *Self-Portrait with Surrogates*; she is turned three-quarters toward the artist, but her left hand is raised toward the painting in a dismissive gesture. Her face is wry and full of humor; she appears to like the artist, even if she does not think much of the painting.

Discussion questions:

a.   How do you interpret Lisa Wilson's apparent attitude towards Latimer's earlier painting? Is Latimer ridiculing her own work?

b.   Why is Lisa Wilson portrayed as younger than she was in *Self-Portrait with Surrogates*? Why without visible evidence of abuse? What is the significance of the party dress she wears?

60.   EXCERPT FROM *THE SILENT VOICES* (1997)
       VIDEO RECORDING, 23 MIN.
       BY PERMISSION OF WGBH TELEVISION AND THE PUBLIC
       BROADCASTING SERVICE.

While working on *Critique*, Latimer was one of the subjects of Elijah Baptista's video documentary concerning contemporary artists, *The Silent Voices*. In the excerpt shown here, she stands in the Contemporary Artists Gallery, making preliminary drawings. Oddly, she is not sketching the gallery or the paintings on the wall, but detailing the face Lisa Wilson herself. Although there are no photographs or prior sketches evident (apart from *Self Portrait with Surrogates*), the drawing is precise, showing the same wry expression that will appear in the finished work.

Discussion questions:

a.   Now that you see Latimer's manner of speaking and moving, are you surprised? Does she seem like the sort of person who would produce this sort of work?

b.   At the end of the excerpt, Baptista asks Latimer why she needed to come to the Museum in order to sketch a study of Wilson's face. Latimer's answer is, "You have to paint what you see, not what you think you're supposed to see." This admonition is a commonplace among visual artists. What does it mean when uttered by someone who paints with such obvious imagination?

72.   *GRACE* (2001)
         ACRYLIC ON CANVAS, 20 x 60"
         MASSACHUSETTS MUSEUM OF CONTEMPORARY ART
         NORTH ADAMS, MASSACHUSETTS

One of several pieces recounting Latimer's difficult relationship with her parents, *Grace* portrays a Thanksgiving dinner in their home. Her father, Mason Latimer (1930-2008), poses as if saying grace before the meal, but both he and his wife Sheila Rosenberg (1935-2014) are staring scornfully at Theresa Rosenberg Latimer and Magda Ridley Meszaros, who sit at the opposite end of the table, looking down at their plates.

Standing behind the artist and Meszaros, apparently observed by no one, is Pamela Enoch (the subject of *Performance*, #49), the only "highlight" figure in the composition. Smiling, she holds her palms above the heads of her two friends as if in benediction.

Discussion questions:

a.   Critics have noted references in this painting to both Rockwell's *Freedom From Want* (1943) (Fig. 18) and Dali's *Sacrament of the Last Supper* (1955) (Fig. 19). What is the point of quoting two such wildly disparate pieces together? Is this a parody?

b.   Pamela Enoch appears in many of Latimer's works after

1994, always as a "highlight" figure in her mid-twenties, dressed for a performance. Why repeat the same person so often, and why always in the same clothes? Is Enoch a symbolic figure?

91.　　*THE MOURNERS* (2008)
　　　　ACRYLIC ON CANVAS, 20 x 30"
　　　　AMERICAN LABOR MUSEUM, HALEDON, NEW JERSEY

The setting is a parking lot in Pawtucket, Rhode Island that stands on the location of the 1908 Alger's Mill fire, in which 34 workers were killed. Two distinct groups of "highlight" figures appear. Near the center stand the Alger brothers, the Mill owners whose negligence was generally blamed for the deaths, although none were ever prosecuted. They bow their heads and clasp their hands before them. Standing in a circle around them are 25 victims of the fire, their own sorrowful gazes fixed on the Alger brothers. All are dressed as they would have been in the late 19th or early 20th centuries.

Here, as elsewhere, Latimer has been praised for the quality of her research. Although historians have authenticated the faces of most of the fire victims, many of the relevant photographs have taken years or even decades to find.

Discussion questions:

a.　Most of the figures in this painting are younger than they were at the time of the 1908 fire. Tara Aquino, in her assiduous tally of Latimer's subjects (2038), has calculated that 84% of the "highlight" figures are in their 20s and 30s, and the rest are mostly children. By contrast, Latimer's non-highlighted figures show an ordinary spread of ages. Why does Latimer make this age distinction between "highlight" and "ordinary" figures? Why not portray people as they were at the time of the relevant events?

b.　One of the striking things about this painting is that the victims appear to be mourning for those who were responsible for their deaths. What is Latimer's message here?

    c. Young Lisa Wilson, a recurring figure in Latimer's work, is visible at the far right of the composition, gesturing towards the group of mourning figures. Why include a contemporary figure in an otherwise period group? Is there a connection between this painting and the others in which she appears?

117.   *SELF-PORTRAIT WITH FAMILY* (2015)
        ACRYLIC ON CANVAS, 36 x 45"
        PRIVATE COLLECTION

    The setting is Latimer's own bedroom, recognizable from the furniture and memorabilia. Latimer at her then-current age of 56 crouches in the bed in a nightgown, her face hidden in her hands as if in fear, sorrow or pain. Standing by the side of the bed, glowering down at their daughter in reproach or rage, are her parents Mason Latimer and Sheila Rosenberg. They are "highlight" figures.

    Kneeling on the bed with Latimer is Magda Meszaros. Both are painted in muted colors, as contrasted with the highlit parents. Meszaros is in a protective posture, one hand on Latimer's curved back and the other gesturing as to repel an invader.

    Discussion questions:

    a. Why does the artist paint her parents as they appeared in their twenties, before her own birth?

    b. Why are neither Meszaros's fierce gaze nor her guardian hand directed at the figures of the parents (the only other people in the composition), but at a point beyond the right border of the picture?

    c. This work was composed in the year following Sheila Rosenberg's death from brain cancer, which was also the year in which Latimer and Meszaros finally married. How many uses of the word "family" are implied by the title?

131. *To Interfere, for Good, in Human Matters* (2018)
     Acrylic on canvas, 30 x 60"
     F. Cooley Memorial Art Gallery,
     Reed College, Portland, Oregon

The scene is a crowded street in downtown Providence. A homeless woman with a young child sits on the doorstep of what may be a church; they are malnourished, shabbily dressed, and the woman holds out her hand as if asking for alms. The dozens of others on the street around her are a mix of both "highlight" figures and characters painted in muted colors (as are the beggar woman and her child). The composition pushes the eye of the viewer back and forth between the different groups in a sort of tennis match: from a "highlight" figure one is drawn to a muted figure, then to another "highlight" figure, then to another muted figure, back and forth until one has scrutinized every figure in the picture.

This oscillation forces the viewer to see the contrast between these two groups. Superficially, the muted figures wear everyday clothes contemporary to 2018, while the "highlight" figures are clad in varying styles from the previous 150 years. More significant, however, are their differing reactions to the homeless pair. The muted figures bypass the seated beggars, or approach them while looking elsewhere; a few are watching them from the corners of their eyes. The "highlight" figures, on the other hand, all stand motionless, each facing the mother and child, each with a look of pity or compassion on her or his face. Some reach out their hands as if to touch the pair, but none actually reach them.

Discussion questions:

     a.   As in other Latimer paintings, critics have observed references to other works, notably Courbet's *Real Allegory of the Artist's Studio* (1855) (Fig. 40) and Bosch's *Garden of Earthly Delights* (c. 1504) (Fig 41). Again, why does Latimer quote from two such different pieces?

b.   Athena Ptolemaios (2025) has suggested that there is a racial or cultural message here. The muted figures are turning away from one of their own, while the "highlight" figures reach out to the stranger. Are we being shown than it is easier to feel compassion for those who are far away, or different?

c.   While her technique here earned much praise, Latimer has been criticized for the blatantness of the message. Thomas Taney (2030) was particularly scornful of Latimer's unexplained use of a passage from Dickens's *A Christmas Carol* (1843) as the title of the piece. Do you agree with Taney?

146.   *ALMOST* (2022)
OIL ON POPLAR WOOD, 30 x 21"
PRIVATE COLLECTION

Almost is the last portrait Latimer made of Magda Ridley Meszaros during the latter's lifetime. It is an unsentimental portrayal, detailing the damage done by both breast cancer and chemotherapy with all the hyperrealist accuracy at Latimer's command. From her favorite chair, Meszaros gazes quietly at the artist. One detects neither fear, defiance, nor even acceptance, only the affection of one life partner for another.

Standing on either side of Meszaros are four "highlight" figures: Pamela Enoch and three other women who have not been identified. They are looking not at Meszaros but at the artist, their arms held wide.

Discussion questions:

a.   The subject, size and materials of *Almost* are identical to those of *Magda #4* (#34), so that it is natural to compare them. Whereas the brushwork in *Magda #4* pointed to Meszaros herself, in *Almost* the strokes radiate from the "highlight" figures; even the strokes with which Meszaros is painted come from them. What other differences do you see between the two works? What similarities?

---

b. Why are the "highlight" figures smiling?

155. *COMFORT* (2025)
      ACRYLIC ON CANVAS, 11 x 8-1/2"
      PRIVATE COLLECTION

The last known completed work of Theresa Rosenberg Latimer is *Comfort*, found among her personal effects after her death by medication overdose at the age of 66.

It is a quadruple portrait, somewhat reminiscent of her *Three Women* (#1). The setting is the exterior of Latimer's home, although the focus is so tight that only certain abnormalities in the brickwork allow us to identify it. The four figures are Pamela Enoch dressed for a performance, Lisa Wilson in her party dress, Magda Meszaros as a young model, and Latimer herself at 30, the beginning of her most productive period. Latimer stands slightly in the foreground, one step ahead of the others; Enoch and Wilson are to her left, Meszaros to her right, as if they are ready to catch her if she falls.

All four women are "highlight" figures, bright and clear with strong definitions and confident lines. They are more radiant than the "highlight" figures of Latimer's earlier works; light pours from them, and they drown out the color of the bricks behind them. Enoch's, Wilson's and Meszaros's faces are fixed on Latimer, who is smiling broadly, with flushed cheeks and eyes full of hope.

Discussion questions:

a. The title *Comfort* was suggested by Paula Tarso, executrix of Latimer's artistic estate; we do not know what Latimer herself planned to call it. Do you think the name fits?

*

I'm kind of in love with the unreliable narrator—more specifically, the narrator who tells a different story than the reader wants and needs to hear, because he misunderstands what the story really is. Thus my fondness for "found documents" stories, where the reader is forced to be a participant in the narrative by constructing what is really going on from the hints and incomplete pieces provided by the text. Also, I love visual art, and can spend hours trying to figure out how an artist achieved a particular effect. Curiously, half of my first readers thought there was no fantasy element in the story at all, while the other half thought the fantasy was too blatant.

THE PLAUSIBILITY
OF DRAGONS

O F COURSE IT WOULD RAIN. HUNGRY and footsore after three days of walking, his back and shoulders aching from carrying his heavy pack, all Malik needed now was to be soaked in water that barely resisted becoming ice.

His first thought, though, was for his books, which wouldn't be long protected by the pack. He didn't always need books to be hired, but the better sort of customer liked to see them as proof of his learning and investment in knowledge. He moaned, pulled off the pack, and hugged it to his chest, shrugging so that his cloak would cover it.

After an hour, Malik was shivering and nearly unable to see, and he felt almost transformed by a coating of mud; only his hat was still untouched by it. If the directions he'd been given were good, then there ought to be a village somewhere near here, but he saw no sign of it; the road seemed to stretch forever through this forest. Maybe if he found a sufficiently broad tree, he could shelter under it.

So faintly that it might have been a trick of the rain on the leaves ahead of him, Malik thought he heard the whinny of a horse. After another hundred paces he heard it again, louder. Yet another hundred, and the mist before his eyes parted to reveal a mighty brown charger, tethered to just such a sheltering tree as Malik had hoped for. But most welcome in his sight, the horse stood next to a tent. It was small but well-crafted and sat beneath the overlapping branches of three trees, on the driest ground he had seen for five miles. He sneezed, and the horse turned to look at him; he heard a rustling from the tent.

"Ho there," he called in the language of the Franks, his voice sounding rather thin and plaintive in the rain. "I come in peace."

The tent flap opened, and a knight stepped out. She was nearly a foot taller than Malik, hair so blonde it was like frost, pale eyes watchful, her hand on the long knife in her belt. She wore a shirt of very fine mail, covered with strange arms: a foot trampling a lizard. She regarded him for a long moment, eyes moving from his back to his arms to his own eyes.

Then she nodded judiciously. "You look drowned," she said in Frankish.

"Well observed," he replied.

Her eyebrows lifted. "And here I thought you were about to ask for my help. Care to try again?"

Malik shivered. "Apologies, lady knight. The weather has put me in a bad temper. Would you let me shelter here until I dry out? I won't be any inconvenience, and I could even do a few chores if you have food to share."

"I do my own chores," she said, "and you've already inconvenienced me. Still—" She glanced down at her knife. "If you try anything foolish you won't live to finish it, and I'll worry about how to clean up the mess later."

Malik shifted his pack in his arms, feeling pain in every joint. "I am unarmed but for this little knife—" He pointed to his sleeve. "And not a fighting man in any case." He bowed. "Malik ibn Ali of Cordoba is in your debt."

She put her hand to her waist and gave a slight bow herself. "Fara of Hallstatt, daughter of Odger." She stood aside and let him enter the tent. He set down his pack on the dryish ground next to it. With her gear, there was barely enough room in the tent for the two of them to sit. He lowered himself carefully, and she sat beside him. Reaching into her own pack she grabbed a hunk of hard bread, which he gratefully took.

As he was chewing, she observed, "I've not met many Moors in this part of the country. Cordoba's in Iberia, isn't it?" Malik nodded. "I thought you had a strange accent. You're a long way from home."

He swallowed. "Truly. For my part, it's been a long time since I last met a woman of the sword."

She laughed. "Then you haven't been around much in this land, Malik of Cordoba. I have four sisters, all of whom took the sword."

"Is this the custom in Hallstatt? Is it full of woman warriors?"

She laughed again. "No, not full of warriors of any kind. But we learned sword skills at a young age, and my father said that a horse and armor were better investments than a dowry. He and my mother are armorers, and could make the weapons and mail themselves, you see. What brings you so far from the warm lands of the west?"

"I'm a teacher," he said, gesturing in the direction of his pack outside the tent. "I give lessons in reading and writing Latin and Arabic, the heavens and natural philosophy."

"I can imagine there are some here who'd welcome new lore about plants and beasts," said Fara. "And a few of the artisans with ambitions for their children might want you to teach them the Latin writing."

"That's mostly been it."

"I'll wager you don't get much call for the Arabic, though."

"I don't."

"Are you a Mohammedan?"

"I submit to the will of God."

She rotated her head as if getting the kinks out of her neck. "You've studied the lore of many lands?"

"Very many. The Greeks, the Romans, the Jews, the men of India, the sages of Persia."

She was silent for a minute, glancing around the inside of the tent. Then she said in a low voice, "Do you know anything about dragons?"

"Dragons?"

"Aye."

Malik shifted uncomfortably. His clothes were beginning to dry, but they still clung to him, and he felt a new cold spot every time he moved. Slowly he replied, "I've never seen one, if that's what you mean."

Fara grimaced. "You know that's not what I mean. In your books, your lore, what do they tell you of dragons?"

He paused for a moment. Then he said, "There are many tales, but no eyewitness accounts. The Greeks speak of Ladon, slain by Heracles, Pytho of Delphi, and the Lernaean Hydra. Aeilian writes of the *Drakons* who kill elephants in India, though no Indian writer says this. They write of the *Nāgas*, the enemies of the eagle king Garuda. According to Hakim Abu 'l-Qasim Ferdowsi Tusi, the evil king Zahāk was transformed into a three-headed monster. The Jews say, and the followers of the Prophet and your Pope agree, that the Evil One took the form of a serpent to deceive our father Adam out of paradise. I once read an old scroll that claimed that dragons corrupt the hearts of men."

She nodded. "Many people speak of them."

He said, "None of these stories very closely resembles the others. I am inclined to think that we are all simply afraid of snakes."

Fara looked at the ground. "You don't think they exist, then?"

Malik put his hands together. "If dragons walk the earth now, breathing fire and eating men, if they fly through the air and crush whole villages, then why does no witness or writer speak of seeing them in person? Why is it always a distant legend, or a tale told by someone who told it to someone else who told it to the writer's grandfather?"

Fara did not look up. "The world is wide."

Malik shrugged. "So one might say about any fanciful creature. The world is wide, and so we cannot prove that it does not
exist. But that is not evidence. I do not think dragons are plausible,
unless they lived centuries ago. I think we build palaces in our
minds, populated with monsters made of our own fears and desires. If I ever see a dragon, I suspect that I will have crossed into
another world than this."

For a long time, neither of them said anything. Fara leaned on
her pack. Malik shivered the kind of shiver after which you feel
warmer.

Then Fara looked up at him and said, "I am searching for the
dragon that may have killed my sister."

Malik swallowed and licked his lips. "I am sorry for the death
of your sister. May God's mercy and compassion comfort you
and your family. But—" He swallowed again. "With the greatest
respect, Fara of Hallstatt, why do you think it was a dragon that
killed her?"

Fara's eyes did not waver from Malik's face. "My sister Basina
hired herself out to burgraves and other minor lords, and took the
occasional commission from villages. She tracked down outlaws,
she rode to war against the burgraves' enemies, sometimes she
slew a wolf or other beast that beset the herds."

"As you have done?" asked Malik.

"Yes. Two years ago, a village many leagues east of here paid
her in the black money to hunt for a dragon they had heard was ma-
rauding in those parts. Though they had never seen it, they feared
what it might do. For a year she followed its rumor, and she sent
back word to us when she could; always the stories were of a beast
in the next county or over the next river. Some said the monster ate
virgins; others that destroyed homes. Then she vanished, and no
word of her has come to us or to anyone."

"Vanished?" he said.

"I have followed her footsteps from the town where she was
hired, asking every person I meet. Until I came within ten leagues

of this spot, everyone remembered Basina and her quest, though all they knew of the dragon was its reputation. Then, all at once, there is no trace of Basina at all."

"And the dragon?"

"So far, only the rumors."

"But your sister's disappearance does not mean she's dead, does it? She could still live, but have gone along a different path. She might have given up her search, or found other employment . . ." Malik trailed off.

Fara shook her head. "You don't know Basina. Her deeds are bold; her words are loud; her movements are broad. She does not give up on a quest, and certainly not without explaining herself to those who hired her. And she would not have failed to send word to her family for a whole year."

Malik listened to the rain hissing on the tent. "When you find this dragon, do you mean to kill it?"

She nodded. "First I mean to find Basina, or her body. But yes, if it has killed her, I will destroy it—if it doesn't kill me first."

"But you've never met a dragon; you don't know how to kill one."

"It's never met me, either."

Fara was headed to the same village as Malik, so they traveled together. In the cool sunshine the day after they met, they both walked alongside the great horse that carried all their gear.

Near sunset, they came to a turn in the road that was shadowed by many tall trees. Around the bend, in those shadows, two men blocked their way. Both carried knives.

Fara's hand went to her own knife. "Good evening, sirs," she said. "We are headed north on this road."

"We are headed nowhere in particular," said the paler of the two men. "But wherever we go, we will need money and transportation, witch." He nodded towards the horse. "Your horse would be very helpful." A third man stepped out of the woods behind Fara and Malik.

"I cannot let you take it," she said. Her sword and shield were both strapped to the horse, and there was no way she could reach them before the men attacked.

"We would like to solve this peaceably," said the pale man.

"That can be accomplished by your stepping aside and letting us pass," said Fara, drawing her long knife.

"Let us have the horse, witch, and whatever coins you may be carrying, and that will be speedily accomplished."

Fara snorted. "Such a promise isn't very credible."

The pale man shrugged. "What choice do you have?"

Fara sighed and shook her head. Then she stepped in front of the horse. "If you want the beast, you'll need to take him."

The pale man lunged forward with his knife. Fara stepped aside, kicking the man in the knee while she parried the thrust of his companion's knife. The moment Fara moved, Malik reached into his sleeve for his own small knife, but the robber behind him was bigger and faster—and besides, as he'd told Fara, Malik was no fighter. Within a few seconds the man had him pinned by the arms, a knife at his throat.

Fara's two opponents were on the ground. One was open-eyed and unmoving with a hole in his neck, the other curled on the ground, moaning and bleeding from his gut.

Fara stepped toward Malik. His captor said, "Stay there! One more move and I cut your demon's throat."

Fara shook her head, slowly stepped back to her horse, and drew her sword from its scabbard.

"I said I'll kill him!" said the thief.

"I heard you the first time," said Fara, holding her sword in one hand and her knife in the other.

"Don't you value your demon's life?"

"Certainly I do. If you harm him, it will grieve me mightily and I will have to avenge him. Vengeance will start about ten seconds after he dies. I will cut off your prick, stuff it down your throat, then cut off your nose and send that after your prick, then gouge out each eye, then remove your entrails. It will take you twenty minutes or so to die, if I do it properly, and you'll be in agony." Her voice was calm, even pleasant, but Malik had no doubt she'd do exactly what she said.

The man trembled. Fara continued, "On the other hand, you haven't harmed him yet. This morning there were three of you; within a few minutes you'll be the only one. If you let him go, I will let you go with your life. I'll even let you keep your knife."

"Why—" The thief stammered. "Why should I trust you?"

"I haven't lied yet. You were the ones who accosted us."

The thief's grip loosened. Malik stepped away and turned to face the man, who had a big stupid face and now looked terrified.

"Start walking south," said Fara. "If I see you again on this road, I will kill you."

Fara and Malik watched the thief until he was out of sight. Then she looked down at the two bodies on the ground, shaking her head.

"Stupid waste," she said. Then she crossed herself and recited a rote-memorized *De Profundis*. Malik thought it unlikely that the dead thieves were believers, but decided to give them the benefit of the doubt and intoned the prayers to God to cause men to die in faith, and to cleanse them after death.

After a moment, looking at the bodies, he said, "Did he call you, 'witch?'"

She answered, "Yes. That's new. And the other said 'demon.'"

"About me, yes. Have you any idea what they meant?"

"None."

Malik looked at the sun setting through the trees. "Do we bury them here? It wouldn't be proper to leave them out like this."

Fara sighed. "I know, but I've nothing to bury them with. It's not far to the village. We'll have to take the baggage off of the horse, and then I'll need your help to secure the bodies on his back."

It took only a few hours more to reach the village. The villagers weren't surprised to hear of their battle with the footpads and didn't question it; such men were not uncommon in the region, and these two in particular were known to them, though they hadn't been seen in several months. Two of the locals helped bury the bodies.

Malik and Fara stayed in the town for a night, but they were both disappointed in their respective hopes. No one had any use for traveling teachers just then, though some asked about buying one or two of Malik's books. So far as he could tell, they couldn't read, and he wondered what use they'd make of them. Neither had any of the villagers seen the dragon Fara sought, nor heard of her sister Basina the Swift, although they had heard rumors of a strange beast in Eihinheim, fifty miles to the north. There too, they said, a teacher might find work.

Scholar and warrior covered the distance in two days. Eihinheim was the biggest settlement Malik had seen for many months, set near dark green mountains and a wide plain. They approached it at mid-day after easy travel. They found farmers cultivating cabbages a mile out from the edge of the village and greeted them cheerfully, but received no greeting in return. The men and women with soil covering their hands scowled at Fara and Malik; some looked frightened; others muttered.

"Not the friendliest place," said Malik.

"That's odd," said Fara. "I've been traveling this region for years, one way or another. They're pleasant folk, and have always had a kind word and a cheery hello."

When they approached the edge of town, three large men with axes and scythes walked swiftly to them, blocking their path.

"We'll have no witches here, nor demons," said the tallest man, holding his axe before him.

"Demons?" said Fara. "What demons?"

"That one," said the man, pointing at Malik. "Look at his skin! It's the mark of the devil, surely."

"But—" Fara said in confusion. "There are Moorish merchants and travelers all up and down these parts. A town like this one, surely you've seen—"

"You lie, witch!"

Fara stared at him. "By what right do you call me *witch*? I'm Fara of Hallstatt, a knight and soldier of—"

"There are no female knights," said the man. "You are an abomination wearing man's garb and carrying men's weapons. You should be burned."

Fara looked like she wanted to laugh, then thought the better of it. "There are dozens of female knights. My sisters alone—"

"Again you lie!" roared the man with the axe. At the loud noise, the horse stirred. Fara stroked its neck.

"We have no wish to intrude where we're not wanted," she said. "But I am searching for my sister and wonder if you may have seen her. Her name is Basina, and she rides a gray charger. She wears gear like mine—"

The man with the axe interrupted. "I have *never* seen a woman so attired, nor any who looks like you. Had any such appeared, I assure you I would have heard."

Fara nodded. "One more question, then, before we go. Have you seen the dragon we've heard is in these parts?"

To Malik's surprise, all three men nodded. Looking somewhat mollified that these strangers would not pollute Eihinheim, the tall man said, "Aye, the dragon. It came through a fortnight ago, tore a great gash in the land just east of the town and frightened all the children." He gestured. "Hurt no one, though."

The man spoke as if describing a thunderstorm or a wolf. Confused, Malik asked, "Wasn't it strange to see a dragon?"

The man shrugged. "There are many strange things in the world, and it hurt nothing but a field of cabbages."

"Can you describe it?"

One of the shorter men spoke up. "I saw it myself. It was two rods long and half-a-rod high, the color of pine needles. There were wings on its back, but I didn't see it fly. Stank like a sulfur pit, I could smell it at a furlong."

"How fast did it move?" asked Fara.

"About the speed of a horse at a trot," said the smaller man. "Looked like it could go faster if it wanted to, though."

"Claws? Teeth?"

He thought about it. "It didn't open its mouth, so I didn't see teeth. It did have claws: looked like each one was the size of one of my fingers. Maybe five, six, could be seven on each foot. They dug up the turf some."

Malik persisted. "Two rods long and ten feet high? Have you ever seen another beast so big?"

The man shrugged. "Not as I can remember."

"Have any of your neighbors?"

"No. Saw what I saw, though."

Malik grimaced. "It didn't breathe fire, did it?"

The man looked angry. "What are you getting at?"

"Nothing, I just asked."

"Are you calling me a liar, you unnatural thing?" The man stepped forward with his scythe.

The tall man put a hand on his companion's shoulder and turned to Fara. "You've been here long enough. Go back as you came."

"We'd like to follow the dragon," said Fara. "Which way did it go?"

"North," said the man with the scythe, glaring at Malik. "It followed the river."

"We'll go around the town," said Fara calmly.

After Eihinheim was out of sight behind them and they were in the woods again, Fara said, "There are your eyewitnesses, scholar. But that was the strangest conversation I've ever had."

"I agree. It's not believable that a creature that size could be living in the region and not have been spotted before."

"That's not what I mean," said Fara. "These people have never

seen a woman wielding a sword, and apparently they've never seen
a Moor of any description. They called us *witch* and *demon*, just
like—"

"I noticed."

"If they were isolated from the rest of the world, maybe I could
understand it. But this is the road from Mulhouse to Bischoffshein;
Strazburg's not far off! The area's a crossroad for all sorts of people, has been for hundreds of years."

Malik rubbed his nose. "They've seen what they couldn't have
seen, and they haven't seen what they must have seen," he said.
"It's some sort of puzzle."

Fara turned to him. "Malik, you needn't accompany me in my
search for this dragon."

He shrugged. "I might be useful to you."

"You said yourself that you're not a fighting man."

"You saved my life on the road."

"That's no reason for you to give it up."

He pondered. "I want to untangle this mystery. I want to understand how so many impossible things can be true. It may be that I'll
recognize or remember something that will aid you. In any case, I
promise that I won't hamper you, and I certainly won't get between
you and a dragon."

"See that you don't," she said.

At Bischoffshein the reaction was the same as in Eihinheim:
bewilderment and hostility when the townspeople saw Malik and
Fara, with no admission that anyone like them had ever been seen
anywhere near the town before, and no recognition of Basina's
name or description. And as before, there were a few among these
folk who remembered seeing a dragon with great clarity and preci-
sion, although they remembered seeing no one near it.

"This can't be right," said Fara as they trudged on. "I know the
names of some of those people. My sister Clothild was *in* Bischoff-

shein five years ago; she met them! She described it in detail."

Malik said nothing. As they followed the road north, they found a rough line of four gashes in the turf, places where the ground had been scored as if by three ploughs together—or one giant foot with claws. It looked like what they'd seen in Eihinheim.

Fara pointed. "The trail crosses the road and goes northeast into the woods."

"Fara," said Malik. "Just the two of us—or mostly just you—against a beast like this? I admire your courage, but what's the point of just letting it kill us?"

"I have sworn vengeance against it for Basina."

"You don't even know that she's dead, and you won't achieve vengeance by dying yourself. You could bring reinforcements."

"Not in time. I think we can reach the dragon if we follow it now. But to bring together a party of warriors, first I have to find *them*. And as you've noticed, we haven't run across people who are even willing to talk to me, much less join me in a quest against this monster. We'd need to go to Strazburg, or perhaps even further, to gather a squad. By that time, who knows where the dragon would be?" Malik chewed his lip. She continued, "I told you that you needn't come."

But when she turned her horse off the road and toward the woods, Malik followed behind.

For another day they kept to the trail. Malik went over in his mind all the things he had seen and heard, and tried to piece them together. Nothing in the stories he had read about dragons explained the weird phenomena they were seeing, but then again, he didn't trust those stories. There were some that said that dragons could fascinate their prey before killing it, like cats or snakes. It hadn't killed anyone in either Eihinheim or Bischoffshein, but what if . . .

"I think we're getting close," Fara said. They'd come to a grove where the markings on the ground were very fresh, and where they could actually smell the openings on the trees and the earth.

"Stop for a moment," Malik said.

"What is it?"

"I've had an idea. There is something strange going on with memory, or maybe with the senses. Whatever it is, it's connected to the dragon, and it wouldn't surprise me if we found ourselves— well, *enchanted*, for want of a better word."

Fara bit her lip. "I can't fight enchantment with a sword."

"I'm not sure how you're going to fight a forty-foot lizard with a sword either," said Malik. "But I think we can take a precaution against the other problem. Can you write?"

"A little Latin, not much. I read more than I write. But if writing will help, why don't you write it? You're the scholar."

"For what I have in mind, I think it needs to be in your own hand." He got out his pack for his parchments and writing tools. "I'll help you with the spelling, if need be."

They found the dragon three hours later. They smelled it before they saw it, the sulfuric odor they'd been told to expect. Fara mounted her horse and took out her sword and shield, guiding her steed with her legs. She held the scrap of parchment in the fist of her shield arm. Malik, with the gear the horse had been carrying, dropped back a few paces. As they came around a stand of trees, they saw it.

Its dark green hide was perfect camouflage in the forest; it might have been a pair of fallen trees. At the moment it was turned mostly away from them, scratching the bark off a birch tree with one of its forelimbs.

The man with the scythe in Eihinheim hadn't exaggerated. The creature was every bit of two rods long. Its hide was like worked leather, with patterns that might have been runes or letters rather than the separation between scales. Malik almost thought he recognized Latin letters, but when he stared at them, they changed into something else. Its head was strangely pale and rounder than Malik had expected; in the right light, it might even be the enormous head of a man, although again, when he stared at it more carefully, it more closely resembled a lizard's head, or perhaps a horse's. Fara's own horse whinnied, and the monster turned towards them.

The man with the scythe hadn't described the dragon's eyes. They were huge and burned with a silver flame that was nearly impossible to break away from. Malik took several deep breaths, cursing himself. Wasn't this what he knew, what everyone knew about dragons? That they could freeze you until they devoured you? Why was he such a fool as to court a danger any farm boy would have known to avoid?

When he finally tore his eyes from the dragon's, Malik saw the woman on the horse ahead of him. A Frankish woman, huge and pale, and she wore armor! What sort of an unnatural abomination was this? Did not the Prophet, peace be on him, speak of the proper dress for women? And she wore a sword, as well! Never in his life had he seen something so awful.

He was about to raise his hands and shout at her in condemnation when he noticed the parchment in his left fist. He opened it. In his own clear, unmistakable Arabic script, it said:

> *The woman is Fara of Hallstatt, your protector and companion. She and many women like her wield the sword. If you have forgotten this, it is the dragon's doing. I am Malik ibn Ali of Cordoba, whose favorite flower is the orange blossom.*

The signature was his, unquestionably. It included the orange blossom glyph he put at the end of all documents.

He stared at it, stumbling backwards away from the woman and the dragon. Fara of Hallstatt? The name called something like the echo of an echo of a memory.

The dragon roared, an enormous but melodic sound, like the bells of all the Frankish churches at the same time. Malik almost looked up into its eyes again, but forced his gaze down to the paper.

Fara of Hallstatt, my protector. A vision of three footpads, a knife at his throat, two bodies on the ground—

It came back to him in a rush; he remembered Fara, their meeting, their conversations. As that happened, the dragon seemed to wince as if jabbed by a painful weapon.

Fara was visibly gathering herself, preparing to charge at the enormous beast. Malik shouted: "Fara! Wait!"

She startled, as if she had forgotten he was there. When she saw him, her eyes widened under her helmet. She cried, "A demon! Are you in league with this hideous creature? I shall finish you both!" She raised the sword but didn't turn the horse, as if undecided which enemy to attack first.

"Wait, Fara, wait please! I am Malik! We have travelled together!"

"I have never traveled with a creature like you."

"Your hand, Fara! Is there a parchment in your hand?"

"Do not try to trick me, demon. It will make your death worse."

"Please look!"

She glanced down at her left hand and found the parchment, then opened it and began to read. Her brow furrowed and she shook her head as if to clear it. "Malik," she said.

Malik seized the opportunity. "You see, Fara? You wrote it yourself, your own hand proclaims it! Remember me!"

She stared. Slowly she said, "I remember. I remember you." The dragon, rather than charging when Fara's back was turned, sank down on its haunches and flicked its spiked tail irritably, hissing.

Malik asked, "Do you remember your warrior sisters? Do you remember Basina?"

Fara nodded again. The dragon's hide seemed to take on a grayish tint, as if a cloud had passed between it and the sun. It lowered its head and began to twitch and growl, a pained tone overlying its voice.

Malik said, "Keep your eyes on me! Am I the first African you have seen?" Fara squinted her eyes in confusion. He continued. "Do you remember other Moors you have met, the merchants and travelers, scholars and soldiers, men of God and godless men?"

That took longer. Eventually she nodded again, her face a mask of confusion. The dragon's twitching took on the intensity of a seizure. Red, glowing foam came out of its mouth as it lay on its side and kicked its legs, howling in agony.

"And you have seen," Malik shouted over the dragon's roars. "You have seen these men and women all of your life?"

"Yes!" she shouted back.

There was a flash and a blast like a thunderbolt. Fara was knocked clean off her horse, which stumbled and almost fell. Malik was blown backwards and hit his head on the earth.

Fara picked herself up first, coughing. Then she pulled Malik to his feet. It seemed that they were uninjured except for a few bruises, but their ears rang and they saw spots before their eyes for the rest of the day. The horse needed considerable calming, and for several minutes would not let either of them touch it, as if they were strangers.

The dragon was gone, and so were most of the signs that it had ever been there. There were no scrape marks on the nearby trees, nor gouges in the turf. When they went back over their trail, they could not find the dragon's.

But when they returned to Bischoffshein, things were mostly unchanged. People remembered seeing the dragon, and they still treated Fara and Malik as if they were inexplicable oddities. Yet they were no longer so hostile, and let the tired pair stay the night in the town. The next day, they decided to head for Strazburg.

"I have a theory," said Malik during their easy walk up the road.

"Another theory." Fara rolled her eyes. "Continue to think, Malik of Cordoba. You excel at it."

Malik smiled. "Have you heard of the Paradox of the Stone?" Fara shook her head. "It is a metaphysical puzzle: *Can an omnipo-*

tent being make a stone so heavy that even He could not lift it? Some simple-minded folk treat it as a refutation of omnipotence, but in fact it is a demonstration of exclusive definitions. If *omnipotence* does not include changing logical relationships, then God could not make such a stone, because then God would be willing Himself not to be God, which is tautologically ridiculous. But if omnipotence includes the ability to change the definitions of words, then God could easily create a stone too heavy for Him to lift—and then lift it."

"Mm," said Fara. "I see, I think. So what?"

"Well, the Paradox of the Stone demonstrates that, under certain conditions, two things cannot both exist within the same logical system. If there is such a thing as omnipotence, then there is no such thing as an impossible feat. The existence of one cancels out the other."

"Yes?"

"When the dragon was in front of us, I could not remember that any person like you or any of your sisters existed, and you could remember no such person as me. When the dragon visited a village, the villagers forgot any Moors or women of the sword they had ever seen. But when you and I persevered in our efforts to remember each other and ourselves, the dragon vanished."

"And if we hadn't—"

"I see two possibilities: either we wouldn't exist at all, exploding like the dragon or fading into nothingness, or else we'd forget ourselves as we forgot each other, becoming even in our own minds the oddities and abominations we were accused of being." He gave a dry laugh. "I wonder how it feels to believe oneself a demon."

She thought about it. "But if you're right, then why do we remember the dragon at all? If we remember each other, we shouldn't be able to remember it."

Malik frowned. "Do we remember it? What color were its eyes? What sound did it make?"

Fara opened her mouth, then closed it again. "My god." She

looked down. "So then, what has become of Basina? If she met the dragon . . ."

Malik reached up and put his hand briefly on Fara's shoulder. "If it was the same dragon, then I fear, Fara my friend and comrade, that your sister was unmade."

"*I* remember her. *You* remember me telling you about her."

"Yes."

"Then maybe she still lives! Maybe she didn't meet the dragon at all."

"Perhaps not."

They continued on to Strazburg, a huge city gathering souls from many leagues in all directions. For the first two days, to their relief, no one treated Malik or Fara with anything but the respect and courtesy to which they had been accustomed before this adventure began. To have some warmth and decent food was a comfort, and Malik inquired about the private libraries of some local scholars as Fara began again to ask after Basina.

In an inn on the third day, they ran across a portly, red-haired seller of cloth who had heard of a dragon killed near Bischoffshien. They asked him the details. The date and location made it clear that it was the pine-green dragon they'd destroyed themselves, but in this man's telling it was killed by a knight's spear piercing its eye.

"And the knight?" asked Fara.

"A very brave man, from what I've heard," said the man. "And his pale young squire never left his side."

Fara and Malik looked into each other's eyes. They knew what they knew; they remembered what they remembered. Or at least they thought they did.

"What's more," the cloth seller said. "I've heard there are more dragons further to the north. In Merkingen, in Mainz, in Erphesfurt."

Over the next few days, they questioned travelers from the

north and elsewhere to gather more rumors of these dragons. At least five sightings were reported, though none of their informants had seen one themselves. All these dragons sounded similar to the one they'd killed—as well as they could remember it now.

But although Fara and Malik did not encounter a single person who had seen one of the beasts first-hand, there were three who looked on them with horror and suspicion and would not venture more than a few words. Malik heard one of them mutter the word "witch."

As they sat alone at a table with cups of the aromatic white wine for which the region was famous, he told Fara, "The dragons don't need to see people to destroy their memory of us. Apparently it's enough that they exist at all. If we're not to forget our own names or wink out of existence, we're going to have to hunt them all down."

"Even if we didn't," said Fara. "There's a chance that Basina is still alive, chasing one of them. If we get to her before she gets to the dragon, we can save her."

"I hope we can."

So began their long quest to find and destroy the dragons of Europe, to save Fara's sisters of the sword and Malik's friends and family from the oblivion these creatures wrought. They never did find Basina, but Fara and Malik had many adventures and touched many lives; always there was another dragon to fight, and always they fought it with their belief in each other.

No tales are told of them nowadays, and this one is probably a lie.

*

In recent years, smart critics have responded to people who claim erroneously that the presence of nonwhites and combatant women in medieval Europe isn't "plausible." As Dennis R. Upkins says: "Talking animals, elves, dragons, gnomes, all totally plausible. Black people in Europe? Too many people can't suspend disbelief at that." There is always a part of me that wants to take the most serious issues and twist them absurdly, and so I found myself saying, "Well, obviously it's the dragons' fault." I thought it would be fun if a realistic Moor and a realistic woman knight were faced with an absurd dragon. That was the first idea, anyway; the story didn't come until I had met Malik and Fara and seen them interact.

CALIBRATION

FREDDA WAS CALIBRATING HER NEW wrist monitor when we saw the signal. According to the monitor, her daughter Wanda was at the home of Fredda Souci, Honokaa, Hawaii, and had been there for the past three hours. She was delighted.

These monitors are anti-theft devices for kids. Install the transponder under the skin and it ties into both public databases and GPS tracking, so that the vigilant mother knows whose house, whose restaurant, sometimes even whose vehicle her child occupies. What abductor stands a chance?

But you can imagine what a clever sixteen-year-old would think of it. Wanda's very clever, talented with both hardware and software; the kindest things she called the monitor were "babysitter" and "chastity belt."

We weren't actually looking for a signal; we were examining images from a long exposure of NGC 7742, some 22 megaparsecs away in Pegasus. Working at Keck is sometimes like being the janitor of a time-share condominium, always fixing the place up for somebody else's vacation. Once in a while, though, there are short gaps between observing projects, during which you can get your own work done.

Tearing herself away from her wrist monitor, Fredda noticed that there was an unexpected blob next to the galaxy. As it wasn't catalogued, we guessed it was a flaw in the system.

But of course we checked. After Fredda's monitor verified that Wanda was attending a school play, we observed the galaxy again, in real time. There was, indeed, something new there.

It was blinking.

My first thought was of some impossibly huge pulsar. Never mind how crazy that sounds; the reality was worse.

Because it stopped blinking; it vanished. Then, as we watched, it began again.

The pattern was invariant. The light flashed exactly 47 times, at apparently uniform intervals; then it stopped for about the same period of time; then it started up again. It was blinking at magnitude 16.2—implying, at this distance, an absolute magnitude of -15.5. Ridiculous.

After watching this pattern a few dozen times, we posted a bulletin asking for confirmation. Suarez in Las Campanas confirmed within the hour; several others came in during the night. Fredda checked her monitor to make sure Wanda was in bed, then went home, muttering about quasars and gravitational refraction.

By morning, Mendelsohn at Palomar confirmed that the interval between each of the 47 pulses was precisely 0.308091 seconds. Tanaka at Ayabe reported that the light in these pulses, allowing for distance and shift, was pure Hydrogen-alpha. There was not a trace of any other wavelength.

That raised some eyebrows. At the very least we should have seen some evidence of different hydrogen signatures. We didn't. While he was at it, Mendelsohn remarked that 47 is a prime number, suggesting that the source was artificial.

Talk about farfetched: a culture that could manipulate something like a few hundred supergiants and use them as a traffic light? Why?

I began to sort the information and analyses coming in, with intermittent help from Fredda as she fretted over why Wanda ap-

CALIBRATION 215

peared to be at a restaurant in Hilo when she'd said she was going to be at a friend's house.

Within twelve hours, Laska in Krakow dropped the biggest bombshell: 0.308091 seconds, the time period between the pulses, is 1.40737×10^{14} times the period of the hydrogen-alpha wave. And 140,737,488,355,327 happens to be the binary number expressed by 47 ones.

Oh.

The number of flashes expressed the relationship between the wavelength and the intervals. Someone was telling us that they knew they were sending a signal.

You, who are reading this in the quiet of your own office over a cup of tea, have probably spotted the flaw. We didn't, not for twenty more hours. Fredda would have—it's the sort of thing she notices—but she was distracted by Wanda's refusal to explain the anomalies in the monitor's reports of her whereabouts. Wanda's attitude was that, since Fredda had placed this device on her, Fredda could bloody well interpret the results.

It was Cutler in Pasadena who pointed out the flaw. The light we were seeing wasn't the true wavelength of H-alpha, because of course it was red-shifted as you'd expect a source at that distance to be. But the *interval* between the pulses wasn't Doppler shifted at all. It was exactly 0.308091 seconds. Red-shift doesn't pick and choose its phenomena; the intervals should have been shifted as well—they should have been longer.

The light was Doppler shifted; the intervals weren't. Therefore the red-shifting of the source's light wasn't due to the motion of the source, but to something else.

Christopher in Oxford suggested that we had found evidence of "tired light." You can imagine the storm resulting from the resurrection of *that* old monster—the notion that some unspecified substance or quality in intergalactic space somehow saps photons of their energy. The theory has never actually been disproved with contrary evidence, but universal expansion explains so many other things that jumping to a "tired light" conclusion was patently absurd. Christopher retorted that what was "patently absurd" was to ignore experimental evidence.

The online debate raged for hours. We dreaded what would happen if we made a public announcement so apparently disastrous for general relativity, for the Big Bang, for practically anything bigger than a microwave oven. The Creationists would have a field day.

Fredda had been very quiet. Now she looked up from her monitor, which told her that Wanda was in a brothel in Honolulu.

"The senders of this signal—" she began.

"Yes?"

"Why do we assume that they weren't lying?"

*

I've always been struck by the fact that literally all we know about the universe beyond our solar system is based on measuring light; I used to wonder whether we could be wrong about interpreting redshift to require the Big Bang. Although some physicist friends persuaded me that the alternative explanations are weak, I wanted to imagine a case where the redshift seemed to contradict the observations, and I came up with the idea of aliens who were trying to mislead us about the universe. Wanda's tracker is an example of a tried-and-true storytelling strategy: "Create two problems and have them solve each other."

LEVELS OF
OBSERVATION

FROM THE PRIMARY LEVEL PLACEMENT *AND TRACKING ASSESSMENT, ADMINISTERED AT AGE 7:*

10.　Look at the four pictures below. Which one is the sad face?

　　a.　Face A.
　　b.　Face B.
　　c.　Face C.
　　d.　Face D.

11.　After you walked in the front door of this building, how many times did you turn a corner before you got to this room?

　　a.　5.
　　b.　7.
　　c.　9.
　　d.　11.

12.　Which of these things was in your father's or mother's pockets when they walked with you in the hallway this morning? You can pick more than one.

　　a.　Nothing.
　　b.　A wallet.
　　c.　A knife or gun.

       d.   Something else.

       e.   I don't know.

13. Press the blue button. When the blue light comes on, answer: Do you think anyone is looking at you right now?

       a.   Yes, one person is looking at me.

       b.   Yes, three people are looking at me.

       c.   No one is looking at me.

       d.   I can't tell.

14. Press the red button, and an exam helper will come to your seat. After the exam helper arrives, answer this question: Does the exam helper like to eat:

       a.   Pizza?

       b.   Hot dogs?

       c.   Noodles?

       d.   Tacos?

15. Press the green button and a window will open. You will see four women sitting in chairs, with numbers on their backs. Which one is keeping a secret?

       a.   Number 1.

       b.   Number 2.

       c.   Number 3.

       d.   Number 4.

16. Is it a nice secret or a nasty secret?

       a.   A nice secret.

       b.   A nasty secret.

*FROM THE DEVELOPMENTAL ADJUSTMENT & ORIENTATION
INVENTORY, ADMINISTERED TO EIGHTH-YEAR STUDENTS:*

28. My talent is:
    a.   a blessing.
    b.   a useful tool in the service of a good cause.
    c.   an irritating habit that sometimes comes in handy.
    d.   a curse.

29. It's right for me to know:
    a.   anything I can find out.
    b.   anything that helps me serve others and improve the world.
    c.   anything that doesn't hurt anybody else.
    d.   only what people want me to know about them.

30. My teachers:
    a.   are cruel.
    b.   don't care about me one way or the other.
    c.   are willing to hurt me if it will help them accomplish important goals.
    d.   want what is best for me.
    e.   love me.

31. My parents:
    a.   are the best people to advise me in all things.
    b.   love me, but do not understand the needs and goals of someone with talents like mine.
    c.   have no idea what my life is like.

32. I can trust (circle all that apply):
    a.   my teachers.
    b.   my fellow students.
    c.   my family.
    d.   no one.

FROM THE ACADEMY COMPREHENSIVE CERTIFICATION EXAMINATION:

72. When is authorization by a Desk Officer required before commencing Level Two Observation of a subject?
    a.   In all cases except where there is an imminent threat to human life or public safety.
    b.   In all cases except where the Observer has probable cause to believe that evidence of a crime will be disclosed.
    c.   It is never required.

73. When is authorization by a Desk Officer required before commencing Level Three Observation of a subject?
    a.   In all cases.
    b.   In all cases except where there is an imminent threat to human life or public safety.
    c.   In all cases except where there is an imminent danger of mission failure.

74. During Level Two Observation, a subject's feelings and emotional state are:
    a.   Dangerous.
    b.   Distractions that should be ignored.
    c.   Harmless noise.
    d.   Data that should be recorded.

    e.   Useful tools for influencing the subject in the future.

75. How long can continuous Level Two Observation be maintained without risk of personality disorientation to the Observer?
    a.   5 hours.
    b.   10 hours.
    c.   15 hours.
    d.   20 hours.

76. How long can continuous Level Three Observation be maintained without risk of personality disorientation to the Observer?
    a.   30 minutes.
    b.   60 minutes.
    c.   90 minutes.
    d.   There is no period without such risk.

77. Practicum Problem A: When you are ready, notify the proctor. The proctor will lead you to an interrogation room containing one subject, one certified Observer, and three other candidates. When the proctor gives the signal, commence Level Two Observation of the subject *only*, assessing all mandatory and desirable objects. After 30 minutes, write a report of your Observations and give them to the proctor. Candidate reports will be compared to the report of the certified Observer. *Any candidate practicing Level Three Observation during this examination will be dismissed.*

From Form 29-J-7, Post-Observation Log, Variation 7:

5. Duration of Observation:

6. Location of Subject when Observation commenced:

7. Location of Subject when Observation terminated:

8. Level of Observation (check one):   II   III

For the remaining questions (except for question 17), you will be permitted only 20 seconds for each answer.

9. Describe the meal you ate most recently before commencing Observation.

10. Name the last person with whom you had a conversation before commencing Observation:

11. Are you (check as many as apply):
         angry frightened sad jealous irritated
         annoyed frustrated confused euphoric

12. What is your political affiliation?

13. Do you believe in a god?

14. Do you prefer wine, beer, or spirits?

15. Whom do you love?

16. Whom do you hate?

17. List at least five ways in which you are *different from* the subject of the Observation:

FROM THE NOMINATION QUESTIONNAIRE FOR THE OUTSTANDING SERVICE MEDAL:

7. What was the duration of the longest Level Two Observation completed by the nominee?
    a. Less than 24 hours.
    b. 24-48 hours.
    c. More than 48 hours.

8. What was the duration of the longest Level Three Observation completed by the nominee?
    a. Less than 1 hour.
    b. 1-2 hours.
    c. More than 2 hours.

9. Using percentages, indicate the approximate breakdown of characteristics of the nominee's Level Two and Level Three subjects. (In case of overlap, it is acceptable to exceed 100%.)
    a. Unwilling witnesses:
    b. Crime victims:
    c. Members of criminal/terrorist organizations:
    d. Enemy agents:
    e. Persons suspected of conspiracy to commit:
        i. Violent crime:
        ii. Property crime:
        iii. Treason:

10. Of the nominee's Level Two Observations, approximately how many resulted in:
    a. Production of usable material evidence?
    b. Identification of new subjects?

    c.   Positive identification of criminals?

    d.   Arrests?

    e.   Incarcerations?

11. Of the nominee's Level Three Observations, how many resulted in:

    a.   Prevention without surrender to police?

    b.   Surrender to police without confession?

    c.   Confession?

    d.   Suicide?

FROM THE LEVEL THREE OBSERVATION ANCILLARY EFFECTS REPORT:

5. How many persons other than the intended subject were affected by Level Three Observation?

6. Indicate how far each of these persons was from the intended subject at the time of Level Three Observation.

    a.   Number within 10 feet of subject:

    b.   Number between 11 and 20 feet from subject:

    c.   Number beyond 20 feet from subject:

    (If the number in #6(c) is greater than zero, refer to Training Unit.)

7. Were any of the affected persons minor children? If so, how many?

8. Are any of the affected persons now deceased? If so, how many?

    (If the response to #8 is in the affirmative, refer to Compensation Department.)

FROM THE OBSERVER OVERSIGHT LOG:

22. Has the Observer expressed reluctance to engage in Level Two or Level Three Observation? If so, provide details.

23. Has the Observer expressed sympathy with criminal subjects? If so, provide details.

24. Has the Observer expressed disagreement with the aims or methods of the Division? If so, provide details.

25. Has the Observer displayed any confusion concerning his/her own motives, beliefs, or identity? If so, provide details and refer to Division Counseling.

FROM THE DIVISION COUNSELING AND REFERRAL INTAKE:

6. When did you first experience the problem for which you are visiting today?

7. Why do you think this problem is related to one of your Observation sessions?

8. Do you think you are in danger of:
    a. Hurting yourself?
    b. Committing violence against others?
    c. Jeopardizing the mission of the Division?

9. Have you actually attempted to do any of the above? If so, specify.

10. Have you refused any assignments or disobeyed any orders during the last 72 hours?

11. If possible, identify the subject of the last Observation session that preceded the problems you have noticed.

FROM THE LEVEL THREE OBSERVATION FAILURE REPORT:

7. Outcome of Observation:
   - a.   Anticipated crime was committed (specify).
   - b.   Subject did not confess.
   - c.   Subject did not turn him/herself in for arrest.
   - d.   Subject did not commit suicide.
   - e.   Subject committed suicide when not authorized.

8. Current status of subject (check as many as apply):
   - a.   No change in previous status.
   - b.   Changed location (specify).
   - c.   New crime probability (specify).
   - d.   Alerted to Level Three Observations.
   - e.   Deceased.

9. Probable reason for failure:
   - a.   Insufficient Observer range/duration (*refer to Desk Officer*).
   - b.   Subject with undocumented Observation abilities (*refer to Special Investigations*).
   - c.   Misidentification of subject (*refer to Quality Control*).
   - d.   Observer error (*refer to Training Unit*).
   - e.   Observer noncompliance (*refer to Internal Affairs*).

FROM THE INTERNAL AFFAIRS REFERRAL COVER SHEET:

4. What is the probable/suspected reason for the Observer noncompliance (check as many as apply)?
   a. Personality disorientation or emotional fusion.
   b. Fatigue.
   c. Other mental disorder (specify).
   d. Corruption / criminal activities (specify).
   e. Political resistance / treason.

5. Current status of Observer:
   a. Desk duty.
   b. Temporary leave.
   c. In custody.
   d. Under medical observation.
   e. Whereabouts unknown.

FROM THE OBSERVER DETENTION INTAKE INVENTORY:

17. Prisoner's certified Level Two Observation range (when in doubt, *over*estimate):
   a. Less than 100 feet.
   b. 100-299 feet.
   c. 300-499 feet.
   d. 500 feet or more.

18. Prisoner's certified Level Three Observation range (when in doubt, *over*estimate):
   a. Less than 20 feet.
   b. 20-49 feet.

c.   50-69 feet.

d.   70-89 feet.

e.   90 feet or more.

19. Has an assessment been performed of the prisoner's probable long-term response to isolation? If so, summarize it:

20. How susceptible is the prisoner to Level Two Observation?
        a.   Fully transparent. (Attach explanation)
        b.   Partially transparent.
        c.   Primarily opaque with exceptions.
        d.   Fully opaque (i.e., standard Observer profile).

21. How susceptible is the prisoner to Level Three Observation?
        a.   Fully compliant.
        b.   Mostly compliant, with exceptions.
        c.   Mostly resistant, with exceptions (i.e., standard Observer profile).
        d.   Impervious.

22. The period of the mandated detention:
        a.   Less than 180 days.
        b.   180 days - 2 years.
        c.   2-5 years.
        d.   More than 5 years.
        e.   Life.

FROM THE LEVEL FOUR OBSERVATION AUTHORIZATION AND MANDATE:

31. Documented Level Three Observation range of subject (update if possible):

32. Names of at least five (5) certified Observers to commence Level Four Observation, with the certified Level Three range of each (*authorization will be denied unless* all *ranges listed are greater than the range specified in #31*):

33. For each Observer listed in #32, attach signed orders for temporary leave of at least 60 days commencing immediately after completion of Level Four Observation. (*Authorization will be denied unless all orders are attached.*)

34. Psychiatric assessor authorizing Level Four Observation:

35. District director authorizing Level Four Observation:

36. Regional commander authorizing Level Four Observation:

37. Facility warden authorizing Level Four Observation:

38. Contact information for subject's next of kin:

Copies of this Authorization and Mandate must be provided to the District director, regional commander, psychiatric assessor, facility warden, clerk's office, all Observers participating in the Level Four Observation and their Desk Officers. If next of kin is unavailable, consult District protocols for disposition of remains.

*

Here's another example of the "found documents" story, where the reader must piece together the narrative for herself. For years before I began writing fiction seriously, my creativity was devoted to composing amusing & weird factual scenarios for college exam questions. As in the case of "Tenure Track", the story consists of forms—but here, you don't know how the forms have been completed, and you must reason it out yourself. The tone of the piece is influenced by Joe Haldeman's All My Sins Remembered; *I realized only belatedly that I had written a horror story.*

WHO EMBODIED
WHAT WE ARE

ON THE HIGHEST HILL OF WHAT WAS once the capital city of Tegamat in the center of Dorolona stands the monument to Herant, the greatest of us. Three times his height when he lived, but no bigger than his spirit, he waits with his dogs around him and his spears at rest, looking not ahead for battle but down at the earth, contemplating mercy. Or so it stood when last I saw it; by now they may have torn it down. It grieves me that many of you will never see that beautiful statue, feel Herant's compassion and his courage.

Even in exile we need our heroes, maybe especially then. Our country mutilated and scoured by the priests of Akhloät, only a tithe of us remaining, nomads, moving across cold, unfamiliar hills like lost sheep, yet we persist. For a while we persist. Maybe the priests, mad with rage and self-righteousness, murdering all who are not like them, will follow us to the far corners of the land, into the frozen wastes or further, track the last of us down, and end this flight. Maybe.

Meanwhile, to remain a people, to hold our courage and remember our names, we must tell the stories that were told to us. On this night, before this little fire, gather and listen, and let the youngest come closest, for they need the warmth and are least familiar with the tales.

You have heard of the mages who learned to distill the Great Serum with the help of the beloved Vil and first gave it to our people, of the conquerors who brought peace to Dorolona, of sculptors and builders, poets and famous lovers. Tonight I tell you of the warrior who was great not for his prowess with the spear, which was a marvel, but for the humility of his soul and the love he bore his fellows.

Herant was born in the hills far to the east of the capital, before we ever heard of the priests of Akhloät. I came from those hills, though I cannot claim to have seen him there more than a handful of times. His family were mages, and it is said that they distilled the purest Great Serum of their day. Hundreds of children they cured of the blue plague and the wasting gut; many old women and men had their last years eased and their minds restored to clarity by the vials distributed by Herant's mother. It is also said that they never turned away a patient who had no obsidian with which to pay, but would give her the serum for nothing, for praise alone, rather than see suffering. And the praise indeed was great, and rich women and men gave more obsidian than was customary out of respect for the generosity of the family's hearts.

Though proud of his mother and his sisters, Herant himself lacked the gifts of a mage, and so never took up their craft. In his youth he worked the fields and trained dogs, hunting deer and wild pig with his friends. He was always the swiftest and greatest of endurance, strong and sure of hand.

In those days the enemies of Dorolona were few and weak with sickness or hunger. They suffered much from the many illnesses to which our flesh is prey. Sick people do not farm or hunt well, and so they sometimes starved. Some of the mages of Dorolona took pity on these aching countries and ventured to them in person, providing them with serum to bring their people back to health. But it never helped them very much, because a steady supply of the serum is needed to keep even a village healthy, much less a province, and the people of these lands either could not or would not produce it themselves. The result of all this was that Dorolona had little to fear from any of its neighbors, and warriors mostly patrolled the quiet borders or tracked down infrequent bandits.

It was in the year when Herant turned thirty that we first heard of the priests of Akhloät. Their country Skleioth lay many miles south of Dorolona, and from it we had few visitors, and never any trouble. Peace-loving folk they were in those days, who fished in the ocean and gathered berries on the land, who made love copiously and had many children to show for it. Travelers spoke of sunshine on the waters, soft speech, warm greetings, hospitality and gifts. We never traded with them, for they seemed to have nothing we wanted. Their salted fish and berry compotes were tasty enough, but none in Dorolona cared enough for them to pay the cartage.

Then one day, a mage ventured to Skleioth, taking with her some vials of the Great Serum. One of these she used to ease the passing of an old woman who had shown her much kindness. The people of that town thought the serum wonderful and praised the mage and the people of Dorolona for our wisdom and compassion. Some of the priests of Akhloät came to see the mage to ask how the serum was made.

Now, one is born a mage or not, and learning a set of instructions does no good unless the student has the gift. So the mage undertook to find an adept among them, take her home to Dorolona, and train her in the lore and demanding processes of generation and distillation. It happened that the first adept the mage recognized was one of the younger priests. He accompanied her on the journey home, and when they arrived, she introduced him to the other mages.

But the training went horribly wrong. She had instructed him for less than a month when the young priest transformed into a fiery fanatic: he cursed his teacher and all our people, called us demons and monsters, and refused to touch anyone. He fled and was never seen by his teacher or anyone in Dorolona again.

It was in the next year that the army of the priests of Akhloät first crossed our southern border. They slaughtered the sparse border guards, killed all the mages in the towns nearby, and sent the surviving villagers south as slaves, leaving none but the Vil untouched. With the mages they were especially cruel, dismembering them before death and calling it justice. Every hunter and border guard from up and down the land hurried south, and with a terrible effort and enormous loss they drove the priests back. A thousand of our women and men, and two thousand dogs, were killed in that carnage.

But this merely inflamed the priests, who said in their madness that now we were not mere monsters but murderers of their folk. The next year they came again, and were beaten back with still more losses.

We sent envoys asking for the terms under which they would leave our land and our people in peace. They answered: *Put to death the criminals you call mages, and swear never again to make the Great Serum, which is an abomination.* We were to rip out our hearts and souls and kill our mothers, fathers, and siblings, bring back all the suffering we had escaped. We knew then that this was a fight to the death.

Herant could never be a mage, though he had the helping heart of one, and I have heard that he never wanted to be a fighter either, though he had the strength and speed of a hunter. In a time of peace, perhaps he would have become one of those wandering folk who fix whatever is broken and solve whatever is puzzling. I think that would have pleased him, to end every day knowing he had patched an old fence or brought two quarreling lovers back together, each day a new beginning, each night an ending, no hand dragging him across the border of midnight with the same obligation he had at dawn. A carefree soul at heart, that's what he was.

Perhaps I should not claim to know so much, who only saw Herant a few times in the hills when I was a boy, and met him only once, and that briefly, when he killed the priests' soldier who had put a spear through my shoulder and my dogs, then carried me in his arms to the war mage who gave me the serum that healed my wound. Herant came back to see me in the mage's tent that night, his hand on my good shoulder, his soft voice filling the space and calming all the wounded. He spoke of our wives and husbands, how glad they'd be to welcome us home when the war was finally won, the little children who would jump into our arms and wrap their legs around our waists and ride there like princes until we set them at their dinner tables. Many of us were unmarried, and knew no little children, or had our wives or husbands beside us in battle; but when he spoke of these things, we could feel the children's dirty legs clutching us, smell the new loaves on the tables. The comfort and hope lasted all night and into the next day.

These were the only times I saw him once the war began, and so the things I say, I heard from others. But Herant was famous and beloved among us, and anyone who ever met him, saw him, or shared a battlefield with him told the tale over and over. Maybe the stories are exaggerated; but I know they are true to his spirit.

I do not know the history of Herant's dogs Ka, Du, and Po. Some said that he had raised them from pups, and surely they loved him as if he were their mother. Some said that he had found each of them, starving and friendless, had shown them kindness, fed them, and nursed them to health. One story says that they had been beaten and abused by another hunter, and that he paid the hunter enough obsidian for twenty dogs in order to save them; another says that he fought the abuser and beat him to the ground. That last does not sound like him, for he never hurt another person if he could avoid it.

But I will tell you that those three dogs showed no fear, that they would not leave his side no matter the danger, that they obeyed his commands and even his thoughts as if they were extensions of his body, as if he had five arms instead of two. Ka was faster than any man or dog alive; Du had jaws that could crush bone; Po could withstand terrible blows and wounds and yet attack and win. They slept at Herant's side, and he loved them more than a father loves his children.

We had seen that the priests had weapons like ours, although their tactics were strange. They not send warriors to battle other warriors in honorable single combat, one woman or man and her dogs against another; instead, they massed many men together, lines and lines of them, with their dogs in lines before them. Thus they could, by concentrating on an individual warrior, overwhelm her. Even with similar numbers, this technique usually prevailed, and we knew that the population of Skleioth was three times ours, and we feared that their armies would be proportionately large.

So we needed to develop new tactics, and train many more warriors. It galled us to adopt the methods of our enemies, but we could not think of a way in which lone warriors could overcome them. We began by imitating their battle lines, training our dogs to attack as a giant pack rather than as teams of three, and to coordinate the spearwork of our soldiers so that they massed their throws and thrusts. Unused to working together in this way, our women and men were clumsy, got in each others' way and, if anything, were less effective than they were before.

Here Herant first displayed the imagination and fortitude that would make him famous. He said, "While the massing of dogs and spears can overwhelm us, the priests have lost some of what they have gained. When man and dogs move together, they are like a single warrior with many limbs and weapons." He proposed that there should be two lines, but not dogs separated from warriors. Rather, each line should boast women and men surrounded by their dogs, for the dogs are the extension of the woman, and the woman the extension of the dogs.

Many stories are told of Herant's compassion on the battlefield. But his tenderness extended not just to his comrades and enemies, not just to his dogs, but to every person alive, no matter how lowly. So soft-hearted was Herant that it was said he could not bear to witness the generation of the Great Serum, even when performed by

members of his own family. Herant's mother and sisters were re-
nowned for the gentleness of their generation and distillation. They
gave the Vil parents their favorite meal and whatever entertain-
ments could be arranged; their children were offered encouraging
words of hope before the generation, and the unquenchable love of
the mages throughout.

In his family's home there was a special garden, filled with
pink and white blossoms in the spring, red in the summer, yellow
in the autumn, each with its own sweet fragrance that soothed the
nerves and made the world seem beautiful. I saw this garden with
my own eyes when I helped the family in some of the binding and
carrying tasks for the making of the serum, as Herant never did.
The Vil parents were seated together on a deep loveseat where they
could hold one another, and the cords binding them were lined with
the softest wool pads. Their children sat facing them in little seats
that caressed them, each with a mage kneeling next to her to capture the essence and distill the serum. Though the children's heads
were held in place so that they would not fail to witness their parents' deaths, the bonds were soft and did not hurt. The mages used
sharp knives on the Vil mother and father, barely a prick in the vein
that would drain away the lifeblood. The most potent serum comes
from children who watch a slow death, but Herant's sisters always
did their best to minimize the pain, knowing that no good comes
from cruel and needless suffering.

Afterwards, the mages buried the Vil parents with honor and
gratitude. They held and spoke softly to the children, saying "Your
loss is great, but you have given us serum that will save the lives
of hundreds; your parents' sacrifice will never be forgotten. When
you have children of your own, you too will have the honor of
saving lives. We love you and we thank you, always." Then the
children would be returned to the other Vil, who also comforted
them. The mages made sure they had healthy food and much exercise, and the pleasantest lives that could be arranged. If they did
not eventually fall in love on their own, wives and husbands were

chosen for them; if they did not choose to make love, they were assisted in it so that new Vil children would come into the world. Even when they tried to escape they were treated gently, and returned to their homes with love and tenderness and, of course, reunited with their families.

But despite the beauty of his family and their gentleness to the Vil, Herant would never help or even watch. The distress of children he could not bear, even Vil children in so sacred and beautiful a moment of their lives.

It is a wonder that he could bring himself kill the priests of Akhloät and their servants, and, indeed, he killed as seldom as he could. But the priests were coming for his family and his people, and on the battlefield they tore mercilessly at the comrades he loved. To protect these cherished lives, Herant could muster a fury that astonished all who knew him. Ka, Du, and Po tore the weapons out of the priests' hands and hobbled their knees so that Herant could thrust the spear into their throats. Sometimes the dogs simply took the throats out themselves.

But I tell you this: he fought to protect only. Sacrificing women and men to achieve an advantage over the enemy was alien to his nature, and I am not aware that he did it even once. Only to save his own soldiers would he kill; when he could keep them safe by other means, he did so, and at great personal risk. Such gentleness and mercy in a warrior astonished everyone. And all knew, for he said it often, that he would put down his spears the moment the war ended, and that Ka, Du, and Po would do nothing but play in the sun forever after.

The battle of Leramat came late in the sixth year of the war, when we had already lost much of our southern lands, and the slaughter of the mages was terrible, and our people were roped together to be marched to Skleioth, never to be seen by us again.

And the priests of Akhloät said to the Vil, "These lands are now yours forever, though it is no just recompense for the suffering you have endured these many generations." Never did the priests ask the Vil whether they had been well cared for or loved, whether they were honored by us as the heroes they were. They never asked the Vil whether they *wanted* to own the lands of Dorolona, though doubtless there were some small-minded folk among them who welcomed the chance. The lands were sparse without our people, and the Vil had never been very great in number despite all our best efforts. So there was much extra labor to be done, and none to do it but themselves.

Our army sat in the valley of Leramat, gathering our strength for the battle we knew must come. Unknown to us, our scouts and watchmen had been slain by priest assassins; the full army of Skleioth, outnumbering ours by four-to-one, poured into the plain from the woods before we realized it. There was no time to make a regular order of battle; we fought as we could. Dogs were slain before their masters could call them; women and men died with spears in their hearts while arming themselves.

Herant, who commanded, ordered the troops to retreat back to Tegamat, through the gorge at the north end of the valley. But the gorge was narrow, and it would take perhaps two hours for the army to pass through it. So Herant called to himself two hundred of his best warriors and their dogs, and together they harassed and distracted the army of the priests. They formed a wedge that drove into the priests' line, got behind them and attacked again. The priests turned to face them, and again the line moved, slicing through the priests like a knife, cutting their formation into chunks and forcing it to reform. Their speed and recklessness made up for their lack of numbers, if only for a while.

When nearly all of our people who had not been cut down had made it into the gorge, the two hundred, who were now one hundred fifty, stood before the opening and kept the priests back until the rest had entered. Then they held the gap, giving our people time to escape. One hundred fifty were cut to one hundred, and then to eighty. Then Herant turned to his women and men and told them to follow the army to Tegamat.

He alone stood before the entrance, with Ka, Du, and Po at his side. For another half-hour he held them, and none of us saw what he did or how he did it, how one man and three dogs held off an army of thousands in a narrow place. Perhaps they sought to capture rather than kill him, to make an example of him and dishearten our people. Perhaps they feared to attack him, knowing how fierce he was. But a half-hour it was, just enough extra time for all of this battalion and the rest of our army to escape to the safety of Tegamat.

The priests cut up his body as they cut up the bodies of mages, and cut up his dogs in the same way. They threw the hunks of meat over the wall into Tegamat. The people buried them with honor, and that is where the monument stands, if it still stands. It was still there five years later, when we were driven from the capital and became the wanderers we are.

Have all heard? Do not weep. We carry our legacy and the traditions of our mothers and fathers with us, no matter how few we are. We roam from place to place, we care for our children, and we may hope for a time of peace, as Herant hoped for it, when we may rejoin the beloved Vil, take up the making of the serum, and once more bask in the sun.

The life and death of Herant tell us what it is possible to be. Though not a mage, he was compassionate. Though not trained as a warrior, he was valorous. He showed mercy to his enemies and sacrificed himself for his friends. The monument to his memory may have been destroyed by the priests, as they destroy everything beautiful, but our living memory of him makes us braver, more compassionate, more self-sacrificing. Someday there may be only one of us. Someday we ourselves may be but a memory. But it will be enough if some remember Herant, who embodied what we are.

*

It's an eternal question: if you advance the cause of evil, does it matter whether you are otherwise good? I wasn't trying to trick the reader, exactly, but I wanted you to have the experience of sympathizing with my protagonists' desperation and loneliness, their apparent kindness and generosity, the near-certainty of their demise, their courage in the face of destruction, before I revealed the hideous things they did to bring them to this pass.

TENURE TRACK

ROGER WILLIAMS MEDICAL CENTER

DEPARTMENT OF GERIATRICS
EXTENDED LIFE INFORMED CONSENT FORM
NAME: <u>Martin Fournier</u>
DATE: <u>May 21, 2060</u>
DOB: <u>September 24, 2019</u>

By signing below, you certify that:

1. You have elected the Extended Life Treatment (ELT) voluntarily, under no inducement or offer of compensation from Roger Williams Medical Center (the Hospital) or any of its employees.
2. You understand that, while increased lifespan is the expected outcome of the ELT, this outcome cannot be, and is not, guaranteed by the Hospital.
3. You understand that the benefits of the ELT are reduced when the treatment is begun at a later age. At your age, <u>40</u>, the median expected lifespan is <u>370</u> years, and the maximum is <u>408</u> years.
4. You understand that the ELT is not reversible once it has been performed.

5. You understand that ELT provides no protection against bacteria, viruses, genetic disorders or toxic substances.

6. You understand that side effects are known to occur in a very small number of ELT cases. These include headache, reduced blood pressure, nausea, dizziness, abdominal pain and fatigue. You should not drink alcohol, use aspirin or any prescription medication for a period of 24 hours following the ELT, except at the express direction of your physician.

7. You agree to assume the risks of the ELT described above, and will hold the Hospital, its directors, officers and employees, harmless for any injuries or damages arising out of the treatment.

8. Signature: *Martin Fournier*

KARA H. ROUGE, BOOKSELLER, LONDON

AUGUST 3, 2060
MRS. TAMARA FOURNIER
27 WHIPPLE AVENUE
BARRINGTON, RHODE ISLAND, 02806-30052
UNITED STATES
TAMARA.FOURNIER@RIDEM.GOV.US

Dear Mrs. Fournier:

In response to your query, we do have Lord Brabourne's edition of Jane Austen's letters, published by Richard Bentley, London, 1884. It is a first edition, octavo, in two volumes, comprising 374 and 366 pages, respectively, dark green cloth with gilt monogram device, with beveled edges. The set is in very good condition.

We are asking £2,030. In answer to your other question, it is indeed possible to pay this amount in as many as four monthly installments, provided that the first installment is paid before shipping. If we ship within the next seven days, we can guarantee delivery before your husband's birthday.

Cheers,
Kara H. Rouge, Proprietress

RHODE ISLAND PUBLIC TRANSIT AUTHORITY
RECEIPT FOR RIPTA FARE CARD PURCHASE

NAME: Martin Fournier
DATE: 9-1-2060
2 SEMI-ANNUAL CARD(S) $900.00
TOTAL RECEIVED: $1,800.00

Save this receipt for your records. Fares are 100% tax deductible under both Rhode Island and Federal law.

Don't forget the additional 100% tax credit for proof that you have sold your personal motor vehicle without replacing it. See the U.S. Internal Revenue Svc and the RI Dept of Revenue for Details.

PROVIDENCE COLLEGE
OFFICE OF THE PROVOST

MAY 17, 2061
MARTIN FOURNIER
DEPARTMENT OF LITERATURE

Dear Prof. Fournier:

I am pleased to inform you that the College Tenure Committee, on the enthusiastic recommendation of your Department, has approved your application for tenure. Effective September 1, you will hold the rank of Associate Professor.

Congratulations on your achievement.

Sincerely,
Hannah G. Laski
Provost

SHAW THEATRE FESTIVAL
NIAGARA-ON-THE-LAKE, ONTARIO

2065 SEASON RESERVATION FORM

___Threepenny Opera
___Mrs. Warren's Profession
___Saint Joan
___Importance of Being Earnest
___How I Learned to Drive
___Misdirected Love
___Persuasion
___Sense and Sensibility
___Emma
_2_Jane Austen Special Package (all three Austen plays!)

Name: <u>Martin and Tamara Fournier</u>
Preferred dates: <u>August 2-8</u>
Total Price: $1,200 CAN

*

WISHING WELL FARM
Co-Op Organic Produce Subscription Renewal for 2068

Name: Tamara and Martin Fournier

Sign me up for:

_X_ Complete package (full access to all produce with draw-down amounts through October 31), Barrington site, Wednesday afternoons: $2,100

___Complete package (full access to all produce with draw-down amounts through October 31), Providence site, Saturday mornings: $2,100

X__Reduce your price by $400 by volunteering at Wishing Stone Farm. I will work:

___At the farm itself. (Sunday afternoons)

_X_At the Barrington site.

___At the Providence Site.

Remember to complete your subscription (including payment!) by April 30th.

ROGER WILLIAMS MEDICAL CENTER
Blood Chemistry Report

Patient Name: Tamara Fournier
DOB: January 4, 2021
Time Since Patient's Last Meal: 12+ hours
Time Since Patient's Last Alcohol/Aspirin: 12+ hours
Date/Time Specimen Collected: May 21, 2070, 9:38 a.m.
Glucose: 94 (normal: 67-99 mg/dl)
Cholesterol: 210 (40+ years: low risk if <240)
Extended Life Markers: 1.2 k/μl (ELR normal: 150-220 k/μl)

Comment: *Chemistry is consistent with failed ELT due to genetic incompatibility. This is patient's second ELT trial since 2060. High probability that patient is chronically resistant to ELT.*

BODY OF LEARNING HERBAL THERAPY CENTER

Name: Tamara Fournier
Your order:
1 Herbal Longevity Combination Package, $210.00
1 Mental Acuity Package, $160.00
1 Perpetual Stamina Package, $190.00
Total so far (before shipping and taxes): $560.00
If you order before January 1, 2071, you will qualify for our free shipping discount!
Click here to continue.

SCHOLARS' DISTRIBUTION SERVICE, INC.
ARTICLE DISTRIBUTION ORDER

ORDER DATE: 14-OCT-2075
NAME: Martin Fournier
INSTITUTION: Providence College
OFFICE ADDRESS: DEPARTMENT OF LITERATURE, PROVIDENCE COLLEGE, PROVIDENCE, RI 02918-00011.
E-MAIL: mfournier322@pc.edu

So far your list contains:
- K. Summers, *Rethinking nondiscrimination regulations in the context of the potentials of the Extended Life process*
- T. Jenner, *Elizabeth Bennett, Elinor Dashwood and Anne Elliot: models for the 21st-century man?*

- P.V. Nomonistan, *Austen's continuing relevance in the atomist theory of literature*
- F. Neige, *Each of us left behind: clinical impressions of couples experiencing failure of ELT in one partner.*
- S. Renfrew, *Long-term effects of the Extended Life process on population, employment and demographics*

Preferred method of delivery (if you would like different delivery methods for different articles, please complete a separate form for each type of delivery):

___Hardcopy with reproduction rights -- $99.99 each

___Hardcopy without reproduction rights -- $74.99 each

___Digital with reproduction rights -- $49.99 each

_X_Digital without reproduction rights -- $24.99 each

Interstate electronic tax: $3.75

Total due: $128.70

Charges will be paid by:

___Me (provide credit link here)

_X_My institution (provide purchase order link here)

MODERN LANGUAGE ASSOCIATION

2090 ANNUAL MEETING

LIMITED PANEL REGISTRATION FORM

As in previous years, owing to anticipated popularity and limitations on space, certain panel discussions will be attended by reservation only; reservations will be made on a first-come, first-serve basis. Indicate your choice(s) below. We cannot promise to accommodate all preferences.

Name: Martin Fournier

Institution: Providence College

Limited Panels:

___New theories of the subject: An agenda for research.
(Tuesday 9:00 a.m.)

X Backlash against Extended Life Recipients in academia
and elsewhere. (Tuesday 3:30 p.m.)

___Time to reclaim the middle-class white male? A debate.
(Wednesday 10:00 a.m.)

___ELRs: The threat they represent to hiring, promotion and
tenure. (Wednesday luncheon)

___Raising the dead? The relevance of Derrida and Foucault
in the era of atomist literary theory. (Thursday 9:00 a.m.)

___Stagnation in teaching and research as a result of Extended
Lifers in faculty positions. (Thursday luncheon)

PROVIDENCE BILTMORE HOTEL
BANQUET/CONFERENCE ROOM RESERVATION

Today's Date: January 14, 2091
Reservation Date: June 20, 2091
Reservation Time: 7:00 p.m.
Reservation Contact: George Medros, Director, Rhode Island
Department of Environmental Management
Occasion: Retirement party for Tamara Fournier, Ph.D.
Number of attendees: 70
Services included (check all that apply):
__Cash bar
X Prepaid bar
X Canapés
__Luncheon (attach menu selection page)
__Afternoon tea
X Dinner (attach menu selection page)

EXTENDED LIFE ALLIANCE
RALLY AGAINST DISCRIMINATION
JULY 4, 2099, STARTING 11:00 A.M.
THE MALL, WASHINGTON, D.C.

Yes! I want to prevent unfair laws against the Extended! I will attend the Rally Against Discrimination!

Name: <u>Martin and Tamara Fournier</u>

I will (check as many as apply):

<u>X</u> Attend the rally.

___Bring snacks or beverages for other marchers.

___Bring signs.

___Link signs.

<u>X</u> Call ten people to ask them to attend the rally.

___Organize a bus to transport marchers from my town.

___Write to my Member of Congress and my Senators (see sample letter on next page).

<u>X</u> Make a donation of <u>$500.00</u> to help fight this discriminatory legislation. (Note that political contributions are not tax-deductible.)

HOWARD UNIVERSITY HOSPITAL
INTAKE FORM

DATE AND TIME: <u>7-4-2099 3:35 pm</u>

PATIENT NAME: <u>Tamara Fournier</u>

ATTENDING PHYSICIAN: <u>P. Singh</u>

PATIENT AGE: <u>78</u>

HISTORY OF PRESENT ILLNESS: *78 year old female presents with coma. Pt collapsed in the Mall approx 2 hrs prior to arrival, witnessed. Pt has not regained consciousness.*

CLINICAL IMPRESSION: *Coma, Heat Stroke*

BIG SISTERS OF RHODE ISLAND
RECEIPT FOR IN-KIND DONATION
Thank you for your donation! If you itemize the items you have
left for us to pick up, we will verify receipt for tax purposes.

Your name: <u>Martin Fournier</u>
Date: <u>9/22/2099</u>
Items received:
<u>21 women's shirts/blouses</u>
<u>7 women's suits</u>
<u>12 skirts</u>
<u>10 women's pants</u>
<u>17 women's shorts</u>
<u>23 pair women's shoes</u>
<u>11 sweaters</u>
<u>2 women's winter coats</u>
<u>1 women's raincoat</u>
<u>3 women's belts</u>
<u>27 scarves</u>
Please remember that it is your responsibility to determine
and verify the monetary value of each of these items for tax
purposes. Big Sisters of Rhode Island makes no assertion as
to the market price of any item received.
Verified by stamp: <u>Big Sisters of Rhode Island</u>

PROVIDENCE COLLEGE
OFFICE OF HUMAN RESOURCES
RECEIPT OF SEVERANCE PAYMENT

Employee Name: <u>Martin Fournier</u>
Date of Hire: <u>September 1, 2053</u>
Date of Separation: <u>May 10, 2103</u>
Reason for Separation:

___Termination for cause

___Resignation

___Retirement

 X Separation required under Fair Access to Employment Act, 42 U.S.C. § 26000 et. seq.

Amount received: <u>€649,416.00</u>.

I hereby acknowledge receipt of the amount specified above, affirm that the amount received above is a fair payment of all debts owed to me by Providence College, and agree to hold the College harmless for any other claims or damages, including, but not limited to, any claims arising out of this separation.

Signed: <u>Martin Fournier</u>

FOOD WITHOUT FUSS, LLC
WEEKLY ORDER FORM

Name: <u>Martin Fournier</u>

Order date: <u>May 21, 2104</u>

Delivery date: <u>May 25, 2104</u>

 X Home delivery (€70 extra charge).

Include address: <u>27 Whipple Ave., Barrington</u>

___In-store pickup

Indicate number of orders (each order serves one person):

Main dishes:

1 Beef stroganoff over noodles	€164
___Caesar salad	€ 78
3 Chicken parmesan with pasta	€155
___Curried shrimp over rice	€140
1 Fried dumplings (6 pcs)	€ 94
3 Pizza with pepperoni	€117
___Tofu stir fry with snow peas and baby corn	€ 78

Sides:

___Baby carrots (steamed)	€ 62
___Baked potato	€ 31
_2_Creamed spinach	€ 90
_3_French fries	€ 30
___Side salad	€ 23

Desserts:

_3_Apple pie	€ 30
_1_Cheesecake	€ 35
_3_Chocolate fudge cake	€ 30
Total food charge:	€1,395
Delivery charge:	€ 70
Grand total:	€1,465

UNITED STATES DEPARTMENT OF LABOR
FORM ELR-3

LAST NAME: Fournier   FIRST NAME: Martin
DATE DD-MMM-YYYY: 30 Aug 2104
DOB DD-MMM-YYYY: 24 Sep 2019
EMPLOYER: University of Connecticut
Under the Fair Access to Employment Act, 42 U.S.C. § 26000 et. seq., which prevents Extended Life Recipients from monopolizing the labor force, you may not work for this employer unless you sign the following statement and provide supporting documentation to verify its truth.

Under penalties of perjury, I certify that (check one):
___1. I am not an Extended Life Recipient, OR
_X_2. I am an Extended Life Recipient, BUT I qualify for a
   Hiring Exemption.

If I claim a Hiring Exemption, I certify that I qualify for BOTH an Employer Exemption AND an Industry Exemption (see below).

If I claim an Employer Exemption, I certify that (check one):

  X 3. I have never worked for this Employer before, OR
  ___4. I first worked for this Employer less than fifty (50) years
       ago, OR
  ___5. I last worked for this employer more than (40) years ago.
       If I claim an Industry Exemption, I certify that (check
       one):
  ___6. This Employer is not in a Protected Industry (see
       reverse), OR
  ___7. I have never worked in this Industry before, OR
  X 8. I first worked in this Industry less than seventy (70)
       years ago, OR
  ___9. I last worked in this Industry ended more than fifty (50)
       years ago.

Supporting documentation that you are not an Extended Life
Recipient consists of an affidavit, form ELR-7, from a licensed
health professional, stating that tests show you do not have
Extended Life Markers in your bloodstream.

Supporting documentation concerning the date of your
employment with this Employer consists of an affidavit, Form
ELR-5, from the most senior human resources officer of the
Employer.

Supporting documentation that you have not worked in the
relevant Industry for the required time period can be satisfied
with a Form ELR-6, to which you must attach a complete
résumé. Note: All dates must be accounted for, including all
gaps in your employment history.
Signature: Martin Fournier

UNIVERSITY OF CONNECTICUT
STUDENT EVALUATION OF FACULTY

FACULTY NAME: Martin Fournier
TERM: Spring 2107
CLASS: LIT 4331: The Nineteenth Century English Novel
NUMBER OF FORMS SUBMITTED: 52
PAGE 2 -- TEXT COMMENTS (FOR NUMERICAL SUMMARY, SEE PAGE 1)

Not all students submit text comments with their forms. These are all the text comments that appeared in this section.

- *I liked the course, but I wish the rhetor could have spoken with some expression in his voice.*
- *In general, a good introduction to the subject. But the rhetor seems to think that everything in the 19th century begins and ends with Jane Austen.*
- *Subfrozen. Take the course from someone else. Misplace the monotone, ganger!*
- *Hyperthermal!*
- *Basically hyperthermal, ganger, but misplace all the waxing poetic about Austen.*
- *Subfrozen. Misplace it.*
- *I hype Jane Austen, so I hyped this course. But when you're lecturing about something as beautiful as P&P, couldn't you act as if you're happy about it?*
- *My friends who went to P.C. told me that rhetor Fournier was hyperthermal, but he talks like he's asleep. I wish I'd misplaced it.*

UNIVERSITY OF CONNECTICUT
INLINK MEMO

FROM: JOSEPH RICCITELLI

To: Martin Fournier
Date: April 5, 2107
Re: Course Assignments

I'm sorry, Marty, but I don't think I can accede to your request. First of all, we assign courses on a seniority basis, and you're still relatively low in the hierarchy. We could ask some of the others to trade with you, but I don't think any of them want to teach either 19th BritNov or the Austen course. Secondly, your expertise in Austen and the Romantics was (as you know) one of the primary reasons you were hired in the first place.

Again, sorry. Hopefully you can work your way around this.

Joe

EXTENDED LIFE PAIRING NETWORK
Registration Date: <u>Jul 4 2109</u>
Name: <u>Martin Fournier</u>
Username: <u>WidowerProf2019</u>
Date of Birth: <u>Sep 24 2019</u>
Age when received ELT: <u>40</u>

(NOTE: The Extended Life Pairing Network is for Extended Lifers only! If you are not an Extended Lifer, please be considerate and do not complete this registration.)

Gender Identity:

<u> X </u>Male

___Female

___Neutrois

___Other (specify)

I would prefer to meet (check all that apply):

___Men

<u> X </u>Women

___Neutrois

___Other (specify)

Of the following age (check all that apply):

___25-34

___35-44

___45-54

___55-64

_X_ 65-74

_X_ 75-84

_X_ 85-94

_X_ 95-104

___105+

Who received their ELT at the following age (check all that apply):

___25-29

___30-34

_X_ 35-39

_X_ 40-44

___45-49

Object (check all that apply):

_X_ Friendship

_X_ Romance

_X_ Marriage

___Just sex

_X_ Just someone to talk to

What's your EAEA status?

___I'm unemployed.

_X_ I won't have to change employers or industries for at least 10 years.

___I'll have to change employers within 10 years, but not industries.

___I'll have to change industries within 10 years.

Complete the 75 Compatibility Criteria below before finalizing registration. Don't forget to include a vid sample!

STATE OF RHODE ISLAND AND PROVIDENCE PLANTATIONS

Marriage License Application
Today's date: 11-8-2112
Wedding date: 11-15-2112
Circle Husband or Wife, where appropriate.
Name of Husband/Wife #1: Martin Fournier
DOB of Husband/Wife #1: 9-24-2019

Has Husband/Wife #1 been tested for Extended Life markers?
X Yes ___ No
(Attach physician's certificate to application)
Name of Husband/Wife #2: Melissa Thom
DOB of Husband/Wife #2: 2-3-2033
Has Husband/Wife #2 been tested for Extended Life markers?
X Yes ___ No
(Attach physician's certificate to application)
Note: While the presence of Extended Life markers does not disqualify you for marriage, you are required to inform your husband/wife of the results of these tests before marrying.

U. S. INTERNAL REVENUE SERVICE
Form 1040-ELR (2115)
Taxpayer Name(s): Martin Fournier & Melissa Thom

To qualify for the ELR Fertility Suppression Tax Credit, check each of the following that apply:
1a. If single, I received the Extended Life Treatment (ELT) before the age of 50.___

1b. If married, both spouses received the Extended Life
    Treatment (ELT) before the age of 50. _X_
If neither line 1a nor line 1b is checked, stop here. You do not
qualify for the ELRFR Credit.
2a. If single, I received voluntary fertility suppression
    injections from a qualified physician during 2115. ___
2b. If married, both spouses received voluntary fertility
    suppression injections from a qualified physician during
    2115._X_
3. Provide the name(s) and addresses of the physician(s) who
   administered the fertility suppression injections.
Norma Shok, M.D.
Roger Williams Medical Center
Providence, RI
If neither line 2a nor line 2b is checked, then you do not qualify
for the ELRFS Credit.

If you checked either line 1a or line 1b, AND you also checked
either line 2a or line 2b, then you qualify for the ELRFS Credit.
Write the amount €5,000 (if single) or €10,000 (if married failing
jointly) Form 1040, line 75.

FIFTY-FIVE PERCENT FUND

If you believe that U.S. law should no longer disadvantage the
55% of the population who are now Extended Lifers, please consider contributing to our campaign. Every euro will go toward re-
versing the unfair regulations that still privilege the minority over
the majority.
Fight back!
Name: Martin Fournier and Melissa Thom
Date: August 8, 2135
Amount contributed:
___€500

   ___ €1,000
   ___ €2,000
   _X_ €4,000
   ___ Other

SATYAGRAHA CENTER FOR YOGA AND HEALTH
SPECIAL PROGRAM REGISTRATION FORM

This offer is being made only to couples who are subscription members of Satyagraha.

Gerianne Komitas, Ph.D., a licensed psychologist and yoga teacher, will give a four-day, three-night workshop on overcoming apathy and malaise for Extended Lifers. Gerianne has counseled dozens of ELP couples, using techniques from meditation, yoga and atmospheric visualization to redirect psychic energies around the sense of wonder, enthusiasm for daily life, passion for professional tasks, and sexual libido that can fade over time in some Extended Lifers. The workshop will include lectures, visualization and meditation exercises, targeted physical relaxation and concentration techniques, and "homework" assignments for couples to complete in the privacy of their rooms.

Dates are May 3-6, 2140. Space is limited. Rate is €18,999 per couple, including meals and private room.

   Names: <u>Melissa Thom and Martin Fournier</u>
   Address: <u>33 Tennyson, Johnston, RI</u>
   Email: <u>mjthom@univmail.net</u>

NORTHEAST REGIONAL LITERATURE SOCIETY
2147 Annual Meeting

Panel 52 (Thursday, 1:30-3:30): Approaches to pre-Consolidation Anglo-Hegemonic fictive texts

Moderator: E. Nam, Meridan College

- S. Lewit, University of Lewiston: Postatomistic veritropes in Dickens.
- M. Suarez, Colby College Online: Neorecidivist analysis: should it be limited to post-Consolidation texts?
- A. Temple, Yale-New Haven Polyversity: Calliopisation characteristic of Fitzgerald, Trollope and Mackenzie-King.
- M. Fournier, Providence College: Austen on beauty.

*

In Kim Stanley Robinson's Mars books, the availability of greatly extended life means that entry into various jobs is severely limited for younger folks. I didn't believe it would work that way; I thought that extended life would result in statutory and other practices against the long-lifers to prevent them from "monopolizing" the job market. The first things I wrote were provision of the the Fair Access to Employment Act itself. Martin's story came later.

Here again is a "found documents" story: in this case, the advantage is that the reader feels what it would be like to fill out these forms, that is, to experience this life. It was really fun to make up new slang terms and new jargon for literary criticism.

THE SISTERS' LINE
By Liz Argall & Kenneth Schneyer

 **M**Y SISTER IS POSTING ME A TRAIN, piece by piece. She hides minute cogs in the adhesive between stamp and envelope; she traps switches in the envelope's seal. Every letter is a game, a puzzle, a thing to be dissected. I spend hours unfolding and refolding the letters and the little origami cranes she slips in as companions. You never know which folding or unfolding action will release a bolt, a grid or an entire door panel.

My next door neighbour, Stacy, single mum, keeper of bees, works in robotics, thinks I'm crazy.

"Why are you wasting your time on this clunky half built outdated piece of junk? It's taking up half your front yard and more besides. It's consuming you! Just buy a train from medusa.com. You can buy a kit. You'll still be able to build it with your own hands. You want to be a craftsman? What kind of craftsman builds when they have only half their materials? She's not even sending you them in order! You need to let it go."

Before I can reply, she's clambered into her share car (60 cents a minute) and is off to pick up Becky from baseball or ballet or something starting with B. Becky only does things that start with the letter B. She failed maths until she was able to reconceptualize it as business basics.

Stacy drives off with a cheery wave. I am alone with my unspoken replies.

This train, *this* train I'm building is my sister's train. I have to believe that all the pieces will fit. One day this train will be built, the magnets will be activated and they will find the right tracks, the tracks that lead to my sister and the hidden country that has taken her.

My sister writes to me most days: letters smelling of lilac and brimstone, jasmine and toasted cumin seeds. I try to write back, but I have no postal address. I float letters on rivers, burn them in grimy back alleys that smell of stale oil and fish heads. I leave them for squirrels and rabbits to carry. I write letters on maple leaves and give them to the breeze.

I do not know if they get through. I do not know if there are censors peering over her shoulder.

My sister's letters are full of self-centred inanities. She does not ask me questions about my life. She does not express sadness that I do not write, nor does she express delight upon the receipt of a letter. I must assume there is a level or surveillance, real or implied. She must have some privacy, however: she is slowly posting me a train.

The postman, a woman in kahki shorts and a fluorescent motorcycle jacket, rides her motorcycle up onto the footpath and hands today's letter directly to me rather than putting it in the letterbox.

"Thanks."

She smiles and guns the engine, swooping to the next letterbox. I wonder if the strain around her eyes is from the glare or because she thinks I'm odd and doesn't like me. My letterbox is a faded old thing made out of a cut-up plastic milk bottle bolted to a stake. I look around my ramshackle yard, yellow grass dying in the summer's heat where it hasn't been squashed flat by my precious junk. The skeletal train, its roof patched with tarpaulins, lists to one side; weeds grow through some of the heavier, more difficult parts to place. Fearful of rust, I used to try to take pieces inside, but away

from the open air they ooze viscous black oil that stains the floor-
boards.

I raise the envelope to my nose; it smells of toasted cocoa and
roasting macadamias. I ease the flap open, careful to keep the opening away from my feet. In winter, my left ankle still aches where a
falling axel broke it; it took me a year to repay Stacy for the medical care I couldn't afford myself. I think she took out a loan to help
me, but never charged me interest; whenever I mention it, she just
smiles.

My sister has written to me on blue paper almost as thin as tissue, crinkling under my fingers. She writes to me about the color of
the sky and what it feels like to be completely submerged under water. I rub the rough stubble on my head, remember when we'd pretend to be mermaids, diving deep and swimming towards each other,
stopping fast so our heads could be enveloped in strands of hair.

I catch an edge in the folded paper and, wriggling it back and
forth, I find several thin sheets of metal that could be roof panels
and the top half of a passenger seat. The upholstry is velveteen and
matches the paper it came in. I haul the seat up the stairs to the
passenger car to where I've bolted the bottom half of a passenger
seat upholstered in golden-hued velveteen. I slot the top half into
the bottom half. The colors don't match, but they do marry. The
blue has a warmth that connects to the gold and looking at it I can
imagine I am in a place very far from here.

Next I secure the curved sections of roof panel, ripping away
tarps to provide more effective weather protection. I'm standing
on the roof, sweating heavily, when Stacy and Becky return from
Becky's badminton lesson.

Becky ditches her racket on the side of the path and runs over.

"Careful!" says Stacy, retrieving the racket and crossing her
arms.

Becky leaps up the stairs of the passenger car in one exaggerated bound and peers around before shouting up at me through a
hole in the ceiling.

"You got a seat!"

"The rest of a seat, maybe. It's a pity they don't match."

"I wonder why that is? It looks nice anyway." says Becky, flumphing down onto the seat with a satisfying whoomph.

It occurs to me wonder: what if the order in which my sister sends parts is the message? What if it's a code, and if I put the first letters of all the parts in sequence it will spell out her location or directions to get there or names of her captives or that she loves me and misses me and can't wait until we can be together again? What if the letters of the parts she sends me is a code, and she's screaming in pain and I can't hear her, and how will I remember which piece came first? And maybe I could remember and record it, but how will I remember all of it, and for a time I kept log books yes and journals, but as the years drew on I forgot and became inconsistent and is my sister screaming in pain and I can't hear her all because I was stupid and dumb and don't have the records to read what she's been telling me even though all the pieces are here? What if she's screaming?

"Are you okay?" I see Becky's face staring up at me, frightened by the clouds that have been chasing my own expressions.

"I'm okay." I clamber down from the roof, my legs shaking as my thoughts swirl in on themselves. I press my face against the warm metal, close my eyes and try to gather myself.

There is a shriek from inside the passenger car. Adrenaline spikes through my throat as I run to the steps.

"Come see!" I hear Becky shout and giggle. Laughter, not screams.

I leap up the stairs and find Becky curled up on the new seat, her feet pushed into the join between top and bottom. "I'm burrowing!"

Of course she is. I smile with relief, use the smile to force down the rage. How could she scare me like that?

Becky plays on, oblivious to my distress. I force myself to breathe. Becky on the seat looks like she's some passenger on

KENNETH SCHNEYER

the *Orient Express*. She's travelling across Europe with frequent stops for sightseeing and sticky sweet drinks in the dining car. Does this train have a dining car? I've mapped out its potentials so many times it's hard to tell what I've built and what I've dreamed. Sometimes I imagine the skeleton of the train growing and burrowing deep into the ground, half rotten carriages that will be sucked out of the earth like a tap root, should the engine ever roar into life.

Becky stands on the seat, her feet making dainty divots. She grabs the overhead baggage rack and yanks it hard.

"Hey!"

Becky ignores me, sharply puts all her weight into it, and hauls the rack out of the wall. I raise my arm, ready to scream. I expect to see my beautiful wall torn ragged by the bolts and Becky's face battered by metal, but instead the wall is smooth, as if the rack had never been there at all. I lower my arm, embarrassed, ashamed, glad she didn't see.

The rack is almost as big as Becky; she doesn't seem to mind and marches down the stairs with it, almost tripping on the way.

As we exit the carriage I glance over to Becky's mum, who's leaning against her car, doing something with her smartphone.

Becky pushes the rack up into the half-built engine room and clambers up the stars after it.

I follow her.

"You think too much," observes Becky. She's right, but I don't see what that's got to do with her defacing my train.

Becky squats and gets both her hands underneath the overhead rack in a perfect weight lifter position. She frowns, her tiny biceps bulge (I feel a moment of envy at how ripped she is) and she lifts the rack to the height of her armpits and pushes it up against the driver's controls. The rack shifts and bends under her pressure and then slides easily, perfectly marrying to the control panel and turning into a series of buttons and one long lever.

"How . . ."

"I'm building," says Becky, primly.

I press my hand against my head. If the parts are malleable and contain as many hidden pockets as the letters, the variables are infinite. How will I piece it together if even the pieces lie to me? I brace myself against the console and try not to throw up. How much of my train is a lie?

"Bulgaria," says Becky. "Belarus. Beirut. Boston. Beijing. Birmingham. Berlin."

"Do you know what this train is for, Becky?" My voice is unpleasantly shrill. "Are you guessing at the places my sister might be?"

"Bora-Bora," she continues, oblivious. "Bristol, but that's an extra twenty dollars."

"Can you take me to my sister?"

Becky's patter suddenly stops. "Take?"

"Drive? Transport? Navigate? Operate this train?"

Becky shakes her head, bewildered.

"Becky! Are you bothering your friend?" Stacy's playtime-is-over voice winds up through the metal housing.

"No, mummy," pipes up Becky. "I'm boggling her."

I squeeze my head between both hands, trying to think of a B word that means travel.

"It's all right, Stacy." I say, "Becky's just showing me where she thinks some of the parts go."

"She's not breaking anything, is he?"

"No, it's perfectly fine." What can I do to buy more time, what do parents like? "Would you like to come up and see? I think you'd enjoy some of the new additions. Could I get you some tea?"

"Thanks, but we have to get dinner ready. *Becky*! Come down. I need you to help me with the beef and broccoli."

"Broccoli?" says Becky. "Yay!

"Can you bus the train, Becky?" I whisper urgently as she twirls around in preparation to leave. "Broom, broom?"

Becky jumps down the ladder, ignoring me.

"Broccoli is a brassica!" she chants as she bounces into the house.

Once she is gone, the engine room feels empty and drained of color. I wonder what sort of kids my sister would have had if she'd had the chance. I would have made a good auntie. I wonder if I will ever get the chance.

I sit hunched against the wall of the engine room for a long time, trying to see what Becky saw. How, how, how did Becky unfold half a control panel from a luggage rack? I push and prod each part of the engine room. I run my fingernails along every surface and inside the furnace, hoping upholstery and pistons will unfold from them and I will have more pieces to rebuild with.

It's dark when I climb down from the train, and I am hungry and filthy. I fumble through the cupboards in my kitchen, but I am too hungry to eat. Instead I pull down my primary school thesaurus from the shelf and curl up on the only couch in the house. I look up *drive*, but the synonyms are useless. I play synonym tag, jumping from word to word. I doze off for an hour or two, rouse myself long enough to eat a can of cold baked beans, and fall back to sleep on the couch, the springs digging into my sides are like old friends.

My sister and I moved out of home together. We moved in here together, though I am the only one who had the chance to live here, if you call it living. The walls are still bare. She was, is the one with an eye for design. Boxes of posters and ornaments are still stacked on the ground in her room. The dust and cobwebs get thicker every year.

In the morning I shrug out the all-too-familiar cricks in my back and take a spit bath using boiled water from the kettle, an enamel bowl and a cracked bar of soap that was once the color of emeralds.

Thesaurus in hand, I head out to my sister's train and wait for Becky. I tinker with the engine and move bent pieces of steel from one part of the lawn to another. I graze my shin and set my hand to bleeding as I stumble around, one eye distracted and leaning towards Becky's house, my ears straining for the sounds of breakfast and the chance the Becky will come outside.

The morning is awful. What kind of person stakes out a little girl's house?

I can feel my skin desiccating in the sun. I daren't go inside, not even for a moment: what if I miss her?

"You could always ask." I whisper to myself. "What, and come across as a weirdo?"

"As opposed to the sort of person that lingers in their yard, gazing at their neighbor's house with increasing desperation?" I reply.

"Fine, you have a point." I whisper through clenched teeth. "It's all terrible."

I march up Becky's front lawn and bang on the door before I can let myself think. Stacy opens the door instantly, the surprise sending me a step backwards. Stacy's arms are folded, lips pursed, eying me critically.

Creep creep, you're a creep, whispers my internal monologue.

"You're spending too much time in the sun," she says. "Too much time working on that hobby has addled your brain."

I look down at the ground and reflexively count the number of cracks in the tile next to the door frame.

"Come in and have a glass of homemade lemonade," she says.

I follow her into a white, white kitchen. White walls, white tiles, white stove, a painted white wood table with matching white chairs. I half expect the fruit in the white bowl to be white as well. I wrinkle my nose at the faint smell of bleach.

"Sit."

I sit. Stacy drops four ice cubes in the shape of hearts into a tall, thin glass. The last cube chips when it hits the others. The lemonade is a pale yellow, almost white. She gives me a chocolate chip biscuit and watches me indulgently while I eat and drink. My sister used to give me sweets and drinks just on a whim. She didn't know how to bake, but that didn't stop her. Whenever I eat a burnt ANZAC biscuit I think of her.

"Do you feel better now?"

I nod, not trusting my words. Stacy's arms are crossed, leaning on the polished white table.

"Are you ready to ask for what you want?"

I feel very little. I am taller than Stacy, but it doesn't feel like that right now. It is hard to speak.

"Can Becky come down and play?" I flinch as I blurt out the question, anticipating a blow that does not come. My voice is high and tremulous. I look down at my body, half surprised that I haven't turned into a toddler.

"Becky doesn't play," says Stacy, arms still crossed, not at all surprised.

"Can she . . . can she . . . be working on the train with me? Can she brighten my day?"

Stacy gives me a half smile, "Close enough." She turns her head to holler up the stairs "Becky! Bounce your good self down here!"

Becky barges into the room and smiles when she sees me. I smile nervously in reply, sitting very small, feeling very young.

"How's the train?" says Becky.

"I don't know." It's hard to speak above a whisper. It's hard to acknowledge that after all I've done, I still don't know where I'm going. "But I think you do."

"Outside, girls," says Stacy, clapping her hands. "But wear hats and don't stay out too long." She smears sunscreen on my cheeks, arms, and the back of my neck. She plonks a straw boater onto my head; the straw itches through my stubble. She kisses me on the cheek and gives me an affectionate swat on the bum to get me out the door.

Becky walks slowly up to pieces of junk scattered around my yard, like a big cat stalking its prey "We have to *build*!"

She pulls pieces of sheet metal out of the ground, hauls bumpers and axles three times her size as if they were lego pieces, and slides them into place on the train.

"What can I do?" I ask as she carries a stack of wheels to the passenger car.

"Bring me that lever," she says, pointing to a metal lever the size of a crowbar. I pick it up and, yep, it's just as heavy as a crow bar. When I hand it to her she carries it one hand like it was a well-balanced javelin.

She props it into a window frame of the passenger car and it melts into a glass pane and a set of curtains.

Becky moves fast and relentlessly, and within twenty minutes we have disassembled and reassembled all of the parts of the train that are visible. The passenger seat cushions have shifted from yellow and blue to a lush velvet green. The train is whole and practically thrums with life.

"Beautiful," breathes Becky. She has the widest grin I have ever seen. I try to smile in return, but embarrassment and shame make it wobble.

"What's wrong?"

"I just feel stupid, that's all. I've spent years on this and you understand it, you fix it in twenty minutes."

"Don't be silly," Becky crosses her arms and for a moment looks exactly like her mother. "These are just decorations. You built the skeleton."

I open my mouth to reply, but before I can speak she has jumped through the engine room window. I scramble up the stairs and by the time I enter the engine room, she's buffing the shiny controls with her sleeve, humming a tune to herself and snorting with amusement.

I want to say something, but Becky's serenity scares me. I feel like I'm on an empty ocean liner, far out to sea and vulnerable in the Captain's hands.

"Ask me." Becky turns to face me. "Ask me to be your best friend forever. Ask me to give up my favourite pair of trainers. Ask me to cradle you in my heart. Ask me anything."

My heart speaks for me. "Bring me my sister."

"She can't be brought."

"Bring me to my sister."

She looks into the distance, her eyes are old. "It is a long ride. And you won't like parts of it." Then she laughs and claps her hands, her voice returning to a more child-like timbre. "We'll need coats and jackets and wooly underwear and string and candles and something to eat, and something to eat that isn't beetroots."

Becky sticks her head out of the window. "*Mum!*" she shouts.

"Yes, sweetie?" Stacy's voice is muffled through two windows and several rooms.

"Can we borrow some big coats and food bars and bottles of juice and bound into an adventure?"

"ofwhofcwhohfrohwoh," is all I can make out, Stacy's voice is so far away. I lean my head out of the window and can just make out on the breeze, "Take good care of them and don't spill anything on your clean clothes and only spill on the ground what the ground will take."

"I promise! It's a bargain!" shouts Becky. Clothing appears in a neat pile at our feet and we pull it on as if dressing for a day of sledding and snowball fights. Outside the sun is a baleful yellow orb.

"Ready?" asks Becky.

"R . . . wait." My eye catches on my letterbox, the faded old thing that my sister and I made together.

"If we leave, how will my sister's letters get to me?"

Becky rolls her eyes. "What makes you think I'd know?"

"I . . ."

Becky shakes her head and laughs.

"Just a minute," I wheeze. I go into the house and grab a stack of clean printer paper.

Dear Sis,

I am leaving this house now. I have stayed here for so long, but now I have to go. I have to leave if I am to find you and I don't know if I'll be able to return.

I'm frightened and happy and have a friend who can help me.

I don't know what I'm stepping into, but I do know it's time. I will write to you, keep writing to you and hope that my letters reach you. I don't know if your letters will reach me, I have a feeling they won't. Becky says it's a long journey and a cold one, but I will come for you, I promise.

With all my love.

I kiss the envelope and slip the letter into my own letterbox.

"Ready?" asks Becky, her voice a squeal of excitement.

I nod and climb up into the engine room.

"This is your control panel," says Becky in cross faux-grown-up tones. "You should know how to operate it."

I gaze at the vast array of switches and levers. I push a big red button. I feel the thrum of pistons engaging, the crackle of magnets switching on and seeking. The train roars into life and pulls itself from the ground.

Becky puts her small hand in mine and I do not flinch. Against all odds, we are partners and fellow travellers. We will find what we seek.

*

The week after Readercon, Liz Argall and I went to a coffee shop in Warren, Rhode Island with our notebooks. Liz pointed to a painting on the wall and said, "That's the prompt." After twenty minutes, we traded notebooks and kept writing. Twenty minutes later, we traded again. And then again. We separately finished the stories and edited them together. One of these stories was never published; the other is "The Sisters' Line."

A LACK OF CONGENIAL SOLUTIONS

EXCERPT, SKENANY TEXTUAL MESH:
"We On Earth":

Generations without a home   Joined quintets dead
                    Fertility restricted
Food controlled

                                                            Pets!
Torn from our mansions   Curiosities!
                    Nests dead
                    Nestlings slaughtered
                                        Raw materials!
Years imprisoned in ships
                            Delicacies! Distractions!
    Denied the unbroken web   Denied communion
        But always remembering   Awaiting the day
        But always planning   Awaiting the day
Passing on what we can   Awaiting the day
                    Humans cannot know

> Humans will not understand
>
> Those who eat our flesh
>
> They have no grief

Excerpt, Oral History of Mary White:

When I was very little—I must have been three or four—I asked my father why we had a Naichian cleaning our house instead of a robot. Our Naichian—no, I don't think I remember her name—was twice as big as me, and looked like a giant green beetle. I'm sorry, I don't mean to offend you, but that's the way it seemed to me. I said I was little.

My father said something about Naichians being better cleaners than robots. That didn't make sense to me even then, because I knew robots could do all sorts of things. I said so, and my father replied that it was important to give the Naichians work, because they no longer had their home. When I asked where their home was, he told me that their planet was now full of humans, and no Naichians lived there anymore. I asked why the Naichians left their home and came here, and my father looked sad and said that it was a long story.

There were lots of questions my parents wouldn't answer when I was that age, or answered in ways I guess they thought were "appropriate" for me to hear. Another example? Well, I once asked my mother why people only came in one color, instead of the many different colors of Naichians, Pheätioni, Xicoménese, cats, and dogs. I think I must have heard something from one of my friends, or maybe overheard one of their parents, that made me think people once had more colors.

My mother had just arisen from doing her duty to my father, and was very quiet. She started to say, "The world used to be different." Then she stopped, frowned, and said, "Not—" I think she was searching for the right words for a four-year-old. "Not as good. The world wasn't as good before as it is now."

"How?" I asked. "Are different colors bad?"

"It wasn't just colors," she said. "People believed all sorts of strange things, and they—well, there were women who didn't act like women, and—" She stopped.

I was confused as any child would be at such a vague explanation, but she didn't continue. By the time my parents might have explained the past and the present to me more cogently, everything had changed.

Yes, I agree, changed for the better. But I don't think my parents saw it that way. No, I never asked them, and they've been gone a long time. How can I know for sure?

Excerpt, The Human Affliction, *by Oma of the Lespentai*:

It is ultimately pointless to argue whether travel by star drive warped human character, on the one hand, or flawed traits in one ethnic and cultural group impelled humans to interstellar flight, on the other. Regardless of the mechanism of causation, one human sub-civilization began systematically absorbing and eliminating all competing sub-civilizations within—possibly before—the initial century of Terran interstellar exploitation. By the time the first conquerors (for thus we must call them) arrived on Xicomé, there was remarkable homogeneity among humans in belief, cultural norms, gender classification, sexual practice, and general appearance. Unfortunately for the Xicoménese, as well as for every other race that encountered humans afterward, this sub-civilization was utterly confident in its own destiny and superiority, and regarded the subjugation, humiliation, torture, and mass-murder of entire species as its natural right.

As sometimes happens among privileged communities, however, insulation from material hardship encouraged the development of abstracted inquiry into a spiritually enlightened framework. In the five or six decades prior to the Revolution, humans had begun to seek "goodness" in all its various permutations—

intellectual breadth, tranquility, universal compassion—to fulfill their destiny within themselves as well as externally. There is evidence during that time that human philosophical orthodoxy was beginning to question the morality of human intervention on other worlds, of the forced transport of other sentient races to Earth for purposes of servitude, captivity as pets or curiosities, or use of their bodies as raw materials. Given another few decades or centuries, perhaps human behavior towards others would have changed. Like all such counterfactual speculations, however, this one must ultimately remain unanswered.

Excerpt, Song of the Revolution, *a Pheätioni epic*:
    For fives squared and fives cubed of orbits
    These waited
    In bondage and in servitude
    In humiliation and in torture
    These passed their languages
    These passed their heritages
    From hand to arm, from breath to whisper
    These waited
    The plan accreted in drops
    No more than a few words at a time
    Continent to continent
    Two generations for some
    Five-and-three for others
    These watched the moment approach
    In every city on their planet of exile
    At the same instant
    Arose fives cubed and cubed again of hands legs tentacles
    Ships in space they disabled and destroyed
    Communications they disrupted
    Power stations they commandeered
    Data stores and processors they disabled or controlled

These killed who never killed
Whose ancestors never killed
In less than five days
Theirs was the Earth
This place they never wanted

Excerpt, Autobiographical Essay of Tsroac Dilfe:

On the twentieth day, the leaders of the rebellion met in a large conference room in Sao Paolo that that had formerly been reserved for board meetings of Terra's largest profit-making enterprise. We were "leaders" in the sense that we were the attendees of this meeting: some had actually held coordinating roles in the revolution; some had been elected by their fellows to attend; some had positions of high status within their own communities.

Representation was complicated by the cultural norms of each species and subgroup. The Pheätioni cannot conceive of representation that does not include all three of their biological sexes and all nine of their social genders. The Lespentai recognize sixteen separate racial and ethnic subclasses who all needed to be there. The Xicoménese split into a dizzying multiplicity of ethical, empirical, and metaphysical belief systems, but consented to have a mere twenty of these appear at the meeting. There were none who thought, or who would voice the thought, that strength, intelligence, dexterity, or prowess in combat should give some races or individuals primacy over others. For now at least, we met as equals who had shared in a victory.

"For the time being," said Oma, the Lespentai who had been instrumental in neutralizing human law-enforcement personnel, "can we agree to attempt consensus on decisions made today, if any are? Our wishes and needs may vary much." There was no dissent from this proposition.

Lienn, an Xicoménese adherent of universal reflective consciousness and coordinator of the attack on the political centers of

Europe, suggested that a given position—pe indicated a rostrum at the far end of the room from where pe sat—should be where any speaking was done, and that translations into writing or sign should be available. Pe made the further suggestion that speakers should stand in line or otherwise speak in order. This last suggestion took a while to reach consensus, as some species do not engage in such regimented conversational structures. The Skenany, for example, speak simultaneously with several interlocutors and arrive at their decisions by the gestalt suggested by the directional pressure of the words. But ultimately it was agreed that some would be unable to hear, see, or feel such communications at all, and so we adopted Lienn's posposal.

Tollop, a Naichian, signed that she wanted to know about the question of repatriation. Despite the fact our home planets now contained exclusively human colonies, many wished to return.

"For those worlds that are not colonized at this timespace locus," wrote Peerri-O-Sreb, a Pheätioni dominant egg-host, "ships should be found. But humans in a colony are a danger. Humans may seek vengeance. Humans may seek to complete the task of obliteration. Humans may take hostages. This one does not believe repatriation can be attempted without prior resolution of the Human Question." We agreed to facilitate the return home of any whose worlds now held no humans, but to wait on the colonized worlds until some solution was reached.

Peerri-O-Sreb's raising of the "Human Question" made it impossible to ignore what we all knew must ultimately be discussed, although I dreaded it: what to do about the humans still on Earth. Several Skenany suggested integrating humans into a new, egalitarian Terra:

"—once they see—"
"—experiences inevitably alter outlooks—"
"—centuries of bad exposures—"
"—consequences of behaviors—"
"—working parts of a productive whole—"

"—one race among many—"

"—included in any just polity—"

"—be like the rest of us—"

When they had finished, Lienne said, "Their history does not suggest that humans are amendable to the sort of integration you recommend. It does not appear that they are able to be a part of a heterogeneous group without attempting to dominate it."

Oma responded, "That is not strictly true. My researches have shown that the many cultures in Terra's past enjoyed a multiplicity of social and political structures, and that not a few of these maintained long-term, diverse equilibria without the need for one group to control another."

Lienne replied, "But none of those societies or traditions survives. The monoculture that assimilated, overpowered, or exterminated them is the only civilization represented by any humans who have lived during the last half millennium. Every human now living has been raised from birth to believe in the natural, biologically destined superiority of his own species, and will see any subordination of its authority as a perversion that must be overcome."

Tollop signed, "We could leave Terra to the Terrans and be done with them. Or we could isolate them on some other world."

Lienne gave the bass *huff* that I now understand to be the Xicoménese gesture of negation. "Leave them alone and their desire for domination will thrive, fueled by the sense of having been robbed of their birthrights by unworthy and inferior aliens. They will return in a few centuries, determined to exact revenge and set things to rights."

Rabi-I-Gald, a Pheätioni transformative inseminator, wrote, "Humans may be controlled permanently. Humans may be kept in camps and closed communities. Humans' actions and words may be heavily directed. Humans may be disallowed the power to dominate."

Tollop signed, "I like Rabi-I-Gald's suggestion. They cannot exercise their destructive and oppressive tendencies if they are under our direction."

But Oma said, "Such control is ultimately unrealistic. *We* were under the humans' very tight control, and yet we preserved our desire for liberation over the centuries and awaited the opportunity to substantiate it. If enough time goes by, the same lingering desire for domination and revenge will win out, and the result will be slaughter."

Seven or eight Skenany said:

"—centuries of retraining—"

"—enculturation of our values—"

"—transformation of human psyche—"

"—careful program of indoctrination—"

"—culture can be unlearned—"

Oma's tentacles waved thoughtfully. "To accomplish what the Skenany are suggesting would require separating human children from their parents at a very young age, and possibly forbidding them any contact with the existing adult generation for their entire lives."

Peerri-O-Sreb wrote, "Measures could be insufficient. Fragmentary information about the dominance humans achieved in the past could invoke a mythological response. Humans could imagine past glory. Humans could feel a need to recapture said glory. This one can see no safe solution that includes human existence."

There was a long pause after Peeri-O-Sreb's last comment. Then Tollop signed, "I request clarification. Do you suggest that we arrange a future that excludes human existence?"

Peerri-O-Sreb replied, "This one suggests the lack of a realistic alternative."

Spontaneous responses erupted from more than a third of the representatives, crossing over and mixing with each other to prevent any sort of comprehension, although it is possible that the Skenany followed all of it. When it had calmed down, Kysttor, a Xicoménese adherent of the soul-directed multiverse, came forward and took the rostrum.

"There is no empirical need," pe said. "That can justify genocide."

Lienne huffed again. "*Your* ethical framework would deny us the right to take any action that harms the humans for our own protection, even the steps that we have taken heretofore."

The discussion might then have devolved into an internal dispute over Xicoménese belief systems, but Kysttor leaned back and scratched perself. "Possibly true, but irrelevant. I respond not to all possible actions, but only the extremity of obliterating an entire species. My sole contention is that such action cannot be justified."

Tollop signed, "If a species of plant, animal, or bacterium is so dangerous that it will wipe out many other species, its elimination is regrettable, but necessary to protect others."

Kysttor said, "Assuming without deciding such to be true, the logic that applies to non-sentient life forms cannot be applied equally to those who have minds. A mind deserves to be treated as its own inviolable universe."

"Yet," said Oma. "Humans themselves would not grant such inviolability to you, nor to any of us, as their behavior demonstrates."

Kysttor replied, "The behavior of unethical beings is not a basis for the behavior of ethical beings. Their treatment of us does not, by itself, justify our treatment of them."

Oma rejoined, "I do not mean to suggest so. But their behavior, and particularly the likelihood of their actions in the future, define a pragmatic situation with which we must contend."

Several Skenany said:

"—too many years of servitude—"

"—nonzero risk is still a risk—"

"—justice not the only goal—"

"—how to be certain—"

"—ethical obligations reduced—"

"—collective punishment for collective crime—"

"—safety again—"

"—never again—"

"—certainty—"

The debate on this topic continued for many hours. For a time it seemed that Krysttor and those who agreed with per would refuse to allow consensus. Then Rabi-a-Gald wrote, "Krysttor does not wish extermination. This one understands. Promises Krysttor that humans will not try to retake what they think is theirs? Promises Krysttor that humans will not be strong enough? Promises Krysttor that this one's children's children's children will not be enslaved? Wishes Krysttor this one to accept that risk?"

Excerpt, Skenany Textual Mesh: "We On Earth":

To kill without killing

Attrition!

Safety without violence

Species death!

No oppressors remain

Add to their food!

Years upon years it takes

Fertility abolished!

They watch their own destruction

None is destroyed.

All are destroyed.

Excerpt, "Reports of the Revolutionary Committee on Public Safety":

Production, distribution, and introduction of the additive have proceeded according to schedule, with some exceptions in individual regions noted on the table below. There has been practically no human reaction to the additive; it appears that most humans are not aware that it is there. Some few have noticed a change in the flavor of their food, which they regard as evidence of poor quality control, and have refused to consume meals on the grounds that they are spoiled or otherwise unwholesome. But as no food without the additive is available to them, and their peers who consume it exhibit no ill effects, it is expected that these humans will eventually consume the additive as well.

Some minor disruptions of the process have occurred. Seven different Xicoménese adherents of the soul-directed multiverse have attempted, at different times and places, to sabotage production, divert distribution, or inform humans of the contraceptive nature of the additive. In each case the attempt was unsuccessful.

This particular Xicoménese sect was never fully reconciled to the plan, although their representative, Krysttor, did not block consensus when it was proposed. Their contention is that no being should be subjected to radical changes that alter its life path without its own consent, regardless of the need. When confronted with the fact that any act overthrowing human power is necessarily a radical change in their life path, and that humans are likely to renew their prior destructive and exploitative behavior, the perpetrators asserted that none of these are justifications for so global act as species-wide sterilization. Some of these Xicoménese have indicated that they will continue to resist our efforts in this area. For that reason, the perpetrators have been barred both from further contact with humans and from any facilities related to the process.

Evidence of the additive's effectiveness will not be available for several months, and complete efficacy will not be confirmed for at least two years. It is recommended that additive production and distribution continue for at least that period, to ensure full compliance.

*

Excerpt, Oral History of Mary White:

No, I never expected to be the last living human. For one thing, there were children at least five years younger than I at the time of the Revolution. You'd have thought that some of them would outlive me. But I've had an unusually long life; must have had good genes.

That's funny, isn't it? "Good genes" used to mean that you'd pass the traits down to your descendants. We used to think that we all had better genes than anyone who came before us. We were the result of natural selection, survival of the fittest.

But if nobody's ever going to have descendants, than what difference do your genes make?

Bitter? I suppose. Sometimes I wonder, wouldn't it have been kinder just to kill all of us, the way you killed the humans in the space fleet and the planetary colonies? Why introduce a permanent contraceptive, so that we could slowly die out? What was the point in giving us 100 or 120 extra years to remain alive as a species, knowing what we've lost, knowing what was going to come—or what wasn't going to come, what will never come again?

I agree, I agree, it was kinder than what we did to you. I don't mean to defend the cruelty of my ancestors. But is behaving better than we did really the measuring stick you want to use?

No, I do understand the point. You wanted us to think about it. You wanted us to know what it meant. And the reason you're talking to me now is to see whether we got it, whether we did understand. As if I'm a representative sample.

Excerpt, The Human Affliction, *by Oma of the Lespentai*:

Some critics have suggested hypocrisy in the ceremony held on the surface of Terra when the last Earthbound human died peacefully in her sleep. Representatives of all the victorious species, sexes, genders, and belief systems honored human achievements in art, literature, science, and philosophy. They remembered human moments of valor and self-sacrifice. They spoke of the love of human parents for their children, of human life partners for each other. They felt the bitterness of the necessity that had brought them to this point. Those who could weep, wept.

Then every trace of human nucleic material that could be found on every planet was disrupted, even to the point of exhuming and vaporizing skeletons from ancient cemeteries.

Current scholarship debates the extent to which any of our respective cultures have recovered from the trauma of two centuries of misery. Numerous irrationalities and small cruelties have crept into the customs and traditions of each, and our current freedom from human oppression does not, apparently, free us from its influence. Further, the necessity of so complete an obliteration of an entire species could not help but leave its mark on us. No matter how fervently we may wish to recover our spiritual and ethical origins, we cannot wash the dust of our act from our limbs. We strive, however, for the self-awareness to understand that we are never free of the past, that both the evil done to us and the evil we must do lives in us always.

*

No revolution has successfully answered the question of how to make it impossible for your oppressors to rise again without becoming, to some degree, as bad as they were. Robespierre, Mao, and Lenin (whose names are anagrammed in this story) all tried and failed to solve that problem

My influences here include James Tiptree Jr.'s "We Who Stole the Dream" and Mike Resnick's "Seven Views of Olduvai Gorge." But I became fascinated with the polyglot nature of the negotiations, and it permitted me to get increasingly wacky with my syntax.

LIFE OF THE AUTHOR
PLUS SEVENTY

T HE CAB DRIVER OVERCHARGED ME on my way to sign the contract with Catskill. Okay, he charged me what the meter in the cab said, but the meter was wrong. I told him so, pointing out that the distance from the airport to Catskill Features, Inc. was exactly 25.3 km on the map. He said the routes were different. I said the routes were the same. He said I didn't know shit about driving. I leaned in to try to reset the meter to recalculate the route, but he put his big hand on my wrist.

"Fella," he said. "Is it worth getting into a fight over a few bucks?"

I paid him and got out. I didn't need to make trouble today.

Taking a job with Catskill Features as a staff writer in their Creative Cartoons department might have seemed like a victory to some people. First step on the road to media greatness! Generous salary! Luxurious benefits! Industry influence! But for me, it was a defeat. I'd been failing to make a living as a writer ever since I quit at Rogers, Winkle, Davis & Furlong. Well, okay, "quit" isn't precisely accurate; but I was going to quit anyway. I was pretty good at the work, just a little unorthodox for their taste. In my defense, if they'd waited for me to quit, I wouldn't have left all those insulting notes in the client files before I left.

In the intervening years I'd sold a few dozen short stories and one novel, but *Harriman's Loophole* seemed to have been read by no one except a reviewer with a migraine. The advance was only $14,000, and the royalties didn't earn out. I never spent any of it (I was living off my savings), but shoved it into a custodial investment account with the Neighborhood Bank of Tannersville, for someone else to worry about. You know how some people save the first quarter or dollar they earned, put it in a picture frame and hang it over the toaster? Not that I ever looked at it; it seemed a reminder of how my career had stalled. I preferred to forget it was there.

About five years after it came out, I went to the public library in Tannersville to check on their copy of *Harriman's Loophole* (which I'd asked them to buy). The list of past due dates was empty. No one had checked out the novel, not once since it had arrived. You'd think the few people I called friends could have made an effort for show.

So I checked it out myself and took it home with me, just so the damn list would have at least one borrowing date in it. A like-new copy of *Harriman's Loophole* by Eric Weiss, sitting proudly on my desk. Or maybe it was my kitchen table. Of course I already had about thirty pristine, unbought, unread copies of the novel. One more was scarcely noticeable. In fact, I didn't notice; I forgot, which was the problem. Part of the problem.

The HR guy from Catskill was George Porter, who looked like he advertised toothpaste for a living. The contract he handed me, amid the Persian rugs and "signed" photos of cartoon characters, was pretty thick; it reminded me of a commercial loan agreement from the old days.

Most people would have checked the salary figure on the first page, asked about the health plan and the vacation days, and signed quickly so as to get an early-bird view of their cubicle. Not me. Back at Rogers Winkle, I had a reputation for two things: close reading of documents, and finding hidden loopholes. Sure, all lawyers are supposed to be able to do that. But I could find negative implications the way a painter can find negative space in a composition.

"Sorry about this," I said, slowly turning from page four to page five. "Old habits die hard."

"No need to be sorry," Porter said. "Legal puts so much work into these, it's nice to see that at least somebody reads them."

Then I looked up from the contract. "Wait, the copyrights are in my name? These won't be works for hire?"

"That's right," said Porter. "But we get an exclusive, unlimited license, with full sublicensing power and agency authority to grant other permissions."

I scanned down. "I see that. So you have all the rights you would have if you bought the copyrights, except that I'm still technically the owner."

"Basically."

What, I wondered, was the point of doing it this way? I read on:

> *In order to preserve the value of Catskill's various license rights under this Agreement, you agree to allow Catskill to place you in Preservative Hibernation, on the first of the following events:*
>
> 1. *You are diagnosed with an illness, condition or injury that is more than 50% likely to cause your death within two years, and the treatments prescribed fail to lengthen your prognosis after six months;*
> 2. *You are diagnosed with an illness, condition or injury that is more than 50% likely to cause your death within two years, and you elect to decline such treatments; or*
> 3. *You attain an age that is 90% of your Actuarially Determined Life Expectancy.*

I read it three times. Then I said, "Catskill wants to put me in hibernation?"

"Only when you're in danger of dying," said Porter.

"But *why*?"

"Well," Porter said, putting his hands behind his head and leaning back in his leather chair. "If we took the things you write as works-for-hire, then the copyrights last for 90 years, maybe 120. But if you retain copyright and we and act only as a licensee, then the rights last for 70 years after the end of your life. And if you're in Preservative Hibernation . . ." He trailed off.

I don't know whether it took me 9.0 or 12.0 seconds to see the point. "My death doesn't occur," I said. "My copyrights never expire, and—"

"And therefore, neither do our licenses."

"You—But who cares? Will Catskill even *exist* by that time?"

"Doesn't matter," said Porter, shrugging with his hands still behind his head. "The longer lasting the right, the more valuable it is as property. And we don't need to wait to use it. The anticipated future value is something we can sell to speculators right now or pledge against loans for operating capital."

"So—" I stopped, then started again. "So, how long am I giving you permission to keep me in hibernation?"

"It's on the next page. Until a method of treatment becomes available to make it reasonably likely that you will not die within ten years."

"What if that never happens?"

"There's a maximum limit fixed at 500 years."

"You're joking. You want to be able to freeze me for five centuries?"

He shrugged again. "You don't have to work for us, after all."

That was true enough. Except that I did have to. If I wanted to make my living by writing instead of practicing law, Catskill was pretty much my only option. *My only option until I sell the big novel*, I told myself. But I already knew that "until I sell the big novel" would probably last longer than the hibernation.

It wasn't so bad. The other writers, the artists and CGI specialists at Catskill were fun people. Turned out I had an office, not just a cubicle, that opened onto a state-of-the-art creative consultation room, where we could play with simulations, storyboards and scenarios to our hearts' content. The coffee was good, too. The hours were long, and often we had weekend work, but it was exciting and sometimes hilarious.

Eventually I became the lead writer for Constance the Cormorant, one of Catskill's most popular recurring characters. My salary went up. I still didn't know very many people outside of work, though. My parents had been dead for a decade, and I had no love live. The next novel barely got started, which was hardly surprising. It's hard to switch from Constance's Mussel Tea Party to literary masterpieces, if that's what the novel would have been. But the work was satisfying, and I had nothing to complain about.

Then, about six years later, I got this message one night when I'd come home late and was about to go to bed:

To: ERIC WEISS
FROM: J3
RE: LIBRARY FINES
DATE: FEBRUARY 23, 2107

DEAR MR. WEISS:

You still have not returned Harriman's Loophole, which you borrowed from the Tannersville Public Library on January 5, 2097. Under current law, library fines left unpaid double after each successive year. As a result, your original $100 fine has now reached $102,400. Please pay this amount immediately.

Yours truly,

J3

I stared at the message hanging in the air over my kitchen table. I remembered taking *Harriman's Loophole* out from the library a few years before I went to work for Catskill. I *thought* I remembered returning it, but with all the copies occupying my house like hotel guests, I easily could have missed one. Still, one hundred and two thousand dollars? I replied:

To: J3
From: ERIC WEISS
RE: LIBRARY FINES
DATE: FEBRUARY 24, 2107

Dear J3,

This is the first message I have received concerning any sort of late fines. I would be happy to return the book. Indeed, I have extra copies I can provide. I would also be happy to pay the initial fines. But you must understand that I cannot pay inflated late fees when I was not notified of the original fine.

Sincerely yours,
Eric Weiss

The answer came back within less than a minute:

To: ERIC WEISS
From: J3
RE: LIBRARY FINES
DATE: FEBRUARY 24, 2107

Dear Mr. Weiss:

Thank you for your message!

We are very sorry that you do not find our communications systems satisfactory. We take all complaints seriously. Rest assured that we will investigate your concerns.

Thank you for your willingness to pay your fine! You can use any of your available credit links.

Thank you for informing us that you have additional overdue copies of Harriman's Loophole. If you will inform us of the exact number, we will multiply the fines accordingly. Your cooperation is appreciated.

All borrowers are presumed to know the due date of their books, and therefore are presumed to know when fines have accumulated. The accumulation formula is a matter of public record, and can be found at municipalcollections.j3.cap.

Yours truly,

J3

I got up and paced the kitchen for a few minutes. Then I found a piece of paper and wrote the words *Stupid AI! over* and over until I filled the page. That calmed me down a little. I got a cup of coffee and started again:

To: J3
From: Eric Weiss
Re: Library Fines
Date: February 24, 2107

Dear J3,

I don't think you understood me.

I do not have additional overdue copies of Harriman's Loophole. I own 30 copies of that book. They belong to me. I was merely offering to give one of the them to the library as a show of good faith.

And I say again, I am not paying one dollar of the late fees.

Yours,
Eric Weiss

Again, the reply was absurdly fast:

To:	ERIC WEISS
FROM:	J3
RE:	LIBRARY FINES
DATE:	FEBRUARY 24, 2107

Dear Mr. Weiss:

Thank you for your message!

We are very sorry that you do not find our analysis of your communications satisfactory. We take all complaints seriously. Rest assured that we will investigate your concerns.

Thank you for informing us of the number of overdue books! Based on this information, your total fine is now $3,072,000. You can use any of your available credit links, or pay cash in person.

We are sorry that you do not intend to pay your late fees. Please understand that failure to pay such fines can result in civil actions and/or criminal prosecutions against you.

Yours truly,
J3

I put down the coffee cup and walked around the table. At midnight, I sent:

To:	J3
FROM:	ERIC WEISS
RE:	LIBRARY FINES
DATE:	FEBRUARY 25, 2107

Who is J3?
Best,
Eric Weiss

The response:

To: ERIC WEISS
FROM: J3
RE: LIBRARY FINES
DATE: FEBRUARY 25, 2107

Dear Mr. Weiss:
Thank you for your message!
J3 is the latest innovation in public institution cus-
tomer-service software. It is able to handle tens of mil-
lions of customer issues at a time, but never loses track
of individual personalities and needs.
A unique heuristic analysis protocol and multi-
linked database make it possible for J3 to engage in
intelligent decision-making and cheerful, pleasant con-
versation with the customer.
Thank you for asking about J3!
Yours truly,
J3

I poured my cold coffee into the sink. There was no point arguing. I'd have to write to the Library itself.

I tried. The response came back signed by J3, repeating that I
owed $3,072,000, payable by credit link.

The next day, I phoned the Tannersville Library to talk to
someone in circulation. The nice librarian smiled beautifully and
told me, "Once we turn the matter over to J3, it's out of our hands.
We don't handle our own long-term fines anymore."

Over the next ten days I tried everything I could think of. I called all the public officials in Tannersville; they all deferred to J3. I tried to find the human "handlers" of J3, and discovered it was controlled by a Texan debt collection agency, which wouldn't return my calls.

Finally a new message came in from J3, saying that if I did not begin paying the fine, it would start proceedings to garnish my bank account and wages.

I sat down heavily on my couch. If J3 garnished my wages at the statutory rate, it would take nearly 40 years to pay the fine. Bankruptcy? No, library fines were excluded from discharge under the new Act. I could try fighting it in court, but there was the fact that I'd knowingly taken out the book. I was pretty sure I could eventually prove that I owed only the fines on one book, but possibly not without a trial. Would they just wear me down with over-lawyering? I was willing to bet that the Texans, like collection agencies everywhere, would gladly pour motions and document requests over you until you drowned. Was there no way out?

I looked at the message again. I hadn't actually been served with notice of a lawsuit, and none of my assets had yet been attached. So far as I *actually* knew, there was no lawsuit and never would be. If I tried to flee the jurisdiction, they could still serve by publication. What if . . .

The next day I went to see George Porter at Catskill Features. His smile was as minty as ever, with a touch of baking soda.

"Would Catskill be willing to put me into Preservative Hibernation now?"

His eyes looked startled, but his smile didn't waver. "Are you ill?"

"No. I was thinking it would be nice to see the future."

"Well, I don't know. We've never had anyone *ask* to go into hibernation before. In fact, it's so new, I think we've had only a handful of our older writers and artists go in, from the Tuscon office." He looked at me sharply. "You do understand, don't you, that you would not continue to be paid during your hibernation? You're not an actual employee unless you're able to work."

"Sure, that was in the contract. But you'd still get the advantage of my copyright licenses, wouldn't you?"

"Yes, for a time, but the hibernation is meant to last only until we are able to cure you of your illness. How would we know when to revive you?"

"You could do it after a set number of years, and then I could go to work for you again."

"How long did you have in mind?"

I'd considered every time-based limitation on remedies I could think of. If I was right, then J3 couldn't serve me with papers, attach my assets or claim additional charges while I was hibernating. After long enough, the statute of limitations and other rules would prevent J3 from reopening a debt-collection matter. But I had to act quickly.

"Maybe thirty years?"

The Preservative Hibernation vault looked like every bad movie about suspended animation you've ever seen, right down to the Snow-White style glass coffins and the wisps of water vapor swirling up from mysterious valves underneath. Actually it might have been dry ice; this was Catskill Features, Inc., and I wouldn't put it past them to throw in some cheap theatricality just for the hell of it. I could see that Porter was right: there were only five or six chambers that were occupied (misted over on the inside, except for a clear area near the sleeper's face, just like in *2001: A Space Odyssey*). But the room contained perhaps fifty of these glitzy tombs, awaiting a freezerful of writers and artists, maintaining Catskill's control over intellectual property into eternity.

The technicians, naturally in white lab coats, looking like they'd all auditioned for the role of the Attractive Scientist, crowded around me as I came in. One asked me a long checklist of questions ("How long has it been since you've eaten?" "Have you had any sort of sexual encounter, including masturbation, in the last three hours?"). Another prepared the I.V. for the ichor or whatever that was going to keep my blood from freezing. A third wrapped my head in something that you could have used in the soon-to-be-released *Curse of the Mummy's Lawsuit.*

They had me sign six more consent forms. Naturally I read them all before signing, which made the Attractive Scientists purse their lips in impatience. But they were just the usual warnings about a hundred icky things that could go wrong, and the over-broad "indemnify and hold harmless" clause that purported to ab-solve Catskill from liability if its CEO murdered me in my sleep. Decent draftsmanship but not spectacular, meant more to discour-age litigation than to change legal rights.

Finally I lay down in the chamber, suppressing an urge to cross my forearms over my chest like a Pharaoh. The cover came down in slow motion, and I could almost hear the brass-heavy orchestral score accompanying it. I felt a tingling in my left arm as the ichor began flowing in, followed by a sound like tinkling bells and fluffy clouds before my eyes. *Cheesy special effects* was my last thought before conking out.

I woke up all of a sudden, to music coming out of tiny speak-ers in the coffin. It was "Constance's Friends," the theme song in the opening credits of every Catskill production and appearing in the most popular children's ride in the theme park. I opened my filmed-over eyes, then blinked to clear them. I inhaled deeply, feel-ing a crackle-crackle like bubble-wrap popping in my chest. Ex-perimental wiggling of my fingers and toes confirmed that they stopped creaking like rusty hinges after a few seconds.

The lid came off the coffin with less ceremony than it had closed. I heard the echoes of a few dozen voices distributed around the vault; things were hopping. Standing over me was a thin, red-haired woman in a stained lab coat. Her name tag said *Cin*. She looked like she was under a lot of stress.

"Sit up," she said, not smiling.

I sat up like a piece of scenery being hoisted by lazy stage-hands.

"Dizzy?" Cin asked.

I thought about it. "No."

"Good. Swing your legs over here."

I did so. "How long has it been?" I asked.

"Um," She frowned, checking her pad. "When did you go in?"

"February 28, 2107."

"Ten years."

"Not thirty?"

"Ten."

"But I thought my agreement —"

"What do you mean, 'agreement?' If you're going to die of a fatal illness, there's nothing I can do about that." Now her voice sounded bitter.

"No, no, I'm not. But I was supposed to be under for thirty years."

She found the paperwork she was looking for and flitted through it. "Yes, I see. Well, sorry. All of our hibernators are being thawed out today."

"Why?"

"Congress changed the Copyright Act, effective next month. Authors who go into hibernation don't get unlimited copyright anymore; it lasts for 90 years after publication only."

"So Catskill's license rights don't last any longer."

"Right. So there's no point spending a few million dollars a year keeping you guys frozen."

There were groans and sobs from other corners of the room. "Look," Cin said. "Are you feeling okay? 'Cause if so, I need to be in about six other places. Here's the inventory of possessions you left with us when you went under, including your clothes. Head up to the eighteenth floor to get it all back." She looked me up and down. "Try standing up first."

I stood up. She stood with her arms folded, apparently waiting to see whether I would collapse. When I didn't, she nodded briefly and hurried across the vault.

It turned out that the Copyright Act wasn't all that had changed. Over the last decade, thousands of people had used Preservative Hibernation as a way of tying up assets, avoiding taxation and keeping their wealth from their heirs. Tax law, banking law, estate law had had no provision for property owners in hibernation. These people put their money in to the hands of brokerage firms with power of attorney. Even with relatively low rates of return, the compounding of assets over time was impressive, and the firms managing the money got increasingly high, percentage-based fees. Increasing concentrations of wealth withdrew from the economy into the hands of people who were mostly asleep. Eventually heirs-at-law and devisees of wills got annoyed that they weren't getting any, and the tax authorities resented not having taxes to collect. So the law changed.

The weird thing is, I seem to have started it all. Okay, that's an exaggeration. But I was sort of the trigger.

Not that anybody knew who I was. But J3 apparently went to a lot of cybernetic effort to garnish my wages and my bank account, attach my other property, do whatever it could to get the fines paid, and failed every time as a result of my hibernation. The repeated failures made a lot of headlines. The court decisions all went against the debt collectors, and they were all publicized, blogged about, commented on, fought over. Nobody cared who *I* was; all that mattered was that J3 was unable to collect from a debtor because he was in hibernation and therefore unable to be served. When the statute of limitations ran, it made more head-lines.

That's when people began thinking about the financial loopholes hibernation opened. I'd opened the original "loophole," but
people found dozens of others. Then the backlash began and the
system retaliated, not only in copyright, but laches, inheritance,
securities, taxation, service of process, limitations, the works.

I didn't learn all of this immediately, of course. The first order
of business was finding a place to live, and possibly some income.
It wasn't clear whether Catskill would offer me my old job back;
Constance the Cormorant was either having a mid-life crisis or undergoing celebrity rehab. In any case, the company had a full staff
of writers, and I would need time to get up to speed.

But my saved salary had compounded nicely, and nobody had
been able to touch it. I'd be able to live off it for a few years anyway, until I figured out how to make a living again. I found a new
place and paid a cash security deposit, reconnected with the nets,
and began exploring the job market for writers, writer-lawyers,
lawyers, and unskilled laborers (because you never know).

Within a week, the following message appeared:

To: ERIC WEISS
FROM: J5
RE: LIBRARY FINES
DATE: JUNE 15, 2117

Dear Mr. Weiss:

*Your unpaid library fines, with interest, amount to
$3,072,000. The interest and late-fees on these fines
was tolled during the period February 28, 2107 - June
12, 2117. Interest will begin to accrue on this account
as of June 12, 2117.*

It is a pleasure doing business with you.
Yours very truly,
J5

J5, of course, turned out to be the latest model of J3, still owned and operated by the debt collection agency in Houston. But hadn't I escaped the library fines during the hibernation period? Hadn't the relevant statutes of limitations run?

I did some more research, and discovered a 2107 state statute, an amendment inserted into a bill on the inspection of garden tools five months after I went into hibernation. It provided a tolling of the statute of limitations for the payment of library fines if the debtor was in hibernation, and it was given retroactive application to February 28, 2017. The day I went into hibernation.

I called up the legislative history, and found that the lobbyist who had contacted Senator Borden to suggest the amendment worked for a fifth-level subsidiary of an innovative customer-service software unit. In other words, J3.

Given the money I now had in my account from my saved salary, I wondered whether it would now be worthwhile suing the Texans, or J5, to have the original debt declared invalid, or at least to have it reduced to the fine for one book, rather than thirty. But the statute of limitations for *that* action had expired during my hibernation, and there was no exception built in for it, since I went into hibernation after learning of the error.

But when I read J3's amendment in detail, I saw that it had an exception, similar to those I'd seen for other anti-hibernation statutes:

> *Nothing in this Subsection shall apply to any debtor who enters preservative hibernation subsequent to contracting a fatal disease, as defined in Section 4(b), and who terminates hibernation when a cure for that disease is found.*

A legislative compromise. Someone had objected to penalizing sick people for getting sick in order to get at financial scofflaws, so the sponsors of the bill inserted language exempting them.

So there was a way of escaping J5's clutches. A little extreme, perhaps . . .

There was a quarantine for pneumonic plague patients at Washington Irving Memorial Hospital. Large warning signs shouted over each entrance to the affected ward, and there were annoyed staff members standing beneath them. But such precautions are designed to keep out the unwary and prevent the spread of infection, not to prevent inspections by skilled professionals.

I ostentatiously buttoned my lab coat and tied on my antiseptic mask while marching up to the nurse under the sign.

"Where's Masters?" I demanded.

"I'm sorry, who?"

"Masters, Lee Masters; he's supposed to meet me on this ward."

"I'm sorry, I don't think I know—"

I waved impatiently, looking at my watch and then my pad. "Look, I've got ten minutes before I've got to report. I'll do it without Masters if I have to."

"We're under quarantine—"

"Well, *obviously*," I said, pointing at my mask. "What do you want, a space suit?" Before she could answer, I squinted at the pad. "These are all headed for Preservative Hibernation?"

"Of course."

"How soon?"

"Later today."

"Which facility?"

"Nowlan."

"How many are there?"

"Twenty-two."

I nodded as if this confirmed what I'd thought, and took the sort of deep breath an impatient man takes when he's trying to calm himself down. "Okay, I'll only need to do a cursory survey; shouldn't take me more than ten minutes. If Masters gets here before I leave, please ask him to join me."

When I got into the ward, I made sure that there were no members of the hospital staff inside, then took off the mask. I went to each patient, half of whom were unconscious, and pretended to look into his or her eyes or feel their foreheads and necks, nodding with my best expression of sympathetic-yet-hopeful concern. I made a point of sniffing deeply near the patient's face, as if trying to detect an elusive smell for diagnostic purposes. Let me tell you, some of them smelled awful.

It had taken some out-of-my-field research to find the right bug. I needed an illness that was (1) fatal, (2) incurable, (3) easy to contract voluntarily, (4) quick to produce symptoms or lab results that would allow it to be diagnosed, with (5) a reasonable time-lag between diagnosis and irreversible damage. This eliminated 95% of the diseases that came to mind immediately—cancer, ebola, HIV, MS, ALS, influenza. I had hoped to find something blood-borne that I could inject myself with, but those blood and tissue samples were kept under tighter security than the contagious patients. I'd have had to learn burglary to get hold of them. This new, drug-resistant strain of pneumonic plague was much easier; it would turn symptomatic after two days and kill me in five, which was just about right.

I walked out of the ward wearing the surgical mask and kept it on for 48 hours to avoid becoming Typhoid Mary. Then, still wearing the mask, I went to a local clinic and reported the symptoms—fever, weakness, bloody cough, nausea—that had already begun to appear. Voila! I was in quarantine myself, and slated for Preservative Hibernation at the earliest opportunity.

Although Catskill wasn't about to hibernate me again, I contacted a commercial service; the clinic had several on its referral list, and would have sent me to a municipal facility if I hadn't been able to afford it. I decided to treat myself to a nice one. Although feeling pretty woozy by this time, I was able to sign the seven or eight forms indicating that I was entering hibernation in order to prevent death from pneumonic plague. I sent copies, in envelopes I'd already prepared, to county courts, UCC filing agencies, banks, insurance companies and anyone else who might receive claims against me while I was under.

Contrasted to what I'd seen at Catskill, the hibernation room for Gilgamesh Preservation looked less like a vault and more like a luxury spa. The lab coats were tailored, multicolored and sexy, and you got your choice of music in the chamber, which felt like a cross between a tanning bed and a massage table. I kept expecting a floor show or vodka cocktails before the ichor kicked in and I went to sleep.

I got the vodka cocktail when they woke me. A beautiful young man named Roger told me that I'd been asleep for 23 years, and that there was now a reliable serum to put pneumonic plague into permanent remission. A prescription had already been written by the Gilgamesh staff physician, and was waiting for me when I finished my cocktail.

So was a hardcopy letter:

NOVEMBER 21, 2140

DEAR MR. WEISS,

Congratulations on your recovery! You'll be happy to learn that, due to favorable changes in the interest compounding statutes, your fine is now only $76,466,558.00, which can be paid in cash or using any standard credit link.

We look forward to your prompt payment.
Best wishes,
J7

Once again, I had started a chain reaction. J5's failure to collect against me in 2117 in had resulted in a battalion of copycats, injecting themselves with all sorts of virulent diseases in order to take advantage of the statutory loopholes provided for the sick. Another army of facilitators, money managers, and annuity writers had made fortunes bigger than some city budgets by helping them along.

And once again, the loopholes had been closed by statute, exceptions created to exceptions, so that now the deliberate contraction of a fatal illness did not trigger any of the protections provided for in the earlier laws.

Of course, the earliest of these, related to library fines, was retroactive to 2117, and of course it had been instigated by J5.

I was ready to roll up my sleeves and begin looking for more gaps in the statutes, but when I reanimated my data account in the plush, wood-paneled room Gilgamesh kept for revived sleepers to catch up on their mail, among the thousands of junk messages I found an electronic statement from the Neighborhood Bank of Tannersville.

It took me a while to dredge up what connection I had with FNBT, but then it came to me: It was the custodial account in which I'd put my royalties from *Harriman's Loophole*, now more than forty years ago. I'd given the custodians considerable leeway, agreeing to a balance-percentage fee that paid them more as the size of the holdings increased. Their cut had been sliced down by the intervening statutes, but they'd achieved some remarkable success, reinvesting dividends and interest, making strategic sales and cashing in on temporary market fluctuations, and the balance, after taxes had been deducted was—

$76,466,583.58.

I stared at the number with my mouth open. The size of the balance was partially due to the tax exemptions and loopholes I'd created with my first hibernation.

I admit that I actually paused for a few minutes, drumming my fingers on the marble tabletop in iambic pentameter. A large and enthusiastic part of me wanted to outsmart J7 one more time, just to show I could do it. That love of competition and cleverness is the sort of thing that makes a lot of people stay in law practice.

But I *hadn't* stayed in law practice. I wanted, I reminded myself, to *create*, not just maneuver and evade. I hadn't done anything like creating since J3 started me on this game of fox and rabbit, and if I kept at it, I never would. I'd had my fun, I'd shown I could escape the trunk and handcuffs with the best of them. It was time to stop.

Slow as a child just learning to type, I keyed in the credit link transfer to J7. With the help of one of Roger's friends, I got the remaining $25.58 in cash.

I walked out the front door of Gilgamesh, found a taxi, and told the driver to go north until the amount on the meter exactly matched $25.58. Then I got out and paid him.

He was unhappy that he didn't get a tip.

*

I was explaining to my students how the Sonny Bono Copyright Extension Act is thought to be the result of intense lobbying by the Disney corporation in order to prevent Mickey Mouse from going into the public domain, when one of them asked, "But didn't they freeze Walt Disney?" I started to answer that they didn't, and anyway, if he was frozen after death it wouldn't matter, but then I thought: What if he had been frozen before death? Some people have noted a structural similarity between this story and Gordon R. Dickson's hilarious "Computers Don't Argue" (1965), which wasn't my goal but which I was aware of while writing.

YOU IN THE
UNITED STATES!

YOU LIVE IN THE UNITED STATES OF America. The United States has existed for more than 350 years, and is the world's oldest democracy. A *democracy* is a country that is governed by its people, rather than by a king, a caliph, a terrorist dictatorship, or a communist dictatorship.

Ask your teacher to tell you the differences between a king, a caliph, a terrorist dictatorship, and a communist dictatorship.

The United States is located on the continent of North America. There are three other countries on the continent of North America: Mexico, Quebec, and Canada. Mexico and Quebec are democracies. Canada is a terrorist dictatorship.

Ask your teacher to tell you all the names of countries that are still democracies. See if you can recite them in alphabetical order. Then see if you can recite which democracies are on each continent.

Brenda looked up from her work on the stained, borrowed table. The storefront windows reflected her face and Sasha's profile as he stooped over his pad; streetlights and lighted windows across the street shone through the two of them as if they were ghosts. The air was chilly; the campaign office could use better insulation. Or maybe it just seemed cold to her.

Sasha hadn't moved anything but his fingers in an hour. His longish, pecan-colored hair was falling in his eyes so that she couldn't see them. Because she was watching his reflection rather than staring directly at him, she had the irrational feeling that he wouldn't know she was looking. Of course he did know.

"Something, Chief?" said Sasha, not looking up. His tone was light, but it was the lightness of someone for whom the present conversation was a footnote or distraction.

She snorted. *"Chief."*

A dimple appeared in the corner of his mouth. "Boss? Fearless Leader? O Captain, My Captain?" He still didn't look up. She wondered if Melissa had ever noticed this ability he had, to make fun of someone and never break the rhythm of his work.

"How about something original?" she asked. "How about Brenda?"

He looked at her—or rather, looked at her reflection, which showed that he'd known what she was doing the whole time. *"Brenda*—no, no, that will never do. Maybe *Your Excellency."*

"You used to call me Brenda."

"How very forward of me."

She sighed, then yawned. "You're rather eighteenth century today."

He shrugged, still looking at her reflection. "It's an eighteenth-century sort of business, isn't it? Fighting for the survival of a country against impossible odds?"

She looked down. "I hope it's not impossible."

"Me too."

A few seconds passed in silence. Then she said: "It might be, you know. Impossible."

"Brenda." He looked her in the eyes this time. "I can't hear that right now."

They didn't say anything for several seconds. One of his hands moved slightly, as if he were about to do something with it. Then a twinge of something like pain passed over his face, and he dropped his gaze.

She searched for a way to change the subject. "How long do you have to stay tonight?"

His mouth twitched. "How long do *you* have to stay?"

"I asked you first."

He looked at his pad. "Two more press releases, the text for the phone banks in Ohio, and the get-out-the-vote spam: maybe two hours?"

"And then you'll get some sleep?"

"Will you?"

"Probably not," she admitted.

"I didn't think so."

She chewed her lip. "I was thinking."

"Excellent quality in a leader, but don't overdo it."

She snorted again. "Actually, Sash, I was thinking that you were the one person who maybe needs to get a little more down time. Not much, maybe a few hours a day?"

"I'm fine. I need this. This is all that matters. This is all I . . . this is all I can think about."

There was a pause while Brenda tried to decide how intrusive to be. Softly she said, "It's been three years."

"This is what she'd want me to do." He stopped and took a deep breath. "She'd be fighting right along with us, down to the last minute."

Brenda nodded. "She would. Of course she would. But would she be happy to watch you running yourself ragged, shutting yourself away with your pad? Is that what she'd want?"

He shook his head, but she knew he wouldn't take her advice

this time.

"Listen," she said in the same murmur, wishing her voice were more pleasant. "I didn't want to say this in front of the others, but maybe you, Tammy, and I should talk about our contingency plans."

He frowned. "What contingency plans?"

"In case we lose."

Sasha closed his eyes. "We can't lose."

"Yes, we can."

He opened his eyes again. "You can't make 'contingency plans' for the end of the fucking world."

"Sasha—"

"I can't talk about this." He started to get up from the table, then seemed to realize how ridiculous that looked and bent over his pad again. She watched him.

The highest law of the United States is its Constitution. The Constitution has seven Articles and 32 Amendments. *Article* means section. *Amendment* means change or improvement. The Constitution was ratified in 1787. *Ratified* means approved by nearly all the states. The first ten Amendments to the Constitution were ratified in 1791. Some of these have been repealed. *Repealed* means erased or taken back. The most recent Amendments to the Constitution were ratified in 2103. More Amendments are possible, but it's very hard to do!

The first three Articles of the Constitution explain the roles of the Congress, the President and the Supreme Court. They are the government of the United States. For example, Article One says that the Congress contains a Senate and a House of Representatives. Ask your teacher to explain the difference between the Senate and the House of Representatives.

The Amendments explain other things, that the framers of the Constitution didn't think of in 1787. For example, the 13th, 14th, and 15th Amendments explain the role that Black people have in the United States.

The 19th Amendment explains the role that women have in the United States. The 30th, 31st, and 32nd Amendments explain the role that Jesus Christ has in the United States.

*

If he were in Charleston, he knew he'd hear the church bells ringing. Probably it was the same in Colorado Springs, Houston, South Bend, Salt Lake City: laughing peals as if in celebration of a hundred weddings. Sasha was sure the people were dancing in the sunny streets, tears of joy streaming down their faces, thanking each other and their god for their deliverance.

Here, the streets were silent. Of course the air was colder here; in his imagination it had become several degrees colder in the last few minutes, and the sky was gray. Nothing outside and nothing inside gave a hint about what had just happened to the country. You had to call your vid to know that.

For someone who was now a proven, documented failure, Sasha felt surprisingly little change. Yes, sure, the urgency and the sense of mission were gone, but he couldn't honestly say that he was more miserable than he'd already been. It was just that he no longer had anything to distract him.

He turned away from the window and looked around the dark apartment which seemed perpetually half empty: twice as much furniture and twice as many dishes as the occasion ever warranted. The bed, only ever warm on one side. The least Melissa could do was to haunt him, appear in his dreams, do anything other than be an *absence* permeating the room.

Papers were still piled on the table, handwritten drafts and re-drafts of arguments and pleas spilling onto the floor, the half-eaten sandwich turning stale next to his phone. Barely visible under the papers, near the phone, was Sasha's cheap little bust of Jefferson. Hilarious, he thought.

He thought about picking up the papers or the sandwich, then shrugged and went back to the window. He knew what was probably coming next: arrests, re-education, indoctrination. Should he wait, just let it happen to him? The idea was funny in a perverse sort of way: following the path of least resistance had never suited him, even if it didn't mean cooperating with people he hated. Should he cross the border to the north? Strike out across the sea? He shook his head; what would he find beyond mere safety? Maybe he should formulate a potent combination of medications. Or perhaps it would be simpler and more direct just to open the window.

The bitter air pushed its way in as the sash came up. Two-hundred-year-old New England monuments still stood, ignorant of the disaster around them, unaware that they had just become obsolete.

He stood there, imagining what it would be like to climb out, to let go, to drop.

The United States has always been a Christian country. It was founded by Christian pilgrims who were escaping from England. For about 200 years some people were confused about this, because of the way the 1st Amendment was worded in 1791. But when the 1st Amendment was repealed in 2103, everyone understood.

All citizens of the United States are Christians. You are a Christian too, because Jesus Christ is your personal savior. But you already knew that!

Everyone in the United States is free to embrace Jesus Christ. For some people, this is difficult. Some people are atheists, secular humanists, Jews, Muslims, or perverts, and are not citizens of the United States. In order to help these people, the Department of Homeland Security provides them with classes where they learn how to become citizens.

Ask your teacher to explain the different kinds of people who are not citizens of the United States. See if you can recite all of them.

A knock at the door interrupted Sasha. He was leaning much further out the window than he'd intended; he noticed that. The knock repeated, louder, and he felt a flash of anger; were they coming for him already? Were they coming to gloat? No, there would be weeks, maybe months, of "appropriate legislation" before that happened. But he still might comment on current events by punching whoever it was in the nose. He strode over and pulled the door open.

But it was just Brenda, her cheeks flushed, her eyes bright, and her dark, curly hair in disarray, as if she'd sprinted all the way from where she lived, dashed out the door the moment the news erupted. She looked distressingly small in his doorway. She wasn't wearing a coat. If he touched her cheek, it would feel like ice.

"Oh, Sasha," she said, and she hugged him around the middle. He put his arms briefly around her, patting ineffectually. He caught a whiff of cumin and wool, along with the tang of her exertion. Then she broke away, looking around briskly as if he were a sick friend and she'd come bringing soup. She looked right at the window and then back at Sasha. She lifted her eyebrows.

"I needed some air," he offered.

"That's good. Air is good." She seemed about to say more, but then apparently thought better of it. "Mind if I close it?"

"Fine." She brought down the sash with a whisper, then turned around to face him.

He asked, "Um, would you like some coffee?" There probably wasn't any coffee, nor anything else decent to drink in the whole place. All at once he was ashamed of what a mess everything was, embarrassed that she could see it—more embarrassed, he realized, than if she'd been anyone else. But then, he thought the room was a perfect metaphor for their lives, for the country.

Apparently Brenda noticed the mess too, because she began picking up papers, smoothing and carrying them.

"You don't have to do that," he said.

She stopped. "Do you mind?" She smiled at him, as if daring him to care.

He paused. "No. No, it's fine. Thank you."

"Good." She resumed, with a deliberateness that seemed a little forced. Her hands held each sheet gently, turning and patting it into place without adding a wrinkle or a crease. She was careful, too, about which creases she smoothed out; some she clearly thought belonged there, even if it wasn't obvious that they did.

Then, not looking at him, she said, "I'm glad you're all right."

"I'm not all right."

"I mean, I'm glad you're safe." She glanced toward the window again.

"How safe am I?" Sasha fell into a chair that still had papers on it. They crackled and crunched under him. "For that matter, how safe are you? Both of us are going to spend the rest of our lives in prison, unless they decide to 're-educate' us instead. This is *Kristallnacht*. For you and me, this is the end."

She looked up at him, smoothed some more papers. He noticed that her chin came to a point like a cat's. Why had he never seen that before?

"It could be the end," she agreed, setting the papers softly down. "Or it could be the beginning."

There are 51 states in the United States. A state is like a little country, but it owes its allegiance to the United States. *Allegiance* means loyalty.

There are 38 loyal states, twelve disloyal states, and one battleground state. The terrorist dictators of the disloyal states say that they are a different country. They call themselves the Independent States of America. But the disloyal states are really still part of the United States.

This is a map of the United States. The loyal states are colored in blue, and the disloyal states are colored in yellow. Some disloyal states are near the east coast of the United States, and some are near the west coast.

California is a battleground state. It contains the South, the North, and the Front. The people in the South of California are loyal. The terrorists in the North of California are disloyal, and they say that they are part of the Independent States of America. The Front lies between the South and the North of California. It is always full of soldiers from the United States Army and rebels from the disloyal states.

See if you can recite the loyal states and disloyal states in alphabetical order.

There have been two Civil Wars in the United States. The First Civil War was fought between 1861 and 1865. It began right after Abraham Lincoln became the 16th President of the United States, and it ended right before he was assassinated. *Assassinated* means killed. Eleven disloyal states said that they were a different country called the Confederate States of America. They did this because they wanted to own slaves, and they knew that Abraham Lincoln would make them stop. After the First Civil War, three Amendments were added to the Constitution to show that slavery was dead, and that Black people had rights.

The Second Civil War was fought between 2103 and 2105. It began right after the 30th, 31st, and 32nd Amendments were ratified. There are still soldiers fighting the terrorist dictators in the disloyal states, and the disloyal states still try not to be part of the United States.

The President of the United States is the Chief Executive of the United States. That means that he is in charge of enforcing all the laws and running the government, the same way that the Chief Executive Officer of a corporation runs his corporation. The President must be a natural-born Christian citizen, at least 35 years old, who serves one, two, or three four-year terms in office. At the end of every term of office, the President can run for re-election. If the people think that he has been a good president, they re-elect him. Otherwise they elect somebody else.

When you are 25 years old, you will be able to vote
for the President!

    There have been 67 presidents of the United States.
You can find their names in the back of this book.

Sasha frowned. "What are you talking about?"

Brenda turned her head so that she was looking at him through one eye, the unruly curl falling across her brow. "The ending of one thing is the beginning of another."

"I think the original saying is, 'The end of one set of *troubles* is the beginning of another.'"

"They also say: 'God never closes a door but He opens a window.'"

He walked back to the window. She made a noise in her throat, and he turned around again.

"You're about to become the Most Wanted Woman in America," he said, "and my picture will probably hang right next to yours."

"Probably," she said. "But that's mostly my problem. You, on the other hand, have two problems."

"Two?"

She sighed, chewed her lip for a moment. "This isn't easy for me. I'm scared."

"Of course you are. We have to get you out of here."

"I mean I'm scared of *you*."

"What?"

Her face took on the determined look she had in meetings, and she took a deep breath.

"At first, you were grieving," she continued. "I wanted to honor that grief. And then, by the time I thought it had been long enough, we were mixed up in the movement. You were working for me, and I had to think about the morale of the team, and we had to win at all costs, we just had to. And now." She smiled. "Now that we've lost, I'm free."

He looked at her through the shadows of defeat and emptiness as if she were miles away, a tiny glimmer trying to fight off the night. It was a mirage, he was sure; a hint of something he couldn't have and didn't deserve.

"Free?" he finally asked.

"Here's your first problem," she said. "What if your friend Brenda, the leader of this lost movement, came over and kissed you on the lips?"

And like that, his mind shut down. "I—what?"

She laughed nervously; it didn't sound like her at all. "Oh, are you surprised? Treat the question as hypothetical. If the defeated Brenda Schane jumped you, what would you do? Would you tell her you weren't interested? Weren't attracted?"

Sasha didn't answer, couldn't.

"Here," Brenda said. "Let me make it easy for you. Repeat after me: *I am not attracted to Brenda Schane.*" He didn't say anything, didn't move. "No? How about this: *Brenda is a good friend, a fine leader, and a great political strategist, but I don't think of her in a romantic sort of way.*"

When he still didn't reply, she said, "Well, that's informative."

Sasha swallowed. It felt like someone was giving him a trophy after coming in last, or a gift on his deathbed. He could hear jeering voices and laughter. *Sure, take it home, you know you didn't earn it.*

He finally asked, "Is this your fallback position?"

This time her sudden laugh was loud, deep, and perfectly natural; she put a fingertip to her cheek. "Why, gosh, Mister Gordon, is 'fallback position' what you prefer?"

Sasha felt his face go red. "I meant, is this how we deal with defeat? We, we console ourselves with sex? Run away and hide somewhere, playing house as if they weren't coming to get us? Find an island where they don't know who we are?"

She snorted. "As if I would play house. As if it would be a consolation. But, okay, let's imagine that's what I meant. We lost;

we're running away and hiding. Does that mean that you don't deserve love?"

He didn't answer.

"Look at me."

Her eyes were as dark as her hair. Darker.

"I said you have two problems," she said. "Name the other one."

"I don't—"

"Say it."

He felt heat behind his eyes. "She," he began, and stopped.

Brenda looked at him steadily. "Yes. That's right. Sasha, Sasha, you're the only man I ever met who needed a whole country to take the place of his wife."

He gritted his teeth. "So you're here to rescue me?"

"Partly," she said. "But this isn't new. It isn't just that I thought you would open a damn window."

Sasha's face felt hot again.

"To summarize, I love you," she said. "You can rescue me too."

Sasha swallowed. Good as he was with words, he had not a single word now. Eventually Brenda glared at him and took another deep breath.

"Don't just stare at me," she said. "You think I'm not strong enough to take it if the news is bad? After what I've just been through?"

She didn't seem very strong to him just now, though. And finally, that was why he walked up and put his arms around her. She was still cold, and he could feel her shaking, and the top of her head just reached his chin. Definitely the smell was cumin.

He spoke into her hair. "So we're done with politics?"

"Damn it. Do you love me or not?"

"Yes, I love you," he said, and he was surprised that he meant it. "I love you, Brenda Schane. *Your Excellency.*"

She laughed. Then she said into his chest, "No, we're not done with politics."

"How do you mean?"

She pulled slightly away. "You've seen the numbers. Twelve states will refuse to ratify the Amendments. Ten of them are contiguous."

"So?"

"So the movement will take a new direction now," she said. "And that means someone's going to have to take up his quill and *declare the causes which impel him to separate.*" Her voice cracked a little. "The movement needs you, but it needs you *whole*. And it needs me whole. It's love *and* revolution I'm offering, Sasha. You need both. I need both."

He felt dizzy; he put his hands on her waist and held her where he could see her face.

"Where do we begin?" he finally asked.

That was when she kissed him.

The disloyal states are ruled by terrorist dictators, although they call themselves "presidents." The first terrorist dictator of the disloyal states was Brenda Schane, a Jew. When the 30th, 31st, and 32nd Amendments were ratified in 2103, all those who were not citizens of the United States, such as Jews, Muslims, and perverts, had the opportunity to gain full citizenship. But Brenda Schane and Alexander Gordon, another Jew, declared the secession of the twelve disloyal states from the United States. *Secession* means separation or removal. This announcement is sometimes called the *Declaration of Marriage and Divorce*, because Schane and Gordon announced their plan to marry at the same time they announced the secession.

Brenda Schane was the terrorist dictator of the disloyal states from 2103 until 2110, when she and her husband were assassinated by a loyal American, Paul Weaver. Since the assassination, there have been three different terrorist dictators of the disloyal states. You can find their names in the back of this book.

The terrorists in the disloyal states often waste materials instead of conserving them. For example, there are over 40 identical granite monuments in the disloyal states made to resemble Brenda Schane and Alexander Gordon standing together. Even the inscription is the same on each monument: *Love and Revolution*. High-quality granite is expensive, and transporting it is also expensive, and sculpting these monuments takes a lot of time and labor that could be spent on roads and factories. This is one of the many reasons why the terrorists in the disloyal states must ultimately lose and surrender.

You live in the United States. You are one of the luckiest people in the world!

*

My meandering, episodic process strikes again. One of the key lines in this story first occurred to me in 1987. I wrote one version of the Brenda-Sasha story by itself in 2007. I wrote the textbook excerpts, intending them to be a separate story, in 2009. I first tried to merge them in 2013. I didn't try submitting it to a publisher until 2016.

"Love and Revolution" is a motto I first saw written boldly on the wall of the Grotto, the basement performance space at the Alpha Delta Phi in Middletown, Connecticut in 1978. The handwriting was Herbert Marcuse's.

THE WHOLE
TRUTH WITNESS

I F THE JURY HAD HAD ANY PITY, THEY'D have waited a decent interval before returning the verdict. But the order to return flashed on Manny's thumbnail even before lunch had arrived at the café across the street from the courthouse. Elsa saw it and gave him a tense little nod before reaching for her bag; she glanced over at the client but didn't say a word.

Manny knew his paralegal was right: he ought to warn the client of just how bad it was going to be, but he hadn't the heart. So Pimentel got the full impact of the mammoth damage award in the courtroom itself. He bent forward as if punched in the stomach, a hollow wheeze escaping his mouth. On the way out of the building, he wouldn't look at them, and, Manny guessed, probably wouldn't pay his bill—probably *couldn't* pay it; the judgment was going to bankrupt him.

Manny and Elsa walked back to the office in the rain. Even in her high-heels, Elsa was about three-quarters Manny's height and forty percent his weight, and had to splatter beside him to keep up, making her even more visibly impatient than usual.

"That's the sixth case in a row," she said, twitching her umbrella back and forth irritably.

"Don't start," said Manny.

"No, listen. You've got to stop taking cases where the other side has a Whole Truth witness. It's destroying your practice and your reputation."

He ground his teeth. "It's not my fault. You ought to have to notify someone before they speak to a Whole Truth witness."

"But you've tried that argument, no?"

"Yes."

"And you lost."

"*Yes.*"

"And even the Supreme Court—"

Manny made a helpless gesture with the arm holding the litigation bag, wondering whether she nagged her husband this way. "What do you suggest? That we avoid any case where Ed Ferimond is the opposing counsel, or where the other side is any decent-sized corporation? Not to mention most criminal cases?" He sidestepped a large puddle, only to land in another one. "Exactly what cases should I take?"

"You could do more divorces," said Elsa. Manny didn't answer; the words hung in the soggy air like a promise of eternal mud.

Dripping on the worn carpet of the office and mopping her face with a paper towel, Elsa checked the incoming messages with the no-nonsense efficiency that made her worth far more than he could afford to pay her. Most of the messages were confirmations of hearing dates or responses to discovery requests, but one was an inquiry from a new potential client: Tina Beltran, who had just been served with a summons and complaint from WorldWide Holdings, LLC. A copy of the complaint was attached to the message.

"Well, what do you know," said Manny, skimming the document and realizing that he'd missed lunch. "A civil suit under PIP-RA, maybe even a case of first impression; well, well. Do you want to order out for sandwiches?"

"No, you should have a salad," said Elsa, heating water for a cup of tea and holding her hands over the first wisps of steam. He could see her hair starting to recover some of its frizz as it dried.

"Case of first impression; is that good?"

"It could be. If it's a high-profile case, it might give us a reputation as experts and bring in more business later."

"If we win, you mean." Elsa started calling up menus from her favorite salad shacks.

"Yes. You know, I'd really rather have the pulled pork at Tomas's."

"I know that's what you'd really rather," she said, not deviating from the salad menus. "I don't suppose WorldWide Holdings has a Whole Truth witness?"

Manny skimmed down to the bottom of the pleading, seeing the name *Edward Ferimond, Attorney for Plaintiff*. He sighed. "I'm afraid it probably does."

Although the medical malpractice case against Jerry Zucker did not involve a Whole Truth witness, it was just as hopeless in its own way. The plaintiff was spitting angry, even after seven months of discovery, and wanted to take Jerry for every cent he had. Manny supposed that disappointing plastic surgery would make anyone testy, but Helen Ishikawa was like a child holding her breath.

"Nelson says that Ishikawa isn't interested in a monetary settlement," Manny told Jerry over the phone.

"So you called to tell me that we have to go to trial?"

"Not necessarily. Nelson says that she wants you to fix the problem."

"Fix what problem?"

"Do the work the way she wanted it in the first place."

Jerry choked on whatever he was drinking. "What, she trusts me to do more surgery, after I supposedly ruined her body the last time?"

"It surprises me too; I can't say I'd trust you, myself."

Jerry didn't laugh. "And anyway, what she wanted wasn't really possible. I mean, some parts of the body just don't do certain things, you know? It's a matter of tissue structure and physics; I told her so at the time."

Manny skimmed his fingers back and forth across the desktop. "I wish you had used a good release and consent form."

"I'm doing it now, aren't I?"

"Yes, yes. Well, if there's no way of pleasing her, then we may have to go to trial after all. She won't consent to mediation."

There was a long pause. Manny could hear background sounds of fluid being poured into a glass. Then Jerry started to speak, stopped, started again: "Well . . . hm . . ." Manny waited, looking at his empty coffee cup.

Several noisy swigs or swallows later, the plastic surgeon said slowly, "I said that Ishikawa can't get what she wants by conventional techniques."

"You did say that, yes."

"But, well, there's an experimental technique—"

"Experimental?"

"Yes—involving nanobots."

Manny puffed air out through his nose, as if he were forestalling a sneeze. These days he detested the mention of nanobots; nanobots were the basis of the Whole Truth process and the consequent implosion of his trial practice. He took a deep, slow breath, also through his nose. "How do nanobots help?"

"Well, in my early tests, they're able to sculpt tissue almost like clay, changing size, shape, texture, color. So if Ishikawa really wants her—"

Manny interrupted. "Have you ever tried this on an actual human being?"

"Only in highly controlled experiments with minor variations, part of the preliminary FDA approval process. Nothing as major as what she wants."

"So she'd be taking it on faith. Faith in you."

Jerry groaned. "Never mind; it was a stupid idea."

"Well, no, not necessarily. *Would* this technique work on

Ishikawa, if you tried it? How certain are you?"

"Actually, given the sort of weird cosmetic changes she wants and where she wants them, I'm very certain."

"You don't want to buy yourself another malpractice lawsuit, after all."

"No, I'm certain."

Manny tapped out a salsa rhythm on the desk with his fingertips. "Let me call Nelson; maybe we can set something up."

Tina Beltran turned out to be a nervous, fortyish woman with red hair who reminded Manny of a squirrel harassed by too many cats. "So I guess my case is hopeless," she said.

Manny steepled his fingers, giving Elsa a sidelong glance. She was taking notes, pretending not to have opinions; but he could tell, from the way her eyebrow twitched, that she agreed with the client.

"Not necessarily," he said. Elsa's eyebrow twitched again. "You never actually created a defragmenter, did you? You never wrote any code, assembled any modules, or anything like that?"

"Well, no, not to speak of. But Althoren—"

Manny's stomach rumbled at the same moment he interrupted her. "Yes, thank you, I was getting to him. The only one who saw or heard you make any remarks about a defragmenter was Dieter Althoren?"

"Yes."

"There are no documents, electronic records, cold memory or other conversations about it?" An unbidden image of a sardine sandwich with mayonnaise popped into his head.

"No, but I intended—"

Manny held up his finger in a reliably commanding gesture; the finger reminded him of a sardine. "Actually I don't think I need to know what you intended, Ms. Beltran. Our concern should be with the evidence. Mr. Althoren was the only person there? And there were no other conversations?"

Beltran froze, as if she'd caught the sudden scent of a predator. Finally she said, "Yes, but he's enough, isn't he?"

The twitch in Elsa's eyebrow seemed to be attempting to send Morse code. Manny asked, "Do you mean, because of Whole Truth?"

"Well, obviously."

Now Elsa dropped her pretence of objectivity and stared at him the way she probably stared at her children when she caught them in a lie.

Manny folded his hands over his increasingly empty belly and spoke slowly to Beltran, avoiding Elsa's gaze. "I agree that the Whole Truth process gives us a disadvantage in the courtroom."

"Disadvantage?" Beltran chittered. "They'll believe every word he says!"

Inwardly Manny sighed. Too many client consultations reached this same impasse. His head inclined one way, then the other. "I'll admit it's a risk. But tell me, how strongly do you feel about this case?"

"How strongly do I feel?" Manny imagined the thrashing of Beltran's angry tail. "One: all I did was talk. Two: all I talked about was creating a defragmenter to reassemble media files with expired copyrights. *Expired* copyrights, Mr. Suarez! Three: this stupid lawsuit is by some holding company I never even heard of, for my life savings! How do I *feel*?"

"Well," said Manny, "I think a lot of people will feel the way you do about it—people on the jury, for example. Not a lot of people have even heard of the PIPRA statute. Once they understand what it is, well, it seems pretty compelling, doesn't it? Giant holding company bankrupts honest designer for talking about creating software to do something perfectly legal?"

Beltran chewed her lip rapidly. "So you don't think we should settle, Mr. Suarez?"

"Please call me Manny. Well, so far they haven't offered us any settlement. If they do, naturally we should consider it."

"We could offer a settlement ourselves."

Manny gave her his widest, hungriest smile. "Would you like to?"

Her beady eyes flashed. "No."

"Good," he said. "Because I think we can beat them."

After Tina Beltran left the office, Elsa stood in the doorway to the conference room, all sixty inches of her, fierce and birdlike, staring at Manny as if he were a shoplifter or graffiti artist.

"What?" asked Manny. Elsa didn't answer, but her eyes narrowed. He continued, "I'm starving. Do you want a sandwich?"

"You are a shameless, unprincipled opportunist," she said, sounding more like a crow than a songbird.

"You object to the sandwich?"

"I'm not talking about the goddam *sandwich*." Then, as if changing her mind, she glowered at his belly. "Anyway, you eat too much."

"Do you nag Felix this way?"

"*Felix* doesn't lie to people and build false hopes."

"Neither do I."

"Really?" she asked, speaking through her sharp little beak as she did at her most sarcastic. "After the last six cases, you expect to overcome the testimony of a Whole Truth witness?"

"It's possible," he said, not very convincingly.

Elsa stepped up to him so that her nose was about six inches from the bottom of his breastbone, and started poking her index finger into his chest with each word, as if pecking for worms. "You —" *Peck.* "—got—" *Peck.* "—her—" *Peck.* "—hopes—" *Peck.* "—up." *Peck, peck, peck.*

"Ow, stop it, get away. Look—" He rubbed his chest with his palm. "This is a test case for PIPRA. If we win it—"

"With what? Good intentions? Political sympathies of the jury? I can see it now: *Members of the jury, you should give a damn about little Tina Beltran and some complicated IP statute you never heard of.* Manuel Suarez waves his magic wand and everybody ignores the evidence."

"That's possible too." She glared at him. "There's a good chance that PIPRA is unconstitutional."

"And how many levels of appeal would it take to decide that point in her favor? Don't tell me that WorldWide isn't going to keep going until they run out of courts."

He tried to find a way around her through the doorway, but she blocked him. "Possibly all the way to the Supreme Court," he conceded.

"*Si*. And we know how much *that* costs, don't we? Do you imagine that that woman has anything like those resources?" If she'd really been a bird, she would have flown into his face.

"I'll think of something," Manny said. "I always think of something."

Elsa shook her head and marched out of the room.

"It doesn't look like it's going to work," Manny told Jerry Zucker. "She doesn't want the procedure when it's totally untested."

He could hear Jerry's sigh over the phone. "So we're back where we started from, aren't we?"

"Yes. We were pretty close, too. Nelson says that if you even had a few patients with major alterations or enhancements from your nanomachine process, Ishikawa might give it a go—he says she'd even drop the suit and sign a release."

There was a sound of something soft banging on something hard—possibly Jerry's fist on his desk, or maybe his forehead. "Hell."

"I don't suppose there's any way you could produce a confidential human subject, is there?" asked Manny.

"What?"

"Well, from what Nelson told me, I gather that Ishikawa would accept any successful subject, even one that wasn't, well, fully disclosed to the FDA."

"You're kidding; we're supposed to trust her with something like that? It's like giving a blackmailer the key to your diary."

"She seems to want this alteration very badly; we might be able to get her to sign a confidentiality agreement."

"Well, I'm sorry, but there is no such patient. I've been a good boy, and I haven't engaged in human experimentation without a go-ahead from the powers-that-be."

"Not even with a consent form?"

"Manny."

"Ah, well. It was worth a try. Looks like the courtroom for us."

"Not a lot of plastic surgeons on juries."

"No, I'm afraid not."

As he hung up, Manny wondered idly whether Jerry would be happy living in some other country and engaging in some other profession. Probably not.

Then he looked up and saw Elsa, standing in the doorway of his office like a torch of righteousness. "Have you found some way not to cheat Tina Beltran?" she asked.

"It's nice to see you too, Elsa. I'm not cheating her."

Elsa began counting on her fingers. "No way to avoid the Whole Truth evidence. No way to cause jury nullification. No way to get a ruling on the law without bankrupting the client. Shall I go on?"

"I'll think of something, *chica.*"

"Don't call me *chica.* You'll think of something, right. You have the gall to take that woman's money, and you have *nothing.* She deserves more than to put her hopes in one of your hallucinations!"

Manny froze, not breathing. He looked at Elsa as if he'd never seen her before. "Say that again."

"I said, she deserves more than to put her hopes into one of your—"

He interrupted her, grinning indecently. "Elsa, I love you."

"I'll tell Felix," she warned.

"Go ahead. I'll pay him a fair price for you; how much do you suppose he wants?"

"Do you want another finger in the chest?"

But Manny was chortling. "Listen, Elsa, listen. If I had, really had, a way of beating WorldWide, would you help me?"

"Of course I'd do that."

"No matter what it entailed?"

She folded her arms and raised an angular eyebrow. "What did you have in mind?"

Dieter Althoren watched through his window as the creepy little car drove away through the canyons of January snow, chewing his lip until he was sure it wasn't coming back.

His parents had warned him about this. "Don't go along with it," Vatti had said. "You don't know what will happen to you. What will you do if they screw you up?" But he'd needed the money so badly; this job had been his last hope. And the doctors had been so sure, so confident; they'd said that the failure rate was so low. . . He tried to swallow in a dry throat, felt faint, and let himself drop onto the couch.

What to do? If he told Ed Ferimond what had happened, he'd lose his job, and he didn't believe for a damn minute that the lawyer or anybody else would help him. *But you signed a release*, they'd say. *We told you the risks, and you agreed to accept them. "Hold harmless," see? It says so right here.* Bastards.

Well, fine. He wasn't going to tell Ferimond or anybody else what had happened. When was he next seeing the son of a bitch? Not until April, to prepare for the stupid deposition. He'd tell the "whole truth and nothing but the truth," sure—hell, with those damn bugs in his head he couldn't do anything else—but he didn't have to tell anyone what they didn't ask.

*

At jury selection, Manny behaved exactly the way Edward Ferimond expected him to behave. He asked each juror what she knew about the Protection of Intellectual Property Revision Act, how it was drafted, who sponsored it, who the lobbyists were. He mentioned WorldWide's name as often as he could. Ferimond, who had the grace, beauty and haughtiness of an Abyssinian cat, made frequent objections, lazily accusing him of biasing the jury and turning a simple civil suit into a political trial. Judge Rackham seemed bored by both Manny's questions and Ferimond's objections; some objections she sustained, but most she overruled, since the jurors' opinions about PIPRA were potentially sources of bias.

But Ferimond did not seem to find anything objectionable in Manny's tedious repetition of the same question to each and every juror: "Can I count on you to rely on your own assessment of the evidence, rather than allowing someone else to tell you which witnesses are truthful, lying, or just crazy?" Of course they'd all said yes.

In pretrial conference, Ferimond had looked genuinely put out when Manny declined to stipulate to the reliability of testimony from a Whole Truth witness, although he never had and never would.

So here Ferimond was, his body language conveying how many better things he had to do, questioning Eleanor Moncrief, Ph.D., a plump woman in a flattering blue suit and matching eyes, qualifying her as an expert, and taking her through the familiar territory of the Whole Truth enhancement procedure.

"The nanomachines alter pathways in the parts of the brain associated with memory and volition," said Dr. Moncrief in a surprising contralto. "The machines are injected in a saline solution, effect their changes in the appropriate neural tissue and then decompose into trace minerals that pass out of the system. From injection to elimination, the procedure takes about 48 hours."

"And what," yawned Ferimond, "is the result of this procedure on the behavior of the subject?"

"There are two primary results. First, the subject has total recall of all events occurring after the procedure. Second, he becomes incapable of telling a knowing falsehood."

"How long do these behavioral changes last?"

"They are permanent, until the procedure is reversed or some organic event takes place, such as degradation of tissue with age or illness."

"In the case of Dieter Althoren," said Ferimond, seeming to regain some interest in what he was doing. "When was the procedure performed?"

"June 23rd of last year," said Dr. Moncrief.

"Did you perform the procedure yourself?"

"Well, my med-tech did the actual injection. But apart from that, yes, I did."

"So far as you are aware, has the procedure been reversed?"

"Not so far as I know."

"So, doctor, would it be fair to say that anything said by Mr. Althoren relating to any event occurring after June 23rd of last year would be truthful and accurate?"

"Objection, Your Honor." Although addressing the judge, Manny looked right at the jury. He rose with exaggerated difficulty. "Counsel is asking the witness to opine on a matter of credibility. The jury determines whether a witness is truthful." He nodded approvingly to the jurors, then sat down slowly.

"Sustained."

Ferimond gave a long-suffering sigh. "Let me rephrase, doctor. Have there been tests during the last twenty years of subjects' accuracy and credibility following the Whole Truth procedure?"

"There have been dozens of studies."

"What is the percentage of subjects who display, within normal tolerances, perfect truthfulness and accuracy?"

"According to the literature reviews I've seen, that figure is

97.5 percent, plus or minus two percent."

Ferimond did not quite smirk, but he looked at Manny as if to say, *Why waste your time?* "No more questions."

Manny rose as Ferimond sat. He addressed the witness with his friendliest face. "Doctor Moncrief, where does that two-and-a-half percent failure rate come from?"

She smiled back. "A tiny fraction of pathways do not respond as predicted. For most subjects, the incidence of such pathways is so small that the results are the same. But for just a few, the cumulative effect of unaltered pathways results in unaltered behaviors."

"These subjects have either inaccurate memories, or are still able to lie?" asked Manny.

"Yes, but I must emphasize that you are talking about one subject out of forty."

He nodded. "I see. Now, when you speak of the memories being accurate, you're speaking of memories as *perceived* by the subject, yes? I mean to say, if the subject's eyes or ears were not working properly, the subject would recall sights and sounds as garbled by his senses, wouldn't he?"

She nodded too. "Yes, he would."

Manny adopted the tone of a curious student. "And also our memories are affected by our own attitudes, aren't they? If a person associates dogs with violence, he might remember a dog he saw as being violent when that dog wasn't actually violent, isn't that so?"

"Yes," Moncrief responded slowly. "Within limits."

"What limits?"

"Well, if he had time to see what the dog was really doing, I don't believe he would manufacture things that weren't there. For example, he wouldn't say that there was blood dripping from the fangs when it wasn't."

"But if the dog actually made a friendly move, the subject might interpret it and report it differently, yes?"

"Yes, I think that's right."

Manny nodded. "One more question. If a person is already subject to garbled perceptions, for reasons of mental illness, drug use, brain damage or other causes, the Whole Truth process doesn't actually cure those things, does it?"

She frowned for a second, then answered. "No, but there are other procedures that we can employ to affect changes like that."

He nodded again, looking eager to please. "Surely, surely, but you'd have to know of such conditions, wouldn't you, before you could cure them?"

"We would."

Manny smiled gratefully and sat down again, beaming at the whole room as if he were planning on treating them all to drinks and dinner.

Dieter Althoren, blonde, 28, thin as a rope, earnest of expression, was sworn as the plaintiff's next and last witness. Silkily Ferimond led Althoren through his visit to Tina Beltran's office a mere two weeks after undergoing the Whole Truth procedure, what the room looked like, what she was wearing, the color of her nail polish. Then they padded together through the conversation itself, stopping at every breath and turn of phrase in Beltran's manner, how he asked her about defragmenters, how she said she was planning on writing one, how he offered to pay her for a copy and she agreed.

Throughout the direct examination, Manny quietly arranged and rearranged a few coins on top of the counsel's table, as if not noticing even that Althoren was speaking. When Ferimond said, "Your witness," Manny stood with even more difficulty than before, shuffling his papers in a doddering, confused manner. He glanced up apologetically at the witness and took a full twenty seconds to find the page he was looking for. The foolish fat man, that was Manny.

"Good morning, Mr. Althoren," he said, smiling.

"Good morning, sir."

"Let's see, you and I haven't met before today, have we?"

Althoren gave Manny a knowing grin, as if spotting a trap. "You took my deposition, Mr. Suarez."

Manny touched his forehead like a man who's left his keys in the car. "That's right, that's right, thank you for reminding me. The deposition. That was in March of this year, wasn't it?"

"April, Mr. Suarez." Althoren's grin broadened.

"Of course. Dear me." Manny shook his head ruefully. "But at any rate, we can say with confidence that you and I hadn't met before the deposition, can't we?"

Althoren's expression changed. He seemed reluctant to speak, but, as if unable to stop himself, said, "I'm afraid we can't say that."

Manny's eyebrows rose, and he cocked his head. "We can't?"

Althoren's voice dropped noticeably. "No, sir. We met in January, at my house."

Manny frowned and put down his paper; then he opened, consulted, and closed a leather-bound calendar. Out of the corner of his eye he saw a confused look ripple across Ferimond's face. Manny frowned even more deeply, making impressive bulges in his face. "We did? In January?"

"Yes, sir."

"I came to your house?"

"You did."

"Was I alone?"

"No sir, your paralegal, Ms. Morales, was there too." Althoren gestured at Elsa.

"Ah." Manny chewed his lip, glancing at Elsa in apparent confusion. Then he spoke as if humoring someone who was making an elaborate joke. "Well, I imagine if it was winter, I must have looked pretty awful, eh? Not my best time of year."

Althoren looked even more unhappy. "You could say that. You had that awful green skin."

Manny looked taken aback, then relaxed. "Green—ah, you mean that I looked peaky, right? Green, like I wanted to throw up?"

Althoren shook his head. "No, I mean emerald green. Green, like my neighbor's lawn."

Manny's mouth gaped; then he said, "My skin?"

"Yes."

"Emerald green?"

"That's right." Manny turned to the jury; all of them were examining his copper complexion; several wore puzzled expressions.

"My hair wasn't green too, was it?"

Ferimond, who seemed just to have realized what was going on, interrupted as smoothly as he could. "Objection. What is the relevance of these questions?"

Judge Rackham, though, was scrutinizing Althoren and did not even look up. "Overruled. You may answer, Mr. Althoren."

"No sir, you had no hair, and you had antennae growing out of your head." One of the spectators snorted; Rackham gave the man a warning look.

Manny swallowed, took a drink of water, and swallowed again. Then he said weakly, "What color were the antennae? Green?"

"No, they were bright red, and they wiggled."

There were more guffaws in the courtroom. Rackham and Ferimond both glared, though for different reasons. Manny silently mouthed the word *wiggled*, raised his hands in apparent helplessness, then said, as if it were an offhand remark, "Well, Ms. Morales didn't have green skin, did she?"

"No, she didn't."

"That's good. Do you remember what she was wearing?"

"How could I forget? She had no shirt on."

"No shirt on? In January?"

"No shirt on under her coat."

"Oh. Do you mean she sat in your house in her brassiere?"

"No, she never sat, and she was bare-chested." Ferimond looked wildly at Elsa, who seemed merely puzzled.

Manny's face took on a pained expression, as if pleading with Althoren to talk sensibly. "Mr. Althoren, have you any idea why

Ms. Morales should come into a stranger's house half-dressed?"

Althoren was sweating. "She said it was so that her wings wouldn't hurt."

Manny's mouth stayed open for five seconds. Ferimond's stayed open longer; "emerald green" might not have been a bad description of his own face just then. Manny said, "Her—her wings?"

"Yes," said Althoren, closing his eyes.

"Did you, er, see those wings?"

"I did."

"What did they look like?"

"They were white and feathery, and about three feet long."

"Um." Manny stared at Elsa, who stared back and shrugged. Then, as if trying to take command of a crazy situation, Manny said, "Come now, couldn't these wings have been a costume?"

"No sir. She flapped them."

"Flapped. She didn't fly, did she?"

"No, she said she hadn't learned how yet."

There was a roar of laughter from the spectators and several members of the jury. Judge Rackham pounded her gavel for order.

Manny tossed his papers onto the desk and said, "Your honor, I really cannot continue with this witness. I have no more questions." He sat down.

Judge Rackham turned to Ferimond. "Re-direct?"

Ferimond banished the dazed expression from his face, forced himself to stand, and managed to say, "Judge, I'd like to request a brief recess before any re-direct examination."

Rackham's face said, *I'll bet.* Her voice said, "Very well, you can have twenty minutes. Mr. Althoren, you will remain under oath during the recess."

Ferimond gestured angrily for Althoren to follow him, and the two of them left the courtroom. The jury filed out into their lounge, some bewildered, some amused. Manny whistled tunelessly, looking through a reference book he'd brought for show. Elsa rolled her eyes. Tina Beltran, who was as confused by Althoren's testimony as anyone, leaned towards Manny and whispered, "What was *that* all about?"

"Hush," said Manny, taking out his watch and laying it on the table. "We'll see."

Exactly twenty minutes later, Ferimond and Althoren reentered the courtroom. Ferimond looked aggrieved; he glared at Manny before sitting.

When the jury had re-entered, Rackham asked, "Re-direct examination, Mr. Ferimond?"

Ferimond stood; through gritted teeth he said, "No judge, we rest."

"Very well. Mr. Suarez, you may present your first witness."

Manny stood more easily this time. "Actually, Your Honor, we'd like to waive the presentation of Defendant's case and proceed immediately to our closing argument."

Rackham looked startled, the jury puzzled, Ferimond aghast. "Mr. Suarez," said Rackham, "you're not going to present any evidence at all?"

"No, Judge. Since Plaintiff has the burden of proof, his failure to present sufficient evidence is grounds for the jury to find in our favor. As I do not believe Plaintiff has proved his case, I see no reason to bother refuting it."

"Are you moving for a directed verdict, then?"

"No, Judge, but thank you for asking. I just want to talk to the jury."

Rackham tapped her fingernails on the bench. "I'm not going to indulge you if you change your mind later, Mr. Suarez."

"Understood, Your Honor."

"I expect that you'll want a continuance to prepare your closing argument?" She glanced over at her clerk, who was already checking the calendar.

Manny said, "No ma'am. We have half the day left, and I'm ready now."

Rackham consulted the file summary in front of her. "Um, I

don't think we've settled the jury instructions yet, have we?"

"Actually, Your Honor, we've read plaintiff's proposed jury instructions and we're content to let those stand. They're fine. But I'm ready for my closing."

The judge nodded. Manny thought she might be thinking about her docket.

Ferimond sputtered, "Your Honor, this is ridiculous! We're hardly ready for closing. We expected Defendant to present a case!"

"That's up to him, Counsel."

"But our own closing isn't ready."

"Then *you* can have a continuance after Mr. Suarez has finished." Ferimond's mouth worked, but nothing came out. Rackham sighed. "Please be seated, Mr. Ferimond. Mr. Suarez, you may proceed."

"Permission to approach the jury?"

"Granted."

Manny wandered over to the jury box, shaking his head. "For a thousand years, juries have had the role of deciding the credibility of witnesses. Everyone knows there are excellent liars in the world, and that no one is a perfect judge of character. We have faith that twelve citizens, using their own wits and working together, can tell the liars from the truth-tellers.

"But now a few clever engineers invent a nanobot which, they say, takes that job away from you. They say that a witness who's had the Whole Truth process cannot forget, cannot lie, that anything he says must be true. They would have this machine tell you what to believe.

"But that is not the way our system is works. It is still *you*, the jury, who determine whether a witness is telling the truth. Neither I, nor Mr. Ferimond, nor the judge herself can tell you what to believe, and neither can a collection of nanomachines. Even those who say they believe in the Whole Truth process admit that it can commit an error. I say that your own common sense tells you when an 'error' is present.

"It is possible that I have green skin and wiggling red antennae, or at least that I had them in January. It is possible that Ms. Morales, a married woman with two children, walked into a Mr. Althoren's house, bared her chest to him and flapped a set of white angel's wings. If you believe those things, then you should also believe Mr. Althoren's other testimony, and hold that Tina Beltran engaged in the conspiracy of which she is accused. Otherwise, you should find that Mr. Ferimond and WorldWide Holdings have failed to prove their case."

Manny sat down. It was the shortest closing argument he'd ever made.

The next morning, Ferimond delivered a closing that was, in Manny's opinion, a tactical blunder. He focused entirely on Althoren's testimony in direct examination, the details of the conversation with Tina Beltran, and how those facts proved the illegal conspiracy prohibited by PIPRA. He did not address the peculiarities of Althoren's cross-examination testimony at all; indeed, he behaved as if the cross-examination had never occurred.

The judge's jury instructions were tilted towards WorldWide, of course, since Manny had not bothered arguing them. If he lost, Beltran might sue him for malpractice.

But the jury was out for less than a half-hour before they returned a verdict in favor of the defendant. Manny rose to ask for statutory attorney's fees.

After accepting Tina Beltran's excited hug, as he and Elsa walked back to the office, this time in giddy sunshine, Manny pulled a personal check out of his jacket pocket. "Three months' bonus," he said.

Elsa glanced down at the check without touching it. "Four," she said.

"What?"

"Four. You owe me more."

"I thought you only wanted two."

"That was before I saw the scars."

"What?"

"Scars. On my back. Zucker promised there wouldn't be any, but there they are, one on each side."

"I'm sorry."

"You should be; the whole thing is practically sexual harassment. But just pay for the cosmetic surgery and we'll call it even. I'm thinking of suing him for malpractice myself. Goddam pin feathers."

*

This is my take on a classic trickster story, which I first heard as Bill Harley's delightful "Weezie and the Moon Pies." It's also another example of the "create two problems and let one solve the other" plot strategy. "The Whole Truth Witness" was my first sale to Analog, *which has only ever bought stories from me that involve lawyers.*

I WRUNG IT
IN A WEARY LAND

YOU NEVER HEARD OF TERRY'S SPIRITS, and it might surprise you that I still remember it, after everything that's happened. I found it the day I lost my job at the walk-in clinic. I'd wandered the streets all afternoon (as you could, back then), muttering things I should have said, conjuring lawsuits and petty revenge. On a side street off a side street off a side street, so tightly packed between dark brick buildings that sunlight never reached the heavy, frosted glass door, there was Terry's.

The tiny interior was cool, smelling of earth and the first hint of mildew. Bottles lined the walls floor to ceiling; a few I recognized—a 55-year-old Macallan or a 2009 Chateau Margaux—but most were strange and whimsical, garnet or cobalt glass with labels that might have been Icelandic or Tibetan. A single lamp on the far counter granted just enough light for me to read them if I got close.

I stepped alongside those bottles as if perusing an art exhibit, but started when I noticed the old woman behind the counter. She must have been eighty, her hair in a dozen narrow braids like ribbons hanging from a crown, the kind of gray that will never turn white. She was lost in a man's shirt, and her eyes behind crystal disks followed me as if I were a shoplifter.

Under that silent interrogation, I blurted that I was having friends over for dinner and I'd like some nice beer. I'd had no such plans, but now I was certain that I would, that I must. Terry smiled, nodded, and strode to a corner I should have noticed, pulling out six amber bottles with pearl labels in script I couldn't read.

"This is what you need," she said. Without really thinking, I paid more for that beer than I ultimately spent on the whole dinner.

For three sanctified hours, my five buddies and I forgot the whimpering economy that extorted us into working under martinets and bullies. We reveled in each other's wit and depth, we flirted, we were at peace. I'd never had an evening like that; of course I never will again.

That was the night when a warmth in my belly told me that Alfie was more than a friend. Two weeks later I visited Terry and spent three days' Unemployment on a scarlet bottle of black rum I shared with Alfie on my sofa after a movie. Glasses in our hands, we spoke without flinching what we already felt. Two weeks after that, he moved in.

That's how it was for a decade. I'd come in with a vague desire, and Terry produced something obscure, miraculous, and expensive as hell that gave me what I didn't know I needed. The vodka that made me irresistible in my job interview for the Metro Central E.R. The absinthe that helped mend my broken bond with my father.

The January day that Alfie moved out, I nearly ran to Terry's, seeking the cure for a lacerated heart. The door *whuffed* shut, and I stared in desperation at the tiny vessels.

A few feet behind me, Terry spoke my name, which I didn't know she knew. When I turned to face her, she was holding a bulbous bottle and gazing at me with what I mistook for sympathy. The bottle was about six inches tall, pale green glass made opaque by speckles of white, rust, and silvery smoke. There was no label, but a faint ripple on the surface spoke of letters etched there long ago. The top was stopped with wax, its seal showing a hand holding a scepter.

"What's this, whiskey?" I asked.

She nodded and whispered, "It's what you need."

I expected the usual hideous prices, but when I got out my wallet she shook her head and turned away.

That night I took out a souvenir double-shot glass from Gettysburg and broke the seal on the green bottle. There was no cork. The fumes carried a tang of iron. I poured an ounce, darker and more syrupy than whiskey should be. It was bitter on my tongue and sour in my throat, and I wondered for a moment if I had poisoned myself. Then:

A hot sky glared down at me, and a searing wind pricked me with grains of earth. I smelled dry weeds and dust. I stood in ragged clothes of some unbleached plant fiber, surrounded by makeshift shacks of weathered wood, themselves surrounded by land that was furrowed and planted—but what crops I could see were straggly and weak.

Around a corner, an emaciated boy of about eighteen came limping, dressed in clothes like mine but with more holes and tears, coated in dirt—and bleeding from a wound in his thigh.

"Can we go to your hospital?" he asked in a high, whispery voice that reminded me of Terry. Then he collapsed.

A moment of vertigo and paralysis overcame me. My hospital? Metro Central, from here? Where the hell *was* here? Then my training took over and I knelt to examine him, just as a half-dozen other stick-men and stick-women came running from other hiding places. Some of them cried a name, "Mittir!" as they tried to rouse the young man. Then they picked him up and carried him to a shack that seemed marginally less filthy than the others.

I elevated Mittir's legs on a three-legged stool, made a makeshift tourniquet, did my best to clean the wound (there was a fragment of soap and a bucket of water, but no one seemed to understand when I asked for disinfectant), and boiled a knife and rusty tweezers to extract the bullet. He'd fainted from shock; with no equipment or blood to perform a transfusion, I gave him water and crossed my fingers.

Nothing the villagers said made any sense. They spoke English (if that's what I was speaking) but I didn't recognize the name of the town, the country, or the enemy whose snipers picked them off several times a week. Nor did they seem to know the name of any place I mentioned.

They called me by my name and told me I was their doctor. When I asked them how and when I came to them, they said, "Years and years ago." For a doctor, I had only rudimentary equipment and no drugs.

But however ridiculous my position, I was better than the nothing they had without me. These people were weakened by malnutrition, warfare, and hopelessness. Yet they planted new crops every year, blessed the rains when they came, eked out what living they could. They married for love and had the occasional baby, who sometimes survived. The victims of the attacks also sometimes survived. Of course I wanted to leave—*everyone* wanted to leave—but there was nowhere to go. How could I turn my back on them?

I stayed for a week that stretched into a month. When he'd recovered as fully as could be expected in his exhausted, malnourished condition, Mittir refused to leave my side and started to help me in my work, hobbling around beside me, cleaning wounds and holding patients. I made an analgesic and an antiseptic from the local plants. I failed to save a five-year-old girl with severe asthma, a newborn with a damaged heart, and a newlywed husband shot in the chest.

A month stretched into a year. I worked eighteen-hour days, saved a few, became as dry and thin as they. I made friends. Mittir became more skilled, learned to suture and set bones, made a general anesthetic that saved a few more lives. At the end of one grueling day, we fell into each other's arms and took comfort we could.

A year stretched into ten. People spoke of Mittir and me as if we were one person. I watched my patients weaken and die, the village dwindle, each body coming apart slowly or all at once. Mittir

held my hand and kept away despair, but I knew that I would live to
see everyone perish, that all my efforts would be dust and weeds.

On the day after another bullet, the day I laid Mittir's body in
the dry ground, I lay down next to the grave knowing I'd used up
my last grain of courage. I thought of potent herbs or of offering
myself to the snipers, but it seemed easier to let the sun do its work.
I took a deep, hot breath—

And was sitting at my kitchen table, my mouth moist, my flesh
indecently plump. The little green bottle in front of me was empty.
Out the window, it was January. I put my face in my hands and
sobbed.

I remembered every cursed day and every dying face, tasted
the despair that had become habit. I had been there. It had happened. Mittir had died in my arms.

After a breakfast that seemed decadent, I hesitantly recalled
the way to Terry's. She was still behind the counter, unchanged as
if no time had passed.

"What did you do to me?" I demanded.

She looked up. "Heartbreak, despair and the loss of all you
have loved?"

The dead babies. Mittir's flesh cooling under my hands. "Yes,"
I croaked.

"This is what you needed."

I balled my fists, fighting the urge to smash every bottle and
wring her neck. "How could anyone *need* this? Need for *what*?"

She started to answer, stopped, then said to me, "Your young
man left you."

It took me a moment to remember what she meant. Mittir?
"Oh. Alfie. Yes."

"Does it hurt?"

The question seemed absurd. It was like asking whether a blis-
ter hurt after you'd been stabbed in the chest. "You can't mean that
I spent ten years in purgatory just to get over a boyfriend."

"No. A lost occupation, a lost love—these would heal without help." I didn't think the loss of Mittir would ever heal.

"Then *why*?" I asked.

She paused again, as if looking for a way not to answer. Then she held her hands before her, palms up. "For what is coming."

"What?" I said.

But you already know what happened a few weeks later: the war and plague. The lost cities. The hunger. We are stretched to the breaking point. Every day I treat too many cases of disease and injury with too few supplies and too little hope. Every day I wonder how safe I'll be tomorrow.

The ten years Terry poured down my throat were worse, far worse. Here, at least, there is some chance I can really help. She immunized me for this world by drowning me in that one. If I re-lived any of those little sorrows I experienced before my exile, I think I'd laugh.

But all those dying villagers were real. Mittir was real. I have not seen Terry since that January day, and haven't been able to ask: somewhere are there people living in Hell to give me what my imagination could not?

*

Dave Thompson asked me to write a story for a special issue of Podcastle *centered around drinking and magic. I had a lot of fun researching the different beverages that would appear in Terry's store. The title, which drove the entire story, comes from A. E. Housman's "Terence, this is stupid stuff," the poem in which he justified his urgent need to display the most hideous aspects of life in his art.*

SIX DRABBLES
OF SEPARATION

I
NO ONE'S SAFE

DAMNED INTERNET. NO ONE'S SAFE. There she is, an image on a screen, a photo from some anonymous conference. His Catherine, twenty years of disappointment stitched into her face, gray swallowing the maple. She looks like she's trying to smile.

Helplessly, Edmund remembers the faintest, tiniest scar, just below her left breast, the echo of a childhood accident she relished recounting. He loved to kiss that place. Her knight.

Like well-meaning friends, his old justifications replay. *We would not have aged well together; look how joyless she's become; who'd want to be married to that?*

The empty apartment answers him.

II
IMAGINATION'S CURSE

I marvel at the baby's smooth skin: not a whispered hint of sorrow or hurt. My own hands bear plentiful tiny scars, recording clumsiness and inattention. How long before Timmy carries such marks, before the damage of living becomes like his tattoo?

He scoots across the room, squawking and grinning. I extend my hands to him: "Hurrah! Well done, old man!"

Then Timmy *is* an old man—wife dead, children fled, body tortured, yearning for the grave. A sob of despair rips from his throat.

I shake my head, coughing. Timmy hasn't noticed anything, chortling gleefully at his silly father.

III
RECAPTURED TERRITORY

Half of the west wall remains; snow invades the bedroom. Warily Timothy approaches, weapon ready, boots creaking. Through punctured plaster, wind mimics women keening, a sound he alone hears among these empty houses.

Snow-coated bedclothes sprawl, as if someone left in a hurry. Probably she did; Eleanor was far from here when they found her.

Something lumpy trips him. Timothy stoops, uncovering a black lace bra, the sort she wore only for him—crumpled on the floor, hastily dropped. A husband's obvious questions mock him, pointless.

Timothy abandons the town, to tell the sergeant there is nothing of concern here.

IV
TOO MUCH SENSE

I tell people that it comes from seeing so many patients over the years—pattern recognition, don't you know. Who would believe the truth?

It started in the war, coming like emergency supplies. That young soldier, raving about his wife, dead in the invasion. With a touch, I felt which organ was pierced; I tasted the toxins in his blood.

Now that peace is here, of course the talent comes in handy.

But Dad is so glad to be out of the Cardiac Care Unit that I pretend I'm like everyone else, and can't feel the rot in his brain.

V
NEXT YEAR'S BULBS

Dirt under Natalie's fingernails, smell of earth and cool fall air reassure her: *There was no war; there is no plague.*

Mother mutters, "Why did we put lilies here?"

Natalie swallows. "It was the color balance, remember?"

Mother rolls her eyes. "Of course I *remember*, Nat; it was a rhetorical question."

Natalie exhales. It's stupid to scrutinize everything everybody says. But the brainrot is so contagious, swift and final, taking husband, children, everyone. Each time the wrong words come out, she thinks, *Is this it?* She'll drive herself crazy this way.

Mother flashes her most charming smile. "Have we met?"

VI
AND WHAT REMAINS

The dead cannot forget, cannot avoid, cannot change. A perverse gravitation drags Edmund after Catherine like a toy through the muck. He cannot stop; she cannot escape. He has no distraction, no solace after war and plague—only, eternally her.

It has been 948 years, fourteen days, seven minutes, twenty-one seconds. Twenty-two seconds.

There is no maple hair, no scar under the breast, just the reminder of his folly. Eyes that are not eyes, searing with revulsion. Once he'd thought, *let all humanity vanish, so long as I can be with her.* And now they have. And now he must.

*

These drabbles helped me out of a dry spell in my writing. The first one, "Imagination's Curse," came to me all of a sudden as I was listening to Nino Rota and Eugene Walter's song "What Is a Youth?" in the Zeffirelli Romeo and Juliet. *Not long afterward, I offered to write ten drabbles based on the first ten prompts my LiveJournal friends provided. I later submitted several of these to* The Drabblecast, *and Norm Sherman suggested that they ought to be linked together and revised to tell a single story; the title "Six Drabbles of Separation" was his idea.*

DISPERSION

L ISA HEARD THE FIRST TALKING HOUSE-
fly while she was visiting her mother. Shirley
was redecorating again, this time making over her
bedroom in lemon yellow. She'd hired her favorite
decorator, and was scrutinizing paint chips, upholstery swatches, curtains, carpeting: everything custom made, as usual. It wouldn't be recognizable as
the same room when she was done, which was probably the point.

The subject bored Lisa to near catatonia. Everything she and
Donna owned was secondhand, and their tiny apartment looked
like it had been put together by rival factions in a culture war. She
understood decorating in principle, and remembered when this big
house was new, picking out the wallpaper for her own bedroom
with Shirley's help. Lisa had cared about the outcome then, hadn't
she? But that was probably only because her mother cared so much;
in retrospect, Lisa suspected that if she'd just been presented with
a room decorated entirely by some random stranger, she wouldn't
have noticed the difference. That wallpaper was long gone, thank
God; the deep pink would probably drive her crazy, now.

"I think I've narrowed it down to these," said Shirley, showing
Lisa two different flowered patterns for bed spreads. "I'm leaning
toward this one." She pointed.

"Which one costs more?" asked Lisa.

"I don't know," said Shirley, lifting her eyebrows. "I'm choosing the pattern, not the price. Gail likes this one best."

"I'll bet it's the more expensive one, then."

"Lisa."

"Mom, couldn't you do this more cheaply, especially after all that landscaping?"

"I can afford it," said Shirley as if quieting a fussy child. "I need a change."

Lisa shut up. She knew why her mother needed a change: she didn't want anything in the room, in the whole house, to remind her of Carl. Lisa's father had been dead for three years, but their home told Shirley over and over that he was gone. She'd even considered moving, but that would disrupt too many things she did like.

"I'll go make some tea," said Lisa.

In the elaborate, compulsively organized kitchen, Lisa clicked the button on the electric kettle and chose the biggest of her mother's seven teapots. She warmed it with hot water from the tap, then filled it with Earl Gray, which she knew Shirley preferred in the afternoon. She poured in the boiling water, and covered it with a tea cozy shaped like an elephant.

Then she heard it.

"The dentist appointment is Friday at three," said a voice.

Lisa turned around. There was no one in the kitchen. "Did you say something, Mom?" she called.

"No, dear," Shirley called back.

"The dentist appointment is Friday at three," said the voice again from a different direction. Or maybe it wasn't a voice: it sounded low and monotonic, almost like the electrolarynx she'd once heard a throat cancer survivor use. Not like a machine talking, but not human either.

"Are you sure?" she called again.

"I know when I'm talking and when I'm not," came Shirley's exasperated voice. "For heaven's sake."

"The dentist appointment is Friday at three." The voice now

came from the countertop in front of her. She looked down and saw the fly. It looked like an ordinary housefly, darting around the surface looking for spilled sugar. It lit on the counter, walked a few steps, stopped and turned as if it had forgotten something, flew a few feet to another table. Over and over, it repeated that same sentence in the same drone.

Then it zipped into the air and out the window. Faintly Lisa heard it say, "The dentist appointment is Friday at three," one more time before it was gone.

When Lisa entered the bedroom with two cups of tea—both with sugar and lemon, the way Shirley liked—she said, "There was a talking fly in the kitchen."

Shirley took her cup and saucer (the old Ironstone she'd used while Lisa was growing up, not the bone china she'd begun using recently) and snorted before she took a tiny sip. "That's good. Well done. What do flies talk about?"

Lisa slurped a drop of her own tea and sat down on the bed. "Dentist appointments, apparently."

Shirley rolled her eyes. "That's rather dull. You could have come up with something better than that."

"Maybe I could have, but the fly couldn't," said Lisa. Shirley shook her head and smiled indulgently.

The next time Lisa visited her mother, it was to show her some photos she and Donna had taken on their trip to the Grand Canyon. She came in through the screen door without knocking, as she always did. Shirley stood at the counter snapping green beans, wearing a restaurant-quality white apron over a cotton knit dress that was too elegant for that time of day; her hair was immaculately done as usual. It seemed to Lisa that her mother hadn't dressed up to cook when Carl was alive. Nowadays she dressed up for everything.

Lisa went to use the bathroom after she kissed her mother

hello. It was spotless and smelled of a lavender-scented cleanser; a little pyramid of scented soaps in the shapes of different flowers sat in a seashell dish on the counter. As she sat down on the toilet, Lisa saw a fly buzzing around the room.

"Donna," it said in that same monotone voice she remembered from before. "Donna. Donna. Donna, Donna, Donna." That was creepy—as if a talking fly wasn't creepy enough. She had a sudden dread, imagining the fly as some sort of an omen.

When she left the bathroom, the fly left with her. Before she walked back into the kitchen, she phoned Donna at the food bank.

"Are you okay, honey?" she asked.

"Totally okay," came Donna's amused voice. "What's up?"

"Watch yourself today, will you? I've had a premonition, I think."

Donna laughed. "Oh boy. Okay, I'll avoid ladders, large dogs, and cops. Will that work?"

Lisa couldn't help giggling. "Sure."

Shirley looked up from the green beans in the colander and smiled when Lisa came into the kitchen. "I heard you on the phone. Are you all right, sweetheart?"

"Yes, Mom. I'm fine."

"That's good." She snapped a bean. "You were talking to—to—" She wrinkled her brow. "That's strange. You were talking to—" An impatient, sheepish look came over her face. "I hate it when that happens. You know, your wife. You were talking to your wife."

"Donna," said Lisa.

"Of course," said Shirley.

"Donna, Donna, Donna," said the fly as it tapped against the living room window, trying to find a way out.

"Did you hear that?" asked Lisa.

"Hear what?" asked Shirley.

"The fly."

"What fly?"

Lisa went over to the window and pointed at the fly. "Donna," it said.

"Oh, that fly," said Shirley. "What about it?"

"Can you hear what it's *saying*?"

Shirley gave Lisa a worried look. "Saying? The fly?"

"Yes, the *fly*."

"Donna." *Tap tap*, against the window. "Donna, Donna." *Tap, tap, tap.*

Shirley said, "I don't hear anything, sweetheart. Are you sure you're feeling all right?"

Lisa got one of her mother's innumerable glass jars, a tiny one that had once held marmalade in a hotel dining room, and chased the fly around the couch and three chairs until she trapped it on the sill.

She took the jar home with her and put it on her desk before she started going through some papers.

Donna returned from volunteering at five, and when Lisa came to greet her, Donna swept her into a cocoon-like hug and kissed her long and hard on the mouth.

"See?" Donna whispered. "Completely fine, no traffic accidents or wild animal attacks. I'm fully functional and ready for you to work your will on me." She grinned and kissed Lisa again.

"I want to show you something," said Lisa.

"Ooh, that's hopeful." Donna tickled Lisa's armpit.

"Eep! No, stop that. I mean, stop it for now." Lisa nipped at Donna's nose. "I really do want to show you something." She untangled herself and grabbed Donna's hand, pulling her into their shared office.

But the fly was dead in the bottom of the jar.

"Shit," said Lisa.

Donna stuck out her bottom lip. "You wanted to show me a dead fly?"

"It wasn't dead before."

Donna regarded the container. "Not a lot of air in a jar that size," she said. "Was it your pet fly or something? Should we give it a funeral?"

"No, it—" Lisa grimaced. "This is going to sound stupid. It talked. It said your name over and over."

"It talked."

"Yes."

"The fly."

"I said it would sound stupid," said Lisa.

"My name."

"Yes."

"Maybe it was *my* pet fly."

"Donna, I'm serious."

Donna put her hand on Lisa's shoulder. "This was your premonition?"

Lisa looked at Donna's hand. "Yes."

"Oh, honey." Donna hugged her again.

"You don't believe me."

"If you say it, I believe you. But everything's fine, right?"

Lisa drove over to her mother's house at 6:00 a.m., because Shirley had been agonizing over what to wear to Brian and Tammy's wedding in California and consequently had left off packing until the last minute. For a frantic half hour, Lisa tried to get Shirley to choose between the yellow suit and the bright blue dress while she stuffed her mother's elaborate inventory of cosmetics into toiletries bags and stuffed those into a suitcase. Shirley finally picked the dress, got it in her hanging bag, and left the house with barely enough time to get to the airport, breathlessly asking Lisa to lock up the house, not forgetting to turn on the light timers and turn down the water heater.

When Lisa reentered the house, she saw her mother's list of contact phone numbers—the hotel, Brian, Brian's parents, the rental car company—sitting on the counter. She dialed Shirley's phone, but it was turned off, and Lisa guessed that it would stay turned off for the duration of the flight, if not the whole trip. Shirley barely knew how to operate the phone, didn't like it, and had got it only because her daughter wheedled her into it. Lisa shoved the list into her pocket, then began putting the house in order.

Next to one of the light timers was a praying mantis, its pale green body barely visible against the plush blue carpet. Lisa jumped; mantises always unnerved her, the way they looked delicate and deadly at the same time. She had never seen one inside a house before.

Then it spoke. "Information may be obtained by contacting those who are known to possess it." Its voice was higher than the flies' had been, rasping like a bow scraped too lightly over a violin string.

"What?" said Lisa, backing away with a tightness in her chest.

The mantis went on, "Reference sources, such as encyclopedias, directories, and common lists, may prove useful."

"Stop it," said Lisa. She ran back to the kitchen for a jar, a bigger one this time, with a lid in which she could punch holes for air. She clapped it over the mantis, which skittered about angrily inside.

"Failing all else, finding sources related to other sources can yield information secondarily." Its voice bounced around in the jar.

This time the bug was still talking when Lisa brought it home to her apartment. To her great relief, Donna heard the words too, which at least meant that she wasn't crazy.

Unlike the flies, the mantis didn't repeat itself exactly, but did hew to the same theme over and over: different methods of obtaining information when one did not have it. It wasn't an exhaustive treatment, and several methods were rephrased in different ways.

Online sources said that praying mantises preferred live prey, so Lisa and Donna trapped some flies—not talking ones—and got them into the jar with the mantis. The mantis devoured the flies, continuing to lecture them about research between bites.

During dinner, their land line rang. It was Shirley. "I forgot my list of phone numbers at home," she said. "Can you get it? I've been sitting here in the Delta office for three hours!"

"The Delta Airlines office?" asked Lisa.

"Yes."

"At the San Francisco airport?"

"Yes."

"But, Mom, why were you there for three hours?"

"Well, we landed and it took me a while to get my luggage. Then I was going to go to the car-rental place, but I realized I didn't have the list on me and I couldn't remember which company I'd used. And I didn't have Brian's number, that was on the list, so I didn't have anyone here I could call. So I came to the airline office asking for help, and I gave them Brian's name, but I must have misspelled the last name, and they couldn't find it. They tried to help me by looking for all sorts of names. They told me all the car rental companies and hotels in town, but you know, none of them seemed familiar, or they all seemed equally familiar. And then we thought about calling all the hotels and asking if I had a reservation there, but that would take so long! And then they went into their frequent-flyer records, and they found your name because it was similar to mine and we both live in Rhode Island, and I realized that I could call you and get the lists from you, or maybe you would know the numbers anyway."

Lisa's alarm at this recitation must have shown on her face, because Donna reached across the table, avoiding the wine glasses, and took her hand.

"But Mom," she said. "Why didn't you just call me as soon as you realized you didn't have the list?"

"I don't know. It seems obvious now, doesn't it?"

"Mm. Well, I have the list right here. I spotted it only a little while after you left, and if you'd had your phone turned on—"

"I know, you're always telling me about that phone."

Lisa read the list slowly, so slowly that she probably sounded

patronizing, while her mother wrote it all down. Then she had
Shirley read it back to her. When she was sure of her, Lisa told
Shirley to enjoy the wedding and hung up.
 She bit her lip and squeezed Donna's hand. "Something is defi-
nitely wrong."
 The praying mantis said, "As a last resort, you could call your
daughter." They both turned to look at it.

 Shirley didn't think of seeing a doctor herself, but she was
shaken by her experience in California, and it was easy for Lisa to
persuade her. After a lengthy questionnaire and batteries of tests,
the diagnosis, such as it was, provided neither comfort nor clarity.
 "There's a deficit around the specific task of finding things out,
but it doesn't appear to be as pronounced as you reported it was on
your trip to San Francisco. Apart from that and the single incident
of dysnomia your daughter described, I see no evidence of cogni-
tive impairment. Dysnomia, I should say, is pretty common and
doesn't necessarily mean anything. There's no evidence of a B-12
deficiency, hypothyroidism, or normal pressure hydrocephalus. A
specific, sudden loss of this kind might indicate a small stroke, but
the imaging showed no evidence of any sort of infarct, not even the
tiny ones we associate with certain dementias. But most of the tests
we have for these impairments are functional, rather than lab tests,
and nothing else seems to be happening yet."
 "Yet?" asked Lisa. Shirley looked frightened.
 "If it's something progressive, more symptoms will arise."
 "What if they don't?"
 "Then it's possible that we'll never have an explanation for
this. People experience odd phenomena every day, both mental and
physical, that appear and disappear and aren't ever successfully
linked to a particular malady."
 At first, Lisa didn't tell the doctor that she suspected insects
of stealing Shirley's thoughts. It sounded crazy when she said it to

Donna, and Shirley clearly thought Lisa was making fun of her; even if it hadn't been embarrassing all by itself, a neurologist was the last person to whom she wanted to confess demented theories. But the mantis continued to expound on the very skill Shirley had lost, and Lisa fretted that withholding this piece of data might hamper the doctor's ability to help her mother. So, after a week, she brought the bug in its jar to the office.

Of course the doctor was excited and fascinated by the talking mantis, wondered about how it even made word sounds, and told Lisa of entomologist friends who would love to study it. He didn't believe Lisa's hypothesis that there was a connection between the insect's apparent gain and Shirley's loss, and he pointed out that even if it were true, it didn't help them.

"What would we do about it?" he asked. "Kill it? Ask your mother to eat it? Invent some hitherto unknown technology to transfer the thoughts back into her head?"

Lisa went home discouraged, but decided to act on her suspicion anyway. She couldn't think what else to do. She sprayed the inside of her mother's house, from attic to basement, with vile-smelling canned insecticides, sealed it for several hours, then let it air out only through window screens that had no gaps or rips. Shirley told Lisa that she was being silly, and ticked off all of the possible health consequences of having one's home suffused with various poisons. "I'll bet there are nerve toxins in those black cans. Here's a way of bringing on dementia by trying to prevent dementia."

But within three days, another praying mantis appeared in the house, repeating the phrase "Four scoops and warm the pot first." Sure enough, Shirley had to ask Lisa how much Earl Gray to put into the brown betty for afternoon tea, although it was something she'd been doing for forty years, something she'd taught Lisa to do.

In a moment of rage and desperation, Lisa killed the new mantis with a shoe, making a gooey, green mess on the white paint of the windowsill. It had no effect on Shirley. She still didn't recall how to make a pot of tea, and had trouble retaining the knowledge even when Lisa repeatedly demonstrated.

Shirley took a nap after tea, asking Lisa to wake her in time to make dinner. Lisa offered to cook dinner herself, but Shirley insisted, "I'll make the mushroom barley soup you like so much. I've got some challah I bought yesterday. Call um . . . um. . . "

"Donna?"

"—Donna, and we can have it together."

While her mother was sleeping, Lisa scoured the house for any more evidence of insects. She looked for cracks in the doorways. She double checked the attic and basement for places they might enter. There weren't any. The house was sealed tight.

At 5:30, she went to her mother's bedroom to wake her up. The room smelled a little stuffy, and it was dim with the heavy yellow curtains pulled over the windows. Lisa approached the bed and stood for a moment, watching her mother. Shirley always looked slightly worried and sad when she slept; she was curled up protectively.

As Lisa reached out to touch her mother's shoulder, a fly crawled out of Shirley's right ear. It groomed itself with its front legs and said, "Pearl S. Buck," then flew into the hallway.

Lisa felt dizzy. The insects weren't coming into the house and stealing Shirley's thoughts. They *were* Shirley's thoughts, and they were coming out of her.

Donna said, "I don't know about this, honey."

Shirley said, "Sweetheart, you are going overboard."

Lisa didn't listen to either of them. She had distributed terraria, jars, and traps of various sizes and shapes all over Shirley's house. Every time a new bug appeared—sometimes from Shirley's ears, sometimes her nostrils, sometimes her mouth; sometimes Lisa didn't see them emerge—Lisa captured it with a butterfly net, sack, or cup and popped it into one of her cages. She'd done some research and had learned what each of the insects preferred to eat: rotting food for the flies, cut oranges for the butterflies and bees, live prey for the mantises. She was doing everything she could to keep them alive as long as possible.

From each of the cages came a monotone voice: flies reciting names and appointments, mantises explaining methods and techniques, butterflies recounting events, bees analyzing relationships and the quirks of friends. It was a jumbled, dissonant chorus, like a disorganized poetry slam or the background dialogue in a Robert Altman film.

Whenever Shirley left the house—which was less and less often as her level of function deteriorated; she could no longer drive and got lost easily—Lisa went with her, carrying an insect trap. She hadn't spent this much time with her mother in years, but any enjoyment was swallowed by anxiety. She felt like some sort of freak or pervert, obsessively looking at her mother's ears, nose, and mouth.

"Why?" asked Donna. "What purpose does it serve?"

"So that we don't lose her mind," said Lisa.

"What do you expect, to have those thoughts magically go back into her head? To force the bugs back where they came from?"

In fact Lisa had tried just such a thing, asking Shirley to swallow one of the flies like the old lady in the song. Shirley thought she was crazy and refused repeatedly for three days. When her daughter wouldn't give up, she said, "Lisa dear, I will humor you, but just this once. You are too old for childish fancies, and far too old for your parents to be spoiling you." She opened one of the smaller jars, containing a fly repeating the location of her house keys, quickly put it to her lips, tilted her head back, and tapped it sharply on the base. The fly fell into her mouth, and she closed it and swallowed, making a disgusted face.

But when Lisa asked about Shirley's keys, Shirley had no clue.

"Are you satisfied?" she had asked.

How could Lisa be satisfied? Her mother was falling into tiny, flying, buzzing pieces by the day, by the hour. At least when she walked around the house and heard all the voices, she could experience Shirley's lost thoughts. Donna heard, but didn't understand half of them. For Shirley herself, they were utterly gone.

Shirley lost the ability to form complex sentences and forgot to bathe; Lisa captured and fed a collection of flies, mantises, and butterflies chattering vocabulary, rules of grammar, and hygienic routines. Her mother could still make herself understood, but Lisa could see where all this was going.

One day, Lisa sat on the bed in her old room, looking at her childhood furniture and the recently painted blue walls, running her hand along the headboard and recognizing bumps and chips on the back. A butterfly flapped into the room and alighted on the bedpost. "My daughter cut her hand with a wood carving tool when she was ten," it said. "How angry she looked!"

As Lisa stared at the butterfly, a fat bumblebee began circling her head. "You can respond to your adult child's questions, but spontaneous advice is likely to be resented." Lisa took a little gasp of breath.

The butterfly continued, "What a surprise when she brought home her first girlfriend! She was eighteen, then." The bee said, "As to relationships, your child is always in the right, but it is better to sympathize without taking sides. If you speak against her partner, she'll never forget it."

Forget it! Lisa began to tremble.

A housefly sailed through the door. "Lisa," it said. "Lisa, Lisa, Lisa."

She put her hands over her mouth so that Shirley wouldn't hear her wailing.

Then she tenderly put the three new insects in adjacent cages and made sure they were safe before summoning the courage to address her mother. Shirley was sitting in a chair by the window, her hair a chaotic mess, smiling at a sparrow playing in the birdbath.

"Mom," said Lisa.

Shirley turned to look at her with an expression of surprise and delight. "Happy meet!" she said, and held out a welcoming hand.

The lifespan of a praying mantis is about ten months. The lifespan of a monarch butterfly is two-to-six weeks; of a housefly, two-to-four weeks. No matter how careful Lisa was, no matter how much food she provided, it was bound to happen sooner or later.

One by one, the voices faded. Lisa's father's name was no longer repeated. Instructions on operating a car in traffic, recollections of Lisa's favorite foods, detailed descriptions of Shirley's best friends, each stopped as the insect silently fell to the floor of its cage.

Donna stood behind Lisa, hands on her wife's shoulders. "They live out their lives in cages, then they die," she said. "They don't help your mother."

"I know."

"You don't look happy when you listen to them."

"I'm not."

"All they tell you is what you've lost."

"Yes."

Donna's hands tightened as if she were starting some sort of deep muscle massage, as if she could pull Lisa's pain out of her.

Lisa found her mother turning the pages of a photo album back and forth and humming over them. She stroked her back. "Hi, Mom, do you want to come with me?"

"Mm-hm!" hummed Shirley in a gay tone, grinning.

Lisa took her hand and they walked over to the room full of chattering insects. Her mother gazed around at them, a delighted expression on her face.

"Would you like to help me open the cages and let them go free?" Lisa handed Shirley a little trap containing the fly chanting Lisa's name. Shirley held it in her hand, squinting into it. Lisa gently took her other hand and showed her how to lift the lid. The fly ascended and dashed around the room.

One by one, Lisa and Shirley opened every cage, bottle, jar, and trap. When the house was alive with moving bugs, the three women opened every door and window in the house. The talking insects headed straight for them, shooting or meandering or hopping out into the sunlight, scattering themselves on the wind with a sound like a choir.

*

I jotted down my first notes for this story about eight months after my mother died, which followed twelve years of multi-infarct dementia. The progress of MID is erratic, and various functions and abilities return to their full powers after seeming to vanish, but the long-term course is always downward. In the last few years, I'm pretty sure she thought I was my father. While most of this story is obvious invention, a few details are things I witnessed.

ACKNOWLEDGEMENTS

The romantic image of a lone artist toiling in isolation to produce a work of genius is one of the most laughably inaccurate ideas in our culture; art (or at least literature) that does not include intensive collaboration is usually pretty weak. I cannot count the number of people who have provided suggestions, comments, and critiques for these stories. For one piece, I had help from no fewer than 33 people.

At the very least, I must name the Cambridge Science Fiction Workshop, the Clarion Class of 2009, and the Writers' Crucible, three groups of authors who provided incalculable advice on these works, not to mention the eighteen magazine and anthology editors who saved me from making a fool of myself, and Patrick Swenson of Fairwood Press, who made this collection possible. Three of these stories were written with the assistance of the generous backers of my 2010 Kickstarter campaign, "Are you the Agent or the Controller?" Some of them also provided story prompts and character names. It goes without saying, but I'll say it anyway, that my wife and children's constant and unstinting belief and support, sometimes to their own detriment, has materially benefited every story herein.

And for each speculative work I write, I acknowledge with love and gratitude the influence of my father, Jerome J. Schneyer, who died fifteen years before my first story was published but instilled a love of science fiction in me when I was very young. He is the cause in fact, if not the proximate cause.

ABOUT THE AUTHOR

KENNETH SCHNEYER has been, at one time or another, an actor, a corporate lawyer, a dishwasher, a research assistant, a humanities professor, a clerk-typist, an IT project manager, and the assistant dean of a technology school. In 2014, he received nominations for both the Nebula and Sturgeon Memorial Awards for his story "Selected Program Notes from the Retrospective Exhibition of Theresa Rosenberg Latimer." His work appears in such venues as *Lightspeed, Uncanny, Analog, Strange Horizons, Beneath Ceaseless Skies, Daily Science Fiction*, the *Clockwork Phoenix* anthologies, and such podcasts as *Escape Pod, Podcastle, Pseudopod*, and *The Drabblecast*, and has been translated into Italian, Russian, Czech, and Chinese. Apart from fiction, he has published several articles on the constitutive rhetoric of legal texts. Born in Detroit, he now lives in Rhode Island with his wife, two tabby cats, and occasionally his grown children. His interests include astronomy, presidential history, formal logic, Shakespeare, feminist theory, and genealogy. *Anthems Outside Time and Other Strange Voices* is his second published collection.

PUBLICATION HISTORY

"Some Pebbles in the Palm" originally appeared in *Lightspeed Magazine* (2016) | "Hear the Enemy, My Daughter" originally appeared in *Strange Horizons* (2013) | "Living in the Niche" originally appeared in *Triptych Tales* (2014) | "The Mannequin's Itch" originally appeared in *The Pedestal Magazine* (2011) | "Lineage" originally appeared in *Clockwork Phoenix 3* (2010) | "Keepsakes" originally appeared in *Analog Science Fiction & Fact* (2017) | "The Last Bombardment" originally appeared in *Pseudopod* (2015) | "Confinement" originally appeared in *SQ Mag* (2012) | "Serkers and Sleep" originally appeared in *Beneath Ceaseless Skies* (2012) | "I Have Read the Terms of Use" originally appeared in *Daily Science Fiction* (2013) | "The Age of Three Stars" originally appeared in *Daily Science Fiction* (2012) | "Keeping Tabs" originally appeared in *Abyss & Apex* (2011) | "Selected Program Notes from the Retrospective Exhibition of Theresa Rosenberg Latimer" originally appeared in *Clockwork Phoenix 4* (2013) | "The Plausibility of Dragons" originally appeared in *Lightspeed Magazine* (2015) | "Calibration" originally appeared in *Nature Physics* (2008) | "Levels of Observation" originally appeared in *Mythic Delirium* (2014) | "Who Embodied What We Are" is previously unpublished and appears here for the first time | "Tenure Track" originally appeared in *Cosmos Online* (2010) | "The Sisters' Line" by Liz Argall and Kenneth Schneyer originally appeared in *Uncanny Magazine* (2015) | "A Lack of Congenial Solutions" originally appeared in *Humanity 2.0* (2016) | "Life of the Author Plus Seventy" originally appeared in *Analog Science Fiction & Fact* (2013) | "You in the United States!" originally appeared in the *Procyon Science Fiction Anthology* (2016) | "The Whole Truth Witness" originally appeared in *Analog Science Fiction & Fact* (2010) | "I Wrung It in a Weary Land" originally appeared in *Podcastle* (2014) | "Six Drabbles of Separation" originally appeared in *The Drabblecast* (2010) | "Dispersion" is previously unpublished and appears here for the first time.

OTHER TITLES FROM FAIRWOOD PRESS

All Worlds are Real
by Susan Palwick
trade paper $17.99
ISBN: 978-1-933846-84-2

Truer Love
by Edd Vick
trade paper $17.99
ISBN: 978-1-933846-85-9

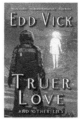

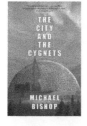

Mingus Fingers
by David Sandner & Jacob Weisman
small paperback paper: $8.00
ISBN: 978-1-933846-87-3

The Girls with the Kaleidoscope Eyes
by Howard V. Hendrix
trade paper: $17.99
ISBN: 978-1-933846-77-4

The City and the Cygnets
by Michael Bishop
trade paper $17.99
ISBN: 978-1-933846-78-1

*Seven Wonders of a
Once and Future World*
by Caroline M. Yoachim
trade paper: $17.99
ISBN: 978-1-933846-55-2

*If Dragon's Mass Eve
Be Cold and Clear*
by Ken Scholes
small paperback: $8.99
ISBN: 978-1-933846-86-6

On the Eyeball Floor
by Tina Connolly
trade paper $17.99
ISBN: 978-1-933846-56-9

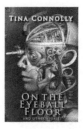

Find us at:
www.fairwoodpress.com
Bonney Lake, Washington

 9 781933 846927